Praise for Sophia Knightly's
Grill Me, Baby

"Sophia Knightly cooks up a delicious sizzling contemporary. The only thing hotter than Michaela's red-headed temper is the sexual chemistry between her and Paolo."
~ *Night Owl Reviews*

"If you're ready for a spirited romance filled with good writing, a smooth flow, passion, desire, family and competition, then *Grill Me, Baby* will be the perfect summertime read for you. I couldn't put the story of these two bantering lovers down, and I would love to see a sequel sometime soon. Hint. Hint."
~ *Romance Junkies*

"Sophia Knightley will have you eating out of the palm of her hand with her spicy new contemporary romance... *Grill Me, Baby* is one of the most delightful romances I've read in a while."
~ *Joyfully Reviewed*

"*Grill Me, Baby* is a fun read for foodies who love romance... At heart, the story is a contemporary romance but Ms. Knightly artfully weaves in the complexities of following your dreams, unconditional love, and loving across socioeconomic and cultural boundaries."
~ *Fresh Fiction*

"This is a romance story pure and simple and it's delicious. I thoroughly enjoyed *Grill Me, Baby* from beginning to end."
~ *Guilty Pleasures Book Reviews*

Look for these titles by
Sophia Knightly

Now Available:

Grill Me, Baby
Paging Dr. Hot

Grill Me, Baby

Sophia Knightly

6912500236867I

SAMHAIN
PUBLISHING

Samhain Publishing, Ltd.
11821 Mason Montgomery Road, 4B
Cincinnati, OH 45249
www.samhainpublishing.com

Grill Me, Baby
Copyright © 2013 by Sophia Knightly
Print ISBN: 978-1-61921-131-5
Digital ISBN: 978-1-60928-754-2

Editing by Tera Kleinfelter
Cover by Scott Carpenter

First Samhain Publishing, Ltd. electronic publication: June 2012
First Samhain Publishing, Ltd. print publication: May 2013

Dedication

In loving memory of my beloved dad, Vittorio Cocco, a strong and compassionate WWII veteran, a glorious chef, and most importantly, my warm and lovable father. Daddy's Sunday meals were legendary. My fondest childhood memories are of sitting with my family at the dining room table, feasting on the delicious meals he cooked up with flair and so much love.

Acknowledgments

This book is a culmination of love and support from my family, friends and critique partners. I am grateful to my generous mom, Emilia, for always being my champion, to my glamorous Aunt Julia for sharing her love of books, and to my creative sister, Johanna, for her support.

A big thank you to my childhood friends and wonderful writers, Maggie Dove and Mariana Betancourt, for giggles and zany moments during our critique sessions, to Marcia King-Gamble for her valued friendship and commentary, and to the other Divine Critique ladies—Sandy Madden, Linda Anderson, Linda Conrad, Debbie St. Amand, and Carol Stephenson. *Mil gracias* to my esteemed friend and beta reader, Martha Paley Francescato, for her excellent observations. And many thanks to Isabel Arias for her fabulous feedback on *Grill Me, Baby.*

Special recognition to Tera Kleinfelter, my editor extraordinaire, who made this dream come true. The stories I love to write are fueled by much enthusiasm from my tight circle of support—my darling husband Paul, my lifetime love, and our beautiful daughters, Genevieve and Jacqueline. Thank you for believing! Huge thanks to Genevieve for the many reads and her eagle eye for detail and to Jacqueline for her insightful comments and advice. You girls kept it fresh and lively. Mere words cannot express how much I love all of you! May our foodie adventures continue...

Chapter One

So *this* was the infamous Paolo Santos.

Michaela sized up her opponent in the waiting area of the producer's office. The seriously hot Argentine seated across from her looked so relaxed, nobody would have guessed he was vying against her to host the hottest new celebrity chef TV show, *Miami Spice*. A confident smile spread over Paolo's rugged face as she assessed him. His large, muscular body was sprawled across the sofa, with one tanned arm draped across the sofa back and long legs stretched before him. A crisp white linen shirt revealed a hint of hard chest beneath a tailored buff suit. He looked like a perfectly caramelized Argentine *churrasco* steak. Good enough to eat—damn him!

Michaela's stomach growled so loudly that Paolo raised an amused eyebrow. A gentleman would have acted like he hadn't heard it and discreetly looked away.

"Hungry?" he asked with a brazen grin. His deep voice and sexy Latin accent sounded as delicious as he looked.

"Maybe just a little," she replied breezily. She was trying to relax before her meeting with the producer, but cocky Paolo Santos was doing his best to disarm her with steady, smoldering looks.

She smiled coolly and looked away. *Focus*, she told herself. In a few minutes, she would have to sell herself to Mr. Blumenthal, the producer, in order to land the host spot. If she did, she'd become an instant celebrity chef and her almost finished cookbook would rack up lots of sales. She would also be able to pay back her parents every cent they had shelled out for her education. Her parents, two successful partners in the same law firm, still hadn't forgiven her for dropping out of Duke Law School in her third year. Adding insult to injury, she had chucked it all to become a chef. Their grimace of shame when friends asked about Michaela's new career never failed to make her stomach churn. At thirty years of age, it still felt awful being a failure in their eyes.

She needed to use her nervous energy to show she could hold her own alongside celebrity chefs Paula Deen's zaniness or Rachael Ray's perkiness or Bobby Flay's wise guy banter. But she wasn't the only one competing. She had Santos to contend with, and for the life of her, Michaela couldn't help staring at his mouth. It wasn't just the pair of deep-slashed dimples that drew her attention; it was his full lips that were probably great at kissing...

Stop, she told herself, *concentrate on the upcoming interview.*

Michaela focused on the stark, modern painting on the wall before her, but the image of Paolo's white teeth gleaming against his bronzed olive skin invaded her thoughts—strong teeth poised to take a bite out of her chances for the job. From the corner of her eye, she caught his black-as-sin eyes giving her a slow and thorough once-over.

Were all Latin men so forward? Could be a cultural thing, but he might be trying to seduce her into losing her focus. She had to be on her toes around this one. From the moment he'd stepped off the airplane from Buenos Aires and burst upon the scene at Flamingo Island, an exclusive country club residence island, Paolo had built up quite a rep as a player. Oh, she'd heard plenty of gossip about the executive chef's prowess, but today was the first time she'd seen him in action.

During the past half-hour, Michaela had watched Paolo chat and flirt with the young, blonde receptionist, and then with the producer's middle-aged secretary, Ellie. His sexy accent and exotic looks had captivated both women, as he charmed them with his impressions of Miami and its beautiful inhabitants— meaning them, of course.

They hadn't even met yet and Santos's attitude was a bit too familiar this morning. She already knew about his magnetic appeal, especially with the wealthy socialites of Flamingo Island who had standing reservations at Bella Luna. But bad boy types didn't tempt her anymore, not after her break-up with Jeff Convers, tennis bad boy extraordinaire. That regrettable part of her life was behind her. *Don't think about Jeff, the two-timing player,* she told herself. She took a deep breath and forced her thoughts back to meeting Edwin Blumenthal.

"Don't look so worried, Maki." One corner of Paolo's mouth quirked up as he regarded her with interest. "Relax."

"If I were any more relaxed, I'd be asleep." She gave him a raised brow look. Usually that squelched the over-confident types. Distance was needed with this one. His smile alone could charm the shell off an escargot. "My name is Michaela. Maki sounds like a girlie cocktail, and I'm anything but."

He cocked an eyebrow and she took instant note of the twitch at the corners of his lips. Paolo had glossy, jet-black layers cut like Keith Urban's, except he wasn't an Aussie country star—he was a hot chef *and* a major player.

"Michaela?" he repeated, drawing her attention to the shrugging gesture of his upraised hands. He gave her hair an assessing glance. "You should have been named Penny, it suits you better. Your hair shines like a new copper penny."

"Are you a hairdresser too?" she asked, smoothing the sides of her long hair that were pulled half up.

Paolo flashed a dazzling grin. "No, just a chef." He leaned forward and gave her a hearty handshake. "Paolo Santos."

Strong grip. Nothing wrong with that, Michaela thought as she snatched her hand back the moment it touched his warm, callused palm. "Nice to meet you."

"*Encantado*, likewise." He leaned back on the sofa looking a little too pleased with himself. "I can't wait to tell Mr. Blumenthal about my gimmick for the show."

She eyed him suspiciously. "Nobody said anything about coming up with a gimmick. Did you just make that up?"

His brow furrowed. "Why would I do that?"

She shrugged as if it didn't matter. "No gimmick can substitute for fine cooking." She had certificates from The Culinary Institute of America and Le Cordon Bleu in Paris to prove it.

Paolo snorted. "Is that what you call your rabbit food?" He gazed up at the ceiling with a pained expression. When he looked back at her, his eyes twinkled with mischief. "I can't imagine anyone feeling satisfied after eating only birdseed."

She felt like pelting him with birdseed after that comment.

Given his lean waistline and muscular physique, Paolo had to possess a high-octane metabolism that counteracted his rich, Italian-Argentinean cooking.

Not everyone was so blessed, certainly not she. She had been chubby until age nineteen when, to her shock and her family's, she'd found out she had high cholesterol and high blood pressure. She'd had to drastically modify her eating habits and start exercising. As a bona fide foodie, she adored food and every nuance of preparing it. After years of experimenting, she'd found ways to prepare delicious, healthy meals—including desserts—and she was eager to share them with others. She was about to set Paolo straight in defense of her spa clients who gained weight merely by sniffing his fattening cuisine, when Ellie interrupted her.

"Mr. Blumenthal will see you both now," Ellie said. "Please follow me."

"Both of us? Together?" The last thing Michaela wanted was to share her interview with Paolo.

Ellie looked mystified by Michaela's less than enthusiastic reaction. "Yes, he wants to see both of you—together."

Michaela nodded and covered her disappointment with a friendly smile. She stood and smoothed the skirt of her jade green, wrap-style dress.

Paolo rose beside her and it was all she could do not to gawk at him. He looked to be about six foot three with wide shoulders and hard muscles that tapered in to a lean waistline. He probably sported a six-pack under his white shirt too. She straightened to her height of five foot seven on her three-inch high-heeled pumps, not wanting to feel at a disadvantage beside Paolo who was so much bigger. She watched him cross his fingers for luck and make a comical face at Ellie. Squaring her shoulders, Michaela blocked out the woman's delighted giggle.

Paolo reached for the door and opened it with a flourish, allowing Michaela to enter before his towering form. "Thank you." She caught a whiff of citrus and soap and inhaled deeply in spite of herself. Startled by her heady reaction to his clean, masculine scent, Michaela looked at Paolo and caught him giving her behind an admiring glance. They locked eyes and he winked. She raised her chin and turned her attention toward the producer.

Edwin Blumenthal, a gentleman of medium height and graying hair who appeared to be in his early sixties, stood behind a massive, granite-topped desk. His sky-blue golf shirt and khaki pants made him look as if he'd just finished teeing off. Lucky man, his spacious office overlooked beautiful Biscayne Bay, currently occupied by massive luxury cruise ships queued up to leave port.

After introductions, Michaela and Paolo stood facing the producer across the desk.

"Please sit down." Mr. Blumenthal motioned toward the gray leather seats before his desk. "We have a lot to cover this morning, so I'll be brief. Although *Miami Spice* will be filmed and produced locally, it will appear nationally on the Food Network in the coveted Saturday morning line-up."

Paolo propped both thumbs up in a gesture of enthusiasm. "Fantastic!"

Mr. Blumenthal nodded. "You two are the final contenders for the competition. Since you both work on Flamingo Island, it would be fitting to feature your cooking talents together in one pilot episode."

"Are you looking for two chefs for the series?" Paolo asked, giving Michaela a quick glance.

"No," he replied. "The show will have only one host, with visiting chefs from area restaurants occasionally making appearances."

"Then why do we have to go on together?" Michaela asked, keeping her tone light.

"After eliminating the rest of the competition, the producers watched your audition tapes again and narrowed it down to the two of you," Mr. Blumenthal said. "They'd like you to do one episode together to see how our viewers react. You, Miss Willoughby, have an elegant style, as opposed to Mr. Santos's earthy approach."

"*¿Sí?*" Paolo's white teeth flashed happily. "*Gracias.* We both thank you, right, Maki?"

Michaela smiled at Mr. Blumenthal. "They could tell all this from a videotape?"

Mr. Blumenthal nodded. "We're not in this business for

15

nothing."

"But my cooking is totally different from Paolo's." She paused, noting that Paolo had leaned forward in his seat. "His cooking is rich and spicy," she said, refraining from calling it bad for you. "Mine is light and quite innovative. I have an amazing gimmick planned," she blurted out, avoiding eye contact with Paolo. Why had she said that? She never used that word and now she regretted it, especially when she saw Mr. Blumenthal's surprised reaction.

"A gimmick? Haven't heard that word in a while. Well, good for you," he said, beaming. "Good for you."

She started to panic over her fib, but she covered it up with a confident smile. "Won't you reconsider and allow me to present a show that focuses on delicious, health-conscious cuisine—one which everyone in the audience can enjoy without worrying about calories?" she asked Mr. Blumenthal.

Paolo let out a robust chuckle. "Why ruin good food by counting calories, eh, Mr. Blumenthal? We're not here to lecture our audience. This is supposed to be a fun show, isn't it?"

"It will be fun, just not...high in calories," she said, trying not to let Paolo's comments annoy her.

Mr. Blumenthal gave her a measured look. "I'm sorry, Miss Willoughby, but my mind is made up. I'm sure you can come up with a menu together to complement your individual styles. We'll need a complete meal that you will prepare together before the audience."

"No problem," Paolo said, before Michaela could answer. "We would be happy to, right, Maki?"

"Right...Paulie," she countered. If he insisted on calling her a nickname, she might as well do the same.

"Good," Mr. Blumenthal said. "I can see you two are well acquainted."

Paolo threw his arm around Michaela's shoulders. "No, we just met in the lobby. But I can tell we're going to be good friends."

Did he have to smell so good? Paolo's muscular arm around her was making her feel as wobbly as one of his *flan* desserts. She moved away from him and put some steel in her backbone.

"After the pilot, one of you will be chosen to come back to make a solo tape. And may the best man—or woman—win," Mr. Blumenthal said. "Based on the results before the live audience, we'll make our final decision. Any questions?"

Michaela had many questions she wanted to ask, but Paolo beat her to it.

"Just one." Paolo leaned forward eagerly. "Actually, it's not a question, but a suggestion. My gimmick is sure to be a hit."

Mr. Blumenthal looked delighted. "That's the type of enthusiasm I'm looking for, but save the gimmicks for later. If you're invited back, you can use it on your solo show."

Michaela wondered what Paolo's gimmick was. He was quite the performer, with a growing fan base. She had heard from her clients about the sexy way he wore a white shirt rolled up at the sleeves and tucked into black jeans, with a bandanna tied over his jet-black hair as he prepared food behind a glass panel in full view of the Bella Luna patrons. The showman didn't only prepare food, he did little dance steps and sang tangos as he sliced, chopped and flambéed.

"We'll tape live before an audience next Monday morning at ten sharp. You have a week from today to prepare," Mr. Blumenthal said briskly. "Ellie will put you in touch with Ted Marton, the culinary producer. He'll need the menu list so the kitchen staff and supporting chefs can prep your ingredients."

Mr. Blumenthal stood, signaling that the meeting was over. Raising bushy brows, he peered at them through steel-rim glasses. "If you have further questions, don't hesitate to call Ellie any time this week."

Michaela extended her hand. "Thank you. It was a pleasure meeting you."

"Yes, likewise, Michaela," Mr. Blumenthal replied, shaking her hand.

The ever-inappropriate Paolo gave Mr. Blumenthal a man hug. "Great meeting you, sir. You won't be disappointed. Maki and I will plan a menu sure to make the audience's mouth water."

Michaela's left eye began to twitch out of control.

Paolo winked at her. "Let's go, Maki." He gently nudged the small of her back with his big hand.

She shrugged his hand away from her back as she strode to the elevator. When the doors were shut, she pressed the lobby button and turned to him. "Listen, Paolo, this is a professional arrangement and we need to get along. You can start by calling me Michaela, not Maki."

He quirked an eyebrow. "Why were you winking at me?"

"I wasn't. You winked at me!"

He pointed at her eye. "Your left eyelid was moving up and down. Don't deny it."

"It twitches sometimes when I'm stressed out." She shouldn't have admitted it. He probably thought he had the upper hand now.

"I thought you said you were relaxed. You don't act like it, Maki."

Normally she could relax, but he had the unfortunate ability to rile her up. They rode the elevator in silence. As soon as they descended to the lobby and the doors opened, she rushed out.

"Hey!" he called. "Slow down."

Michaela didn't stop until she reached her car and her eye had stopped twitching. "*Nena*," he said once he reached her. "What have I done to upset you?"

"First of all, stop calling me *nena*."

He threw his hands up in exasperation. "Why? It is an endearment in Spanish."

Endearment? "We just met, so there's no need for endearments. And don't call me Maki. You did it again after I told you to call me Michaela."

Paolo's roguish dimples snagged her attention. "I couldn't help myself. I think Maki is cute—like you. It suits you."

She looked away from the seductive twinkle in his eyes. That was a first. Nobody ever called her cute. Her sister Tiffany was cute, but not Michaela. "Save your charms and gimmicks for someone else, Santos. I'm on to you."

Paolo laughed out loud. "Is that the worst you could come up with?"

She lifted an eyebrow. "Would you like me to curse?"

He gave a casual shrug of his wide shoulders. "It works for

me when I'm mad. Let me warn you, little spaghetti—" Paolo's genial expression turned serious, "—I don't get angry easily or often, but when I do, you won't want to be there. And you won't like hearing me swear in Spanish."

"Ooh, I'm terrified. I don't care if you curse in Spanish or Japanese."

He smiled, his dark eyes crinkling at the corners. "Good."

"We need to come up with a menu as soon as possible."

"I'll leave my sous chef in charge tonight. How about we meet at my place at seven?"

His place? Uh uh. "Can't tonight. Let's meet tomorrow...at my apartment."

He chuckled. "Pretty bossy aren't you?" He surprised her by handing her his business card. "Call me."

She read his card aloud, "Paolo Santos, magnificent chef." She chuckled. "We'll see about that."

"I'm not bragging. It's true."

She waved his card. "Who came up with your title?"

"My immigration lawyer. I came to this country with a visa that states I have extraordinary ability."

"Oh brother."

His gaze turned sharp and his smile faded. "I'm planning on winning," he stated as if it was a done deal.

"I plan to knock 'em dead," she said confidently. "I want this job more than anything in the world."

Paolo's eyes glinted like onyx stones. "Me too, and I always win."

"You hadn't met me yet," she said, poking his chest with her pointer finger.

He rubbed his offended chest. "Your cooking is more suited to anorexic socialites. Mine is purely for pleasure."

"I guess the sky's the limit when you're clogging arteries," she retorted.

"I don't only prepare Italian and Argentinean cuisine. I can make everything and it is delicious." He kissed his fingertips with a resounding smack. "Grilling, or *parrillada* as we say in Argentina, is my specialty. Now you're probably going to say that grilling isn't healthy."

"Scoff all you like, but my conscience is clear. My clients eat well and feel great. Many of them have serious conditions such as diabetes and heart disease."

"You forgot boredom and too much money," he said, with a wry twist of his mouth. "What can you do that Weight Watchers hasn't done?"

The man was getting on her last nerve.

"My cooking wins hands down," he added blithely.

"Ha!" she huffed. They were getting nowhere exchanging barbs. She spun on her heel and stalked away.

Paolo caught up with her in two strides. "Until tomorrow. *Ciao*, Maki. Can't wait to see your gimmick." His dimples flashed to taunt her as he turned and ambled toward his tomato red Alfa Romeo convertible. How fitting that he drove that car; he was an Alpha Romeo, all right.

Michaela watched him take off his jacket and fling it on the back seat, her gaze drawn to his broad shoulders and wide back that tapered into a lean waistline above a compact butt. Try as she might, she couldn't stop staring as he got into the car and drove away. Damn the man for looking so hot as the wind ruffled his thick hair.

As Paolo exited the parking lot, he turned to wave good-bye with a confident grin. Michaela quickly looked away and got into her car. She glanced up at the April sky and noticed a cluster of purple clouds closing in on the clear blue expanse. It would be fitting if he got caught in the downpour. Smiling to herself, she took great pleasure in an image of Paolo, sopping wet and bedraggled as he drove his flashy convertible back to Flamingo Island.

He was so full of himself, she was itching to take him down a few pegs and roast him over his own *parrillada*.

Magnificent chef, indeed!

Chapter Two

Paolo drove his convertible onto the Flamingo Island ferry, put it in Park, and then turned off the engine. He leaned his head back on the leather seat and soaked up the sunshine with pleasure. Turning his gaze across the bay, he noticed the waterspout over the island and wondered if Michaela had been spared a drenching. A little water would definitely cool that temper of hers. What a little spitfire! So tantalizing, he thought, smiling as he closed his eyes and got a vivid picture of her lush pink lips forming an O as she watched him drive away.

The appetizing redhead's slim body had just the right curves. Michaela's dress had shown off her figure to perfection—not too tight, it skimmed over her pert breasts and the sweet curve of her bottom. And those legs, damn, that was a whole other matter...

He was used to women using their looks to their advantage, but Michaela didn't seem to realize how appealing she was. It was refreshing; the camera would love her. All she had to do was loosen up and she'd have the audience eating out of her hand.

Her features were deceptively angelic, but her personality wasn't. Maybe it was true what they said about redheads and their fiery tempers. He had certainly gotten a rise out of her. Not that he hadn't had fun goading her. Who could blame him for wanting to shake her up a little to see that small patrician nose raised in disdain and her fair cheeks turn pink? He'd enjoyed watching her intelligent, blue-green eyes flash with fire at his teasing.

Michaela's striking aquamarine eyes, clear one moment and tempestuous the next, had captivated his attention. But it was her luscious, plump lips that had really turned him on. She had the kind of mouth that invited fantasies and he'd had a few while waiting in Blumenthal's office. Her seductress's mouth might have enticed him, but her dismissive response to his flirting had puzzled him. Not that he was Casanova, but women, as a rule, liked him. And he liked women. However, Michaela didn't seem to like him. Paolo was used to women and their mercurial moods, but the pretty redhead's feistiness had gotten under his skin.

Paolo had been raised as the sole male among a household of women: his widowed mother, his four sisters and his grandmother, Nonna, all had lively personalities. His love of cooking was nurtured at a young age, from hanging around in the kitchen with these women as they cooked and gossiped. As the only boy, the women had spoiled him with an outpouring of affection and devotion. He loved women and felt he understood them, and he was tolerant of their dramas when it came to matters of the heart.

But for all his experience with women and their moods, he had been taken aback by the bossy redhead. When he'd tried to get her attention before the interview, Michaela had sat upright, her graceful hands folded on her lap, high-heeled pumps planted on the floor and slim ankles pressed together. Her thick copper hair had been secured half up making Paolo eager to see how she would look with it tousled about her flushed face.

Señorita Willoughby was going to be a real pain in the ass, but he could handle her. He had no intention of letting her ruin his excellent cuisine with her rabbit food. Paolo's mood brightened at the prospect of dueling with the tempting peach. He would beat the fancy pants off his fiery competitor—literally—with her own spatula if necessary. That fantasy led to hearty chuckles as he started the ignition and shifted gears when the ferry arrived at posh Flamingo Island.

Paolo loved working on Flamingo Island, lavish playground of millionaires, sports figures and celebrities. He had really lucked out on being hired as executive chef of Bella Luna Restaurant on the exclusive tropical resort encompassing over two hundred acres. The whole island operated like a private country club to its residents—some American, but the majority from Latin America and Europe. Residents owned a piece of the island and of the par thirty-five, nine-hole golf course, and they had full access to all the amenities including four first-class restaurants, a state-of-the-art spa and fitness center, fourteen tennis courts and a private beach and marina where they could dock their yachts.

Paolo heeded the required thirteen-mile per hour speed limit as he drove past verdant hedges, royal palm trees and rows of crimson, coral and white petunias and impatiens. Vibrant fuchsia bougainvilleas cascaded over low stone walls encircling Mediterranean style villas and opulent homes that bordered the island with unfettered ocean views. When he reached the massive Art Deco waterfront mansion rumored to be haunted, he waved at the two elderly Bryce sisters who were steady lunch clients at Bella Luna. A wealthy, debauched Italian count, Salvatore Giamano, had once owned the 1920's mansion situated in the middle of a beautiful park where peacocks roamed freely and huge banyan trees offered cool shade even on the hottest summer day.

Turning the corner, Paolo saluted a trio of joggers leaving The Island Spa. He veered to the right a few blocks farther and pulled into the restaurant lot. He parked his car outside the back door and found Gil, the sous chef, taking a cigarette break.

"*Hola*, Gil," Paolo called out, ambling toward him. "How's things?"

"Going good." Gil took a drag of the cigarette. His round, swarthy face and thick, prizefighter's neck was in stark contrast to his gentle disposition. He was the closest thing Paolo had to a brother and he cherished their friendship. "How did it go with the producer?"

"My meeting with Mr. Blumenthal went great. But the chef from The Island Spa was another matter. Michaela Willoughby is one tough *biscotti*."

"Oh? How so?" Gil's rotund belly shook with merriment as he regarded Paolo.

"I tried to be friendly, but she's not looking forward to doing the show with me. I don't think she likes me," he said with a wry grin.

"Maybe you're losing your touch," Gil taunted, slapping Paolo on the back.

Paolo snorted. "She might think she's all that, but I plan to be the next celebrity chef." He paused for a reflective moment. "I owe it to the family—mostly to Papá."

"Come on, Paolo. Don't start feeling guilty. All that's in the past." Gil took a drag of the cigarette and exhaled slowly. "You help your mom by being like a father to your four sisters. It's not an easy job with you here and them in Argentina."

"Yeah, but if I become *Miami Spice's* chef, it will be a fine tribute to Papá's memory." Paying tribute to his dad's memory wouldn't erase the sad regret he felt over the circumstances of his passing, but it might bring him some sort of closure. "If I win, I can stay in the States longer and help Mamá and the girls with their expenses—including my sister Gina's wedding."

"I'm sure you'll win over Michaela," Gil said loyally. He patted Paolo's shoulder. "Let's go inside. I have some questions about tonight's menu."

A little under five hundred square feet in size and scrupulously clean, the Sublime restaurant kitchen at The Island Spa had everything Michaela desired, including state-of-the-art appliances and a full staff reporting to her. She usually arrived by nine in the morning to check that the fresh supplies had come in. Whenever possible, she bought locally and in season, ensuring the utmost freshness. It was a luxury to order the best produce, fish, poultry and meat for her clients. Flamingo Island patrons were used to eating only the best, often to excess. It was Michaela's joy to introduce them to the art of eating for wellness *and* pleasure.

Once she was sure the shipment met her standards, she would plan the day's featured dishes. By ten in the morning, everyone in her staff, from prep cook to sous chef, was in position and ready to work.

Today's lunch special would be sesame crusted ahi tuna sliders and citrus slaw. For the daily lunch special, Michaela often took a comfort food and put a healthy twist to it. She prided herself in offering fun food like a slider, where one could still enjoy biting into a little dinner roll, yet the unexpected filling surprised and delighted one's palate. She discussed the meal prep with Elliot, her sous chef, and then stepped outside to call Paolo.

After meeting the boastful chef yesterday, Michaela planned to take the lead in scheduling to ensure that things were done efficiently. She dialed his number and was about to hang up when he finally answered on the fifth ring.

"*Hola*," a sleepy male voice intoned.

"Paolo, it's ten o'clock in the morning. Did I wake you?"

"Ah, it's you, Maki." Paolo yawned loudly.

"Michaela," she corrected automatically. He was still calling her Maki, but this time uttered in Paolo's deep, slumberous voice and sexy Latin accent, it didn't sound quite so bad.

"How are you?"

"I'm fine, thank you. I've been up since bright and early and I already planned the menu list for the pilot episode."

"Oh, you did, eh?" Paolo's voice rumbled with amusement. "When do I get to see this list?"

"I'll email it to you now. We need to get it to the culinary producer as soon as possible." Hopefully, that would propel him out of bed and into thinking about their show. The careful planner in Michaela had a hunch that Paolo was a seat-of-the-pants kind of guy—in everything.

"I work better in person. What time do you leave work?"

"Around six."

"*¡Perfecto!* Come to my place after work. I'll cook dinner for us. I insist."

"Yesterday we agreed to meet at my place. Aren't you working tonight?"

"My sous chef, Gil, will cover for me."

It might not be a bad idea to let Paolo cook for her first. That way she could observe the culinary skills he boasted about. "Fine, we'll meet at your place. What should I bring? Dessert?" She would be sure to bring one of her light creations, to show him a thing or two.

"Don't bring anything. My address is on the card. See you at six. *Ciao, linda.*"

Michaela shook her head as she stared at the receiver in her hand before hanging up. He had just called her beautiful in Spanish. Not that she minded the compliment, but it came off as glib since he'd just met her. She looked up and saw one of the salon's massage therapists, Lisa Grieves, approaching her. Lisa's compact, petite frame was strong and fit. Her sleek blonde hair was pulled back in a clip, showing off big green eyes and a pretty smile.

"Hey, Lisa," Michaela said.

"Did I hear you set up a date with the hottie Argentinean chef?"

"It's not a date. I have to go to Paolo Santos's apartment tonight and plan the meal we're going to cook together."

"Ha, just listen to you. I *have* to go to Paolo Santos's apartment tonight," Lisa mimicked. Her eyes sparkled playfully. "As if that's a hardship. Better watch out. The word is he's quite the player. Last week when I massaged Bernice Blumenthal, she had just come from having lunch at Bella Luna. She couldn't stop gushing about Paolo and calling him a stud." She giggled. "She even described his body in vivid detail."

Michaela's feelers went up. "Are you telling me that the producer's wife knows Paolo?"

"Hello? Every woman on this island knows Paolo...and they lust after him."

"Not me." Michaela pursed her lips thoughtfully. "Hmm, I wonder if that's how he made it to the finals."

"Probably. Bernice is the one who sponsored him."

"I didn't know that." Michaela tried not to let it worry her. Bernice wouldn't be picking the winner. Mr. Blumenthal and other culinary producers would be judging their performances. The Island Spa was sponsoring Michaela, and she was grateful for the staff and her spa clients who were enthusiastically pulling for her.

"Paolo doesn't need inside help from Bernice. He does pretty well on his own. Your Argentinean has become quite a celebrity here."

"He's not *my* Argentinean," Michaela said quickly. "Frankly, he's infuriating. He flirts and teases...and he is so full of himself. I know his type."

"I wouldn't mind flirting with a hottie like Paolo. It would take my mind off of Tommy."

"More problems?" Michaela asked gently.

Lisa nodded and her green eyes suddenly clouded. "It's over...we're over. I asked Tommy to move out this weekend." Her voice caught and she swallowed hard. "He said he doesn't feel the 'passion' anymore. I think he's cheating on me."

"Ugh, I'm so sorry you're going through this. You deserve better." Michaela's insides roiled at the memory of her ex-fiancé, Jeff's, betrayal. She put her arm around Lisa's slumped shoulders and gave her a supportive squeeze.

Lisa sniffled and wiped her eyes. "This is silly, I must be PMSing, but I'm beginning to doubt I'll ever find Mr. Right. I just don't seem to fall for the good ones."

"Me neither. Anyway, it's not worth being with someone who doesn't respect you, right? Remember what I went through with Jeff."

"That was different. He asked you to marry him."

Michaela snorted. "Only because he wanted me to be the 'respectable' cover for the press."

"What do you mean? Are you telling me Jeff was *gay*?" she asked, shocked.

"Nooo, just the opposite. He was a sex addict—with everyone but me," Michaela said, still smarting from the memory.

"Ew, you're better off without him. You never told me about that part."

It was true. Michaela hadn't told anyone but her family. But seeing the shock on Lisa's face, she knew it was time to qualify what she'd just said. "It was too raw for me to tell you about it when it was going on."

"I understand. You don't have to tell me if you don't want to."

"No, it's okay. I know I can trust you." Michaela took a deep breath and exhaled as she gathered her thoughts. She hadn't talked about Jeff in so long, it was strangely cathartic now. "Before we started dating, Jeff got a socialite teenager pregnant. He was thirty-two at the time. Ashley was only eighteen and he wouldn't marry her. He made her get an abortion."

Lisa's eyes shot open. "Oh no."

Michaela nodded, the memories making her feel sick inside all over again. "They managed to keep it out of the tabloids, but

Jeff's dad and his manager ordered him to clean up his act. That's when he went after me—the nice girl," she said, making quotation marks with her fingers. "I had no idea about his past, but he was so sexy and confident, different from any guy I'd ever dated. Jeff swept me off my feet and before I knew it we were engaged." She paused and swallowed hard. "Until the day after our engagement party when I caught him having sex with Ashley."

Lisa gasped. "No! Was she the one he got pregnant?"

Michaela nodded grimly. "One and the same."

"What did you do?"

"I dumped his sorry ass. Unfortunately, I found out later that Jeff had been hooking up with other young girls too." All the old anger and outrage rushed back, hitting her full force. A year ago, she'd gone from crying to raging over what she'd learned about him. Michaela strove to shake off her anger—no sense in reliving past heartache. "I'm stronger and hopefully wiser now. That's why charismatic players like Paolo are poison to me—he could be as bad as Jeff."

"Or maybe not. Paolo might be different."

"I doubt it. Players are selfish and they usually end up breaking some poor girl's heart. I don't want to ever be that girl again."

"I don't either. I was just teasing." Lisa looked wistful. "I want to get married and start a family."

"Me too—some day." Michaela chuckled and hugged Lisa. "Just look at us, moping about men. I hope we both find the right one some day. I know you will, at least. You're pretty and fun—and you give a great massage."

Lisa managed a wobbly smile. "Aw, you're sweet. I needed that. I still want a full report on Paolo tomorrow."

"Hmph, well he's coming across as a bit of a chauvinist. The type who thinks the little woman should cater to him and be kept barefoot and pregnant."

Lisa's eyebrows shot up. "Really? Most women *love* him. Paolo must have some good qualities."

"He might, but I need to keep my guard up. There's too much at stake. Remember, I'm self-pubbing my cookbook. If I get chosen for *Miami Spice*, my book sales will be off the charts and I won't have to hear one more 'I-told-you-so' from my parents about all the rejections from the New York publishers."

Lisa gave her arm an encouraging squeeze. "I'm rooting for you to win." She was as loyal as they came. That's why it was doubly rotten of Tommy to tell Lisa he didn't feel the "passion" with her anymore. The jerk.

"Thanks. Paolo is very ambitious and overly confident. I'm setting some ground rules tonight."

"Good for you! If anyone can handle him, it's you."

Michaela felt a surge of sly anticipation as she smiled back. "I plan on deflating the Latin lover's puffed up ego." She made a stabbing motion with her pointer finger. "I'm going to flatten the air out of that Argentinean soufflé."

Lisa eyes popped open. "Wow," she breathed.

"I am not kidding. I will slice and dice him until I've made mincemeat out of his oversized conceit. By the time I'm finished with Paolo, he'll be reduced to *petits pois* size."

Lisa took a step backward and giggled nervously. "Your eyes look a little scary, Michaela. What are you planning to do to him?"

"I'm still deciding. But one thing's for sure. I'm going to be the new host of *Miami Spice!*"

Chapter Three

At five minutes to six, Michaela stood outside Paolo's door and rang the doorbell. Was that him singing inside? Intrigued, she leaned in to listen and almost fell forward when the door was flung open. Looking ruggedly handsome and freshly shaven, Paolo grasped her shoulders and greeted her with a kiss on each cheek.

"*¡Querida!*" he boomed. "You're early."

"I'm on time," she corrected, caught off guard by the intoxicating whiff of his subtle citrus cologne mingled with the mouth-watering scents wafting from the kitchen. Oh God. She was famished—not just for food, but also evidenced by her racing pulse, for male company. Unfortunately, her work schedule left little time for dating.

Who was she kidding? This was no date and there was nothing ordinary about the hot Argentine. Michaela raised her hand to her cheek where his lips had been only seconds earlier. Most social kisses were air kisses. Not Paolo's...he made sure his lips touched skin. *Whoa, calm down,* she told herself firmly. *He's your opponent.*

Paolo took her wrist in his big hand and glanced at her watch. "I'm running a little late."

"Do you want me to come back later?" She snatched her wrist out of his warm grasp.

"No, of course not. Come in, come in." He cocked his head and sized up her starched turquoise chef's tunic. "Did you come over straight from work?"

"Yes, I didn't have time to go home and change."

Michaela sized him up too, taking in the white cotton shirt rolled up on his brawny forearms and casually tucked into a pair of snug jeans. Glancing down at his feet, she noted he was barefoot. A little too comfy for a business meeting. His black, deep-set eyes crinkled at the corners as he watched her checking him out.

"I can lend you a blouse if you want to change into something less stiff." He waved his hand at her eloquently.

She arched a brow. "Oh? You keep women's clothes here?"

His dimples deepened. "My mistake, *querida*. I translated wrong. I should have said shirt. One of my shirts."

Michaela's fingers fiddled with the top button of her tunic chef's apron. "No, thanks. I'm comfortable." She squared her shoulders and pulled a paper out of her briefcase. This was a business meeting, nothing more. "Why don't we get down to business? Here's the menu that I..."

"Put that away." Paolo frowned at the paper she held out. "We'll look at it later."

"Fine." Michaela stuffed the paper back into her briefcase, shut it with a snap and set it on the floor. Clearly, Paolo wasn't going to talk business until he was good and ready. The macho Argentine in him probably wanted things done his way and the Italian in him preferred to do it on a full stomach.

Michaela took a quick inventory of his small living room. She had expected to find a bachelor pad complete with a big, flat-screen TV, black leather couches and the latest issues of *Maxim* magazines lying on his coffee table, featuring hot girls in bikinis.

Instead, his apartment was kind of cozy in muted tones of ochre, accented by two brandy colored leather couches, a man-size espresso-colored recliner, and a large coffee table. The butter-colored walls were jammed with autographed photos of a grinning Paolo posing with A-list celebrities. In all the pictures, Paolo's tanned arm was amiably slung over each celebrity's shoulders. Michaela's jaw dropped. Had that many superstars eaten at Ristorante Bella Luna? The Latin lover sure knew how to schmooze.

"I've made a lot of friends here," he said with a casual nod at the photos.

"Friends?"

He flashed a confident grin. "Of course."

"Of course," she repeated, walking toward the couch competing for space beside an upright piano. She noticed the array of thriving herbs in terracotta pots on the shelf under the window. So Paolo had a green thumb and he played the piano. Interesting...

"Nice place," she murmured.

"Thanks. It's not big, but it suits my needs. Come to the kitchen. I'm making *crostini*."

Michaela followed the tempting aromas into his surprisingly large kitchen.

"Please sit down. *Salud*." He handed her a glass of chilled pinot grigio and clinked it with his. Gesturing toward the cobalt-blue tiled kitchen counter, he pulled out a barstool for her. The counter was set with square straw place mats and sleek white dishes, a clean, simple setting for his meal. Ripe figs rested in a white bowl at the end of the counter.

Paolo followed her gaze and gestured to the bowl. "Figs are my favorite fruit." He bared perfect white teeth in a lopsided grin. "I love to pull apart the delicate skin and devour the plump flesh inside."

His vivid description made Michaela's toes curl and she sputtered her sip of wine. Their gazes locked and the smolder in his dark eyes made her sizzle like the hot skillet where he was grilling slices of Tuscan bread. After drizzling them with olive oil, he lovingly rubbed each slice with a split clove of raw garlic and topped it with a thin smear of cannellini paste, followed by chopped, ripe tomatoes. Her gaze was captivated by Paolo's large, brown hands when he took a sprig of basil from a potted plant on the windowsill, plucked the leaves, and roughly tore them up.

"Your herbs look so healthy. What's your secret for growing basil?" she asked.

"I take the leaves and pinch, pinch, pinch." He winked. "But always on the bottom."

"I'm sure you're a pro at pinching bottoms," she murmured dryly.

He grinned shamelessly. "I like to think so." Paolo finished sprinkling the basil over the *crostini* and handed one to Michaela.

Before she could respond, the front door flung open and three giggling girls in bikini tops and sarongs sauntered into his apartment.

"Hey, Paolo, got enough for us?" a Pamela Anderson wannabe asked.

"Yeah, smells delish," added her identical twin. "We couldn't resist popping in."

"Paolo, *amor*, the aroma in the hallway would tempt a saint. What are you making?" a sexy, tanned brunette asked as she sashayed toward him.

"I would invite you to stay and eat, but I'm in the middle of a business dinner." He indicated Michaela. "This is Chef Michaela. We're competing for the new cooking show I told you about." He passed around a platter. "Here, have some *crostini*."

"Hi." Michaela tried to sound friendly, but she wasn't thrilled about the interruption or the familiarity of the sexy babes.

The three of them sized up Michaela's buttoned-up chef tunic and barely acknowledged her with a polite nod. Evidently, she posed no threat.

"Maki, these are my neighbors. The twins are Sasha and Suki. And this is their roommate, Elena," he said, nodding toward the brunette. "Elena owns Cheeky Chic, a Brazilian bikini shop in South Beach. Elena's like me, we both have Italian mothers."

Michaela smiled politely and watched the girls eat the *crostini* and lavish compliments on Paolo. He, in turn, was basking in their flirting and enjoying himself immensely.

"Paolo, can we tempt you for a little swim?" Elena sidled up to him. "We were on our way to the pool."

"Not today, Elena." Paolo's smile broadened and those rakish dimples appeared, seeming to wink at her. "I really am in the middle of a business meeting. Maybe tomorrow night."

Michaela told herself not to be bothered. She didn't know why the idea of Paolo carousing in a pool with three bikini-clad bombshells annoyed her, but it did. She was glad when they finally left.

Determined to seem unfazed, Michaela asked, "What part of Italy is your mother from?"

"Mamá was born in Buenos Aires, but her mother was from Firenze. When my grandmother's family moved to Buenos Aires, she met my grandfather, who was from the States."

"No wonder your English is so good."

"Thanks. Have you been to Italy?"

"I spent a year in Paris, studying at Le Cordon Bleu. That summer, I toured Europe, but spent most of my time in Spain and Italy. Tuscany was my favorite region." Michaela took a final, crunchy bite of *crostini* and sipped more wine.

"Mine too," he said, beaming. Paolo grabbed a dishtowel and tucked it in the front of his jeans, apron-style. He turned to the stove. "We're almost ready to eat."

Michaela watched him sauté fresh *haricots verts* in a liberal amount of garlic and green olive oil. She checked out the grill section of the six-burner, Jenn Air stove. "You're not grilling tonight?"

"Nah, only the *crostini*. I prefer to grill meat outdoors or at the restaurant."

She got up from the barstool and peeked through the glass oven door. "Roast pork tenderloin and potato-fennel gratin." She inhaled the savory aroma. "You must have added cream and flavored the gratin with vermouth. Am I right?"

His eyes gleamed with admiration. "You have an amazing sense of smell."

Michaela smiled. "My taste buds are even better."

"I'll have to remember that." Paolo's glance rested on her mouth briefly and then returned to gaze into her eyes. "Move aside, *mujer*, I need to work."

His warm breath tickled her sensitive ear. That and his firm hand on her waist sent a hot thrill coursing through her. He was a lethal combination—an exotic chef with sexy hands making killer food. To her surprise, he suddenly launched into a Spanish ballad as he turned back toward the oven. She had to hand it to him—Paolo was pure entertainment, but he oozed too much Latin charm and hot sexuality for his own good—or hers.

When he bent over to open the oven door, Michaela couldn't help but notice that his jeans did justice to a tight, muscular butt. Her face flamed with embarrassment when he turned from his bent-over position and caught her ogling the seat of his pants.

Paolo flashed a knowing grin. "Is it too warm in here? You look flushed, Maki."

"It's the wine." Michaela looked away from the devilish twinkle in those dark eyes as she opened the top two buttons of her tunic. Paolo's gaze dropped to the hollow at her throat and her pulse tripped up. An image of him kissing her and unbuttoning the rest of her tunic came out of nowhere. He smiled slowly, the sensual invitation in his eyes sparking sweet heat that spread from her face and neck to a place deep in her belly. Flustered, she looked away and rapidly fanned herself. "Can't wait to taste the tenderloin," she said lamely.

"It's my mother's recipe. Mamá's family in Firenze grills a whole pork loin on their outdoor spit every Sunday afternoon. They stud it with lots of garlic and rosemary, and then baste it with red wine. The best part is the crackling rind." He pressed his fingertips together and smacked them with a kiss. "*¡Delicioso!*"

"Yes, well, it might be delicious." She tore her gaze away from his sultry mouth and swallowed hard. "But it's too rich to indulge in on a weekly basis."

"That's silly." Paolo's appreciative gaze slid over her figure. "With your shape, you shouldn't be worrying about rich food, little spaghetti. Women are supposed to have curves." He moved his hands in an exaggerated hourglass shape.

You certainly know all about female curves, she thought, recalling his near-naked neighbors as she headed toward the overflowing sink. What a disaster—so different from her habit of washing, drying and putting things away as she used them to avoid a messy overload at the end.

"I'm going to clear things up a bit," she said.

Paolo shook his head of shaggy, black hair. "Don't. I'll do that later." He placed his hand on the small of her back, the heat of his skin sending a tingle straight to her toes as he led her back to the barstool. "Sit down. We're ready to eat."

There it was again, that dazzling, white-toothed smile against dark olive skin, the type of smile any sensible person would do well to ignore, Michaela thought, looking away.

"Please refill our wine glasses while I serve the gnocchi," he said.

Michaela obliged and then sat back and enjoyed having Paolo serve her. She speared a tiny dumpling and tasted it. Rich and creamy, the gnocchi tasted delicious bathed in tomato basil sauce, but it had whole ricotta and egg. She could tell on the first bite. It was possible to achieve a lighter, airy gnocchi without the yolk or ricotta. She would have made it with potato instead of flour and used one egg white.

"Very nice," she said politely, liking the hint of nutmeg in the gnocchi.

"*Gracias.*"

The glazed pork tenderloin emerged from the oven with a perfectly crusted outside and tender and herb-studded inside. Paolo served two thick slices beside a serving of the golden gratin and fragrant *haricots verts*.

When he drizzled extra virgin olive oil over the gratin, Michaela switched her plate with his. "No oil for me."

"Nonsense, I insist." Ignoring her resistance, he drizzled the olive oil over the *haricots verts* as well!

Michaela made a mental note to discourage his heavy-handed use of olive oil. The additional calories were an unnecessary indulgence.

Paolo gestured to the feast before them. "*Buen provecho*, let's eat."

She wanted to purr with sheer bliss after the first taste of succulent pork, but she didn't, it would feed his ego too much. "This is lovely." Damn. It was more than lovely—the pork was tasty and juicy—just like its creator.

During the rest of the meal, she encouraged Paolo to share his recipes, but he was casual about instructions and measurements. When they cooked together, she would insist on the exact recipe and not "a little of this and a pinch of that".

He served small white cups of strong espresso with first-rate crema and a rich mascarpone and dark chocolate-laced tiramisu.

"Just a tiny piece for me," she said weakly.

For once, Paolo complied. One taste of the luscious, Sambuca-infused layers made her wish he had cut a bigger piece, but she had to be moderate or she wouldn't be camera ready next week. Everyone said TV added at least ten pounds to your figure.

Michaela took another sip of espresso and gazed around, savoring the combination of creamy tiramisu and strong coffee on her palate. There wasn't one inch of clear counter space and the sink overflowed with dirty dishes. Empty dessert plate in hand, she headed toward the sink and turned on the faucet, only to have Paolo's warm hand cover hers and shut off the water supply. She peered into his deep-set, inky eyes and a shiver teased the length of her spine. She needed space from him, especially when his long fingers lightly squeezed her hand and her body reacted pleasurably, against her will.

He led her out of the kitchen. "Come into the living room for a little *vin santo*," he said, sounding like a wolf luring the lamb. *You are not his lambie,* she reminded herself.

Michaela removed her hand from his and perched on the edge of his couch. "Everything was great, but I would have cut each portion to a third of what you served me and eliminated most of the olive oil."

Paolo gave a derisive snort. "That's not eating, that's dieting! No wonder the women on Flamingo Island don't look feminine, more like dried-up little breadsticks."

She stared at him with a flash of annoyance. "So now I'm a dried-up little breadstick?"

"Not you, Maki. You are round in all the right places. For my taste, that is," he added with a devilish grin.

"We're not here to discuss my figure or your taste."

"Hey, it was a compliment."

"Thanks, but I don't appreciate your remarks about my clients. They work hard to be healthy and fit."

"It's one man's humble opinion," he said with a not-so-humble smile. "Thanks to your bullying, most of the women on Flamingo Island look like they're starving."

Blood rushed to her face. "I do not bully and they're not starving!"

He shrugged. "Perhaps...but they don't look like real women should."

"That's your macho opinion." Too late, she heard his robust guffaws. "Oh, shut up. You're impossible." She headed toward her briefcase in the living room. Returning to sit beside him, she pulled out the menu list she had prepared this morning and handed it to him. "Here, please look this over."

"I don't need to. We just sampled the menu for the show." He tried to hand her back the list, but she refused to take it.

"No, we have not." She articulated each word to get through his dense head. "Don't assume that I'll blindly go along with anything you say." She shoved her list back at him. "We are going to showcase *both* our cuisines and cooking styles— equally. *I'll* cook the meal tomorrow. Then, we come to an agreement," she said decisively.

Paolo sat back and studied her with a grin. "Are you always this bossy?" Somehow, this seemed to amuse him. "And you say that you don't bully."

She ignored his bait and took a business card out of her wallet. "Can you arrange to be at the spa restaurant tomorrow around six?"

He paused for a moment and read the card. "Executive chef. How long have you worked at Sublime?"

"Two years. Can you make it tomorrow at six?" she prodded.

"Sure, why not?" He gave a nonchalant shrug. "Gil will cover for me. The restaurant owners are bending over backward to accommodate me. They're very excited at the publicity they'll get from *Miami Spice*. What are you cooking tomorrow?"

"Mahi mahi." That was all she would tell him about her menu.

The corners of his mouth curved upward. "Can't wait to sink my teeth into the firm, white flesh."

There was no mistaking the glimmer in his black eyes, especially since he was looking at *her* white flesh. Oh, he was a devil, naturally charming and hot enough to melt her composure. Feeling a bit unhinged, Michaela rose from the sofa. She needed to get out of his apartment.

Paolo shot to his feet and was beside her in a moment. "Why are you leaving so soon?"

Before she could respond, his cell phone rang and he answered it.

"Hello?" His genial expression turned serious and his body stiffened with alertness as he listened to the caller. Before

Michaela's eyes, Paolo's face blanched under his tan. "Hold on a sec." He covered the mouthpiece as he spoke to Michaela. "I have to take this in the bedroom. I'll be right back."

Michaela sat back down and waited, wondering what was so urgent that Paolo had to rush out of the room. Just as he shut the bedroom door, the front door opened again. This time a dark-haired older woman strutted inside, resembling a plump partridge stuffed into a coral Lululemon athletic warm up suit.

"Paolo, honey, I need you to feed me, *pronto!*" she wailed plaintively. "I've just come back from the spa and I'm starving. My trainer forced me to eat another boring salad with no carbs again!" She stopped abruptly when she noticed it was Michaela, not Paolo, in the living room. "Where's Paolo?" she demanded.

"He's in the other room on a phone call." Michaela was not thrilled at hearing one of her spa salads described as boring— the ultimate insult to a chef. "What was wrong with the salad you ate?"

"Ugh, too much healthy stuff mandated by the spa's Food Nazi, Michaela Willoughby." She grimaced and made a dismissive gesture, her diamond tennis bracelet twinkling on her tanned wrist. "I'd rather eat pasta any day!"

"Why didn't you try one of the spa's pasta creations? They're delicious," Michaela said, horrified that anyone would refer to her as the Food Nazi.

"Says who?" Bernice challenged.

"Me. They're nutritious and low cal too," Michaela said.

"I'd rather eat Paolo's cooking, calories or not." The woman's heavily made up green eyes scrutinized Michaela with a haughty, up and down motion. "May I ask what you are doing in Paolo's apartment?"

This loud, pushy woman was just about the rudest person Michaela had met in a long time. "That is none of your concern."

The matron pressed together her coral glossed lips and drew back, offended by Michaela's retort. Her double chin quivered with high indignation. "Just who are you?"

"I'm who you just referred to as the Food Nazi," Michaela said smugly. The crass woman would regret having trash-talked Michaela's cooking to her face. "Who are *you?*"

The woman was not the least bit put off. Her attitude implied Michaela was the intruder and not vice versa. "Bernice Blumenthal," she announced imperially, as if she were the queen of England and expected Michaela to curtsy.

Great. Michaela groaned inwardly. Bernice Blumenthal— the producer's wife!

Bernice's eyes narrowed. "You're the one competing with Paolo for *Miami Spice?*"

Michaela's heart sank as the realization hit her full force. She squeezed her eyes shut and hoped for a miracle to erase the last few minutes. But when she reopened them, Bernice was glaring at her with unconcealed dislike.

Michaela was doomed!

The bedroom door suddenly swung open and Paolo emerged looking grim. He absently accepted the two noisy kisses Bernice bestowed on his cheeks, but he didn't react with his usual sexy charisma.

Bernice fluttered her fake lashes. "Paolo, darling, I came to discuss my little soiree and the menu you'll be preparing for our dear Palmentieri."

Bernice was a close friend of Palmentieri's? The young Italian tenor was already on his way to becoming the next Pavarotti.

"I'm conducting a business meeting at the moment, Bernice." He didn't bother to hide the fact that he was suddenly gruff. "If you don't mind, I'd rather chat about this tomorrow at Bella Luna."

Michaela couldn't believe Paolo was dismissing the *producer's* wife. Had he lost his mind in the other room? Her spirits perked up when she realized that he'd just leveled the playing field. Maybe she wasn't doomed after all.

"But what about tonight?" Bernice's lips turned downward into a petulant pout. She fiddled with a strand of hair that artfully escaped the confines of her teased and lacquered hairdo. "I came all the way over here to finalize things."

"Please understand, tomorrow is better, my dear." Michaela heard the softening in Paolo's tone. He was speaking to the middle-aged woman as if she were a child. "I'll make your favorite pasta and a decadent dessert and give you my full attention. What do you say?"

Paolo's cajoling tone seemed to work, because Bernice gave him a benevolent smile. "Oh, all right. I'll be there tomorrow at eleven thirty before the lunch crowd arrives. *Ciao*, Paolo." Her bejeweled hands squeezed his biceps as she got up on her tiptoes to kiss his cheeks.

Forget it—Michaela was still toast. Who could pass up homemade pasta and a decadent dessert in the form of a hunky chef? Bernice was acting excessively chummy with Paolo. What was their real connection?

"*Perfecto.*" Paolo's smile didn't quite reach his eyes, nor was it as warm as usual. His dimples barely made an appearance before returning to grooves beside his stiff mouth.

Bernice gave Michaela a malevolent stare. "Good-bye."

"Good-bye, Mrs. Blumenthal," Michaela said quietly.

When Bernice left, Paolo turned to Michaela with a grave expression. "I'm afraid we have to end the evening now. I have some personal matters to attend to."

"Oh...okay." Michaela felt awkward and wondered why Paolo was dismissing her the same way he had Bernice. "So...we'll meet tomorrow evening at the spa and I'll cook?"

"Yes." His voice sounded strained, as if he was holding something back.

She lingered for a moment, taken aback by his hardened demeanor and the taut lines of his suddenly stern mouth. Michaela hardly recognized him. Gone was the carefree Paolo of earlier, replaced by a man on edge.

"Is everything okay? You look upset," she said cautiously.

"A big problem has come up, but I can't get into it now."

Michaela nodded. "I understand. I'll gather my stuff." She got her purse and briefcase and headed toward the door. The air was charged and not in a good way.

"Well...good-bye, then." Michaela turned the handle and let herself out.

"*Ciao.*" Paolo stood at the open door as Michaela waited for the elevator.

She was surprised when he didn't offer to go down with her. Something was definitely wrong.

The elevator doors opened and a beautiful blonde girl burst forward holding a small suitcase clutched against her very pregnant belly. Huffing and puffing, she pushed another suitcase with her foot.

"Paolo!" The girl dropped her bag and ran into his open arms. He enveloped her in a tight hug and stroked her long hair, murmuring something in Spanish. The blonde's crimson, flushed face scrunched up pitifully. "I'm worried about the baby. I can't raise him alone! I need you." Her plea made Paolo flinch.

Michaela got in the elevator and watched them, riveted to the drama.

"Everything will be fine." His face bleak, Paolo patted the girl's back. "Don't worry."

"I should have stayed away, but I don't want to be a single mother!" she sobbed.

"Don't talk like that," Paolo said firmly.

The elevator doors shut just as Michaela's jaw dropped to the floor. This young, pregnant girl was Paolo's "big problem"? My God, he was just as bad as Jeff was.

The cad!

Chapter Four

Michaela stretched her neck and rolled her shoulders, working out the kinks and tension of the long day spent in the spa kitchen. She had worked steadily on the lunch preparations and hadn't stopped to take a break in order to prepare for tonight's cooking session. She was glad her staff had already left for the day, giving her a breather before Paolo arrived. She took a sip of passion fruit iced tea and tried to relax in the quiet solitude of the spa kitchen, but she couldn't let go of what she'd witnessed at Paolo's apartment last night.

She hadn't slept a wink, tossing and turning with recurrent dreams of Paolo's very pregnant baby mama sobbing on his doorstep. Given his good looks and sexy Latin charm, Michaela could understand his player reputation, but when an innocent baby was the outcome of his fooling around, it was unacceptable. Last night's sad scenario had left a bad taste in her mouth. No wonder he had been in such a rush to get rid of her and Bernice.

Good thing she'd found out what Paolo was like before she'd allowed him to draw her in. Truth was, she had enjoyed his cooking immensely and their banter had been invigorating. Against her better judgment, Michaela had begun to take pleasure in his engaging company—that is, until his pregnant lover arrived.

The snake charmer.

Michaela heard footsteps and for a second, thought it might be Paolo. She put down her clipboard and turned to find Lisa, her massage therapist friend, approaching her with the graceful stride of a born athlete.

"Hey, how did it go with Paolo yesterday?" Lisa asked.

Michaela gave her a pained look and shook her head. "Not good. Let's just say Paolo has shown his true colors."

Lisa's brow creased. "What do you mean? Wanna take a break and chat?"

"I wish I could, but I'm waiting for Paolo. Let's catch up tomorrow. Are you working late today?"

"Yeah. Bernice Blumenthal changed her usual four o'clock Swedish massage to six thirty. Millie has a night class and can't take her, so I have to stay." Lisa flexed her hands and stretched her toned arms in front of her. "I could use a massage myself."

The mere mention of that crass woman made Michaela cringe inside. Being referred to as the Food Nazi by Bernice and her snarky comments about the spa's food still irked her.

"Is she your regular customer?" Michaela asked.

"Yep, she's a real chatterbox. It's hard to keep her quiet long enough for the massage to take effect, but she fills me in on all the juicy gossip."

"What about Mr. Blumenthal? Is he your client too?"

"The TV producer?" Lisa nodded. "He comes in once a week, but early in the morning. He is the total opposite of his wife—high-powered and very type A. Barely says anything while I work the stiffness out."

"Arthritis?"

"That and the stress from living with Bernice."

Michaela grimaced. "I hear you. I got a taste of her last night at Paolo's apartment."

Lisa looked baffled. "Wait a minute, both of you were at Paolo's—together?"

"No, she showed up at the end of the evening and wasn't thrilled to find me there."

"No surprise there. You're young and beautiful and tough competition for Paolo's attention."

Michaela made a wry face. "I'm not seeking his attention. I just want him to be professional so we can impress the heck out of the producers." She glanced at her watch. "He should be arriving any minute. I'm going to prepare the meal I'd like to feature on *Miami Spice.*"

Lisa's eyes lit up. "Ooh, what are you making?"

"Grilled mahi with nectarine salsa, baby asparagus with blood orange vinaigrette, roasted shallot and grape tomato kebabs..."

Lisa grabbed her midsection. "Stop, my stomach's growling already." She grinned. "I wish I could stay and watch you and Paolo in action."

"I'll fill you in on the details later."

"Can't wait. I'm sure it'll be more fun than having to hear Bernice's complaints about lumpy cellulite. Maybe I'll get lucky and she'll gossip instead."

"I'll save you some left-overs."

"Thanks! You just made my day. See ya," she said and left smiling.

Lisa's enthusiasm for her cooking gave Michaela a boost in morale. Who cared what Bernice thought, or Paolo for that matter? She had her fans too.

Michaela glanced at a framed article in the *Miami Herald* on the wall above the phone. The exacting food critic, Ms. Apple Famesworth, had given her the highest "apple rating" in her review.

"Michaela's cuisine is bold and seductive and a little deceiving. Who would have guessed that the luscious key lime pie I ended my satisfying meal with was actually low cal? I couldn't resist and indulged in a second helping. I give Michaela's cuisine at Sublime, The Island Spa restaurant, five out of five apples, for originality, taste and presentation. This is a definite winner on my list of 'Must Dine, Can't Miss Restaurants' in South Florida..."

Michaela glanced at her watch again. Ten minutes after six and no Paolo in sight. What was keeping him—another crisis?

For the second time, she picked up her clipboard and double-checked that all cooking utensils and ingredients were in order. She looked about with satisfaction. All the pots and pans were polished to a gleaming shine, cutting knives sharpened, and stainless steel counter tops scoured to a sparkling clean.

When six thirty rolled around, Michaela exited through the side door and crossed the black and white marble floor toward the reception area. She passed the white leather couches and long glass coffee tables in the lavender and mint scented waiting area and approached the reception area.

"Has a Chef Santos called for me?" she asked Francine, the spa receptionist.

Francine looked up from her computer screen. "You mean Paolo?" she inquired, as if she knew him personally.

"Yes." Michaela was not surprised by the sly smile on the flashy blonde's face.

"Nope, he hasn't called. You want me to text him?" Francine pursed her glossy, bubble gum pink lips. Her protuberant implants strained the neckline of a hot pink, stretch camisole.

So, Francine had his cell...somehow that didn't surprise her either. "That won't be necessary," Michaela said in a brisk tone.

Francine returned to the computer screen, rudely dismissing Michaela.

Michaela stepped behind her and noticed she was IMing someone called *ConMan69*.

"ConMan69?" Michaela asked.

Unfazed, Francine glanced up at Michaela. "I don't usually IM when I'm at work."

"Glad to hear it. Please buzz me as soon as Chef Santos comes in or calls."

"Sure," Francine said distractedly as she ended her chat with ConMan.

Michaela couldn't understand how Francine took her job at the luxury spa for granted. It was a privilege to work for someone as fine as Amy Merkle, the spa director and Michaela's longtime friend.

When she returned to the kitchen, Michaela called Ristorante Bella Luna. "This is Michaela, the chef at Sublime. May I speak with Paolo Santos?" she asked when the *maître d'* answered.

"Paolo isn't here. Would you like to speak with Gil, the sous chef?"

"No, thank you." Michaela hung up and paced the kitchen. It was already a quarter to seven. Why hadn't Paolo called to tell her that he would be late? It was a three-minute drive by car, at most, between the spa and Ristorante Bella Luna. She would have to cook the mahi soon, since it was resting in a key-lime marinade.

With mounting impatience, she began preparing the mahi without him. Another fifteen minutes passed and Michaela started pacing again. He was already an hour late. She had a sinking feeling he was going to stand her up. Even if his pregnant lover had complicated things for him last night, Paolo had had all day to let Michaela know about it. They could have made other arrangements. It was inconsiderate of him not to call.

A wicked thought crossed her mind as she stabbed a shallot with relish. Slowly and ever so thoroughly, she imagined slathering the swaggering Casanova with a habanero chili concoction, skewering him like a shish kebab, and roasting him over red-hot coals.

Chapter Five

Paolo shifted the parcel in his arms and rang Michaela's apartment doorbell a second time. Why wasn't she answering the door? She had to be home by now; her apartment on Biscayne Bay wasn't far from the Flamingo Island ferry. He knocked on the door. When she still didn't answer, he put the bag on the floor and leaned against the wall. If he knew Michaela, she would be arriving soon and she wouldn't be happy with the change in plans. She probably thought the worst of him after yesterday, but it couldn't be helped. He had been up most of the night trying to reason with Claudia.

Michaela arrived a few moments later, carrying her briefcase and a large take-out bag from Sublime. "What are you doing here? Didn't we agree to meet at the spa?" Her elegant nose tilted skyward as she narrowed glittering aquamarine eyes at him. One lock of copper hair lay against her cheek, having escaped the confines of her immaculate French twist.

"*Hola*, Maki." Paolo clasped her slim shoulders and greeted her with a kiss on each cheek and then tucked the silken strand behind her ear.

"Stop that." She balanced the bag on her hip as she shoved her key in the lock.

"I'm sorry I'm late."

She gave him a blistering look. "I don't appreciate being stood up, especially after I've worked a twelve-hour day."

"You *do* look a little tired. Here, let me get that for you." Paolo took the bag from her arm.

"No, I can...oh, all right." Michaela's lush lips flattened into a tight line as she fumbled with the lock.

"I ran late because I had to put out a few fires."

"You seem to have a lot of fires in your life." She stared pointedly at the iPhone in his pocket. "You could have called me, or doesn't that work?"

"It works. I did call, but you'd already left the spa."

"By then you were more than an hour late!" She lifted her chin. "How did you know where I live?"

"Francie told me."

"The receptionist gave you my address?" Michaela's hand stilled on the doorknob as she stared up at him with an incredulous look.

Paolo nodded. "What's the big deal?"

"Francine knows she's not supposed to give out my personal information to strangers," she huffed. "I'm going to set her straight first thing tomorrow morning."

"I'm not a stranger," he stated calmly. "Francie and I are friends. When she mentioned you were expecting me, I explained we had a date tonight."

Michaela gave him a daunting look. "This is not a date."

"You're right, it isn't," he said. Truth was he'd had no intention of meeting her at the spa restaurant. Having her cook a meal for him in her home was far more appealing. If the bossy redhead even suspected he had purposely ignored her plan to meet at the spa, she would have his head on a platter. He gave a contrite shrug. "I'm sorry I kept you waiting and changed the plans on you. Let's try to get along and cook now."

"Not tonight. I'm tired and I want to turn in early. What time can you meet tomorrow?"

"Hey, not so fast. It's only seven thirty." He gave her his most persuasive smile. "May I come in? I promise not to waste your time."

She stared at him as if mulling over her best course of action. Finally, she turned the doorknob and opened the door. "I'll only let you in if we stay on track."

"We will," he promised.

"Come in then," she said over her shoulder as she walked ahead of him.

Paolo lifted his parcel from the floor with his free arm and followed her, happily noticing the saucy sway of her bottom under the chef's tunic. Although her figure was slimmer than what he preferred in a woman, his appreciative gaze glided over her toned legs, from her trim calves beneath the knee-length skirt down to her ankles. He wanted to reach out and stroke her bare legs. It gave him a jolt of pure pleasure to imagine how soft they would feel.

When they reached the kitchen, Paolo placed the bags on the counter.

"What did you bring?" she asked, eyeing the bags.

"A few surprises."

"You're just full of them aren't you?"

"Of course," he said cheerfully as he retrieved a bottle of wine from the bag. "Sit down and let me pour us a glass of Chardonnay."

"The wine opener is in the drawer in front of you and the glasses are above your head on the wooden rack—where your neck belongs."

Paolo burst out laughing, not a reaction Michaela expected, from the look of surprise on her face.

"I'll be right back. I have to check on my baby." Without elaborating further, she headed toward her bedroom.

Baby? Paolo stared at her retreating back in shock. Michaela couldn't possibly be so blasé about a baby! Maybe that's why she was giving him the cold shoulder. If she was a single mother, he had better explain about Claudia ASAP!

Paolo contemplated how he would broach the subject while he waited for Michaela. She was probably saying good-bye to the nanny, but it was odd she hadn't said anything to him earlier about having a child. He unpacked the prosciutto-wrapped melon balls he had brought for her and placed them on a plate. He took a small bouquet of wildflowers out of the bag he'd brought and found a crystal vase in one of the cabinets. After filling it with water and the flowers, Paolo set it on the dining room table.

He had just finished setting the melon balls on the coffee table when Michaela returned wearing a white tank top, black yoga pants and flip-flop sandals.

She gestured to the dining table on her way to the kitchen. "You brought flowers? Thanks."

"My pleasure. Where's your baby?" Paolo asked, raising a quizzical eyebrow at her empty arms.

"You'll meet him in a second. I have to feed him." Michaela reached into the fridge and pulled out a small Tupperware container. Paolo followed her into the living room where she opened the sliding glass door and stepped out on the balcony.

"*¡Hola, Mami!*" a wisecracking voice called out.

Surprised, Paolo turned toward the source to find a colorful parrot watching him with its head cocked to the side.

"*Hola*, Baby," Michaela cooed as she reached inside the cage. She took it out and crooned silly endearments as she gently stroked the parrot's feathers. Paolo had never seen this tender side of her and he liked it—a lot.

"How's my little love? Are you hungry?" Her face glowed with affection as she carefully fed the parrot small bits of cut-up apples.

"Be careful, he might bite you," Paolo warned, eyeing the bird's large, black beak suspiciously.

"Nah, Baby would never do that, would you?" she cooed. "Macaws are very gentle. They're also smart and sociable. And this one is good company, aren't you, Baby?" She kissed the top of Baby's head.

"Kiss me, baby," the bird crowed.

"Do you have any other pets?"

"I wish I did, but with my schedule I can only handle caring for Baby. What about you?"

"No pets. I'd like to have a dog, but not with my work hours."

"My aunt gave me Baby this year for my thirtieth birthday. It's typical of her off-beat humor. Aunt Willow is the black sheep of the family, but she's my favorite aunt."

"Why is she your favorite?"

"She always went to bat for me when I was little and wanted to cook, even though my parents disapproved. Whenever I went to her house, we would bake cookies or make pretty cakes."

"Why didn't your parents want you to cook?" Paolo asked, bewildered.

"They discouraged me from eating sweets." She looked uneasy. "Never mind, it doesn't matter now. Aunt Willow is a bit kooky, which drives my parents crazy. They frown on her free lifestyle."

"Why?"

"Because Aunt Willow still lives in the sixties. She owns a small gift shop in Coconut Grove where she sells homemade candles, incense and stuff like that. Sometimes she has mysterious tasting brownies…"

Paolo chuckled. "I'd like to meet her. She sounds like a character."

"She is—a loveable one." Michaela fed Baby a meaty walnut. "Isn't that yummy?"

"*¿Quién es tu papí?*" the macaw cackled. "*¿Quién es tu papí?*"

Paolo grinned. "He just said 'who's your daddy' in Spanish. Who taught him?"

"My aunt's Cuban boyfriend, Manny. Aunt Willow raised Baby from when he was a baby, and hence the name."

"Ah, I get it." Paolo's index finger stroked the parrot from its red crown to its green and blue tail. "Nice feathers," he said, admiring the big bird's magnificent plumage.

"*Mueve la colita, así, así, así,*" the parrot sang out.

Paolo burst out laughing. "Your parrot just said, 'Shake your booty' in Spanish."

Michaela smiled. "Okay, enough, Baby. Time for beddy-bye." She put the bird back in the cage and covered it with a blue cloth. "*Buenas noches*, Baby."

"*Buenas noches, Mamacita,*" the macaw called back.

They headed back to the living room and when they reached the sofa, Paolo turned to Michaela with a smile. "Sit, relax and enjoy," he said, motioning toward the glasses of chilled wine and the honeydew melon balls covered in prosciutto he had placed on her coffee table.

She gestured toward the appetizers. "What's all this?"

"A little something I brought from the restaurant."

"Thank you." She helped herself to a melon ball, and then took a long sip of wine. "I usually don't drink much during the week and last night I might have overindulged." Paolo felt like pulling her into his arms and telling her not to be so tough on herself. "Good thing I had a few glasses, given what I saw before leaving."

"Let me explain," Paolo began, noting the censure in her voice. He heaved a deep sigh. "It's a delicate family matter."

"I'll say," Michaela mumbled.

"It's not what you think—"

"It's really none of my business," she said, looking away.

Paolo stood behind Michaela and rested his hands on her delicate shoulders. "Your neck is all bunched up. Let me ease out some of these knots and then we'll talk."

She edged forward, dislodging his touch. "Please don't do that. I, I...have to get started cooking." Damn, she was as skittish as a wet kitten.

Paolo dropped his hands to his sides. "How about I cook for you and you put your feet up?"

"No, thanks. You can join me if you like," she said between bites of the melon.

"I'm looking forward to it." He kept his tone pleasant. As soon as they ate, he'd explain about Claudia.

"Don't get excited. It will be something simple, not the meal I planned on making earlier. When you didn't show up, I gave it to Lisa."

Puzzled, he studied her. "If you were starving, why didn't you eat too?"

Michaela gave him a disgruntled look. "If I'd eaten while I was mad at you, I would have ended up with a stomachache."

He shrugged. "Oh, too bad." Nothing gave him a stomachache.

Paolo turned his attention to Maki's elegantly appointed apartment where everything was immaculate, neat and organized. Ivory walls, adorned by abstract watercolor paintings surrounded her cream-colored silk sofa and loveseat. Her feminine touches were everywhere, from the candles, to the fluffy pillows on her sofa, to the blooming orchids on the glass side tables.

"You're very neat."

"I like things to be tidy and in their place," she stated, as if warning him not to be messy.

Paolo suddenly wanted to muss *her* up, rattle her composure and kiss her senseless. "I can see that. Have you lived here long?"

"About three years." Michaela rose from the couch. "Excuse me, but I have to cook something or I'm going to pass out." She sailed into her kitchen.

Paolo followed her there. "Let me give you a hand, *querida*. Two chefs are quicker than one."

"No, thanks. I'm doing the cooking tonight."

His mouth twitched. It was obvious that she didn't like being told what to do. No sir, she was more comfortable issuing orders. One thing was for sure—she would need an attitude adjustment before they taped the show. For now, he would bide his time and pretend to go along. But once they were in front of the camera, he would take the lead.

Michaela felt restless as Paolo's broad-shouldered physique invaded her personal space. Did he have to be so tall and imposing and ooze so much testosterone? She took a measured step away from him, but he moved in closer until she could feel the tiny, soft hairs on her forearm graze the skin of his hard muscled arm. A spurt of excitement raised goosebumps on her skin. She steeled herself against it by downing a large gulp of wine. Things were getting off to a wrong start and her treacherous body was reacting to him. She replayed the image of Paolo's beautiful, pregnant girlfriend crying in his arms. *Paolo is a cad*, she told herself sternly. She would do best to boot the horny devil's pointed tail out of her kitchen.

She set the wineglass down. "I'd rather work alone, if you don't mind. Please go back to the living room."

Paolo looked chagrinned. "Maki, I sense a lot of animosity from you. If you must know...the pregnant girl you saw last night is my little sister Claudia."

"Your sister? Really?" She hadn't expected to hear *that* excuse. "But she's blonde," she blurted out.

"So what? My sister Mafalda is blonde too, like my father was."

"Oh." She suddenly felt ridiculous. Of course there were blonde Argentines. She had jumped to all kinds of terrible conclusions about Paolo without having the facts.

"Claudia is driving me crazy." A muscle ticked in Paolo's jaw and his voice sounded strained. "No matter how much I try to reason with her, she refuses to make up with her husband."

Michaela studied Paolo. His eyes looked sincere and caring. "Why?"

"It's complicated. Claudia is a newlywed. She should have never gotten married so young. She was only nineteen when they eloped. I wish I had been there to stop her, but now that they're having a baby, she needs to forgive her husband for taking a job so far away. The baby deserves to have a father!"

Michaela remained silent. She did not want to open that can of worms. The less she knew about Paolo's personal life, the better, especially since his concern for his sister was an appealing trait. What he'd said about a baby deserving to have a father had also pleased her. But she didn't want to dwell on Paolo's good qualities at the moment, especially when the earnestness in his dark eyes was drawing her in.

"I should have kept closer tabs on Claudia. Whenever we talked, she said things were going great and that she'd visit Miami when she and Bobby could get away. I had no idea she was alone and pregnant."

"Oh, I'm sorry to hear it," she said.

Paolo rubbed the back of his neck. "Ah, well...there's nothing I can do about it now. Call me when you're ready."

Michaela watched him retreat to the living room and saunter over to her stereo, where he turned the radio to a Latin station. She enjoyed the sound of Brazilian jazz as she finished the wine and poured herself another glass. Well, at least Paolo wasn't a deadbeat dad, but instead, a protective brother. Peeking through the kitchen pass-thru window, she watched him study her family photographs on the shelf. He leaned forward and examined each silver-framed photo.

"Hey, Maki, is this little freckle-faced, carrot-top you?" he called out. Michaela could hear the amusement in his deep baritone.

"I do not have freckles."

"I'll have to do a closer inspection to see for myself. You were no spaghetti in those days, Maki. More like a little

55

meatball," he teased merrily.

"Ha ha, you're hilarious," she replied, her lips twitching in spite of herself.

Paolo's loud rumble of laughter filled her living room. He already felt at home and was having fun teasing her.

"Who's the adorable little girl with the blue eyes and blonde curls?" he asked.

"My sister, Tiffany. She takes after my mother's side." She couldn't understand why her parents had given her a formal name like Michaela, instead of something fun like Tiffany. But she had to admit, the name Tiffany suited her cute little sister perfectly.

The doorbell rang and Paolo rushed to answer it before Michaela could get out of the kitchen. She heard Tiffany's cheery voice when Paolo let her in.

"Hi, there. And who are you?" Tiffany's naturally flirtatious tone was laced with curiosity and delight.

"Paolo Santos, and you are?"

"I'm Tiffany, Michaela's younger sister," she replied. "Speaking of which...where is she?"

Michaela sighed. She would have been happy to see Tiffany any other day. Her sister's bubbly personality usually entertained her, but this was no time for sisterly fun. Hopefully, Tiff would get the message and leave when she realized that they were having a business meeting. But she wouldn't hold her breath. Tiffany had been known to turn a blind eye when it suited her.

Knife in hand, Michaela emerged from the kitchen. "What's up, Tiff? I was just thinking about you."

Tiffany gave her a surprised look. "Cool. We had ESP then because I was thinking about you too! What are you making?" she asked, staring at Michaela's knife. "I've been so busy shopping, I haven't eaten anything since breakfast and I'm about to pass out."

Michaela smiled. "Me too."

Paolo immediately said, "You must stay and have dinner with us." He smiled at Michaela. "The more opinions we get on our menu, the better. Eh, Maki?"

"Maki?" Tiffany repeated, raising her brows with delight as

she glanced at Michaela.

Michaela tried to show in her eyes that it wasn't a good time for Tiffany's visit, but her meaningful look went unheeded.

Tiffany lifted a two-handled, glossy white paper bag with a pink hibiscus sketched on it. "I went shopping on Lincoln Road and discovered this funky little boutique called Faloola. They have the cutest stuff and it's just a five-minute drive from the studio." Tiffany worked as a makeup artist for Stefan Falcone, South Beach's go-to fashion and celebrity photographer. She also did freelance modeling whenever Stefan needed someone in a pinch.

"What did you buy?" Michaela asked, wishing she could somehow usher her out without hurting her feelings.

Tiffany's blue eyes twinkled. "A sexy red dress for your show on Monday. You're going to look fab-u-lous!" she crowed in a singsong voice.

Sexy red dress? Michaela glanced at Paolo and caught the blatant wink he sent her way. "Thanks for thinking of me, Tiffany. I'll try it on later and reimburse you."

"No need to." Tiffany gave her a tight hug. "It's my gift."

"Aw, that's very sweet of you." Michaela returned her hug. Her little sister's impetuous generosity always warmed her heart. Tiffany had a sunny disposition and was always up for fun, even if her impulsiveness often got her in trouble.

"I bought this outfit there too. What do you think?" Tiffany gave a little twirl for their approval, her long blonde curls floating around bare, tanned shoulders. The clingy turquoise halter dress fit her hourglass figure to perfection.

Blessed with a gorgeous face and a leggy model's slim figure with just the right curves, Tiffany could wear anything. She was sexy without even trying and she often dated several guys at once. At twenty-five, she had never had a serious relationship because the boys she went out with always ended up being "too lame". In spite of her flirtatious personality, Tiffany held stringent standards for whomever she was going to end up with. Michaela could not have been prouder of her little sister for not falling into a destructive relationship like Michaela had with her ex-fiancé, Jeff. Maybe seeing how much Michaela had suffered had made Tiffany extra cautious when it came to commitment.

Tiffany loved dating and meeting men, but when the guys got serious, she ran. The only good-looking guy who hadn't tried to put the moves on her was her boss. It was a good thing, too, since the enigmatic Stefan was at least a dozen years older than Tiffany and dated most of the models he photographed.

"Great outfit." Paolo sent Tiffany a ravishing grin as he admired her from head to toe. He nodded toward Michaela. "I hope you got one like it for your sister."

Seeing the appreciative gleam in his eyes made Michaela wish she were wearing something more appealing than a tank top and yoga pants. *Stop that,* she told herself firmly. *Don't care so much about attracting Paolo.* The man was a known player, and most importantly, her adversary. They were competitors and that was the only reason she had let him in her apartment.

"It sure smells good in here," Tiffany said, grinning shamelessly. "Hint, hint."

Michaela couldn't turn her sister away after the generous gift, so she caved. "You can stay for dinner, if you like, Tiff. Wanna help me set the table?"

"Sure. Should I do it now?" Tiffany asked eagerly.

"Not yet," Paolo boomed. "Come into the living room and have some prosciutto melon balls."

"I'd love to," Tiffany said, trotting after him.

Michaela stood in the kitchen doorway and watched Paolo pour a glass of wine for Tiffany, then return to sit beside her on the living room couch. She waited for the male charm sure to surface any moment, this time directed at her ever-so-delighted sister. Amazing how at ease he felt after a mere half-hour at her place.

"So...tell me all about yourself, Paolo." Tiffany settled comfortably on the couch after a sip of wine. She crossed one tanned leg over the other and gave him her undivided attention. "How do you know Mic?"

"Maki and I are doing a show together. Hasn't your sister told you about me?" Paolo asked, turning to give Michaela a reproachful look.

Tiffany looked enchanted, as if she was uncovering a delicious secret. Her eyes lit up with interest. "I didn't realize you were her competition. I thought you were a new boyfriend."

"He isn't," Michaela said quickly. "Our meeting tonight is strictly business."

"Suuure...if you say so, Mic," Tiffany teased.

With no time for banter, Michaela listened to her grumbling stomach and returned to the kitchen to finish cooking. She picked up the wineglass and tossed back the contents. A rush of warmth spread from her cheeks, down her neck, to the tips of her hands and toes. She needed to prepare an entire meal in record time.

She could barely make out what Tiffany and Paolo were saying above the music, but they seemed to be getting along great. Well, at least Tiff would keep Paolo entertained so Michaela could concentrate on her meal. Tiffany had always been the cheerful, vivacious one, while her family and friends had referred to Michaela as the "serious little bookworm". But what had they expected when even her parents had misread her pensive nature and labeled her as uncreative? She had always wondered what it would be like to be her sister, whose playful nature could coax a smile out of anyone. Tiffany's sentences always ended with a giggle, whereas Michaela only laughed if she was genuinely amused.

With a pang, Michaela remembered her sixth birthday when she had asked for an Easy Bake Oven with all the trimmings to make pretty cakes. Instead, her parents had bought her something "sensible" they hoped she would enjoy more than an Easy Bake Oven: a complete set of encyclopedias. They declared that baking cakes would only make her fatter, while the encyclopedias would open a whole world of knowledge. That was when Aunt Willow, bless her kind heart, stepped in and bought Michaela the coveted little oven, ignoring their objections.

The first thing Michaela did when she graduated from high school was donate the encyclopedias. With the Internet, she didn't need them anymore. But she'd done it mostly because every time she glanced at them it was a stinging reminder that her parents had imposed their will on her, dousing her creative spirit. They had meant well, but they had done more damage than good with their practical gift.

Michaela spent her teen years glued to her books trying to please her demanding parents who wouldn't be satisfied unless she made class valedictorian and was admitted to a top Ivy League school. To cope with the stress, whenever she felt anxious, she ate cookies or candy bars she kept stashed under her bed. But as soon as she finished indulging, she felt sick inside, knowing it wasn't good for her. Her wake-up call came in her sophomore college year when her doctor told her she had to drastically change her diet or risk health problems. She took a course in nutrition and met Dr. Robin Wells, a brilliant professor who changed her outlook on food...and life. Under the wise woman's mentorship and guidance, Michaela blossomed and became empowered. Now, years later, they still kept in touch and Dr. Wells had generously offered to add a foreword to Michaela's cookbook.

Michaela pulled out two Sabatier chef knives and held them side by side as she made short work of slicing the crimini mushrooms before throwing them into the pan with the shallots and minced garlic already sizzling in the olive oil cooking spray. After stirring a few times, she added a cup of dry Chardonnay and waited for the stock to reduce while she lightly dredged the grouper filets in Panko and seasoned them with freshly ground pepper and coarse sea salt.

"Something smells good, Maki," Paolo called out.

Michaela deftly sliced the zucchini and acorn squash lengthwise and coated them with a scant amount of olive oil before seasoning and brushing freshly chopped rosemary leaves over them.

She looked up and spied a lovely box of chocolate truffles beside her refrigerator, no doubt one of Paolo's "surprises". Chocolate was her biggest weakness, so she tried to limit it, except for once a month when her hormones demanded more.

She was jarred from her work by a loud shout of laughter. Giving in to curiosity, she peeked out to find Paolo and Tiffany bent over one of her high school yearbooks, laughing. She bolted out of the kitchen, hoping it wasn't her senior yearbook. When she neared their side, she froze.

"Tiffany! How could you?" Michaela asked, feeling betrayed and hurt.

Tiffany's eyes widened. "What do you mean?"

"You were laughing at my picture. I can't believe you would do that!"

"I wasn't!" Tiffany protested, looking shocked. "I was just boasting to Paolo about all your accomplishments. He didn't believe me when I told him that you were class valedictorian, president of National Honor Society, debate team leader, Key Club president, etc., etc. I had to prove it to him. Here it is in black and white, Paolo. Read for yourself."

"Wow, Maki, you are a smarty-pants!" Paolo said, giving her an admiring glance.

"Yep, she inherited the brains in the family," Tiffany said proudly.

"Your little sister admitted that she can't even balance a checkbook." Paolo shook his head and chuckled. "That's why we were laughing."

Michaela plucked the open volume from her sister's lap. She stared at her unsmiling senior picture that showed her with an unflattering bowl haircut that emphasized her puffy face. Her thick, straight bangs were so long they covered her eyebrows, giving her a gloomy look. For a long, aching moment, she stared at the somber face, wishing she could turn back time and bring a smile to it.

Her senior year had been fraught with pressure and unhappiness as her parents had tried to steer her to Yale instead of to The Culinary Institute of America. But not all was lost, she reminded herself staunchly. She had persevered and gotten an excellent liberal arts education at Yale. When she graduated, she attended Duke law school, but dropped out in her third year and headed straight for the CIA in New York and then to Paris, where she studied at Le Cordon Bleu. Her parents had never forgiven her.

"Yikes, smells like something's burning!" Tiffany suddenly cried out, darting up from the sofa.

Chapter Six

"Oh, no!" Michaela saw the flames flickering inside the cast iron skillet the second she ran into the kitchen.

Tiffany gave a high-pitched squeal and dashed toward the sink where she grabbed the faucet hose, struggling to pull it out. She wildly sprayed water from afar, not only dousing the flaming pan, but Michaela as well.

"Not me, the pans!" Michaela cried, when the stream of water drenched her face. Frustration welled up inside her as she surveyed the charred zucchini strips and withered mushrooms stuck to the cast iron skillet. The once meaty grouper filets looked like shriveled sardines. "What a disaster! Everything's ruined," she moaned.

Michaela's hair was dripping from Tiffany's careless play with the water hose. Paolo's lips were twitching and so were Tiffany's as they struggled not to laugh. Michaela couldn't help but join in their mirth, but then she sobered. No chef worth her salt left a meal unattended and let it burn. She felt drained and mortified as she grabbed a dishtowel off the hook and blotted her face dry.

"I'll help you clean up," Tiffany said in a soothing voice. "Why don't we order pizza?"

"I'm not hungry anymore," Michaela said quietly. "Maybe you guys should leave."

Paolo took the dishtowel from Michaela and carried the charred pan to the sink. He tucked the towel in around his waist, turned on the faucet, and made short work of emptying the burnt remains into the garbage disposal.

"What are you doing?" Michaela was at his side in an instant.

"You're tired and upset and this is partly our fault." Looking concerned, Paolo smiled at her before turning back to his work. "You've had a long day. Go relax in the living room and I'll clean up for you."

"It's okay. You don't have to clean up my mistakes," she said, taking the towel from his waist.

"I insist," Paolo countered, his voice deepening with firmness as he tried to take the towel from her hands, but she held on and a tug of war ensued. "Let go and do as I say, *nena*. You're being stubborn."

"It's my kitchen." She knew she sounded grouchy, but she needed to be alone in her kitchen, to compose her tattered emotions.

Paolo gave her an uncompromising look and then turned to the sink and resumed washing the dishes.

As if on cue, Tiffany scrambled toward the living room and picked up her Tory Burch handbag. "C'mon, Mic, walk me out."

Michaela followed her to the door and Tiffany gave her hand a quick squeeze. "We were not poking fun at your picture. I swear I would never do that!"

"I know," Michaela said. "But you shouldn't have brought out my yearbook. You, of all people, know I don't treasure those memories."

"Oh, stop it. You're the only one with the fat complex. Look at you! You're a knockout, you fool," Tiffany chided.

Michaela sighed deeply. How could she stay mad at her sister after that? "Thanks, I guess I'm just tired."

"I understand, sweetie. But before I go there's something I have to tell you." She paused. "I'm sorry to bring it up now. I know it's a bad time—"

"What is it?" Michaela felt a frisson of alarm at the look on Tiffany's face.

"It's not good..." Tiffany trailed off with a doleful shake of her head.

Michaela hoped this was just Tiffany's penchant for drama and nothing truly dire. "Then why do you have to tell me now?"

"Dad insisted that I personally deliver a message to you, which is part of the reason I stopped by."

"Okay, spill," Michaela said, anxious to get her going.

"He's coming to the pilot show and he said he expects you

to win. I think he might show up with his latest girlfriend," Tiffany confided.

Michaela's heart sank. "That was Dad's uplifting message? Oh well, don't worry about it." His parenting style was a lethal combination of high pressure and towering expectations. Although she wasn't a teen anymore, it still hurt her.

Tiffany fidgeted. "There's more. Mom's planning on being there too."

"I figured she would." Sylvia Willoughby was very competitive by nature and would be determined to see Michaela win.

"Don't kill the messenger, but she's bringing Aunt Magda."

"Aunt Magda too?"

Tiffany nodded sympathetically.

Michaela loved her aunt, but the woman was a hopeless romantic. An English Lit professor at the University of Miami, Aunt Magda thought everything could be resolved like a Jane Austen novel. She had vowed that neither of her nieces, particularly Michaela as she was the oldest, would suffer the same fate as she. After Michaela's break-up with Jeff, Aunt Magda had appointed herself matchmaker. She doled out prospective matrimonial candidates with the same fervor and consistency as a breeding rabbit.

"I hope she's not bringing a new one...is she?" Michaela asked.

Tiffany squirmed. "'Fraid so. He'll be at the show too."

"Please call her as soon as you leave and tell her the comp tickets are only for family."

"Okay and I'll tell Dad not to bring a date."

"Good. When I told Mom I could get comp tickets, I never imagined everybody would want to come."

"Of course! We're family," Tiffany said, nearing the front door. "You're gonna look amazing on camera. You can wear the sexy red dress and I'll do your makeup," she offered. "I'll give you smoky eyes and some coral-pink blush and lots of lip gloss to highlight your lips. I can just picture how pretty you'll look."

"Thanks. We'll talk about it later."

"You're a spectacular chef," Tiffany said loyally. "The only thing Paolo has going for him is his good looks. He is smokin' hot!"

From behind them, Michaela heard a loud "ahem". She and Tiffany whirled around to find Paolo watching from the kitchen doorway.

"Oops, sorry you heard what I said about you," Tiffany said with a guilty giggle.

"Bye, Tiff." Michaela gave her sister a quick hug. "Thanks for your support."

Tiffany responded with a thumbs-up gesture. "Anytime." She grinned at Paolo. "Bye, Paolo, it was fun meeting you. I'll see you at the taping?"

"Sure thing." Paolo smiled back. "*Ciao*, Tiffany."

Michaela opened the front door. "We'll chat tomorrow. Please don't forget to call Aunt Magda, so she doesn't bring anyone."

"As if you'd let me forget!" Tiffany said, scurrying out the door.

When Tiffany left, Paolo's dark eyes scrutinized Michaela. "Are you still mad?"

"No. I know I overreacted, but when I saw you laughing at my senior year picture, it hit a raw nerve."

"I wasn't mocking you. Who cares about an old picture anyway? You should see mine someday. I laugh every time I look at myself—even my mother used to call me raviolini, I was so stuffed. You, on the contrary, were only a little overweight."

There was nothing stuffed about Paolo's muscular physique now.

"It took a lot of willpower to get where I am. You have no idea," she said.

"You look perfect the way you are." His dark eyes twinkled. "*Querida*, there's no need to starve yourself with rabbit food."

"I'm not in the mood for teasing." He would never know the painful memories she kept locked in her heart. "Raviolini" was mild compared to being called "Miss Piggy" by her unrequited crush, Todd, a boy who had been her chief competition for valedictorian. When her best friend Kimmie had told her about Todd's name-calling behind her back, Michaela had been devastated, especially since she'd been blinded by his looks and hadn't realized how mean and shallow he was.

The grooves beside Paolo's mouth deepened into maddening dimples. "Tell me something. Why does your Aunt Magda want to marry you off?"

"That is none of your business. I need to clean up the mess in the kitchen."

"No, you don't. I already took care of that."

"You did? Thanks. I guess we should call it a night. Don't forget—we meet at Sublime tomorrow evening—six o'clock sharp. We can't afford to waste any more time. Please don't be late."

"Yes, ma'am," Paolo saluted. "Good night, Maki. Hope you feel better tomorrow."

He leaned forward and when Michaela abruptly turned to face him, her mouth caught a kiss intended for her cheek. Paolo's warm, firm lips lingered ever so slightly before pulling away, making her breath catch in her throat as a ripple of pleasure washed over her. She took a shaky step backward and nearly lost her footing. His strong hands caught her waist and gave her a little squeeze before releasing her.

They locked eyes and Paolo's magnetic, dark-eyed gaze drew her into his spell. She would have willingly sunk into his arms if he'd put them around her. She shivered at the sexual, demanding tension emanating from him. Did he feel it too? The intense energy radiating between them, making her dizzy with desire? It had to be that she was famished—not just for food, but for love. That explained the gamut her emotions had run tonight. First, she had felt annoyed with him, then later, upset and hurt, and now there was no denying the hot spark between them. He was driving her slowly mad, and there she was, standing before him hopelessly speechless—a rarity for her.

"Good-bye," she managed, finally finding her voice as she stepped away from him.

She watched Paolo leave, his large shoulders hulking slightly forward. How did he really feel toward her? The accidental kiss had left her dazed, along with the smolder in his eyes and the solid squeeze of his hands on her waist.

Heeding her growling stomach, she trudged to the kitchen and grabbed the box of chocolate truffles he'd brought her. She picked up the bottle of wine and carried it into the living room. She tossed her yearbook from the couch and took a swig of wine straight from the bottle.

Michaela lifted the box cover and inhaled the hypnotic chocolate scent. She popped a truffle in her mouth and let the chocolate melt against her tongue. What the heck, she might as well finish them off. She took more sips of wine and then got a sudden attack of the giggles when she remembered Tiffany wrestling with the faucet. Keeling over on the sofa, she spilled the remaining truffles on her lap. Oops, well now that they were out of the box, she definitely had to eat them all. Michaela devoured five more luscious truffles, one by sinful one as she drank more wine.

She was starting to feel woozy as she pulled the rubber band off her ponytail and fluffed out her hair. She kicked off her flip-flops and curled up on the couch, all the while assuring herself that nothing was lost. She would make up for her ruined meal tomorrow at the spa restaurant.

Paolo had been so nice and patient tonight when she had been grouchy. Not that she hadn't had sufficient cause...but she would have preferred if he'd gotten exasperated and left, instead of branding her with his kiss. He was like the velvety truffles—intoxicating, seductive and sinfully addictive. She had to keep him at arms' length or she'd end up devouring him too.

She polished off the remaining wine and then hiccupped softly as she set the empty wine bottle on her coffee table. She needed to stay focused on her ultimate goal to be top chef of *Miami Spice* and not let Paolo get to her, but it was proving to be harder than she thought.

She'd have to think about that tomorrow because right now, flung on her side on the comfortable sofa, she could barely keep her eyes open.

Chapter Seven

Claudia Santos carefully stretched in bed and then kissed the palm of her hand and placed it over her pregnant belly, greeting Robert Adam Woodbridge, Jr., her unborn baby, as she did every morning. She snuggled her face against the pillow and sighed. Paolo's bed was so comfy, she felt guilty that he'd relinquished it to her. But he wouldn't hear of her taking the couch, where he had slept for the past two nights.

She had one more lazy stretch before turning on her side to hoist herself up from the bed when she suddenly felt a cramp in her belly. She squeezed the pillow until it subsided. The tightening sensation lasted longer than usual, but she wasn't overly concerned. She had felt Braxton Hicks contractions before, so she didn't think they were the real deal. It was two weeks before her due date—too early for a real contraction.

With this in mind, she carefully got up and padded on bare, swollen feet toward the kitchen. Paolo had already left for work, but not before leaving her a scribbled note tacked on the fridge: *"Ham frittata in the oven and fruit salad in the refrigerator. Buen provecho. Call me when you're up. We need to finish our talk!"*

Dios mío, her big brother could be so relentless sometimes! Paolo had been adamant last night that she call Bobby and ask him to come home so they could work things out. But Paolo didn't know the half of it. Bobby had no idea she was pregnant, neither did Bobby's parents or her family, for that matter. Her ears still felt blistered by Paolo's tirade when she had shown up at his door. He hadn't been angry with her for being pregnant, he'd been furious that she'd kept it a secret from him and the rest of their family who loved her.

She'd had good reasons—ones that Paolo had scoffed at, making her upset with him and all men in general. Looking back, she should have realized it wouldn't be smooth sailing when she had eloped with Bobby. But from the moment he'd walked into her family's bakery in Buenos Aires, she had fallen hard for the cute exchange grad student learning Spanish. That afternoon, Claudia had just put the final touches on her specialty—a three layered vanilla sponge cake with *dulce de leche* filling. When she placed it in the window display, Bobby walked by and stopped to watch her. He came inside, bought the whole cake and ordered a double espresso. He invited her to join him as he devoured a huge slice of it, proclaiming it was the most delicious dessert he had ever eaten and that she was the princess of cakes.

Bobby's rugged American physique, chestnut hair and crystal blue eyes had attracted her, but it was his appealing personality that had won her over. After three months practically joined at the hip, they had eloped in one reckless moment, to both their families' vehement disapproval.

His wealthy parents, commercial real estate developers, had disapproved of him marrying a Latina instead of a socialite and when he refused to annul their marriage, they cut him off financially. Bobby had been so incensed, he had taken Claudia to live in Destin, Florida—much to her chagrin. It was the first job he could find, so he relocated them to the small coastal town. Claudia had liked being near the ocean, but very soon she had become homesick in the predominantly Anglo city. With few friends, she had felt isolated, pining for her close-knit family and Latin customs.

Before marrying, she and Bobby had made plans to start a yacht chartering business and sail the world, one adventure at a time. He would captain the vessels and take wealthy jet-setters to exotic destinations. That dream had been waylaid when his parents had disowned him and backed off from financing the venture. Before long, they started to run out of money. Bobby, a civil engineer, had been able to get an entry-level job, but Claudia couldn't find steady employment. Her English was decent, but heavily accented, and many gringos had a hard time understanding her.

In a desperate attempt to make a lot of money quickly, Bobby had taken a job in the oil sands of Alberta, Canada. When Claudia had balked at his plans, he had admitted he would be entrenched in a very remote area, but had tried to convince her with the excellent salary.

"We need the money, babe. Six months will go by quickly, you'll see," he had told her. She had positively begged him not to go, but his stubborn response had been, "My mind's made up. I'm doing this for our future." Well, he had ruined their future by abandoning her—the longer Bobby was gone, the more she resented him, especially since he had left a ticket for her to go to her family in Argentina until he returned. For all he knew, she was living back home. Running to her family and admitting defeat was the last thing she would do. He should have known her well enough not to expect it.

Claudia swallowed hard, willing herself not to cry. Lately, her emotions were getting the best of her and she found herself tearing up too easily. She wiped away her salty tears but they wouldn't stop, especially when she reflected on the bleakness of their marriage. She and Bobby hadn't spoken since he left for Canada after a terrible fight. He had called her several times, but she had refused to answer his calls, instead sending him a text message to stop calling her or her family. Shortly afterward, she began to suffer extreme nausea and found out she was three months pregnant! Many pregnant women got morning sickness, but in Claudia's case, she had all-day sickness with nausea and vomiting that lasted well into her third trimester.

It had finally subsided, but she felt emotionally spent and terrified at the thought of being a single mom far from her home with no real friends or family for support other than her big brother. Despite the ticket sitting in her suitcase, she refused to run home. It was too late now and too humiliating to admit she had done a stupid thing by eloping with Bobby and then getting pregnant so soon. Claudia had lived frugally on the money he had left her in the bank account, not wanting to deplete his savings because, as far as she was concerned, they were separated. When her family had heard the Woodbridges had turned against their son for marrying Claudia, they had urged an annulment. *I'll never leave Bobby,* she had cried, fiercely defending her husband. Ironically, *he* had left her.

When she spent her twentieth birthday alone last month, it was the final straw. Lonely and homesick, she gave up trying to be heroic and headed for Miami in hopes of staying with Paolo until the baby was born. Her big brother would help her figure out what to do.

She blew her nose, took a deep breath and tried to think positively as she served up some frittata and poured orange juice into a small glass. She dug into the frittata and counted her lucky stars that Paolo had taken her in. He was so strong and protective, almost like a surrogate dad, given the fourteen-year difference between them. As the youngest of the Santos clan, she held a special place in his heart, and he in hers. Paolo had been the first one to discover she had dyslexia when she was eight. He had arranged for after-school tutoring so she wouldn't fail the school year. Even when he was overworked or had a hot date to go on, he had carved out time to patiently work with her. He had never made her feel inept or dumb, instead praising how smart she was and what a talented baker she was becoming. He had explained that dyslexia had nothing to do with intelligence, and she adored him for it.

Whoops, there it was again, the annoying Braxton Hicks contraction...a tight sensation, gripping the small of her back and wrapping around to squeeze her belly.

Hmmm, maybe she should stop eating...

Michaela could not ignore the ringing telephone another minute. She forced one heavy eyelid open even though it felt like a sandbag held it anchored down. When she tried to lift her head from the couch, her temples throbbed in protest. She cast a bleary glance about her disheveled living room and noticed the usually tidy area was strewn with chocolate candy wrappers and an empty wine bottle on her coffee table. Wondering why her answering machine had not kicked in, she pushed herself up, but had to hold on to the back of the couch as she trudged toward the phone in her kitchen. Every step made her head pound.

"Hullo," she mumbled, balancing the receiver on her ear as she tried to tamp down the nausea.

"Michaela! Is that you?" Amy Merkle, the spa director asked.

"Yeah, what's left of me," Michaela mumbled, trying to

organize the jumbled thoughts in her mushy brain.

"What do you mean, 'what's left of you'?" Amy asked in an alarmed voice. "Are you okay? It's not like you to be absent from work and not call in."

"I hate to admit it, but I just woke up."

"Really? Now I *am* worried. You haven't missed a day since you started and you've never been late, either. You're one of the most dependable people I know."

"You wouldn't think so if you saw the sorry state I'm in and what my apartment looks like this morning." Michaela shut her eyes and tried to remember what happened last night to make her feel like a category five hurricane was roiling around in her body, wreaking havoc on her stomach and inside her head. But the details escaped her. "I don't feel very well. My head is pounding and my stomach's upset."

"What's wrong, honey? Some sort of stomach virus?" Being the earth mother type, Amy loved nurturing the people she cared for with homeopathic remedies.

"Sorry I didn't call you earlier. Truth is, I have a whopping hangover," Michaela whispered, casting a disparaging glance at the empty wine bottle. So much for restraint.

"Would you please repeat that?" Amy choked out between giggles.

"I seem to have polished off a whole bottle of wine by myself last night." Michaela stared at her senior yearbook on the floor. "But I'm having a hard time remembering details."

"*You* drank a whole bottle of wine and you can't remember details?"

"You know I'm a lightweight. And now I'm suffering the consequences," Michaela groaned.

Amy chuckled and wheezed. Usually her unabashed way of laughing amused Michaela, but today it just made her head hurt.

"Please, I feel awful," Michaela said.

"Sorry." Amy's humor subsided. "Hang in there, honey. I'll come over with an herbal tea guaranteed to make you feel like new."

In the dreadful state she was in, Michaela did not want to imagine what the natural remedy guru would concoct. She shuddered, remembering how Amy had once grown a huge Colombian mushroom and let it ferment in tea. It had looked scary, like something out of *Little Shop of Horrors*, and Michaela was certain it tasted just as vile. Amy had drunk the elixir every night, swearing by its rejuvenating qualities until the mushroom grew too big for the glass jar and she had to throw it out. Luckily, she moved on to a different homeopathic recipe for energizing herself. Nevertheless, Michaela did not want to be her guinea pig.

"Thanks for the offer, but I have to hurry up and get to work. It's ten already."

"I know, but don't worry. Elliot has already taken charge of everything."

"I'm sure he has." Michaela breathed a small sigh of relief. Elliot Ramsey was her efficient sous chef. "Oh my gosh, I just remembered the school kids are coming in for their lesson today!"

"Don't worry, there's plenty of time before they get here. Elliot is making sure we have all the ingredients for their meal."

"It's Thai food today, right?" Every month, "Munchin' Munchkins", a class of energetic fifth graders from an inner city school came for a tour-around-the-world cooking lesson. In a popular series that included coaching in good nutrition, they had fun learning to cook a complete meal that they took home to share with their families. For the past year, this had been Michaela's pet project.

"Yep. Tasty Thai month," Amy confirmed.

"I'd better talk to Elliot," Michaela fretted. "Would you find him for me?"

"He's standing next to me waiting for a compliment on his new lavender suede shoes and matching tunic and pants." Amy started to laugh. "Hold on, Elliot's taking the phone away. Unfortunately, he heard me mention your hangover. Sorry."

"Great," Michaela muttered. Knowing Elliot, she would never hear the end of it.

"Feeling woozy, my culinary goddess?" Elliot quipped. "If I'd known you'd be hung-over this morning, I would have gotten here at least an hour earlier. I mean, hello? Did you forget our little munchkins will be arriving at three, hungry and ready to cook?"

"Yes, I'm rushing. I'll be there as soon as..."

Before Michaela could finish, Elliott gave a high-pitched squeal and suddenly shrieked, "Kitty, is the orange vinaigrette ready yet? No? Why not, you lazy debutante?"

"Elliot, don't talk to her that way," Michaela said, clutching her head while he continued to shout.

"Waldo, get your worthless ass over here and stir this sauce! Quit flexing your muscles, Dan, I've already noticed you! And please control those ham fists. You're handling delicate button mushrooms, not portobellos! I can't do everything myself and be the master chef too!" he ranted. "Goddess, why did you have to get drunk last night? You're the most dependable girl I know."

There was that word again—dependable. Normally, Michaela would have prided herself in being dependable, but this morning the description depressed her. Being dependable equated being predictable. Well, predictable was better than drunk!

"I'm warning you, Elliott. If you don't keep this strictly between us..."

"Stop it, diva! My lips are sealed tighter than Dan's ass."

Shocked by his crudeness, Michaela drew in a sharp breath. "My God, Elliot, shut up! Did Dan hear you say that?" When she heard him chuckle wickedly, she warned, "Better be careful or he might shut you up personally." Dan was at least a foot taller and weighed fifty pounds more than Elliot—in solid muscle.

"Ooh, don't get me excited, naughty girl. Now hurry up and get here. I'm going crazy."

Michaela started to roll her eyes, but stopped when the action made her eyeballs ache. "Better lighten up on the staff or they'll walk out on you, or worse yet, sue you for harassment."

"Hah! I doubt that. They need discipline. You're too considerate with the lot of them."

She grimaced. "I'll be there as soon as I can. No daily special today. Please make sure you're ready to serve lunch by eleven thirty."

"You don't have to remind me. You know how capable I

am," he sniffed, sounding affronted.

"Mmm hmm," she murmured in a placating tone. "Please put Amy back on."

"Fine," he huffed.

"I'm going to jump in the shower, then head on over," Michaela said when Amy took the phone from Elliot. "I'll fill you in on things when I get there. Bye."

Michaela hung up and closed her eyes as she braced herself against the counter. After taking several deep breaths, she got a bottle of aspirin from the pantry and downed two with a full glass of water. She looked around her kitchen and cringed, as little by little, she remembered the events leading to last night's debacle. Once everything came back to her in vibrant detail, she thanked God that she had finished off the wine after Paolo left or there was no telling what she might have done.

Never in her thirty years had anyone gotten to her so swiftly and made her lose her composure so completely. When Paolo had first strolled into her apartment, all sexy charm and macho testosterone, she'd felt the potent force of his charismatic presence. But by the end of the evening, he'd witnessed her mortification over being a chubby, awkward kid and she felt vulnerable. He'd been kind and understanding, but she couldn't allow him to get close to her heart or she'd be lost. She had already been a fool for love once in her life; she couldn't, wouldn't let it happen again.

Agreeing to meet at Sublime had seemed like a safe way out last night, but the more she reflected on it, the more Michaela realized that she needed to reposition herself professionally on her home turf. She decided to call Paolo and change the location of their meeting to her apartment. And she wouldn't allow him to be there while she cooked. He would come over when it was almost ready and her meal would be awesome!

There was no time to lose. She fixed herself a double shot of espresso and then tidied up the living room and lit a few vanilla scented candles to kill the burnt smell from last night's ruined meal. Satisfied that things were in order, she flicked on her answering machine and headed for a hot shower.

Paolo stood before Michaela's front door and rang the doorbell. He waited a few moments and tried again. No answer, but her car was in the parking lot. Weird. Michaela was nowhere to be found this morning, not at Sublime or at her apartment.

Francie, the receptionist, had said Michaela might still be at home, but she hadn't answered any of his calls or responded to the message he'd left on her answering machine. Francie had confided that everyone at the spa was worried when Michaela hadn't shown up because it was so out of character for her.

Now he was beginning to wonder if she was okay. He banged on the door several times.

Suddenly, the door whipped open and Michaela faced him with her hands on her hips. "Please—I've got neighbors! Don't bang on my door that way," she said in a low voice. "Why are you here? We don't have an appointment—do we? I don't remember…"

"I'm relieved to find you here, *querida*. Francie told me you were missing this morning."

"Missing? Why that little gossip!"

Paolo took a step forward, and then stopped in his tracks when he saw Michaela was scantily clad in a short, coral terry cloth robe.

"Don't you know better than to open the door practically naked?" His gaze took in her bare legs and he couldn't help but grin. "Not that I mind."

Michaela's face turned pink. "You got me out of the shower. Don't you believe in calling before showing up?"

"Check your voice mail. I've been trying to reach you all morning, but you've been ignoring my phone calls."

She sighed. "I wasn't ignoring them." Her graceful hands massaged her temples as she closed her eyes briefly and gave a little moan.

"Headache?"

She grimaced. "My head feels like it's splitting at the temples."

"I'm sorry to hear it, Maki. May I come in?"

She didn't open the door further. "It's not a good time. I'm in a rush to get ready."

Michaela might not be feeling well, but that didn't diminish how fetching she looked in the little robe, even with a headache. Her long copper hair lay loose and damp upon her shoulders. Her arms and cleavage were sprinkled with tiny freckles that turned him on more than he dared to admit. Michaela's creamy skin tantalized him, especially now that he had seen the dainty freckles. There were sure to be others on her hidden curves.

His appreciative gaze slid over her pert breasts, her tiny waist and nicely rounded hips barely covered by the robe. His gaze returned to admire her face, but Michaela's troubled expression stopped his straying thoughts cold.

Her aquamarine eyes glistened with tension. "Why are you here?"

"I can't come tonight."

"You can't come tonight," she repeated flatly. "The show is on Monday and we *still* haven't decided on a menu. We absolutely have to get a productive session before the show, Paolo."

"I know, *querida*, that's why we need to talk." Forget talking, what he really wanted was to wind his hands in her hair and hold her still while he kissed the pout off her plush lips, but he forced his gaze away from her mouth and collected his thoughts.

"All right, but please make it quick. I am very late for work. Today is Tasty Thai day and there are thirty fifth-graders coming to cook with me," she said in an agitated voice as she yanked the door open and gestured for him to enter.

Paolo grinned when Michaela turned her back and self-consciously tugged at the hem of her robe, making sure everything was properly covered.

"Don't worry about it. I was just at the restaurant," Paolo said, forcing his gaze away from temptation. "Your sous chef is on a real power trip."

"Ah, so you've met Elliot." A flicker of amusement lit up Michaela's eyes. "You still haven't told me why you can't make it tonight," she pointed out.

"Claudia just called. She's having contractions, but she's

not sure if she's in labor."

The frustration in Michaela's tone disappeared, replaced by alarm. "What are you doing here? Go to your sister, she needs you!"

Paolo was drawn to the genuine concern in her eyes.

"Does your sister have anyone to help her other than you?" she asked.

"Only me, but my mother is trying to get a flight in as soon as she can."

"Okay, that's good." She expelled a deep breath. "I guess you'll have to let me know when we can finalize our plans."

"Yes. Don't worry about the show, Maki. We'll be magnificent together."

"I'm counting on it."

"By Saturday, we'll have the whole menu set," he said confidently.

Michaela walked toward the door. "All right. Good luck with Claudia and the baby. Call me when you can."

"I will."

Paolo leaned forward and kissed her on both cheeks, enjoying her feminine, rose scent. His fingertips grazed the silkiness of her arms until he reached her soft hands and entwined his fingers with hers. Her eyes darkened as his gaze held hers and it was all he could do not to kiss her. Michaela's mouth looked like a ripe strawberry, lush and sweet and he was dying to have a taste. The urge became a distinct ache as he shifted his stance.

She finally broke the lingering eye contact and slid her hands from his.

"I, um—" she cleared her throat, "—I have to get ready. I hope Claudia and baby are okay."

"Me too. Thanks for understanding." His voice came out rough-edged and gruff. "*Ciao, linda.*"

"*Ciao,*" she said quietly before closing the door.

Paolo leaned his shoulder against the door and gave a wry shake of his head. It was a damn shame that he and Michaela were in stiff competition for the same job. Now that Claudia was about to deliver her baby without Bobby by her side, Paolo needed the high-paying job more than ever to cover her needs and the baby's too. He also had to send money to Mamá and pay for his sister Gina's wedding. His whole family was depending on him to win.

Whether Michaela liked it or not, he fully intended to be the victor. Once she saw how aggressively he competed, she would no doubt double her efforts to hold the upper hand. Nevertheless, she was bound to lose to him. With all the fat trimming and calorie cutting she boasted about, Paolo couldn't imagine how Maki's cuisine could be as delicious as his. She might cook with precision, but he cooked with passion. Paolo was intrigued to taste her cooking, but not nearly as much as he craved a taste of *her.*

As he got into his car, his cell phone rang with his home number in caller ID. "*Hola*, Claudia," he barely got out before he heard her labored breathing.

"Ay, ay, owweee. This is it! I think the baby's coming! Come home now!" she cried, panting loudly.

Paolo felt the blood drain from his face. As the oldest of five children, he had heard what his mother had gone through in childbirth and he didn't want to think of Claudia suffering that way.

"I'm on my way," he said through clenched teeth.

Chapter Eight

Paolo stormed into his apartment as if a bull was chasing him. "Claudia, where are you?" he called out. "Are you okay? Is it the baby?"

"No, it's your food," Claudia retorted as she struggled to sit up on the sofa. "Of course it's the baby! I thought you'd never get here."

"Are you still having contractions?"

"Yes!" she exclaimed, wild-eyed. "I just had another one a few minutes ago. They don't feel like the Braxton Hicks ones I've been having on and off." She rubbed her swollen belly in a circular motion and then stopped and winced. "Here it comes again." She took shallow panting breaths while her white-knuckled hands held the sides of the sofa cushion. When it subsided, she cried, "The baby is going to come if we don't leave now! *¡Vamonos al hospital!*"

"*Sí*, let's go." Paolo carefully helped her up, steadying her with an arm around her shoulders.

"Wait! I need my hospital bag." Claudia pointed to a blue canvas carry-on next to the front door. "It's over there."

"We'll get it on the way out. Lean on me."

Claudia supported her bulging belly with one arm as she linked her other arm with his and held on tight.

When they got to the door, Paolo hoisted the hospital bag onto his shoulder. "What do you have in there? Rocks?"

"You never know what you'll need in the hospital," she said, suddenly sounding giddy. Her mood shifts were puzzling to say the least. "Magazines, playing cards, cute outfits for baby and me to go home in, pictures of my family to make me strong. I've been collecting things here and there. Aiyee!" Her body went rigid against his side. "Here comes another one!"

Paolo watched his little sister's face turn red as she panted rhythmically, her cheeks puffing up with exertion. "Have you been timing them?"

"Yes, but they're not coming regularly yet."

"Hang in there, *nena*." Sweating bullets, he waited until Claudia's contraction subsided and then led her outside. "Lean on me while I lock the door. Forget about walking, I'll carry you. We need to get you to the hospital ASAP!"

The moment he hefted Claudia in his arms, she turned awkwardly and grabbed his neck. A sharp spasm shot from the right side of Paolo's neck down to his shoulder. *Ouch*, that hurt. Adding to her tall and athletic figure, Claudia had put on at least another thirty pounds of baby weight. Normally, he could have carried her with no problem, but this morning he had woken up with an annoying crick in his neck from sleeping on the couch. Paolo forced himself to ignore the shooting pain as he took the front steps of the building, two at a time.

Claudia had said she felt the baby coming! He silently prayed for her baby to take a little longer.

Michaela hummed as she sprinkled a liberal amount of chopped cilantro, basil and mint leaves around the grilled yellowtail snapper. Her headache was gone and she was feeling better, in spite of her hangover this morning. The clinking of pots and pans and the frenetic pace of her staff pleased her. Ironically, chef was French for boss and Michaela loved being the ringleader of her domain.

"Why are you smiling, Michaela? Is that a drop of moisture I see on your lower lip?" inquired Elliot. "Salivating over your Italian Stallion or should I call him your Argentinean Chorizo?"

"Neither, you Flaming Baked Alaskan," Dan, the brawny, good-looking line chef, mumbled under his breath, surprising both Michaela and Elliot.

Elliot snickered. "It's called Baked Alaska, darling."

"The kids are going to be here any minute, Elliot," Michaela said.

A pout played on his lips as Elliot replied, "Forget the munchkins. When are you cooking with your succulent lamb chop?"

Michaela tried not to smile. "I don't think Paolo would like you to call him that."

"Too bad. He and Dan have a lot in common." Elliot gave the strong, athletic man beside him a sidelong glance. Dan Haden hailed from El Paso and he was way taller and stronger-built than Elliot. Dan once owned a thriving Tex Mex restaurant until he lost everything to his ex-wife and partner in a contentious divorce. "Isn't that right, cowboy? Love your boots," he drawled, sending Dan a daring wink.

From the grim look on Dan's face, Michaela could tell the big Texan wasn't amused. He had probably been dealing with Elliot's banter all morning.

"Don't make me shut you up, Elliot," Dan snarled, not looking up from stirring the Jamaican conch chowder. "I'll kick your scrawny ass back to your crib."

Elliot giggled. "Ooh, tough love, my Texas Longhorn? But I don't have a crib, it's more like a throne. I also don't have a scrawny ass—"

"Get back to work, Elliot," Michaela said. "Behave yourself and stop the nicknames."

"*You* don't seem to mind when I call you a culinary goddess," Elliot pointed out.

"That's because I am," Michaela declared, smiling benevolently as she used a clean kitchen cloth to wipe up any remaining herbs that had fallen on the edge of the plate. She placed the towel in a laundry bin just as the phone rang on the wall beside her.

"Spa kitchen, Michaela Willoughby," she said into the receiver.

"Hey, it's Lisa. Any chance you can come to the massage room now?"

"Can I come later? The kids are about to arrive."

"It'll only be for a few minutes."

Michaela wondered what was up with Lisa. It was out of character for her to call the kitchen. They usually chatted in person after work.

"Okay, I'll be right there." Turning to Elliot, Michaela said, "I have to leave for a sec. I'll be back before the kids get here. Please set everything out on the counters so we can get started right away when I get back."

Elliot gave a queenly sniff. "You don't have to remind me of my duties."

"If you don't, I will," Dan muttered.

Elliot's face brightened as he puffed up his chest and straightened to his full five foot six inch frame. "There you go again, always toying with me."

"Give it up, Elliot," Michaela whispered. "Stop trying to get a rise out of him."

"A rise is exactly what I was hoping for. Party pooper," Elliot grumbled, not bothering to hide his sly grin.

Michaela left in search of Lisa. When she passed by the reception desk, she stopped in her tracks at the sight of "the succulent lamb chop" sitting in the desk armchair, hunched over, with Francine massaging his broad shoulders.

"Paolo? What are you doing here?" Michaela asked, not thrilled to see Francine's hands all over him. The expression on the receptionist's face was positively dreamy.

"Maki! I was just asking for you." Paolo peered at her from his bent head position. His hair fell forward, shading his face in ebony layers.

Michaela regarded him dubiously. "While you were getting a massage?"

"Poor Paolo has a stiff neck. I was helping him get the kinks out."

"Looks like your hidden talents are wasted at the front desk," Michaela observed dryly.

Francine didn't respond. She just kept digging her hands into his shoulders, eliciting contented groans from Paolo.

"Yes, right there, Francie," he said. "Thatta girl. That's the spot."

Michaela couldn't believe that after all the commotion this morning about his sister going into labor, Chef Casanova found the time to flirt with "Francie" and be massaged too!

"How is Claudia? Why aren't you at the hospital with her?" Michaela asked, giving him a pointed glance.

"It was false labor. She wasn't even dilated. That's why I came looking for you. We can meet tonight," he said, sounding quite pleased with himself. He closed his eyes as Francine continued to work on him. "Yes, right there, Francie."

Francine smiled smugly. "Okay, gotcha. I'll concentrate there. Just tell me how hard and for how long."

Michaela didn't care for the way the two of them were enjoying the impromptu massage, oblivious to how inappropriate they looked. At this point, she didn't feel like meeting with Paolo, but she reminded herself of her greater goal—winning *Miami Spice*.

"So, we're back on for tonight then? No more unforeseen interruptions?" Michaela asked.

"I'm all yours," Paolo said amiably.

"Good, then please be on time. We don't have a minute to waste," Michaela said, all business.

"Hey there. What's going on?" Lisa called out, approaching them from the massage area. "Since when are you a masseuse, Francine?"

Francine's hands dropped to her sides as she gave Lisa a sheepish grin. "Paolo's neck is in bad shape and he's in pain. I thought I'd ease it a bit until he could make an appointment with you."

"Paolo, you deserve a proper massage. Why don't you schedule one with me?" Lisa suggested with a friendly smile.

"I think I will. My neck is stiff and sore." He groaned as he got up from the chair and joined them in front of the desk. "It's been a crazy day. I'll try to squeeze in some time for a massage soon."

"Yes, please do. Francine, the phone's ringing," Lisa said.

Francine returned to her chair and answered the call.

"Thanks, Francie. It feels better already," Paolo called out, his dimples deepening on either side of his sexy mouth.

When Paolo aimed his killer smile at Francine, her whole demeanor brightened and she ended the call fast. "Anytime, Paolo. Really...anytime at all!" She had the nerve to send him a seductive wink from beneath her lowered eyes.

"I was on my way to see you just now," Michaela said to Lisa.

"Don't worry, we can chat later," Lisa replied, giving

Michaela a private look. "I have a client arriving for her appointment now."

"Okay, sure," Michaela said.

"Bye, Paolo. I hope you feel better soon," Lisa said before turning to leave. "In the meantime, alternating hot and cold compresses will help your neck. And you might want to take an anti-inflammatory like ibuprofen."

"I will, thanks," he said.

When Lisa left, Paolo took Michaela's arm and led her away from the reception desk toward the glass doors at the entrance. "What time should I come back here?"

"Actually, I'd rather you come to my place...if you don't mind."

"*¡Perfecto!* I don't mind at all." He seemed to love the idea. Of course, he would. Paolo liked to keep everything on a personal level.

Just as Paolo leaned forward to kiss her good-bye, his iPhone buzzed and he answered it right away.

"Bernice! How are you?"

He looked heavenward with exaggerated patience. "*Sí, sí,* of course, my dear. Don't worry. Your dinner party will be perfect. Remember, you have hired the magnificent chef," he said, winking at Michaela.

Oh, brother, she had forgotten about his business card with "magnificent chef" under his name. Enough was enough; she needed to get back to the kitchen. Michaela waved at Paolo and turned to walk away, but he pulled her back.

"Don't go yet," he said, covering the mouthpiece so Bernice wouldn't hear.

"I have to. The kids just got here for their lesson," she said, waving at the fifth-graders as they walked in an orderly line, led by their teacher, the effervescent Miss Devereux. Ketsia Devereux, their young Haitian teacher, adored food. She was all smiles from the moment she arrived at the spa kitchen until she left with her little charges and a delicious meal to enjoy later.

Michaela walked toward the children and began greeting them. Just as she was about to usher them into the kitchen, Paolo ended the call with Bernice.

He ambled over to Michaela and kissed her on both cheeks. "*Ciao, querida.* See you tonight."

Paolo's comment was met by squeals and giggles from the children.

"Is that your boyfriend, Chef Willoughby?" asked Ruffi, the tallest and most outspoken.

"Mr. Santos is a colleague, *not* my boyfriend," Michaela said.

"Aww, too bad," was the collective response from some of the girls.

"Yeah, it is too bad. Maki wishes things could be different," he said, lowering his voice to a conspiratorial tone. The playful glint in his eyes seemed to say he also wished things could be different.

"You wish," she called out as she watched him saunter away with a self-satisfied swagger.

Paolo turned once more and sent her a brazen wink.

Later that afternoon, Michaela and Lisa sat at the far end of the spa juice bar drinking mango peach smoothies.

"I swear I never get tired of mango and peach together. Talking about an interesting combination...how did everything go last night?" Lisa asked.

Michaela glanced at the server who was busy filling take-out orders for a group of teenage girls. "It was a disaster," she said in a low voice. "Paolo stood me up at the restaurant and then later showed up at my apartment. He seemed to think nothing of changing our plans at the last minute."

"How inconsiderate," Lisa said between sips of her smoothie. "What happened next? I hope you gave him hell."

"I tried. But once he apologized we began to get along until Tiffany stopped by." Michaela set her glass on the counter and grimaced. "Unfortunately, I totally ruined the meal."

Lisa's eyes widened in surprise. "No way. You're a perfectionist! How did that happen?"

"I burnt it." Michaela shook her head. "I don't want to go into details, but it was awful."

"I can imagine. How did Paolo react?"

"He was really nice about it. He even cleaned up the mess in the kitchen."

"So he does have some good qualities."

"Yes, I'm seeing a side of him that's thoughtful and considerate. He's also fun to be with." Michaela made a wry face. "That is, when he's on good behavior and not teasing me or being unreliable. He has interesting layers to his personality. Even though he's cocky about his talents, he listens and is understanding. He's also very caring toward his sister."

Lisa studied Michaela with a bemused smile. "Sounds like Paolo has won you over."

"I wouldn't say that." Michaela felt a moment of panic. Lisa was right, Paolo *was* winning her over, but she didn't want to admit it—to Lisa or herself, and definitely not to Paolo. "Let's not forget he has the reputation of a major player. There's no doubt he is hot, but I already had my heart broken by another player. I can't afford to let down my guard and trust him."

"Stay strong then. That sexy Argentine is hard to ignore, much less turn down."

"Jeff had the same magnetic appeal at first. I'd be a fool to open myself up for that kind of hurt again."

Lisa looked bewildered. "In the player department, no one can compete with your ex. Do you really think Paolo is like Jeff?"

Michaela thought about it. "No, he's not like Jeff. Paolo isn't heartless. He was very sweet when he found out about my weight problem as a kid. He didn't tell me to 'get over it', like Jeff used to. Come to think of it, Paolo is nothing like Jeff."

"It sounds like Paolo is into you. I know you two are competing, but maybe it's worth giving him a chance."

"He's hard to resist," Michaela admitted with a sigh. "And he does act as though he's attracted to me. But I don't know if it's sincere. Lisa, what if he's trying to sidetrack me from winning the competition? I can't allow myself to trust him."

"So what are you going to do?"

"Wear a chastity belt, I guess," Michaela quipped.

Lisa made a mock sad face. "Aw, too bad. Just think of the fun you'll be missing."

Chapter Nine

Michaela leaned against the kitchen counter of her apartment and closed her eyes as she listened to the opening notes of her favorite Yo-Yo Ma CD. His rendition of Bach's "Unaccompanied Cello Suites" was the perfect panacea to bolster her for the evening ahead. She hadn't been able to put her conversation with Lisa out of her mind. As much as she hated to admit it, Paolo was getting to her. No banter and no alcohol for her tonight, she vowed. She would have to stick to business.

Michaela glanced at her wristwatch again. In ten minutes, Paolo would be arriving—if he showed up on time. Everything was set. Even Baby had been fed and was happily asleep in his cage on the patio. She'd gotten a lot done today, considering the disoriented state she had woken up in. Tonight's meeting would go just fine, she told herself, as she went over the menu in her mind. The strawberry soup was chilling in two crystal bowls topped with a dark green mint sprig. Baby artichokes nestled beside tiny polenta cakes waiting to be drizzled with her warm vinaigrette. Before the main course, they would cleanse their palates with lemon-Frangelico sorbet decorated with a tiny slice of pear. Then she would serve the aromatic lavender-crusted roasted rack of lamb accompanied by wild mushroom risotto, infused with a touch of cognac. She was getting hungry just thinking about it.

She peeked into the refrigerator and felt proud when she gazed at the glossy white, raspberry-filled meringue torte decorated with violets and fresh raspberries—the crowning touch to her meal.

The doorbell rang and Michaela glanced at her watch. Five minutes before seven. Surprised by Paolo's promptness, she rushed toward the door as she patted the sides of her hair held half up in a clip. She took a deep breath and opened the door.

Paolo's broad shoulders filled her doorway. He looked casual, yet nicely dressed, in a white linen shirt and tan pants.

"Hi," Michaela said, enjoying the feel of his strong hands as they closed over her bare shoulders and drew her in for a kiss on each cheek.

His admiring gaze swept over her sleeveless silk tank tucked into a flowing maxi skirt. "You look pretty."

"Thank you." Might as well look good, it gave her an edge of confidence. Who was she kidding? She'd purposely worn the outfit because she wanted him to think she was pretty.

"Purple suits you, *princesa*," he teased.

"Why thank you," she murmured. "Come in."

He followed her into the living room and handed her the bag he was carrying. "I brought you a little something."

Paolo didn't seem to believe in arriving empty-handed. She had to admit it was a nice quality.

"You shouldn't have." She glanced inside. "Champagne and figs?"

"*Sí*, Calimyrna figs. They're shipped to the restaurant from California."

"Yum." The combination of champagne and figs conjured all kinds of sensual images. *Don't go there,* she told herself. That was exactly what he had planned. She could bet her best knives on it.

"Shall we have some champagne then?" she asked, moving away from his exhilarating scent of soap and subtle citrus cologne.

"Absolutely. It's already chilled."

She carried the bag into the kitchen and took out the bottle and figs. Turning toward the cabinet behind her, she nearly collided with Paolo's solid chest. "Oh, excuse me. I need to get the champagne flutes."

"I'll do it," he said, opening the cabinet door and setting two flutes on the counter. His warm smile made her stomach flutter. "After last night, I know my way around your kitchen." With a deft movement, he uncorked the bottle and it let out a loud pop. Sparkling bubbles of pale yellow nectar fizzled merrily as Paolo filled the long flutes.

The champagne looked too enticing to pass up. "I'll have just one glass," she said.

He handed her a glass with a surprised look. "Why just one?"

"We have work to do."

"We can still enjoy it," he said, raising his glass in a toast. "*Salud, dinero y amor.* Health, money and love," he translated.

Michaela clinked her glass with his and took a long sip. When he lifted his glass to his lips, she noticed he was moving with stiffness in his shoulders and neck. "Are you still in pain?"

"Yeah, a bit," he admitted, wincing when he attempted to shrug his shoulders. "Crazy day at the restaurant. I took some ibuprofen but it barely helped."

"Oh, too bad. When I injured my shoulder last year playing tennis, I took a painkiller that worked like a dream." Truth was, when she had found out about Jeff's cheating ways, she had gone to the tennis courts and banged so many balls against the wall pretending it was Jeff, she'd ended up with a painful, pulled ligament. "I think I still have some in my cabinet. Do you want to take one?"

"Sure, thanks," he said. "I'm sore from my neck down this shoulder. It feels like someone's stabbing me there."

"Sounds awful. Let's eat now and then you can take the pill. It's best taken on a full stomach."

Paolo placed his hand on Michaela's waist and squeezed softly. "Aren't you going to finish your champagne?" he asked with a disarming smile. His gaze slid over her with a languor that left her breathless. Tiny tingles teased the flesh beneath her skin where his hand lay.

She cleared her throat and looked away from his hypnotic eyes. "No, thanks. No more for me."

"C'mon, Maki. Live a little."

Paolo's mocking tone prompted her to take an extra large sip of champagne. She almost choked when the tiny bubbles burst in her mouth and tickled her nostrils. She erupted into a coughing fit.

"You okay?" Paolo patted her back with his large hand.

"I'm fine," she choked out between sputtering coughs. "Drank too quickly...went down the wrong way."

The feel of Paolo's warm palm lingering on her back made her pulse race. Michaela rested her hand on her chest as she cleared her throat. Paolo's gaze dipped to the neckline of her blouse where her hand lay. He stopped patting her back and began a slow rub instead.

"You can stop now. I'm not coughing anymore," she managed in spite of her pounding heart.

Paolo followed her into the dining room and gave a nod of appreciation toward the table. "Looks great, Maki. You shouldn't have gone to so much trouble for me."

"No trouble. I love everything to look nice," she said, pleased he had noticed. She wished it didn't matter so much that she wanted to impress Paolo. "Presentation makes everything taste better."

"True," Paolo agreed amiably.

The dining room table was draped in a luxurious, muted gold Florentine tablecloth and accentuated with coordinating napkins bordered in dusky rose and bronze. Michaela's fine ivory china sat atop antique bronze chargers. Sleek crystal goblets and a glowing hurricane lamp lent elegance to the room.

For the next half-hour, she sat across from Paolo as they ate and discussed her meal. She basked in his many compliments. He took obvious pleasure from the food and its presentation, asking questions about the ingredients and preparation. His easy-going manner made her relax and enjoy his company.

"I'll serve dessert and espresso in the living room and then we can discuss the show," she said.

"Okay." He winced when he got up with his plate in hand. He was moving stiffly and she suddenly remembered she hadn't given him the painkiller. "Leave everything there, Paolo. I'll clear it. Why don't you go to the couch and I'll bring you the painkiller now?"

"Good idea."

Michaela went to her bathroom cabinet and just as she was reaching inside to take out two prescription bottles and check the labels, the doorbell rang. She grabbed both medicine bottles and headed toward Paolo in the living room.

"Don't get up. Stay there. The pain pill is one of these

bottles," Michaela said, handing him the little plastic bottles before hurrying to answer the door.

"Thanks. Which one?"

"Not sure. Read the labels first and take only one with a full glass of water."

Michaela peeked through the peephole. Oh no, Aunt Magda! Normally, Michaela would have invited her in, but not today with Paolo in her living room. Immobilized, Michaela stared into the peephole. Stylishly dressed in a royal blue fitted dress, Aunt Magda fidgeted from one high-heeled pump to the other and fanned herself with her hand.

"Honey, it's Aunt Magda," she called out.

Michaela turned to look at Paolo.

"Who is it?" Paolo called out, chasing the painkiller with wine.

Michaela bolted to his side. "My aunt. Stay there and I'll try to get rid of her." She frowned at the wine goblet in his hand. "I said to take the painkiller with water, not wine. You're not supposed to mix alcohol with it."

"Don't worry about it." Paolo grinned. "Is it the famous Aunt Magda that Tiffany mentioned last night? The matchmaker?"

Michaela nodded and put her fingers to her lips in a shushing motion.

The doorbell rang again and Paolo burst out laughing when her aunt began banging on the door. Michaela gave him a disapproving shake of the head before rushing to answer it.

"Hi, Auntie," she said, leaning forward to kiss her aunt's perfumed, powdery cheek. "Sorry to keep you waiting."

"It's okay, honey," Aunt Magda said. "I don't normally stop by unannounced, but I got worried when you didn't return any of my phone calls."

"I'm sorry. I was planning to, but I've been really..."

"Busy," Aunt Magda finished with a rueful smile. "But you should take a break once in a while, dear. Your mom is downstairs waiting in the car. We want to take you to dinner with us."

"Thanks for inviting me, but I've already eaten."

Aunt Magda gave her a cajoling smile. "You can still come and keep us company. We're long overdue for a visit."

"I know, but I can't today. I'm actually in the middle of a business meeting." Michaela didn't budge from the door, even though she knew it was rude not to invite her inside.

"Really?" Aunt Magda tried to peek over Michaela's shoulder. "Who's that in your living room?"

Paolo ambled to the door and joined them. Michaela had to step aside as he held his hand out and introduced himself. "Paolo Santos. And you must be Maki's favorite Aunt Magda."

"Why yes! I'm surprised you know my name," Aunt Magda said, looking utterly delighted. "Did you just refer to my niece as Maki? I've never heard anyone call her that."

"It's my nickname for her. She loves it," Paolo said, winking at Michaela.

"She does? Well...isn't that interesting?" Aunt Magda shot Michaela a curious look.

"I'd invite you in, but you don't want to keep Mom waiting downstairs. Right?"

Aunt Magda was too busy sizing Paolo up to protest. "Oh, right...I shouldn't keep Sylvia waiting. Well, call me tomorrow, dear. I was hoping you could join us for dinner tonight."

"I would have loved to. We must do it soon," Michaela said.

Aunt Magda turned to Paolo. "Please continue with your business meeting with my niece," she said with an impish grin. "Not only is Michaela a wonderful cook, but she is also a very smart, loyal and dependable girl."

"Thanks, now I sound like a Golden Retriever," Michaela quipped under her breath.

"What do you do for a living, Paolo? Are you single?" Aunt Magda inquired boldly.

"Aunt Magda, please!" Michaela gave her a discouraging look. "Paolo is a chef. We really are having a business meeting."

Aunt Magda looked like she didn't believe Michaela's protests one bit. She held out her hand to Paolo. "Charmed to meet you, Paolo. Next time I hope to get to know you better."

"It would be my pleasure," Paolo said gallantly. He took Aunt Magda's proffered hand and kissed the top of it like a dashing Spanish *caballero.*

Aunt Magda giggled. A second later, she leaned forward and whispered into Michaela's ear, "Your Paolo is scrumptious. And those dimples are positively wicked!"

Unfortunately, Aunt Magda's comments were loud enough for Paolo's ears. Michaela watched his mouth ease into a slow grin, his dimples deepening rakishly on either side. Shaking her head, she waited until Aunt Magda reached the elevator before shutting the door.

Just as she closed it, her phone rang and she rushed to check caller ID. She gave Paolo an apologetic look. "I'm sorry for the interruptions, but it's my mom's third call today and now, thanks to Aunt Magda, she knows I'm home."

"Go ahead and answer. I don't mind."

"Thanks." Michaela gave him a grateful smile and answered the call. "Hi, Mom. Sorry I can't join you and Aunt Magda for dinner, but I'm in the middle of a business meeting."

"I've been trying to reach you all day. I'm just as busy as you are, Michaela. The least you can do is spare me a few minutes of your time."

Michaela sighed. She hated when her mom took that tone. Sylvia Willoughby wasn't a top litigator for nothing.

"I haven't been avoiding you, I've been absolutely swamped," she said, watching Paolo go into the kitchen and come out with a plate of figs. Nooo, she had wanted to serve her meringue torte first!

"It's about Tiffany." Mom sounded agitated. "Your sister is dating an illegal alien."

Michaela rolled her eyes at her mother's description. "An illegal alien? What are you talking about? Who is it?" Tiffany hadn't mentioned anyone special last night, but then there hadn't been the opportunity for her to, with the way the evening had ended.

"Paco...Pedro...what does it matter? He's the Mexican tennis pro at the Club," Mom replied, her voice laden with disdain. "Your sister has no sense when it comes to men. I'll bet you he's after a green card!"

"You don't know that for sure," Michaela said, hoping to end her rant.

"Don't be naïve. Tiffany is being taken for a fool by Mister Super Taco."

"Mom!" Michaela protested, appalled. "Please don't call him that—especially in front of Tiff."

"Fine, but I want him out of your sister's life. Remember when she was dating the Cuban rafter? I thought she'd never get rid of that good-for-nothing."

"Chill, Mom," Michaela said in a placating tone. "By the way, congrats on the case you just won. I saw it in the *Miami Herald.*"

"Don't change the subject on me. You need to talk some sense into Tiffany because she won't listen to me."

"I'll call you back tomorrow and we can talk about it. I really have to go. Bye, Mom." Michaela hung up before her mother began a cross-examination.

She exhaled loudly and tried to shake off the unpleasant exchange. Mom had a knack for sucking out all her energy with just one phone call. Michaela resolutely put the conversation out of her mind and went into the kitchen. Moments later, she emerged with the meringue torte in one hand and two dessert plates and forks in the other.

Paolo's face lit up as he took the dessert from her and placed it on the coffee table. Michaela sat beside him. "You have beautiful hands," he said, taking her cold hands and warming them with his. He turned them over, palms up. "So slim and delicate. But a chef's hands and wrists must be strong."

He traced the inside of her palm with his fingertip and her pulse went wild. As Paolo languidly studied her palms, Michaela had a crazy wish for him to kiss them. Seduction Paolo-style was dangerous, she reminded herself as she reluctantly removed her hands from his warm grip.

"They *are* strong." She formed a fist and mockingly shook it a few inches from his jaw. "You'd better not distract me from my dessert presentation or you'll get this."

He chuckled and covered her fist with his big hand, giving it a light squeeze. It was a simple gesture, but having her hand engulfed in his felt sensual and intimate.

"Nothing would be more fun than to wrestle with you, *querida*...with real whipped cream."

Michaela got a vivid mental image of them wrestling naked on the kitchen floor covered in whipped cream. Paolo hadn't even mentioned naked, but the gleam in his eyes showed he was imagining it too. She looked away and concentrated on serving two slices of the torte.

Paolo tasted it and gave a rough-edged purr of satisfaction. "*Delicioso.*" He ate another mouthful. "Is this really low calorie? It can't be."

"Of course it is. I'll tell you the ingredients later."

Amazed, he polished off the rest and regarded her with approval. "Light and luscious, just like you. Very nice, Maki."

"Thank you."

Paolo's molten eyes left no doubt of his desire. Michaela forced herself up from the sofa and reached for the dessert plates on the table, only to have Paolo snatch her wrist and pull her back down. The corners of his lips turned upward and she found herself staring at his indolent grin.

Summoning the last shred of willpower, Michaela rose again and this time got away. She headed toward her bedroom in search of a legal pad and two pens. When she returned, she assumed a businesslike stance as she took a seat across from him. "Let's come to an agreement on what we'll cook together."

He took the pad and pen from her. "It's simple." He scribbled as he spoke, "*arista di maiale, gnocchi...*"

"Just a minute. Give me that," she snapped, retrieving the pad from his hands.

"What's wrong?"

"What do you think is wrong? Those are all *your* recipes. One hour isn't enough time for us to cook separate menus."

"But, Maki, your diet food isn't for everyone," he said patiently.

"Why not? Everyone can benefit from healthy eating."

"The viewers will not be thinking of calories when they tune in to our show. They'll want recipes for delicious food."

She started to get annoyed, but tamped it down. "My food *is* delicious. It's Floribbean, a mixture of Florida and the Caribbean."

They had arrived at the inevitable standoff Michaela knew

was coming. Paolo had been agreeable until now and she didn't want to end the evening on a sour note. She sighed. They would get nowhere if he wasn't willing to budge. As long as she was able to feature a few of her signature dishes, she would compromise for the joint pilot show. But when it was her turn to cook solo, she would pull out all the stops.

"I'm willing to compromise," she declared magnanimously.

Paolo eyed her with a hint of suspicion, hesitated a moment and then said, "Fine, I'll compromise too. But not too much."

For the next half hour, they went back and forth until they came up with a menu that was mutually satisfactory. First thing tomorrow morning she would send the list of ingredients to Ted Marton, the culinary producer in charge of their segment.

Paolo finally took the pad from her hands and placed it on the coffee table. "There, we're finished. No more work," he said firmly.

Michaela gave a rueful shake of her head. "I'm glad we got through this without more family visits or phone calls."

"Your Aunt Magda is quite the matchmaker. Tell me, Maki, why hasn't some guy married you and given you a house full of kiddies to tug at your apron?"

We are not going there tonight, she thought, not thrilled by the turn in conversation. Of course, she wanted all those things, but he didn't need to know it. "I'm too busy for a husband and kids at this point in my life. What's your excuse?"

Paolo shrugged. "I still haven't found the girl who will put her family first, before her career and everything else."

"Are *you* going to put your family first?" Michaela challenged. As a macho Latin, he was probably intent on ruling the roost his way.

"Of course," he said, surprising Michaela with his emphatic tone. "My wife and children will always come first and I'll expect the same from the girl I marry."

She blinked. His declaration hit her between the eyes and somewhere deep in her heart. That wasn't exactly what she'd expected from Paolo, and he'd said it with such conviction. "Oh," she said, suddenly robbed of speech and hard pressed for a response.

"My father died young—too young. I come from a very close-knit family. That's what I miss most about living in the States."

Michaela suddenly felt dispirited and a little sad. "Well, my family is different. My parents are divorced now, but when Tiffany and I were growing up, they were both workaholics. We spent most of our childhood being schlepped around by a different nanny every year. My mom was so demanding of them, they kept quitting."

She refrained from adding that her parents had *always* put their careers before family. Paolo's strong, traditional beliefs were admirable and daunting, to say the least. She had never seen firsthand how a real marriage worked, kids and all. In a perfectly harmonious family it made sense, but not in Michaela's disjointed family unit. It seemed unattainable and unrealistic. All she'd heard growing up were heated arguments followed by extended periods of icy silence.

"Must have been tough. Don't you want to have children?" he asked.

"Someday, but what's the point of thinking about it now? I'm not even engaged." Somehow admitting it made her feel even worse. Why was it that everything he said tonight was making her rethink her personal choices? He was digging deeply for answers to questions she'd rather not explore with him.

"But if you were engaged?" he persisted, studying her intently. The soulful look in his eyes slayed her as she strove to regain her composure. She was unraveling before him.

"I would love to have children someday," she said after an awkward pause. Talking about wanting kids somehow seemed better suited to intimate moments between a man and woman in love, making plans for their future together. This wasn't the time for that topic, nor for baring her heart's desire. "How did we even get into this conversation?"

He gave a casual shrug. "It's normal to discuss these things."

"It is?" Michaela couldn't believe her ears. Most guys she'd dated after Jeff seemed to break out in hives at the mere mention of marriage or children, so she normally avoided the topic.

Paolo patted the space next to him. "Come sit beside me." His dark eyes glowed with invitation. "I'll prepare a fig for you to enjoy."

"No, thanks. I can't eat another bite. I'm full." She patted her stomach as she joined him on the couch. He moved in so close she could feel the steely strength of his thigh muscles pressed against hers.

"Do you know that the inside is an inverted flower? In Italy, they refer to the fig as a feminine flower." He paused. "I grew up eating figs."

Michaela stared at Paolo's sensual lips, perfectly sculpted and adept at eating anything. "I'm sure you did," she said in a strangled voice as her defenses surrendered to the attraction sizzling between them.

Paolo's eyes crinkled at the corners as his mouth eased into a deep-dimpled grin that could melt an iceberg. His hand curled around her nape and pulled her forward, settling her into his arms. A restless wantonness engulfed Michaela as hot desire coursed through her body. She peered at him from beneath the veil of lowered lashes, wondering if he could hear her heart slamming against her chest or feel the simmering heat trapped inside her. His knuckles grazed the side of her jaw as his dark eyes gazed at her mouth. She held her breath, waiting, aching for his kiss.

He cradled her face in his hands and held her still as his mouth covered hers, slowly and deliberately deepening the kiss, nibbling and suckling with a thoroughness that left her gasping. Her body inundated with voluptuous pleasure as Paolo's tongue entered her mouth and she got her first delicious taste of him. Demanding, yet tender, he kissed her until she was breathless.

With a blissful sigh, she wrapped her arms around his neck and threw her head back as he kissed her cheeks and jawline and nibbled her earlobe. Her breath caught in her throat when his tongue lightly traced the outer shell of her ear, causing tiny pinpricks to tease her skin.

Paolo nuzzled the crook of her neck and whispered Spanish endearments in a rough-edged voice. Every fine hair on Michaela's skin stood on end. Her body quivered, hot and jittery and hungry for more. He tasted and then gently nipped the side of her bare neck with his teeth. A shuddering moan escaped her lips. She wanted to scream, *yes, more—please!*

Michaela's back arched when he kissed her cleavage just above the neckline of her blouse. He cupped the soft underside of her breasts and lifted upward, plumping them before his mouth as he sampled their tender peaks. Paolo's warm lips closed over the silky fabric and lightly tugged at one nipple and then the other. Her fingers tangled in his thick, satiny hair as she held his face close to her bosom.

She held her breath as Paolo's hands slid under her blouse and up her bare back to unclasp her bra. She shivered when he freed her breasts and lifted her blouse. Laying his warm palms over her cool breasts, he savored their shape before his callused fingertips gently tweaked her nipples. Michaela bit down on her lower lip as Paolo's tongue swirled over her nipples and suckled, drawing out a strangled moan from her parched throat.

"*Delicioso.*" His voice came out a throaty, ragged growl.

Michaela tried to think straight, but her self-control was slipping away. She couldn't pull away, couldn't bring herself to stop him. She melted against him. Paolo's lovemaking was everything she had dreamed of and everything she had never felt with Jeff, the only other man she'd ever made love with. She put her hands on Paolo's darkly aroused face and urged it upward to meet her kiss, to slow down his ardor, but his reaction was almost savage, crushing the last vestiges of her self-control.

Hot and insatiable, Paolo's hands slid beneath her skirt and into her silk panties, cupping her bottom. His bold fingertips inched perilously close to the slippery, aching warmth between her thighs. Michaela's body cried out for fulfillment, but when he shifted his position pulling her beneath him, his hard erection jutted against her, jolting her back to reality.

It was madness.

There would be no turning back.

She would surely regret it.

She was on fire and so was he.

She had to stop now!

Forcing herself back to reality, she cursed softly and

reached back, dislodging his hold on her bottom.

"Please let me up," she choked, pushing against his chest. The solid imprint of Paolo's desire pressing against her pelvis made her feel guilty for stopping. Filled with regret and feeling unhinged, she took a deep breath and tried to calm her galloping heart. He pulled away with a groan as she struggled to sit up and adjust her clothing.

"I'm sorry, but I had to stop," she rasped, her voice cracking from the effort of keeping her wits when all she wanted to do was sink back into his embrace and let him finish what he had started.

"Why stop?" Paolo exhaled a harsh, jagged, breath. His black eyes flashed with frustration. "I thought you liked it."

"I did, I do...too much." Michaela's face flamed as she met his scorching gaze with a pathetic attempt at self-composure. If he only knew she was *this* close to succumbing to his lovemaking! "I mean...oh, God, I don't want you to think I'm a tease...I just—"

"Why did you stop me?" Paolo's taut mouth and the rigid set of his jaw evidenced his struggle to tamp down his lust. The tightly coiled tension in his large frame unnerved her as he leaned into her space. He took hold of her chin and turned her face to meet his intense gaze. "Talk to me."

"This was supposed to be a business meeting," she said for lack of a better explanation. She felt awkward and at a total loss as she got up from the sofa and sat in an armchair across from him. "I'm sorry I let things get out of control."

"Yeah, me too." His voice sounded hoarse with dissatisfaction and hot passion still flared in his midnight eyes.

"It's just that I don't take lovemaking lightly and that's where we were headed." She paused. *Oh, God, don't look at me that way,* she silently implored. "Paolo, you're a complication I can't afford. My goal this Monday is to win the competition. I know that's your goal too."

He frowned. "I wasn't thinking about the competition just now."

Michaela sucked in a deep breath and looked him square in the eyes. "This will probably sound ruthless and unfeminine to you, but winning this contest is the *only* thing I'm focused on right now. I can't allow you to distract me."

He looked annoyed and unconvinced. They were getting nowhere. She suspected this was the first time Paolo had been rebuffed by a woman. She had been close to giving in to reckless abandon when she finally stopped and listened to her conscience.

"In order for this show to work, we must get along. Don't you agree?" he asked.

Michaela noticed that Paolo's words were beginning to sound a bit slurred.

"We can't afford to get involved now," she said.

He came forward and hunkered down in front of her, cupping the side of her jaw in his hand as he peered into her eyes. "And later?"

She tried not to let his midnight eyes enthrall her, but one glance and she relived everything he had just done to her. Hot desire swamped over her again as she hankered for more of his slow, deep kisses and the feel of his warm, strong hands on her body. She *wanted* Paolo, there was no denying it.

He straightened and reached for her hand. When he tried to pull her from the chair, she noticed his grip wasn't as firm as usual and he didn't seem steady on his feet.

She gave him a curious look. "What's wrong with you?"

"Nothing." He frowned and settled back on the couch, across from her. "Can't you let loose at all? Do you always have to be in control? Why are you so bothered by a little harmless flirting?"

A little harmless flirting? Paolo's flippant remark sliced through Michaela's vulnerable heart like a sharp dagger. Had that been all it meant to him? What a fool she'd been to succumb to his seduction and believe she was different from all the other women he had dalliances with! Good thing she had stopped or she would have ended up as just another notch on his belt. Paolo's way of expressing himself was naturally sensuous. He was the master of the chase, and tonight the irresistible serpent had lured his prey.

Michaela suddenly felt no different from his other conquests and that cut deeply. She had allowed Paolo's lusty charisma and hot appeal to make her lose her head.

"Why so quiet? It's not like you. You usually have plenty to say." His brows crinkled over eyes that suddenly looked like he was having a hard time focusing.

Michaela wondered just how much he'd had to drink while she'd been dealing with Aunt Magda's visit and then Mom's phone call. When she didn't answer right away, Paolo gave a profound sigh and closed his eyes. For a minute, Michaela thought he might have fallen asleep. She looked at the half-empty wine bottle on the coffee table. Surely, he couldn't be drunk!

Paolo's cell suddenly rang, jarring both of them. "*¿Allo?* What is it, Claudia? No, please, not againnn." His words sounded oddly slurred.

Claudia said something to which he mumbled, "Not tonight. It's false labor again. Go to sleep." Michaela noticed his eyes looked glazed. "I'll take you to the doctor in the morning. Then you...can have...your...baby."

Why was Paolo reacting so bizarrely? What if Claudia really was in labor? Michaela fretted, starting to panic. She felt like wringing her hands...or better yet, wringing his thick neck! She heard every word Claudia yelled back at him as Paolo held the phone away from his ear.

"Get me to the hospital! NOW!" Claudia shrieked. "The baby is coming. My water just broke!"

The phone slipped from Paolo's hand as he grappled with it. Closing his eyes, he laid it on his chest and nestled his head against the back of the sofa without responding to Claudia.

"Give me that!" Michaela cried, grabbing the phone as Paolo's mouth grew slack and he slumped over. "Claudia, this is Michaela, your brother's friend. I'll take you to the hospital. Paolo is a little, uh, indisposed right now."

"Hurry, please! I already called the doctor."

"Okay. Hang in there. I'll be right over," Michaela promised, shocked that Paolo had passed out on the sofa. She noticed the prescription bottles nestled beside him and picked one up with shaking hands. Dear God, how much had Paolo taken? Had he taken a muscle relaxant instead of a painkiller? Or had he taken both?

Chapter Ten

Paolo's heart pumped hard with adrenaline as he rode to the hospital in a speeding taxi, clutching Maki's scribbled note in his hand. At seven in the morning, he had woken up in her apartment, alone on her couch with a throbbing headache. It had taken awhile to get his bearings. What the devil kind of medicine had Maki given him? That had been no ordinary painkiller! Man, he had never been so knocked out. His sore neck felt better now, but his unsteady legs were still feeling the after effects of the pills.

At four in the morning, he had tried to get up from the couch but had toppled backward, feeling woozy—too woozy to get up. He had zonked out again and had woken up hours later. Then he'd found the note pinned to his shirt front. *Claudia in labor. Took her to Mercy Hospital.*

Maki must have gotten back from the hospital, showered and left for work, but why hadn't she woken him?

Poor Claudia. He wondered if she'd had the baby yet. If not, then hopefully she was having an easy labor. Traffic was hell this time of the morning, but the young Cuban cab driver looked like he knew how to tackle any problem.

"No problem, sir. I'll get you there," he said, hitting the accelerator.

Paolo sat back against the vinyl-covered seat and hoped he'd get there alive. Good thing Mercy Hospital wasn't very far. They sped over the Julia Tuttle Bridge as memories came flooding back of Claudia as a child. She was almost five when they had lost their father. Following Papá's death, their mother had sunk into a deep depression. Paolo, fourteen years older, had held Claudia's trembling body in his arms and rocked her when she had woken up crying on many nights. Cradling her on his lap, he had dried her tears, patted her back and consoled her as much as he could.

In those middle-of-the-night moments, Claudia had asked hard questions, demanding to know where Papá was and when he would come back. Paolo had always replied that Papá was happy in heaven and watching over them. He wasn't sure how much Claudia had finally understood, but he hoped that being comforted in her big brother's arms had helped.

"I'm scared," Claudia had cried, burying her little face against his chest.

"Hush, nena, I'm here," he had said, hugging her tighter.

"You won't leave me like Papá did?" she had always asked anxiously.

"I won't leave. I'll be here for you, no matter what," he had promised.

He had kept his word until last night. Why had he passed out like that? He couldn't believe he wasn't with Claudia the one time in her life she needed him the most. Over the years he'd helped raise his baby sister, she'd gone from being an incorrigible prankster to a fun-loving young woman. Yet she was a mother now, facing huge responsibilities for the first time in her life.

The taxi screeched to a halt in front of the hospital, jarring Paolo from his musings. He quickly paid the driver and then rushed to the information desk where he was directed to the maternity ward. When he arrived at the fourth floor maternity center, Paolo went straight to the nurse's station.

"Is Claudia Santos here?" he asked the tall, wiry nurse manning the counter. "I mean Woodbridge...Claudia Woodbridge. Did she already give birth?"

The nurse put on horn-rimmed reading glasses and peered into the computer screen. "Just a minute. I'll check for you. Are you her husband?" she inquired, checking the list of maternity patients.

"No, I'm her brother—Paolo Santos."

"Oh." She furrowed her thin brows and took her time to check the list.

"Please, I'm Claudia's only relative here. I need to see her now!"

"Your sister is fine." The nurse's weathered face broke into a warm smile. "Congratulations, Mr. Santos, your nephew was

Sophia Knightly

just born."

"Thank you!" He was so happy he almost grabbed her and kissed her right there. "Is my sister all right? Did everything go well?"

"Everything went just fine. Mrs. Woodbridge is still in recovery. She'll be taken to the post-partum room soon."

Paolo felt as if an elephant's foot had been lifted from his chest. "Where is recovery?"

"Downstairs—second floor. Turn right after you exit the elevators."

Paolo sprinted to the elevator and punched the button for the second floor. *Hurry up! ¡Apurate!* he thought as the elevator slowly descended.

Good thing Maki had taken charge of Claudia. How could he thank her enough for helping his sister? What would they have done without her? Maki was so responsible. He remembered how she had left the note pinned to his shirt so he would see it as soon as he woke up. Knowing her, he'd never live that one down.

He arrived on the second floor and explained to the attending nurse that he was Claudia's older brother. After a bit of interrogation, she finally led him to the recovery room area.

"Is she okay? Can I see her?" he asked.

Nurse Ramirez, an efficient, young woman, barely five feet tall but with an authoritative presence, smiled at him. "Don't worry, Mr. Santos. Your sister did well for a first labor. Let me just make sure she agrees to letting you come in," she said, turning the door handle.

"Fine," Paolo said patiently, even though he felt far from patient. Poor Claudia—forced to give birth alone in the hospital while her big brother was passed out on the sofa. He felt like the biggest heel.

Nurse Ramirez returned shortly. "You may go in now. The baby has already been taken to the nursery. You must be a very close-knit bunch. It's wonderful to see a family that cares so much for each other. Your other sister has not left Mrs. Woodbridge's side. She was there during the entire labor, encouraging her."

Other sister? The nurse was surely mistaken and referring

106

to another patient, but Paolo was in no mood to correct her or make small talk. He only wanted to see Claudia and make sure she was all right.

"Thanks." Paolo stepped into the room and stopped in his tracks at the sight of Michaela standing beside the bed, holding Claudia's hand. Gratitude and relief washed over him when he realized she had stayed with his little sister throughout her ordeal.

He smiled at Michaela and then rushed to Claudia's side, taking her other hand in his. Beaming into Claudia's wan face, he said, "Congratulations, *nena*. How are you feeling?"

"I'm okay." She paused and smiled. "Actually, I'm more than okay. I'm head-over-heels in love with Michael!"

"Michael? Who the hell is Michael?" Paolo asked, bewildered.

"My baby, silly. You should see your face, Paolo!" Claudia giggled. "I was going to name him Robert Woodbridge, Jr., but after last night I changed my mind."

"Why?" Paolo searched his sister's face for clues that she might be reacting to whatever drugs they had given her.

"Bobby doesn't deserve to have his son named after him. I decided to name him after Michaela. It's the least I can do after the way she took care of me."

Paolo turned to Michaela. "Thank you for staying with Claudia," he said, touched by her generosity toward his sister, who until last night had been a stranger to Michaela.

She smiled. "No need to thank me. I was happy to do it. It got intense toward the end, but everything worked out fine."

"What happened? Did you have any complications?" Paolo asked, alarmed.

"You tell him, Maki," Claudia said wearily. "I don't have the strength."

Michaela nodded. "Claudia's labor seemed to stall in the middle and they gave her Pitocin. The contractions started coming closer together after that, faster and harder." She smiled at Claudia. "But she pulled through like a trooper and delivered a gorgeous little boy."

Claudia gazed at Michaela with adoring eyes. "I am so grateful to you for staying with me. You didn't leave my side once until the baby was born. And you were so calm and strong while I was panicking and screaming." She turned to Paolo. "Maki was the glue that held me together."

Paolo's searching gaze connected with Michaela's and he felt the stirring of tender feelings deep in his heart. She had never looked more beautiful. Her lustrous copper hair lay tousled about her face and shoulders, her makeup was smeared under her shimmering aquamarine eyes, and her silk blouse and skirt were wrinkled. She looked exhausted, but the radiant happiness on her face held him spellbound. She had remained beside his baby sister the whole night, giving her support and rallying behind her with strength and encouragement. Michaela Willoughby, for all her tough competitiveness and strict rules, was a real softie deep down and he was captivated by her, couldn't take his eyes off her.

"Thank you, *querida*," he said in a hushed voice.

"You're welcome, Paolo. And you too, Claudia. It was my pleasure—really. I had no idea how truly awesome childbirth is. It's life-changing to watch—unforgettable!" she said, visibly moved by the experience.

For several charged moments, Paolo and Michaela stared into each other's eyes as if nobody else was in the room. He wanted to take her in his arms and make love to her until she admitted she felt the same way about him.

Claudia cleared her throat and speared her brother with a quizzical look. "So why did you bum out on me, *hermano?*"

"I didn't mean to," Paolo said, collecting his wits. "Your birthing coach here drugged me. Or maybe it was her food," he teased, turning to wink at Michaela.

"Very funny, Paolo," Michaela replied dryly. "You should have known better than to drink more wine with the painkiller I gave you. Or the muscle relaxant. Which one did you take?"

"I took one of each for good measure."

Michaela drew back in shock. "You took both? No wonder you passed out!"

"I'm a lot bigger than you are, *querida*. I never expected those medicines to knock me out like that." He wagged a finger at Michaela. "You should have warned me they were so strong."

"Didn't I? How remiss of me."

"Maybe you did it on purpose...so you could have your way with me," he teased, black eyes twinkling.

Michaela laughed. "Guilty as charged—not!"

Paolo enjoyed watching her cheeks turn pink and wondered if she was remembering how enjoyable things had been until she had stopped him. "How do I know what other tactics you have up your sleeve for winning the show?"

"You don't and you won't be finding out any time soon," Michaela countered, full of sass. "All's fair in love and war, as they say. So you better be careful what you eat and drink from now on, hotshot...at least until the winner is chosen."

"I know I've just had a baby and I'm a little groggy, but you've lost me." Claudia looked confused as she glanced from Paolo to Michaela. "What are you two talking about?"

"Maki, why didn't you tell Claudia about our pilot TV show?" Paolo gave her a reproachful look.

"I tried telling her between contractions, but she wasn't paying attention," Michaela said. "She had more important things on her mind."

"That's true," Paolo conceded, turning to Claudia. "Maki and I are competing against each other to be top chef of a new cooking show."

"So you're the one he's been muttering about." Claudia grinned. "He said you were driving him nuts."

"Claudia, please, where is your loyalty?" Paolo chided with mock affront.

"I love you, Paolo, but after last night, I'm kinda siding with Michaela," Claudia teased.

"Okay, enough of that. You need to rest, *nena.*" Paolo turned to Michaela. "We should go now."

"You're right, we should," Michaela said.

Claudia started to giggle as she regarded Paolo and Michaela. "I can't wait to hear more about this competition."

"You will, but not now." Paolo kissed the top of her head.

"Don't you want to see Michael?" Claudia asked.

"Of course! Why do you think I'm itching to get out of here? I can't wait to see my nephew. Maki will take me to him," Paolo said.

As if on cue, Nurse Ramirez flung the door open, followed by an attendant. "Mrs. Woodbridge, your room is ready and your baby is waiting for his first nursing."

Michaela stared into the nursery window, her heart filled with tenderness and longing as she pointed toward Claudia's newborn. "There he is! Isn't he the most precious baby?"

When Paolo turned to gaze at her, his gaze was filled with such bursting pride that for a moment she wondered what he'd be like as a dad. "I can't believe my baby sister is a mother. Good-looking kid. He kinda resembles his uncle, don't you think?" he asked, angling his head with a boastful grin.

Michaela cocked her head and crinkled her brow. "You think? He's blondish and looks more like Claudia..."

"What are you talking about? Look at him, handsome, cuddly, sweet..."

"Modest?" she prompted, tongue in cheek.

Paolo pulled her in and kissed her soundly. "I've wanted to do this since I saw you with my sister. Thanks for taking care of Claudia. I really owe you one."

Did he have any idea how much an impromptu kiss sent ripples of pleasure through her? Michaela steadied her knees that had suddenly turned to liquid. "Please, you don't have to thank me again. Claudia's the one who labored hard." In her mind, she kept reliving the beautiful moment when Claudia gave birth, but it was time to hit reality. She gave a heartfelt sigh. "I wish I could stay longer, but I have to get to work."

"Me too. Gil is covering for me today, but I have a meeting tonight that I can't miss." Paolo rubbed the back of his neck. "Claudia will be coming home soon and I know nothing about babies."

"You'll learn as you go along." Michaela tried to sound encouraging, but the truth was she didn't know much about babies either. The whole thing seemed pretty daunting. "Nurse Ramirez told Claudia that she would probably be released tomorrow."

"So soon?" Paolo asked, looking apprehensive.

"Yes. What are you going to do about a crib and all the

baby stuff she needs?"

"I don't know, but I'll figure it out. The stuff she needs is the least of my problems. Claudia is going to need help taking care of the baby while she recuperates." Paolo looked genuinely panicked now.

"She will need help. What about your mom?"

"I'm sending her a prepaid airline ticket, but in the meantime, I have to track down Bobby. He had no idea that Claudia was pregnant and now he needs to know that he has a son."

"How are you going to find him? Claudia said he was far away, in some remote place."

"I'll find him," Paolo said with a determined gleam in his eyes.

"You better clear it with Claudia first. Last night she was pretty vocal about not wanting to see him," Michaela warned.

"She was in labor. Women resent their husbands when they're suffering through childbirth, don't they?"

"I guess, but I'd never witnessed it until today," Michaela said. "I don't know what happened between the two of them, but Claudia kept crying and saying that he had abandoned her."

"She's hurt and mad at Bobby, that's all. After a few days alone with her baby, she'll realize she has to put her pride aside for her son's sake."

"Maybe, but I wouldn't get into it with her now, Paolo. Let Claudia and Michael bond first. Maybe she'll soften toward Bobby...she did say the baby looks like him."

Paolo nodded. "It's true. Claudia had huge dark eyes when she was born. Bobby's eyes are blue just like Michael's."

Michaela wondered how Paolo had looked as a baby. Stifling a smile, she imagined a baby with a mop of dark hair and a set of rakish dimples. She turned her attention to the sleeping infant and wished she could hold him in her arms. "He is the most beautiful little thing I've ever seen!"

"*Sí*, he is a handsome one," Paolo said proudly. "Like I told you, exactly like his uncle."

Michaela smiled indulgently. "If you say so."

Paolo's genial expression turned serious. "I'm going to tell Bobby he has a son. As soon as he knows, he'll come and get them. And I'm going to tell his parents too. They should know their first grandchild was born, even though they opposed the marriage."

Michaela thought it ironic that given his reputation as a notorious player, Paolo was acting old school. Claudia was an adult and should be allowed to decide how to proceed. It was her life, after all, and her baby. But it wasn't Michaela's place to talk Paolo out of it. She had only met him a few days ago and she was already getting entwined in his personal life. That wasn't where she should be, given their upcoming competition.

"Maybe you should ask her first. Claudia is a grown woman."

"She's only twenty and has a lot of growing up to do." Paolo's jaw tightened. "I'm doing the right thing."

Michaela threw her hands up in the air. "Okay, on to another subject. Would you please let me know when we're going to rehearse for the taping on Monday?"

"As soon as Mamá arrives—hopefully tomorrow morning— I'll be free to meet with you." Paolo's gaze grew intense as he regarded her with a thoughtful expression. "Don't worry. I won't let you down."

"Good to hear. I appreciate it. As soon as I get back, I'm going to fax our menu to the culinary producer."

"Thanks." Paolo pulled her in for a tight hug.

Nestled in his strong arms and pressed against his broad chest, Michaela melted against his large form. She could hear his heart beating as rapidly as hers and was suddenly reminded of his passionate kisses last night. Still holding her, Paolo's searching gaze traveled from her eyes to her mouth. Her breath caught in her throat at the anticipation of his kiss, but when his warm lips finally grazed hers, it was different from last night's kisses.

Michaela's fingers rose to her mouth, remembering how his firm lips had feasted on hers, leaving them red and swollen yesterday. Waves of pleasure pulsed through her just thinking about it. *Dear God.* She shivered, imagining how he would make love—vigorous and uninhibited, unabashedly dominating, yet tender. She closed her eyes to the memory of his hands and mouth on her. Her legs wobbled when she stepped away from his embrace, her body hot, antsy and wanting more, much more.

When she looked up, she caught the devilish twinkle in Paolo's eyes and suddenly recalled his flippant comment last night about theirs being a "harmless flirtation". All desire vanished as quickly as it had built up, replaced by a wariness she hated to acknowledge. She couldn't risk falling under his spell. Michaela sighed heavily and looked away from him. Paolo was a known player and she could not afford to forget that. What he considered a harmless flirtation had the power to break her heart. She was already falling for him, enjoying his company, looking forward to spending more time with him and lusting for his touch. The more time they spent together, the more she wanted to be with him.

"I'll wait to hear from you," she said, resolutely wrapping a protective shield around her heart before she turned away.

Late that afternoon, once she had showered, tidied up her apartment and eaten a quick lunch, Michaela headed to the spa to make sure everything was ready for Monday's patrons since she would be out all day with the taping. As soon as she arrived, she took a moment to read the many emails that had come in since last night and noticed one from Mr. Blumenthal's assistant, Ellie, sent to her and Paolo:

Change of venue...taping will be at a house in Mashta Island. Address, directions and details attached. Dry tech at 7 a.m., followed by run-through, and then taping before live audience. Questions? Call me anytime this weekend. Ellie

Well, that changed everything. Now they would be taping in a house, in a regular kitchen, not in a studio with all the necessary equipment on hand—not exactly the environment she had hoped for. Michaela dialed Paolo's cell number and he answered it on the second ring.

"*Hola.*" He sounded out of breath and terse.

113

"Hi, what're you up to?" she asked cautiously.

"I just left from meeting with Claudia's in-laws."

"Oh…how did it go?"

"Terrible. The Woodbridges are the most pompous, annoying people I've ever met. You should see their house, or I should say monument. It's as big as a hotel," he said sarcastically. "They were so cold, I felt like I was in a mausoleum."

"Weren't they happy to hear they have a grandson?"

Paolo gave a derisive snort. "Hardly. Bobby's father only complained about his reckless son's disappearance and how inconsiderate he was. But his wife started to cry as soon as she heard about the baby. And they were *not* tears of happiness!"

"Why would they act like that?" Michaela asked, perplexed. She heard the vehemence in Paolo's voice and could tell he needed to vent.

"They told me they were furious when they found out their son had eloped with a Latina. They had planned on him marrying a high-society debutante. I can't believe how callous and selfish they are. They didn't even want to know how Claudia was doing, or their first grandchild!" he ranted. "What kind of family is that?"

"A cold, unfeeling one," Michaela answered. Poor Claudia. Having judgmental in-laws was the worst thing for a newlywed. It was unimaginable that they wouldn't be over the moon about little Michael. By the time Paolo finished filling her in on everything, Michaela was shocked. "Wow. I'm sorry to hear that," she groaned. "No wonder Claudia seemed so desperate last night, and so alone. Poor thing!"

"Poor nothing!" Paolo bit out angrily. "Claudia is not alone—she has a family. It's a good thing she finally came to me! When I think that she might have…"

"Calm down. She doesn't need more people upset with her," Michaela said, "even if you have a reason, Paolo." She sighed. "I hate to change the subject, but the reason I'm calling is that they've changed the location of Monday's shoot. Did you read Ellie's email?"

"Not yet. What did it say?"

"We have to be on set by seven Monday morning, ready for

the dry tech. Paolo, I know you have a lot on your plate, but we absolutely have to practice together before that. The cameramen have to get the lighting cues from the blocking and..."

"I can't meet tonight," he cut in abruptly. "I have a business meeting I cannot afford to cancel. How about tomorrow?"

"Tomorrow?" Michaela hated waiting until the last minute to meet, but she had no choice. At least they could get one decent run-through. "Okay, tomorrow, then. How is Claudia doing?"

"I just talked to her. She sounds a little nervous about going home with her baby. She's not the only one. I'm nervous as hell. I know squat about babies. *¡Nada!*"

Michaela couldn't help grinning, and at the same time, finding his nervousness endearing. Funny how one tiny baby could stress out a big guy like Paolo. "When is your mom arriving?"

"Who knows? She has a problem with her visa and will have to pull some strings to get here. I need to find someone to help Claudia while I'm gone. The sooner the better."

"I'll ask around. I've heard plenty of women complaining about their hired help at the spa. Ha, we should be so lucky," she quipped. "Anyway, maybe one of them knows of a nurse or a nanny who is available."

"Thank you, *querida*," Paolo said, his voice softening. "I would really appreciate it. I'm heading to Babies"R"Us now. I have one hour to figure out what to buy. Wish me luck."

Michaela giggled at the mental image of Paolo running amok in a huge baby store, amidst cribs, strollers and stuffed baby lambs. It was really too much!

She choked back a chuckle. "Good luck."

"Glad someone thinks it's funny."

Chapter Eleven

Early Sunday afternoon, Michaela attempted to relax as she reclined on the outdoor rattan loveseat on her balcony. She had cleaned out the big steel birdcage and was feeding Baby his favorite treats of nuts and mixed berries.

"*Gracias, Mamacita, qué buena estás*," Baby crowed in Spanish from his perch on Michaela's arm.

Michaela rolled her eyes at the bird telling her she was hot—thanks to Manny, Aunt Willow's on-again-off-again lover. Manny, a Cuban-American firefighter with a snake tattoo on his thick biceps, had taught Baby all the politically incorrect innuendos in his bird vocabulary. And Baby knew precisely when to use them.

"You're welcome, Baby," Michaela replied.

On this gloriously warm and balmy April day, she should have been feeling relaxed, but every time she chatted with Baby her thoughts drifted to another baby—Michael. Right about now, he was probably getting adjusted to his new home and bonding with his mommy and uncle. Ever since she had held him in her arms briefly after Claudia had given birth, Michaela yearned to hold his tiny body again—just for a little while.

She glanced at her watch. Two thirty. They had to be home by now. She didn't want to be pushy and she understood that Paolo was overwhelmed with bringing his sister and new baby home, but she had to get him on board for their rehearsal before the big show tomorrow. Just thinking about it made her stomach pitch with nerves. She wouldn't feel nearly as anxious and a lot more confident if they could have just one run-through.

On her end, everything was set right down to the aqua wrap-style blouse and slim tan slacks she would wear. The wardrobe girl had suggested she wear something in a shade of blue, referring to it as a "friendly" color. She planned on doing her own hair, half-up with a side part, and on wearing small gold loops on her earlobes. She wondered what Paolo was planning to wear. Whatever he chose, he'd be quite a draw for the ladies, that was for sure.

Maybe she should just stop by for a few minutes, drop off the baby gift for Michael she had bought this morning and get Paolo to commit to a meeting tonight. She wanted to give him the benefit of the doubt, but it did not bode well that it was already two-thirty and he hadn't called her.

"*Dame azúcar, mamacita,*" Baby demanded, saying, "gimme sugar, little mama" in Spanish.

Michaela complied by kissing the top of Baby's red-feathered head.

"*Gracias,*" Baby cackled.

"You're welcome," Michaela replied, smiling at his silliness. "Okay, back to your crib now. " She placed him in the cage and closed the door, content that he would be entertained all day chewing and tearing apart his new toys.

Baby cocked his head. "*¿Qué pasa?*"

Qué pasa, indeed, Michaela thought, concerned about Paolo's silence. But why should that surprise her? So far he hadn't done any of the things she had expected him to do. She would wait another few hours to hear from him. If by four-thirty he still hadn't called, she would take matters into her own hands—her future was riding on it. Even though Paolo was convinced he was going to be great, they still needed all the practice they could get, especially to perform in front of a TV camera. One way or another she would drag that Argentine by the horns to a productive practice session!

Michaela didn't bother knocking when she noticed Paolo's front door was ajar and she heard the commotion coming from inside. Between the baby's crying and Paolo and Claudia's raised voices, she was sure they wouldn't hear her knock anyway. She pushed the door and walked in, sidestepping the trail of packages and boxes littering every inch of the floor from the entrance to the living room. The place resembled moving-day chaos. Several packs of disposable diapers were stacked on the kitchen counter, enough to outfit a daycare center for a month. Paolo had clearly gone haywire. Where was he going to store all this stuff?

"Paolo," Michaela called out as she headed toward the bedroom. "Paolo...Claudia."

A disheveled Paolo appeared through the doorway, looking like he had just emerged from a boxing match. His white shirt was tucked half in and half out of his pants, his hair was tousled, his face covered in afternoon stubble, and his eyes looked bleary.

Relief flooded his tense face when he saw her. "Maki. Am I glad to see you!"

Claudia appeared from behind him, looking wild-eyed and just as disheveled. Bone-tired too.

For a split second, Michaela considered running out the door while she could. Suddenly, the whole scene overwhelmed her and she felt like she was rapidly going to be sucked into a black vortex.

Claudia came forward and enveloped Michaela in a tight hug. "Thank God you're here! I really need you. Paolo is going crazy. So am I!"

"What's wrong?" Michaela asked, alarmed.

Claudia gave her a frantic look. "Mikey won't nurse and he won't stop crying. I don't think I have any milk. What should I do?" she wailed, pointing to the little bassinet where her baby lay, his tiny face mottled purple as he howled while his arms and legs made sharp, jerky motions.

"Did you buy any baby formula?" Michaela asked Paolo.

"No. How was I supposed to know that Claudia's milk was dried up?" he asked.

Claudia looked on the verge of tears. "I tried to feed Mikey one of the infant formulas they sent home with me, but he only drank a little. He doesn't want it. I don't know what's wrong. I was able to breastfeed in the hospital, but ever since we got here the milk won't come."

"How long have you been home?" Michaela asked.

"We got here around two and then all hell broke loose," Claudia said, her voice rising.

"Calm down. Everything's going to be fine," Michaela soothed. She was trying to stay calm herself, but she knew practically nothing about babies. She deliberated a moment, trying to gather her thoughts. Of course—her best friend—Google!

"Where's your laptop, Paolo?" Michaela asked.

"Over there." He pointed to a corner of the kitchen counter before retreating to the bedroom.

Michaela ran over and Googled "breast-feeding support for new moms". As soon as La Leche League popped on the screen, she dialed it. From the corner of her eye, she could see Paolo in the untidy bedroom, pacing with Mikey in his arms, trying to quiet him. Seeing big, strong Paolo tenderly holding a tiny, squalling infant stirred a deep longing inside of her. No doubt, he would make a wonderful dad. Michaela exhaled her pent-up breath and looked away to dispel any weakening. *Enough of that mushy stuff or you'll cave,* she reprimanded herself.

"This is Beth Ramsey of La Leche League. May I help you?" a friendly female voice on the line asked.

Michaela gave Beth a brief summary of Claudia's problem, and then handed Claudia the phone so she could pour out her troubles to the counselor. After washing her hands at the kitchen sink, Michaela headed toward the bedroom to tend to Mikey. "Let me hold him," she said to Paolo, reaching for the baby. "Do you have a pacifier for him?"

The moment she held Mikey in her arms, Michaela was floored by an instant rush of emotions—protectiveness, yearning, sheer pleasure in the feel of his soft, tiny body snuggled against her chest.

"Pacifier? I think there's one in there." Paolo searched the bassinet and found one. "Here, give it a try. But I doubt Mikey will be fooled. He is a Santos. That boy wants the real stuff!"

Michaela gently tapped the rubber-tipped pacifier over Mikey's lips and for a second he sucked it in, but then he spat it out and started rooting against her blouse like a hungry little bird.

"See? What did I tell you? He's no fool, he wants milk!" Paolo raked his fingers through his hair. If he hadn't looked so unsettled, Michaela would have laughed at the way his hair was ruffled like a wet parrot's feathers, with the ends pointing in every direction.

"If Claudia could breastfeed in the hospital, she should be able to do it here." Michaela hoped it was true for Mikey's sake. "Shh, shh," she crooned, shifting Mikey to rest on her shoulder as she patted his fragile back.

"I have to take a shower. Can you stay for a while? Claudia could use your encouragement," Paolo said, raising his voice to be heard over the baby's crying.

"Sure, go ahead." Michaela hadn't planned on staying very long, but she could spare a little time. She rocked back and forth and Mikey's cries turned to soft whimpers.

With a look of supreme gratitude and relief, Paolo dashed to the bathroom and closed the door. Within seconds, she heard him whistling a tune and then the sound of the shower water running. Miraculously, Mikey quieted on her shoulder after a few hiccupping sighs.

Claudia returned to the bedroom, looking relieved. "Oh, good. He finally fell asleep." She nodded at Mikey. "That Leche League lady was amazing. Beth told me to lie down on the bed and do some relaxation breathing to de-stress. She said breastfeeding is all about supply and demand."

"That makes sense," Michaela said.

"*Sí*, everything she said made sense. The more I nurse Mikey, the more milk I'll produce. But I have to be calm so the milk will let down."

"You already seem a bit calmer."

"I am. Beth said not to feel overwhelmed because nursing is no big deal and completely natural. And that I can call her at any time."

"She sounds like a treasure." Michaela couldn't believe the change in Claudia after just one phone call. That Beth was a miracle worker. "I'll take Mikey to the living room while you chill. He seems content sucking his thumb. Close the door and call me when you're ready to nurse him."

"I will, thanks." Claudia's eyes suddenly welled up. "You are amazing. Once again, you've come to my rescue and I only just met you."

"Hey, we're friends now! Looks like your little angel likes

sucking his thumb. Maybe he was just cranky and tired. Get some sleep. I'll bring him in when he wakes up, okay?"

"That would be great. Thanks."

"Sure thing. I'm going to enjoy holding him." Michaela kissed the downy fuzz on Mikey's sweet little head.

Just then, Paolo emerged from the bathroom dressed in a freshly laundered white shirt and snug jeans with his handsome face cleanly shaven. Michaela's nostrils perked up at the whiff of his citrusy cologne.

"Where are you going all dolled up?" Claudia asked, regarding him with a raised brow as she placed her hands on her hips.

"I have a business meeting I can't miss."

"On Sunday?" Claudia asked.

"When are we going to practice, Paolo?" Michaela lowered her voice not to awaken Mikey, but she felt like bellowing at him. Claudia was right. It was odd for him to have a business meeting on a Sunday afternoon. "It's already five o'clock."

"I'll be back in an hour...or two," Paolo said.

"That long?" Claudia looked distraught. "Maki, can you stay with me until Paolo gets back? I don't want to be alone with Mikey on my first night here." Her anxious tone and the desolation in her eyes tugged at Michaela's heart.

"Yes, I'll stay with you," Michaela said kindly, even though she wasn't feeling very kindly toward Paolo at the moment. Where was he going "all dolled up" as Claudia had put it?

"Good. I'll bring dinner for all of us." Paolo looked supremely relieved. It was obvious he was itching to leave. "Once Claudia and the baby are settled in, we can go back to your place, Maki."

"Promise?" Michaela asked, doubting him the minute she asked. She narrowed her eyes at Paolo, noting how good he looked after a mere shower and a shave.

"*Sí*, I promise. *Ciao, querida,*" he said and dashed out the door as if a red-hot coal was buried in the back pocket of his jeans.

Driving into the parking lot of Ristorante Bella Luna, Paolo was annoyed that Bernice Blumenthal had insisted on meeting today of all days. Why couldn't she have waited until Monday, after the show? Why interrupt his Sunday and ruin his plans to meet with Maki? Good thing he had circumvented Bernice's plan to meet at his apartment.

No sooner had he begun to open the restaurant door, than he felt two soft, pudgy hands cover his eyes from behind.

"Guess who?" a mature, throaty voice purred.

"Bernice?" he asked wearily.

"The one and only." She gaily appeared before him, her full figure swathed in a flower-printed sheath and a hibiscus tucked behind her right ear. One jeweled hand reached up to smooth her highly teased hairdo. Beaming at him, she clasped his shoulders with fuchsia-tipped hands and kissed him on both cheeks, leaving a cloying trace of flowery perfume. She tilted her head and gave him a flirtatious smile. "Ready for our meeting?"

"Yes." Anxious to get it over with soon, he stepped away from her grasp and flicked on the lights before gesturing for her to enter ahead of him.

Bernice teetered inside on fuchsia stiletto sandals that laced up to mid-calf, decorated with silk butterflies at her bare ankles. She stood beside the table and waited for Paolo to pull out her chair and join her.

"Ooh," she said, fanning herself. "I'm warm and tingling all over. Is the bar open?"

Paolo noted the naughty twinkle in her eyes. Starting Bernice off with a drink probably wasn't a good idea because she had probably already had a few, but he'd have to offer one anyway.

"What would you like?" he asked.

"Belvedere martini, *por favor.*"

"You got it," he said, retreating to the bar.

"With two olives, darling." Bernice's broad grin caused her upper lip to lift and reveal her gum line above her long, rabbity front teeth. She joined him on the other side of the bar, hoisting herself onto the leather barstool. She took a long, gratifying sip of the drink Paolo placed before her and sighed. "That hit the spot, and I don't just mean the g-spot," she said shamelessly.

"Thank you, darling."

How many drinks had she imbibed already, he wondered, put off by her sexual flirting. "You're welcome. What can I do for you?" Once the words were out, he wished he had rephrased it.

Bernice's hand stroked her plunging neckline, which exposed a bountiful décolletage. She had an exaggerated hourglass figure—tiny waist with huge breasts above and a curvaceous ass below.

"You really want to know?" The corners of her heavily made-up green eyes crinkled with shrewd amusement.

"We're here to discuss Palmentieri's dinner party, aren't we?" Paolo kept his tone polite, but cool.

Bernice pursed her glossy lips. "Yes. Next month, I want to give a party for my dear friend Domenico Palmentieri. You've met him, haven't you?"

Paolo nodded. He was well aware of the famous tenor's effusive love of food. The man had the belly of a whale and the lungs of a gorilla, but his voice was rich and sonorous.

"Palmentieri ate here at Bella Luna last December," Paolo said.

"A serendipitous coincidence," she cooed. "I'd like you to prepare an extravagant meal for Domenico and his big family. They will be here for his gala concert on Saturday night. I know you don't work on Sundays, that's why I wanted to speak to you personally about this, away from Edwin's ears."

"I'm sure I can arrange something special for you. Where would you like to host the party, here or at your home?"

"My house—it's much nicer to eat on the terrace overlooking the bay. Don't you think?"

"Sure. How many in the party?" he asked in a formal tone.

"Around twenty-five. I'll confirm the exact number later this week."

"I would be happy to accommodate your group," Paolo said courteously.

"Marvelous! Splendid!" Bernice gleefully clasped his hands in hers. "I knew you'd come through for me. This very morning I had to endure a stern lecture from Edwin who told me to wait until after the show to approach you. But I told him that you could handle anything."

Paolo chuckled and carefully withdrew his hands from her tight grip. "*Gracias.*"

"My pleasure," she gushed. "I'd like to set the menu now."

"Now?" *Caramba*, this was going to take longer than he thought.

Bernice's eyes shined with overflowing enthusiasm. "No time like the present, darling."

For what seemed like an eternity, they discussed food and menus. Any dish Paolo mentioned sparked a tangent from Bernice—a recent trip or love memory that the food brought to mind. Before he knew it, three hours had gone by and he was frantic to get out of there. He had prepared her favorite *fettuccine carbonara* as quickly as possible, but it was Bernice's chattiness that extended their meeting so long. He tried to end it several times, but she continued to prattle about her love of Italian food and Edwin's appreciation for her ample curves. It struck Paolo as ironic that Edwin, a somber, no-nonsense type, was so enraptured with Bernice, but she kept bringing it up.

Would the chatterbox ever stop? By the time Bernice took her last bite of dessert, a thin golden crepe slathered in *dulce de leche* and dusted with powdered sugar, Paolo was ready to bolt.

Peeking coquettishly from beneath her fake lashes, she hesitated a few moments and then blurted, "I hear you've been meeting with the spa chef lately."

"Yes, Maki and I are preparing for your husband's show on Monday."

"Maki? I thought her name was Michaela." Bernice studied him with open curiosity. "Is your relationship anything more than professional?" she inquired with a wicked twist of her mouth.

"Strictly professional," he replied, irked that she was prying into his personal life.

"I'm glad to hear it, darling. That girl is not for you."

"What do you mean?" Paolo studied Bernice from beneath furrowed brows. He got the distinct feeling she wanted to tell him something she considered important.

She leaned forward with great relish. "The Food Nazi, as I call her," she said maliciously, "once had a long-term relationship with our resident tennis bad boy, Jeff Convers. But she got cold feet at the last minute. Rumor has it that..."

"I don't listen to rumors," Paolo cut her off brusquely.

"Pity Jeff didn't fall for her younger sister, Tiffany. She doesn't share her older sister's ball-breaking ambition, pardon my French." Bernice made a moue of distaste and shrugged.

"Maki's private life is none of my business, and neither is her professional one." Paolo could barely refrain from adding that they were none of Bernice's business either. The woman was a troublemaking pest and she was wasting time.

Bernice's sharply penciled eyebrows snapped together at his quelling tone. "It *is* your business, Paolo. Michaela is competing against you. In order to beat your opponent, you must know her weaknesses. Just remember I'm the one sponsoring you and I plan on you winning!"

"I plan on winning too. I have a magnificent show planned for Monday. I am not worried about Maki and you shouldn't be either, Bernice."

"You have all my support, darling," she said, retreating into her previous high spirits. "I have already put in a good word for you with Edwin." She giggled mischievously. "But I can't go too overboard because he'll get jealous and forbid me from meeting with you. Edwin can be very forceful and possessive when it comes to me. I don't want him to distrust you."

"No, we wouldn't want that," Paolo said decisively, before she went any further. He put her empty glass in the sink and walked around the bar toward the door. "I must go now," he said firmly.

Bernice frowned. "So soon? How about a little Sambuca to top off the night?"

"Not a good idea. Those martinis were strong. I wouldn't want you driving off the ferry," Paolo said, even though the prospect was tempting at the moment.

She slapped his arm. "Those teeny martinis? I don't even feel a buzz."

"I have to leave and get ready for tomorrow's competition." Paolo glanced at his watch. It was close to nine o'clock, damn it.

"Oh, all right." She pouted dejectedly. "But can we meet again tomorrow afternoon to finalize the plans? Say, after you tape the show?"

Paolo opened the door and motioned for her to exit before him. "Uh, let's make it Wednesday. Tomorrow's going to be a little difficult..."

"Wednesday it is then. Confirmed!"

"*Ciao*, Bernice. Until Wednesday."

Sliding her hands up and down his biceps, Bernice squeezed his flesh along the way and then kissed him on both cheeks, one wet kiss landing on the corner of his mouth. "*Ciao, churro.*"

It was all Paolo could do not to roll his eyes. The last thing he wanted was to encourage the producer's wife, especially after her warning about Edwin's possessiveness. As if he even wanted a romp with the sly old vixen, but he couldn't be rude to her either.

Wiggling her hips, Bernice teetered off toward her silver Jag and turned with a jaunty wave before getting inside. She rolled down the window and blew him another kiss before driving off, leaving Paolo with a bad taste in his mouth. He had not liked her tacky attempt at seduction. But mostly, her cattiness toward Maki had really bugged him. He had kept his cool because the stakes were high.

Paolo had dealt with women like Bernice Blumenthal before—bored, matronly socialites who chased after younger men and thought they could lead them around by the *cojones*. He tamped down his annoyance and decided to bide his time until he won *Miami Spice*. He could handle Bernice. He was most concerned about Maki. There would be hell to pay if they didn't get a rehearsal in before the taping tomorrow morning.

Chapter Twelve

Michaela could barely see straight, she was so furious with Paolo for standing her up again last night. When he finally showed up, she had to force herself to keep her voice low not to wake up Mikey and Claudia as she hissed, "You have no concept of time. You're irresponsible and inconsiderate and I never want to see you again after tomorrow. Thanks to you, we'll have to wing it without a proper rehearsal!" After her blistering tirade, she had run out of his apartment, ignoring his lame explanation about a flat tire. Paolo had chased after her in the dark parking lot, but she tore out of there before he could say another word.

She hadn't gotten back to her apartment until past midnight and then had tossed and turned in bed, wishing him all kinds of evil. She still could not believe he'd had the nerve to blame a flat tire on his lateness—especially with the unmistakable smell of a woman's perfume lingering on him. She wished she didn't have to see Paolo's face today, let alone cook with him.

But she couldn't dwell on it now; she had to concentrate on the taping ahead. As she drove down I95 on her way to Key Biscayne, she took deep breaths and tried to assuage her nerves, but they were stretched to the breaking point. Aunt Willow's encouraging phone call this morning had managed to bolster her confidence, in spite of her annoyance at not being prepared.

She arrived at the Rickenbacker Causeway and paid the toll. This was a fortunate route, she realized, as her thoughts drifted to happy childhood memories of weekend beach outings with her Aunt Willow. A free-spirited hippie at heart, Willow had mysteriously changed her name from Nadine after attending Woodstock in 1969. She and the love of her life, Stephen, had been as different as two people could be, but they had been happily married for eighteen years until he died young of a heart attack, leaving her a widow at thirty-eight. She had never remarried nor had any children and dearly loved Michaela and Tiffany as if they were her own daughters.

Michaela remembered the countless times she and Tiffany had made this trek as children. They had crammed inside Aunt Willow's red Volkswagen bug and headed for the palm-fringed beaches of Crandon Park in Key Biscayne where they lolled until sundown, grilling burgers, collecting seashells, playing volleyball and feasting on ripe mangos and watermelon. Aunt Willow had always worn her multi-colored macramé bikini, which she had proudly made herself.

As she drove along the Rickenbacker Causeway, the sun was beginning to rise slowly over the horizon, glistening on the silvery blue water with specks of gold. Along the bridge, weathered fishermen were already casting their reels, joggers were sweating, and a trio of cyclists were attempting the steep ascent. Ahead, the thirty-eight acre Seaquarium was ready for busloads of tourists that would soon be coming to visit Lolita the Killer Whale. Perhaps she could interest some hungry shark in Paolo as a tasty treat...

She arrived at Key Biscayne, turned right on Crandon Boulevard, and followed it down to Mashta Island. A CREW sign pointed left and she followed it to a huge ornate iron gate with a man standing guard outside. The number on the concrete wall matched the one on the email.

"Good morning, I'm Michaela Willoughby," she said.

The guard pushed the remote in his hand and waved her in. Michaela followed the winding path of sea grape bushes that led to the Bahamian style mansion. Chalk-white with blue-shuttered windows and flowering bougainvilleas in fuchsias and pinks, the house had a lush, vacation feel. She wondered who were the lucky ones who lived there.

Michaela's iPhone rang just as she parked her car on the crushed oyster shell driveway, alongside two trucks. She answered it right away when she saw it was Lisa. "Hi, Lisa."

"Hey, just wanted to wish you luck," Lisa said. "Break a leg or an egg or whatever they say in TV land."

"Yeah, I need all the help I can get," Michaela muttered.

"Why? What happened?"

"Paolo blew it last night. He arrived too late for a run-through and by the time he got there, I was so mad at him, we had a fight."

"Oh, no," Lisa groaned.

"I am beyond furious with him. We're taping today and we haven't even had *one* rehearsal together!"

"That's unforgivable, but don't fret, you'll do great anyway. Much better than Paolo. Remember, he's not nearly as organized as you are," Lisa said loyally.

"Thanks, I hope you're right. Last night I babysat his nephew so his sister could get some rest while Paolo was at a so-called business meeting." She paused and drew in a sharp breath. "He had the nerve to show up reeking of a flowery, sweet perfume."

"Ew, I hate Bernice's perfume, don't you?" Lisa said, surprising her.

"How do you know it was Bernice's perfume?" Michaela's stomach took a nosedive as her suspicions climbed.

"Yesterday, I drove by the Bella Luna parking lot and saw Bernice with Paolo while he was opening the restaurant door."

"What?" So that's where he'd been—schmoozing it up with the producer's wife! Just when Michaela had begun to let down her guard and trust Paolo, he pulled a fast one. "Are you sure it was Bernice?"

"Yes. She was draped all over him with her hands over his eyes, giggling and whispering in his ear."

Michaela's ire went from simmer to full boil. It was a miracle steam didn't shoot out of her ears. She forced herself to take deep, calming breaths before she choked out, "Thanks for the heads up, Lisa. I'm here now. Gotta go."

"Knock 'em dead, honey. You deserve to win. I know you'll beat Paolo."

"*Beat* doesn't even describe what I'd like to do to him right now," Michaela said grimly before hanging up. She got out of her car and slammed the door. How would she deal with Paolo—roast, broil or barbeque? At the moment, a slow roast sounded the most torturous and it was exactly what he deserved! Squeezing her eyes shut for a brief moment, she told herself not to let her red-hot temper get the best of her—not today. There was too much at stake and she, not Paolo, would be the one to suffer if she didn't rein in her temper.

She pasted a courteous smile on her face as she greeted the uniformed valet who opened the door before she knocked. As soon as Michaela entered the mansion, the full waterfront view overlooking an infinity pool made her gasp. She felt as if she had stepped onto the pages of *Architectural Digest*. Every detail was luxurious and expensive looking. It even smelled rich, she thought, momentarily amused before she turned her thoughts to today's taping.

How would her family behave? Tiffany had tried to talk Dad out of bringing his new trophy girlfriend, but he hadn't agreed not to. If he did show up with her, her mother would be livid. Aunt Magda would be there too. She had been raving about gorgeous Paolo to the whole family. According to Tiff, Aunt Magda had decided Paolo was the perfect match for her niece, contest or no. Aunt Willow had also promised to be there. Thank God, Willow would provide emotional support; she always did. And that left Tiffany, who would be cheering her on, but Tiff tended to run late...

This was the most important event in her career. She had to focus and stay on top of her game. Today was the clincher, it was now or never to shine. She was not going to let Paolo's dalliances with the producer's wife rob her of this dream come true.

Breathe deeply. Stop stressing over what you can't control, she told herself. *Think of the opportunities. You can finish repaying Mom and Dad. The cookbook will be a hit and you'll get brand endorsements and appearances at the Wine and Food festivals in South Beach and NYC.* Michaela ended her personal pep talk with a fervent prayer filled with all kinds of well-intentioned promises if she nailed the audition.

She paused for a moment to visualize herself as the winner as she patted her pants' side pocket where she hid a secret. Today was war and Paolo would be in for a surprise if he thought he could distract her from winning with any of his "gimmicks". The gloves were off. She'd distract the hell out of him with her own gimmick!

Paolo arrived a few minutes late for the pre-taping session, but it wasn't his fault. The spare tire he'd replaced his flat tire with last night had taken a nail on his way to Key Biscayne. Luckily, he passed a tire store en route to the Rickenbacker Causeway, and within thirty minutes, he'd bought a new one, had it aligned, and was on his way. He felt ready to take on the world, despite very little sleep last night thanks to Mikey, who kept waking up every two hours.

He had Señora Fuentes, the elderly Cuban widow two doors down from his apartment, to thank for his peace of mind this morning. She had stepped out to pick up her newspaper just as Paolo was leaving. When she heard Mikey crying and learned that Claudia was alone after giving birth, the kind woman insisted on staying with her until Paolo returned. With that huge concern taken care of, Paolo felt relaxed and ready to wow the audience today. After their argument last night, Maki would probably still be in a snit, but he would deal with her later. Today, he was on a mission and nobody, not even delectable Maki, would stand in his way. With growing excitement, he made a mental list of all the benefits he would gain from winning today's taping.

I'll be able to pay for Claudia and Mikey's bills, send money to Mamá, launch my new grill pan idea and become a celebrity chef. This taping will be such a success, even Maki will benefit. She will have to concede defeat, but she'll get good exposure from it.

From the look on Michaela's face when he strolled into the pool patio, he wouldn't be surprised if she had been the one to leave a spike beneath his tire last night. But there was no way that he'd let the little *rabiosa* ruin his chances today! Underneath her icy façade, she was probably simmering with resentment. Somehow, he had to get her to relax enough for their segment to be fun and entertaining for the audience gathered there. With a friendly wave, Paolo breezed by the group of fifty or so audience members who were listening carefully to the young production assistant's instructions on applause and enthusiasm.

Paolo approved of the cooking set-up that consisted of a long, tile-covered island, complete with a wood-burning oven on one end, gas burners on the other end and ample prep space in between, including a deep, stainless steel sink. Behind the island was a spacious, oblong pool with a cascading waterfall and Jacuzzi and behind that, a panoramic expanse of the inviting ocean, topped by a blue, cloudless sky.

He smiled at the audience, took his place behind the counter and greeted the tech crew. Beside him, Michaela looked rigidly composed in an aqua top and tan slacks. She gave him a curt nod that spoke volumes. He raised an eyebrow at her hands, noticing how tightly they clutched the counter in front of her. Maybe she wasn't as composed as he thought. Small wonder they weren't curled into fists ready to take aim at him.

Ignoring Michaela's biting stare, he gave her a wink. "Ready, *nena*?"

"Don't you *nena* me," she hissed beneath a frozen-in-place smile. "Look at the first row, lover boy, your girlfriend's there."

Paolo's eyebrows shot up when he noticed Bernice sitting in the front row making eyes at him. She gave him a fluttery little wave with her long fingernails and blew a kiss. Bernice's toothy, flirtatious grin was turning his stomach sour. That and the fact that Mr. Blumenthal was watching him like a shrewd hawk made him wish he could pop an antacid.

Paolo and Michaela acted in forced camaraderie for Mr. Blumenthal and the audience's sake as they went through the motions of a run-through. Once their positions were marked, the director, a goateed, stocky man in faded jeans and a Rolling Stones T-shirt, gave them specific notes. As soon as everything was clarified, the cameras began to roll.

Ten minutes into their presentation, it was clear Michaela was incensed with him. Despite Paolo's attempts to lighten the mood with a few jokes, she was not buying any of it. The more he clowned around and had the audience laughing, the more daggers she sent his way when the camera was on him and not her. He completed a dance move to show how easy it was to prepare the gnocchi and ended it with a flourish, which drew another enthusiastic round of applause.

"And that, my friends, is how easy it is to make a delicious gnocchi that will melt on your tongue." Paolo savored the pillowy dough in his mouth with a look of bliss and smacked his fingertips lustily.

While the camera filmed the audience's animated reaction, Paolo caught Michaela surreptitiously reaching into her pants pocket to extract a white paper. When the cameraman turned the lens on her, she smiled and seamlessly explained how to make low-fat Mediterranean vinaigrette with fresh herbs and tiny capers while she lowered her hands beneath the counter top. Puzzled, Paolo watched her pull the backing off thick, double-sided tape on the piece of paper she had taken out of her pocket. *Was she going to consult a recipe?* he wondered, surprised that an accomplished chef would have to revert to that.

Then suddenly, surprisingly, Michaela slapped her right buttock and proclaimed, "This vinaigrette will never fatten your booty and neither will the dreamy dessert I'll be serving up later. So, girls, you can wear your favorite pair of skinny jeans and still eat happily."

The audience clapped, but only Paolo could see the paper Maki had attached to the seat of her pants. BITE ME taunted him in bold, black letters and he would have happily obliged if he thought she really wanted him to. *Caramba,* was that her idea of an insult, he wondered, grinning wickedly at the pleasure he would have doing just that. He leaned into her space, drawing her immediate attention.

The cameraman moved in for a close-up of the two.

Paolo's gaze lowered to Michaela's cute backside and back to the camera. With a suggestive wink, he bared predator teeth in a broad smile and goaded, "Just *one bite*, Maki? There you go again, skimp, skimp, skimping in the name of dieting!"

From behind the counter, he squeezed her right bottom cheek as he tore off the paper and crammed it into his shirt pocket with a wolfish smirk. Michaela gasped and stomped her foot. *Ouch!* Her sharp heel landed on Paolo's instep, almost causing him to lose his balance. He quickly recovered and was amazed when she went right into her segment as if nothing had happened.

"Lemon is an ingredient I include when making my feather-light gnocchi," she said. "Just one squeeze will bring radiance to the simple little dumpling." Paolo leaned in closer just as she squeezed the lemon and a drop landed in his eye.

"Argh!" Paolo roared, covering his stinging eye with the guilty hand that had just squeezed Michaela's sweet cheek. "Damn."

"Oh... I'm sorry," Michaela said.

The cameraman turned his lens on Michaela, whose left eye was twitching out of control.

"Cut," Jim, the director said. "Let's go to commercial."

Paolo splashed cool water in his eye to wash out the lemon juice. "That was a low blow, Maki," he muttered under his breath. "Try that again and I'll drown your 'feather light' gnocchi in a pound of butter."

"It was an accident and you know it. It wouldn't have happened if you hadn't been hovering over me," she retorted, her face turning pinker by the minute. "And don't think you can get away with groping me, you...you..."

"Then don't paste tasty notes on your behind. Next time I'll follow the instructions."

Red-faced, she snapped, "Paw me again and I'll fry you in a vat of lard!"

Jim advanced upon them with a disapproving frown. "Let's keep things civil, Miss Willoughby. This is a cooking show, not a showdown."

"Precisely what I was thinking." Paolo gave a disapproving shake of his head.

It was all Michaela could do not to fling herself at Paolo and pummel his chest.

Chapter Thirteen

Michaela refused to heed the knock on her door when she looked through the peephole and saw Paolo standing there with a self-satisfied smile on his face. The *nerve* of him to show up! Hadn't he bedeviled her enough during the taping? Was he planning to rub it in that he'd been the victor today?

"Maki, open up. I know you're in there," Paolo called out.

"Go away!" she yelled, turning from the door and walking away.

"I have something important to tell you. I hear your footsteps."

Michaela ran back to the door. "I said *go away!*"

She didn't want to see Paolo, or anyone else, for that matter. All she wanted to do was burrow in her kitchen and eat a pound of chocolate, especially since she was still tormented by visions of her family's dismayed faces in the audience. She closed her eyes against the memory of her father's stern and disillusioned look. He had made an impatient hand motion she was all too familiar with that said, "Focus. You're making a fool of yourself, Michaela!"

Mom's reaction hadn't been any better than Dad's. She had caught her mother rolling her eyes and shaking her head in disapproval when it became increasingly obvious that Paolo was outperforming her. Mom's presence in the audience had dredged up unpleasant memories of when she had attended Michaela's high school government debates and sat in the first row of the audience, rigid with steely determination for her daughter to win.

"I'm not leaving until you open the door and hear me out." Paolo lifted a magnum of champagne and held it in front of the peephole. "We have reason to celebrate."

Michaela wrenched the door open and stared at him in

disbelief. "Are you some kind of a sadist? We have nothing to celebrate, now please leave." She struggled to get the words out through clenched teeth. When he didn't budge, she demanded, "Is this your idea of celebration? Showing up here to gloat?"

"That's not why I'm here." Nonplussed, his black eyes regarded her beneath furrowed brows. "I never realized what a little *rabiosa* you are."

"Don't call me names. What is a *rabiosa* anyway?" she asked, giving in to perverse curiosity, even though by the way he said it, it was certain not to be a compliment.

He shook his head. "A *rabiosa* is a bad-tempered firecracker like you. Now be quiet and let me tell you why I said we should celebrate."

"Forget it. You should be here to apologize, not celebrate!"

Paolo threw his hands up in the air and gave her an incredulous look. "Me, apologize? For what? *You* are the one who didn't play fair today."

"Why should I play fair when you are a womanizing trickster?" The thought of him and Bernice together made her want to clobber him.

"Now who's calling whom names? You owe me an apology, Maki," he stated evenly, his eyes sharp lasers of accusation.

"Forget it! I know you're half-Italian, but that doesn't give you the right to grope a girl's behind. You did that to trip up my performance."

"You stomped on my foot and then almost blinded me with lemon juice," Paolo countered, chucking her under the chin with a flick of his forefinger.

"I already told you the lemon was an accident! It was your fault for crowding over me. Don't you have any sense of personal space? Now, thanks to you, the producers think I'm unprofessional and bad-tempered."

"I doubt that." Paolo gave a dismissive shrug and strolled past her with loping strides, entering her kitchen as if he owned it. While she gaped at him open-mouthed, he deftly opened the champagne, poured it into two flutes, and handed one to her.

He lifted his flute in a toast to her. "Lucky for you, I'm in a generous mood. I forgive your quick temper, Maki. I know you don't like to be outshined," he taunted devilishly.

Michaela's hand tightened around the glass stem. How could he tease her over something that meant so much to her? Paolo had not only outdone her with his over-the-top performance, but now he was acting like she should be celebrating his success!

He would probably laugh if he knew the number of chastising phone calls she'd received from Mom, Dad and Aunt Magda. This was turning into the worst day of her life. Where was parental loyalty and support when she needed it most? Ironically, Aunt Magda's sole worry was that Michaela had lost the opportunity to rope in such a handsome and perfectly "charming" catch.

After the show, dear Aunt Willow had pressed her treasured Tibetan Mani Stone into Michaela's palm as she consolingly patted her back and urged her to rub the stone for good karma.

Tiffany had tried to offer comfort with a few compliments on her appearance—even though Michaela hadn't worn the sexy red dress Tiffany had bought her. She knew her sister meant well, but Michaela hadn't wanted compliments on her appearance; she had wanted to outperform Paolo and she had failed—miserably.

"I'm in no mood for your champagne." She looked Paolo in the eye and she emptied her champagne flute into the sink. With wicked satisfaction, she watched his smile turn into a scowl.

Paolo's eyes darkened with displeasure. "You just threw away an excellent Perrier-Jouet."

Michaela lifted her chin with as much dignity as she could muster. She knew it was rude of her to toss his champagne in the sink like dirty water, but she didn't feel like apologizing.

Paolo slanted a hard look at her. "What is wrong with you?"

"Hmm, let's see. For starters, you never met with me to rehearse, knowing how important it was to me. You probably never intended to rehearse in the first place. You were just humoring me, right?"

"Wrong," Paolo replied, his mouth flattened into a grim line. "I had every intention of rehearsing with you, *querida*. Can I help it that Claudia decided to have her baby at the most inopportune time?"

"Maybe you couldn't help that, but you could have kept your pants zipped when it came to Bernice Blumenthal last night!" Michaela's blood boiled at the image of Paolo seducing the older, fleshy flirt for his personal gain.

Paolo's mouth spewed the champagne as he doubled over in mirth. "Bernice Blumenthal? You think I was sleeping with Bernice?" he roared in disbelief, his broad shoulders shaking as he erupted into guffaws.

"Damn you, it's not funny!" Michaela turned on her heel, stomped to the front door and flung it open. "Get out!" Her index finger trembled as she pointed to the hallway outside her door.

Paolo forcefully set his glass down on the countertop and joined her in the foyer. He reached for her arm, but Michaela angrily shrugged out of his grasp.

"Calm down, Maki," Paolo said. "I never slept with Bernice. Whatever gave you that idea?"

"Don't act innocent. I know the reason you were so late last night is because you were with her!"

"We were having a business meeting," he stated in an even tone.

"You expect me to believe that?"

"Damn right I do. It was only a business meeting, nothing else," Paolo said implacably, his eyes hardening to onyx.

"Oh, *really*? More like monkey business. I heard she was all over you in the parking lot of your restaurant," Michaela huffed, seething with distrust. "And then you arrived all disheveled and late and stinking of her perfume!"

"I'm not sure what your sources saw or who they are, but I met with Bernice to plan her dinner party for the tenor, Palmentieri."

"And it took you until midnight?" she asked in a cynical tone.

Paolo's jaw tightened. "I cooked dinner for Bernice and then we planned the menu. If you had listened to me last night, Sherlock, instead of tearing off in the middle of my explanation, you would have known that I was late because I had to change a flat tire. End of subject," he stated tightly.

"I still don't see why—" Michaela began to protest.

Paolo ignored her and shut the door. "I have something important to tell you and you are going to listen to me." She wasn't amused when he firmly grabbed her arm above the elbow and propelled her into the kitchen. She stood rigidly beside him, ready to pounce if he dared make light of things as he lifted the champagne bottle and refilled his glass.

"I don't want to hear anything you have to say."

"You *will* listen and you won't interrupt," he said firmly. He skewered her with a stern look. "Not a word until I've finished, Maki, or I won't give you the good news."

"Good news? Ha!" Michaela planted her fists on her hips and rounded on him with narrowed eyes. "I'll give you two minutes and then I want you to leave."

Paolo looked like he wanted to wring her neck. "The good news for you is that we are both still in the running for *Miami Spice*. The producers haven't made a final decision."

"What?" Michaela's chest expanded with hope and her heart began to hammer against it with excitement. "Did you just way we're *both* still in the running?"

"You heard right. Mr. Blumenthal invited both of us back to do another taping. The next one will be in a studio."

Michaela froze; she could barely believe her ears. A surge of joy made her want to jump up and down and repeatedly squeal "yes!" with accompanying fist pumps. "For real? Are you telling me the truth? This better not be some kind of practical joke," she warned.

Paolo looked heavenward and shook his head. "*Dios mío,* you try the patience of a saint."

"Your last name might be Santos, but you are no saint."

"Damn straight I'm not." Paolo grinned. "Ellie called this afternoon and said that Mr. Blumenthal has decided to have the two of us back for another taping."

Michaela felt the wind under her sails fizzle as she regarded Paolo dubiously. "Why didn't Ellie call me?"

"Because I told her I'd take care of letting you know."

"Oh." For once, she was speechless and then giddy relief mushroomed inside her until she thought she would burst.

Paolo held out his hand. "Truce?"

In a daze of euphoria, Michaela shook his hand. "Truce." A sexy current sizzled between them making her quickly release his hand, but Paolo's exotic eyes held her captive. "When is the taping?" she asked through suddenly parched lips.

"At the end of next month. But this time we get a solo show each."

"Yay!" she cried. "I can't wait to call Ellie for more details."

Michaela grabbed the champagne bottle from his hand, put her mouth on the bottleneck and drank deeply. Champagne had never tasted so good! She closed her eyes, choking as the sparkling froth cascaded down her throat, spilling over the sides of her mouth and onto her cheeks, and drenching the front of her blouse. When she opened her eyes, she caught Paolo watching her, his handsome face lit up with amusement. But she didn't care. She was bubbling over with joy, flying high with the thrill of getting a new chance at winning!

Chuckling indulgently, Paolo grabbed a paper towel and mopped her wet cheeks before taking the bottle from her. He took a long swig and handed it back to Michaela, waiting while she slurped more of the delicious bubbly. For the next few minutes, they took turns polishing off the champagne.

Michaela's head whirled as she sprinted around her apartment on bouncy legs, humming the triumphant tune from *Rocky. Ta ta ta, ta ta ta...*until she collapsed on the sofa in a fit of giggles. Paolo joined her on the sofa and stretched his long legs in front of him.

"Tell me, Maki. Why did you become a chef?" He eyed her giddy enthusiasm with a bemused expression.

"I've always loved food. When I was growing up, we never ate home-cooked meals. I didn't learn to cook until we had a Costa Rican nanny. Her food was so delicious, with flavors I'd never tasted, that I wanted to learn more. That was the catalyst." She cocked her head and looked at him. "What about you?"

"I love food too. Cooking is as natural as breathing to me. I grew up surrounded by women who are great cooks— Mamá, my sisters and my Italian Nonna." Paolo's eyes were warm and inviting as he regarded her. "Why is winning this competition so important to you?"

"It means the world to me. If I win...no let me rephrase that, *when* I win, I will be able to repay my parents for all the investment they made in the law degree that I never finished. Maybe I'll finally gain their respect." Normally, she didn't tell others about her difficult relationship with her parents, but Paolo's solid presence made her feel comfortable opening up.

He appeared mystified, but before he said anything, she continued, "Winning means my cookbook will make tons of sales." Michaela's stomach fluttered with excitement at the myriad possibilities. "Not only that...maybe I'll be invited on the *Today Show* and I can showcase my light and healthy cuisine. I can also introduce my..."

"Wait a minute. You dropped out of law school to become a chef?" he interrupted.

"Yes."

"No wonder your parents didn't look happy today." Paolo gave a wry shake of his head.

"They are ashamed of me," Michaela admitted, feeling a bit ashamed herself that she couldn't live up to their high expectations of her.

"Impossible! You are very accomplished." Paolo's compliment pleased her immeasurably.

"No, really, they are embarrassed by my career. To them, I went from being white collar to blue collar, and I wasted their money in the process." She felt embarrassed revealing how snobbish her parents were.

"Do they feel the same way about your sister?"

"Pfft. Tiffany? No. They gave up on her a long time ago. After she threw a few tantrums making it loud and clear that she preferred Barbies over the Mozart tapes and Smithsonian puzzles they gave her, they had to accept that she would never be an intellectual. Tiffany has other talents. She's not only an amazing makeup artist, she sings and plays the guitar like a dream. Since she is the younger child and stunningly beautiful, they let her get away with most things."

"You're beautiful too."

"Thank you." Surprised and touched by his compliment, Michaela realized with a pang that she loved hearing Paolo say that. "But beauty isn't what my parents respect. They believe that you're either born with it or you're not. They admire hard work and the results of that labor, not something as nebulous as beauty."

"Is that why you work so hard to be perfect in everything?" he asked, regarding her with fond bemusement. "Maki, nobody is perfect. I think you're pretty terrific just as you are. Your parents sound like tough ones to please."

Paolo's supportive words made Michaela want to grab him and kiss him. His dark gaze remained on hers, soulful and genuine, as he aimed to make her feel better.

"It's true. My parents are tough to please, but that's inevitable when you're as driven as they are. Do you know how it feels to be reminded all the time that you're a major disappointment to your parents?" she asked bleakly. "Probably not. You come from a big Latin family who celebrates everything you do."

Looking uneasy, Paolo cleared his throat. "Well, I wouldn't say *everything...*"

"I'm sure you are their hero. The apple of your parents' eyes."

"My father died when I was a teenager," Paolo said quietly.

"Oh, I'm sorry." Michaela saw the sadness in his eyes and felt a stab of guilt. He had graciously come over to celebrate the news and so far, she'd been a real downer. "Tell me...why is winning this competition so important to you?"

"I owe it to my father's memory," he said, his expression stricken.

"What do you mean?" She wondered at the regret on Paolo's face and wanted to know what troubled him. She'd like to return the favor and somehow ease his personal pain as he'd eased hers just now.

"The day Papá died, instead of helping with the family business like I was supposed to after school, I was out fooling around."

"I'm sure there was nothing you could have done to prevent his death," Michaela said kindly, feeling bad that her question had dredged up painful memories. "What did he die of?"

Paolo's face looked drawn and pale beneath his tan. "He

died of a massive, bleeding ulcer. I had taken the family car out for a spin with my friends. By the time they got him to the hospital, it was too late. He had lost too much blood."

Filled with compassion, Michaela touched his hand. "I'm sorry."

"When my sister, Sonia, finally found me, Papá was already dead," he said, his voice low and tortured. "I didn't know he hadn't been feeling well. He was the rock of the family, a pillar of hard work. I wish he had known that I would be responsible enough to take care of the family after he died."

Michaela listened intently, sensing his need to talk. She wished she could find the right words to lighten his burden.

Paolo's eyes clouded over, troubled by the memories. "As the only and eldest son, I was his favorite. Papá used to tell me, 'You are the joy of my life.'"

"I'm sure you were," she soothed.

His face taut with guilt, he shook his head. "No, I was irresponsible and selfish, goofing off with my friends when I should have been working at the restaurant. Poor Papá, he was stressed out and overworked—that's why he died too young," he said, his voice gruff.

"How old were you when he passed?"

"Eighteen. Almost overnight, I grew up and took over running my family's restaurant and bakery in Buenos Aires."

"Oh, I had no idea," Michaela said, seeing Paolo with different eyes. Gone was the carefree braggart. He was a strong, responsible man intent on providing for his family and honoring his father's memory. She wished he wasn't her opponent for something that meant so much to her. It was times like these, when they weren't arguing, that she found Paolo appealing— and utterly irresistible. She was touched he had opened up to her and wished she could alleviate his anguish.

"I'm sure your dad is watching you from heaven and very proud of all you've done for your family." She cupped the side of his face with a gentle touch.

"Thanks." Paolo took Michaela's hand, turned it palm upward and placed a soft kiss in the center.

The warmth of his lips on her sensitive spot disarmed her. Spellbound, Michaela met his sizzling gaze with wide-eyed anticipation as her pulse galloped like a runaway filly. He placed another kiss on the inside of her wrist and flicked the skin with his tongue. Michaela leaned forward and kissed him, a whisper-light touch that landed briefly on his mouth. Paolo's mouth dragged over hers lustfully while he eased her onto his hard lap. She could barely catch her breath as she tilted her head back and welcomed his ardent kisses on the cool column of her neck.

She shifted at the tender assault and heard something crackle. She noticed the paper stuffed inside his shirt pocket and pulled back to peer at him. "What's that?"

Paolo gave her a cryptic smile. "There was a second reason for my visit today."

"What?" she asked breathlessly.

He drew a piece of paper from his shirt pocket. "I've come to collect on your offer, *querida*."

"What offer?" she croaked, recognizing the paper at once.

"This." With unconcealed delight, he handed her the paper that she had written BITE ME on earlier.

Michaela sucked in her breath sharply. The paper slipped out of her hand just as Paolo's tongue lightly touched the soft outer shell of her ear.

"I am going to devour you, *querida*," he whispered roughly, nipping her earlobe. "One bite at a time."

Michaela's body prickled all over with gooseflesh and her feminine core pulsed with dizzying pleasure as Paolo's hoarse voice lured her with throaty Spanish endearments. She gazed into his gorgeous eyes, helplessly drawn into their black depths. A low, ragged moan escaped her when Paolo's mouth covered hers and he began to feast on her, tasting her lips, sliding an insistent tongue between them to explore her mouth. Giving a shuddering sigh of surrender, she allowed him to deepen his kisses and molded her body against him, searching, reaching, yearning for more.

She kissed the bristly side of his lean jaw and the seductive grooves beside his mouth, fumbling with his shirt buttons until his shirt gaped at the waist, revealing his muscular chest. She couldn't resist pressing an open-mouthed kiss between his hard pecs. Paolo tasted so delicious she wanted to lap him up greedily, just as she had done with the champagne. She was drunk with passion and yearning for more—there was no turning back now. Michaela's mouth roamed over his caramel-colored chest, learning the hard planes with her lips and tongue until Paolo cradled her face and stilled her.

"No more, *nena*, not yet," he rasped, breathing heavily as he lifted her in his arms and held her against his chest. The room began to spin as he carried her into her bedroom, kissing her with maddening thoroughness.

"Ooh, Paolo, I had too much champagne. I feel a little lightheaded. Better put me down." She broke away from his kiss and burrowed her face in his smooth, strong neck, inhaling deeply of his appealing scent as she nuzzled the warm hollow at his throat.

"Hold on, baby, it's going to be a long night," he promised huskily when they reached the bed.

Paolo's mouth descended on hers, primal and hungry and demanding in its possession. Every inch of her body throbbed, ached for full domination. The feminist in her cringed, but she couldn't help it, Paolo was so large, so sexy, she wanted to be devoured by him, as he'd wickedly promised her.

Within seconds, they were tearing off each other's clothes and before Michaela knew it, she lay before him, unabashedly naked and moaning with pleasure as Paolo lustily feasted on her fevered flesh. Every inch of her was explored and revered as Paolo delighted in the softness of her breasts, the slight curve of her belly and indentation of her navel, the suppleness of her thighs, lavishing her with compliments and endearments in Spanish.

Michaela was beyond rational thought; her whole being ached for deep, sexual intimacy with Paolo. She pulled his lean hips toward her with urgent hands and wrapped her legs around him. His erection pressed against the cradle of her pelvis.

"Now, Paolo, now." Her body arched upward, eager for his penetration.

"Not yet, *linda*." Paolo's voice came out in a guttural rasp, his face dusky with passion and neck muscles strained as he turned her over, lifting her hair from her nape.

Michaela bit into the pillow and moaned when his damp lips touched her sensitive nape and bit her ever so lightly. Exquisitely torturous moments passed as his greedy mouth traveled along her spine, nipping and kissing the summit of her buttocks, the back of her thighs, down her calves to her tingling toes, before he turned her over again.

Unhinged and beside herself with desire, she reached down to caress him, but his steely hand formed a manacle around both of her wrists, holding them captive above her head as his passionate kisses turned to gentle love-bites, alternately kissing her, driving her wanton and wild as he pleasured her. Michaela's head thrashed from side to side. She squirmed and whimpered, out of her mind, desperate for release. Just when she was about to climax, he let go of her wrists and slowed down to tenderly stroke her breasts, his callused fingertips rubbing the tips.

"Don't slow down...don't stop! Please!" she urged shamelessly.

"*Qué bella*," Paolo said, his voice thick as molasses. "So beautiful."

His molten gaze held her transfixed. At that moment, Michaela was his—*completely*. Holding her hostage at the sweet threshold of release, Paolo worked his magic. He brought her to the edge, prolonging the exquisite pleasure-pain again and again until every pore screamed to let loose and threatened to implode.

And just when she thought she would die, she climaxed with lusty, shuddering cries—*twice*.

Chapter Fourteen

Waking up with a raging hangover was the least of Michaela's problems as she tried to piece together last night's events. She blushed when she reread Paolo's note left on the pillow beside her scrawled in his large, expressive handwriting. As if *everything* about the man wasn't large and expressive, she thought, her heart racing at the scribbled evidence of last night's salacious lovemaking.

Sorry I had to run off, but Claudia needed my help with Mikey. I'll be back for seconds. You are delectable, querida.

Michaela closed her eyes and tried to remember all that they had done. Erotic, carnal images came rushing back of Paolo making love to her, wringing out one shattering response after another until she lay limp with pleasure and shamelessly spent. All she could remember was that she had never felt so close to a man in her entire life—or so uninhibited. She put her hands to her hot, flushed face, trying to visualize the moment when they'd had intercourse, but she couldn't seem to. Had they fully made love, she wondered?

She searched the room for a condom wrapper. Finding none, she ran into the bathroom and checked the little garbage pail—empty. She was not on the pill, so he'd better have used some precaution. Panicking, she suddenly felt more like an irresponsible teenager than a femme fatale.

Michaela fell back on the bed, clutching her throbbing head with both hands. She prayed to God that Paolo had used protection, but she wouldn't know for sure until she asked him. The prospect of having to ask him worsened her king-size headache, that and the fact that her sheets still held the sexy man's scent. She tried to banish self-defeating recriminations as she massaged her temples. Clearly, he hadn't forced himself on her; she had been more than eager to participate. She had even begged for more, she recalled with mounting embarrassment. They had been quite intimate, but she still had no recollection of actual intercourse. Had she been that far gone from the champagne not to remember the final act with such an amazing lover?

She inhaled deeply of Paolo's manly scent lingering on her pillow. Closing her eyes, she relived the opulence of being held in his strong arms. She rolled onto her belly and covered her head with the pillow as erotic images invaded her mind and taunted her senses. Her position dredged up vivid recollections of Paolo kissing her as she lay before him, a bare banquet of curves and valleys. In the privacy of her bedroom, she flushed from head to toe, remembering the sexy things he had said and done, caressing and kissing her into a pleading wild woman, but for the life of her, she still couldn't remember if they had gone all the way.

Why oh why did she and Paolo have to be rivals for something so important to both of them? He drew her like no other man had. Generous, passionate, tender, masterful...all the things that were making her long for him again. But the timing was wrong—very wrong! She had allowed herself to cave just as the dizzying effects of way too much champagne had taken over. Yet in all fairness, it wasn't just the champagne that had unleashed her inhibitions; it was Paolo who had drugged her with his potent allure and he'd been insatiable when it came to her body!

Paolo's passionate lovemaking last night had fed her spirit with hope. Jeff had never shown such passion. He was the only guy she'd ever slept with and their lovemaking had been tepid at best. Deep down, she had always worried that she wasn't very good in bed and that she had a low libido. She had blamed herself for not being sexy enough to captivate and hold on to the tennis world's superstar. That was before she had learned he was a sexual addict. But after receiving Paolo's ardent lovemaking and responding to him so keenly, she was surprised and flattered that she *was* sexy...at least to Paolo.

Nevertheless, she had to be prudent and never drink too much alcohol again when she was with him. Was she such a lightweight that getting drunk meant letting go wantonly? This had never happened to her with anyone but Paolo. He must have noticed she was far gone on the champagne. As hot and irresistible as he was, she had to remember to steer clear of him physically from now on, because the moment he started kissing her, all ration left her brain and her body took over. Yet she couldn't really blame him. Michaela remembered she had been dancing and singing and slugging down the champagne as if it were iced tea on a hot summer day. But what else could she have done? She had been celebrating fresh hope for what she'd thought was a lost cause.

Michaela pushed herself to sit upright. *Miami Spice* loomed before her like a blinding pot of gold. She swung her legs over the edge and contemplated her next move and tried to summon the discipline that had gotten her so close to her goal. Yesterday, she had been given another chance at winning and she would not allow herself to spare another second obsessing over what had happened with Paolo. From now on, she would concentrate solely on winning and somehow put her feelings for him out of sight, out of mind. Except she couldn't really do that until she clarified one pressing, screaming question: Had they had unprotected sex?

Cringing at the thought, she trudged to the kitchen, straight to the espresso machine. Only a double shot would clear her fuzzy head and give her the nerve to question Paolo. Once she got her answers, she would avoid him no matter how much he drew her. She could not afford to be distracted; especially since she'd been given another chance to do a solo show—all by herself. This time she had to pull out all the stops if she wanted to win. Paolo was a formidable opponent, a charming and charismatic personality quite comfortable before a camera and live audience.

Michaela grabbed her phone and nervously punched in Paolo's cell phone number. She was surprised when Claudia answered with a groggy, "Hello?"

"Hi, it's Michaela. Hope I didn't wake you."

"*Hola*," Claudia said on a loud yawn. "Don't worry, you didn't wake me up. I'm so glad you called. When are you coming to visit us?"

"Um...I'm not sure." Given the turn of events, the last place Michaela wanted to go was Paolo's apartment. "How is Mikey?"

"He's doing well. He is a cutie, but he doesn't sleep very much and he always wants to eat." She yawned again. "We haven't been getting much sleep around here."

"Oh, I'm sure that'll only be temporary," Michaela said soothingly even though she wasn't sure about anything anymore. "How are *you* doing?"

"I'm hanging in there," Claudia replied dispiritedly.

"Just hanging in?"

"Well, I'm feeling a little homesick and Mamá can't seem to get a visa."

"Oh, I'm sorry to hear it. Has Paolo found anyone to help you with Mikey?" Michaela asked, concerned about the desolation in Claudia's voice. She wondered if Paolo had been able to reach Bobby.

"There's a lady down the hall, a widow, who sometimes watches him so I can get ready for the day."

"That's good. I'll try to stop by this week when Paolo isn't in," Michaela said kindly.

"Yes, please do. But I'm sure Paolo would like to be here when you visit."

"Is he there now?"

"No, he already left for work. He forgot his cell phone again."

"Does he have a habit of leaving it behind?"

"Sometimes, but you can't blame him. Mikey and I have turned my poor brother's place into a nursery. You can only imagine how his life has been flipped upside down. Try reaching him at the restaurant."

"Okay, I will." Michaela paused. "Claudia, if I can help you in any way, please let me know. In the meantime, try to get some sleep whenever Mikey naps."

"I'll try. I can't wait for your visit," Claudia said, sounding wistful.

"Me too. See you soon. Take care." Michaela hung up with a heavy heart. She felt bad that she dreaded going to Paolo's apartment. She was dying to see Mikey and give Claudia whatever support she could, but she was in danger of getting too close, too involved. It made her sad to have to distance herself from them.

Paolo hid a smile as Michaela stood before him, hiding behind big sunglasses that covered half of her glowing face. He had wondered what was so pressing when she had called him earlier to say she would be stopping by the restaurant and needed to talk to him ASAP.

Lurking at the back door of Ristorante Bella Luna, Michaela glanced over her shoulder before she asked, "Are we alone?"

"Yes, only Gil is inside. But what kind of a greeting is this? Don't I get a kiss first?" Paolo chided, noting her impatience. He leaned forward to kiss her, but she turned her face and his mouth landed on her soft earlobe instead, giving him a jolt of pleasure. Last night he hadn't been able to get enough of her and damned if he didn't want to have her sweet surrender now, while she was sober. Everywhere he had stroked and kissed her last night, her pale skin had turned pink as if she were blushing from his touch. *Incredible.*

Michaela stood rigidly before him, her pretty face struggling for composure. "I want to know just one thing and then I'm going to leave," she proclaimed, her chin jutting forth as she articulated her words. She was acting so high-strung, it was obvious she needed to get something urgent off her chest—a rather beautiful chest, he reflected, smiling at the memory.

"Come in, *linda.*" Paolo placed his hand on the small of her back and nudged her inside. "We'll talk there."

She took a step sideways, shaking off his hand. "No. I'd rather talk here."

"Okay, fine," he agreed, wondering at her prickly mood. "What's up?"

"I want to know the truth." Michaela's face turned salmon pink before she blurted out, "Did we have sex...I mean intercourse...last night?"

So that was it. She was filled with morning-after regrets after getting naked with him and allowing him to pleasure her, welcoming his lovemaking with wild abandon. This mortified her?

"Don't you remember anything?" he asked in amazement.

"Only parts of it," she admitted, her voice muffled.

"*Querida*, my ears are still ringing from your cries of ecstasy."

"Lower your voice, Paolo," she hissed, looking around as she blushed again. "Please answer my question." She bit her lower lip and waited for his response. "I'm not on the pill!"

Paolo took pity on Maki; her torment was so palpable. She was clearly worried about getting pregnant. Little did she know that a baby was the last thing he wanted at the moment, given his lack of sleep since little Mikey had entered his life—and his apartment.

"We played a little last night. That's all." He smiled and shrugged, not making a big deal out of it so she would relax.

But the opposite happened. Michaela clenched her jaw as she tilted her face upward. She whipped off her sunglasses and sent him a scathing look. "You call that *playing*? You haven't answered my question. Did we have unprotected sex?" she articulated between clenched teeth.

Paolo looked into her sparking eyes. "We did not have intercourse," he stated, smoothing a lock of hair from her cheek.

"Ohhh," she breathed, sputtering on the word. She searched his face earnestly. "Are you telling me the truth, Paolo?"

"Yes, of course! You were too far gone on the champagne for me to go any further."

"I am not touching that stuff for a long time. Especially around you," she vowed. "I mean, thank God, we didn't...you know."

He leaned in close. "Believe me, *querida*, when we do, and we will," he growled low into her ear, "you'll be sober and willing. And you will remember every delicious detail in Technicolor." His fingertip traced her delicate jaw line. "I promise."

Michaela's mouth dropped open and the muscles in her throat worked before she croaked, "That is all I needed to know. Good-bye." She turned to leave, but Paolo grabbed her slim waist and pulled her close. She stiffened in his arms, as if his touch scorched her. "Please don't do that, Paolo."

"Why not?" He kissed her warm neck, inhaling deeply of her rose scent, loving the silken softness of her skin.

Michaela heaved a shaky breath and pushed at his chest. "No more *playing*. We are competitors and can't be anything else. My ultimate goal is to win *Miami Spice*. Now please let go of me."

Exasperated, Paolo's hands dropped to his sides, releasing his hold on her enticing body. Too bad last night's temptress had turned into a laced-up businesswoman. "So, we're back to that, are we?" He ran his fingers roughly through his hair in exasperation.

She lifted her chin. "Yes. And nothing you can say or do will change my mind."

"Too bad we started with dessert and never got to the main course," he said, thinking the "main course" would be the best he'd ever had. "But I'm patient. For now, I'll concentrate on my gimmick and you can work on yours."

"You bet I will." Michaela pushed her sunglasses back on her upturned nose.

Paolo grabbed Michaela by the shoulders and held on to her despite her struggles. He wanted to kiss her senseless, to make love to her until she couldn't walk, to make her realize the futility of denying them pleasure. Instead, he kissed the tip of her snooty nose, turned her around and gave her a playful swat on her bottom. "Better get started then." He chuckled. "And lay off the booze."

"How dare you!" If she could have turned any redder, she would have caught on fire. Michaela whirled around with her slim arm raised to slap him, but he ducked and she swung at the air instead. "Beast!"

He mouthed a kiss. "*Bella*."

"You are impossible." Michaela turned on her heel and stomped away with her fists balled at her sides.

From the doorway, Paolo watched her get inside her car and slam the door. Michaela had a flaming temper to match her hair, but she was delusional if she thought she could turn off their attraction, just by ordering it. He would bide his time until they taped their respective shows. After that, there would be no stopping him; he would come after her like a tornado.

In the meantime, he had to get a hold of Bobby. He had tried reaching him at the email address he had discovered in Claudia's online address book, but it had come back as undeliverable. He must have changed his account. Paolo felt bad for his little sis. She was feeling down and lonely, housebound with Mikey. He was a newborn, too tiny for her to take outside on walks yet. Claudia needed friends and family surrounding her, celebrating the arrival of her new baby. Unfortunately, Mikey was colicky in the evenings and seemed to be feeding on his mom's moods, along with her milk.

If Bobby didn't come home soon and accept his responsibilities, she might sink into a depression. Paolo had tried to research post-partum depression online last night when he had arrived home after Claudia's frantic text. But he'd fallen asleep at the laptop, only to be awakened by Mikey's wailing cries for his next feeding. The kid was turning out to be a little glutton, he thought wryly, shaking his head at the irony.

"Paolo, your sister's on the line," Gil called out, ending Paolo's musings. Gil covered the phone's mouthpiece and held it out to him. "She sounds upset," he confided when Paolo reached his side.

Paolo nodded and took the phone from him with a feeling of impending doom. "Claudia, is everything all right?"

"No. Bobby's parents, Mr. and Mrs. Woodbridge, were just here. They want to take Mikey away from me!" she cried. "I don't know how they found out where I live."

Claudia's words made Paolo see red. After they reacted with displeasure after hearing about Claudia and Mikey, Paolo had written them off as pompous and rude. So now they were coming around to take Mikey away and not provide support or love for Claudia too? What a worthless pair!

"Over my dead body," Paolo vowed. "Don't worry, Claudia. I won't let it happen."

Paolo consoled her as best he could, and then hung up aggravated by the Woodbridges and agitated over his present limited resources. Adding to the huge medical bills, it looked like he'd have to get a lawyer to protect Claudia and Mikey from the Woodbridges.

The *Miami Spice* competition suddenly took on greater meaning, with even higher stakes. It was no longer a case of Paolo triumphing and gaining accolades and making pots of money. It was for his little sister and his nephew. Papá would have been proud to know that Paolo was caring for and championing Claudia and her baby.

With hard-nosed determination, Paolo set his thoughts to the gimmick he'd been working on. He *had* to win—Claudia and Mikey were depending on him to protect them.

Later that week, Michaela left work an hour earlier than usual. She drove by Ristorante Bella Luna and noticed Paolo's red convertible parked outside. Perfect! Now that Paolo wasn't home, she could visit Claudia.

Claudia answered the door on the first knock and threw her arms around Michaela in a tight hug, as if she were her long lost relative. "Maki, I'm so glad you're here! Come in, come in."

Hearing Claudia call her Maki made Michaela think of Paolo, but she quickly banished thoughts of him from her mind. "Where is Mikey?"

"He's sleeping." Claudia gestured toward the bassinet in the living room where he lay, dressed snugly in sky blue terry pajamas, sucking his thumb.

"Aw, he looks adorable! And he's gained weight too."

"Yes, he has. I've already lost some baby weight because of his appetite. He's insatiable," Claudia said with a rueful smile.

Claudia hadn't only lost baby weight, Michaela noticed, but the trademark Santos luster in her expressive eyes had dimmed and there were dark shadows beneath them. She studied Claudia's wan smile and pale face. She looked different from the robust girl she had been before giving birth.

"Are you taking good care of yourself? Eating nutritiously, sleeping more?"

"As much as I can, I guess. I'm just feeling a bit depressed," Claudia said, motioning for her to follow.

"I'm sorry to hear that." Michaela joined her at the kitchen table.

"Do you want some *mate?*"

"What's that?" Michaela asked, wondering at the smoky aroma coming from a small, silver-laminated gourd Claudia held up.

"It's the national drink in Argentina. We make it by infusing an herb called *yerba mate.*" Claudia took a sip through a metallic straw. "We drink it with a *bombilla.* That's this straw. Would you like a sip? It's good for you."

"Sure, I'd love to try it." Michaela took a sip from the straw and smiled. "Tastes good, kind of like strong green tea but with orange and honey in it. Am I right?"

"Yes, exactly. In Argentina, we normally drink it plain, but I like to add honey and a bit of orange rind for flavor."

Michaela regarded Claudia kindly. "Tell me what's bothering you. You mentioned you were depressed just now."

Claudia sighed deeply. "It's because I have big decisions to make. I'm worried about how I'm going to provide for Mikey. The hospital bills are astronomical! I can't depend on Paolo forever. I already feel guilty about invading his space."

"I'm sure he loves having you here," Michaela assured her. "Have you gotten in touch with Mikey's dad yet?"

"No, but Bobby's parents came by earlier this week." She made a winding motion next to her ear. "*Ellos están locos.* Crazy. They wanted to take Mikey to live with them!"

"With you too?"

Claudia grimaced. "No, just Mikey."

"What?" Michaela asked, shocked. What kind of people were they?

"Yeah, can you believe it? They said their mansion was a better home for their grandson than Paolo's bachelor pad. Paolo was furious when he heard."

"I'll bet," Michaela sympathized, stunned by the latest turn of events. "Claudia, you have to get in touch with Bobby right away! What's holding you back?"

Claudia shook her head morosely. "My husband doesn't love me anymore. If he did, he wouldn't have deserted me."

"Paolo said he's working in the Canadian oil sands. Isn't he coming back at some point?"

"I guess so. But he thinks I went back to my family in Argentina. He left me an airline ticket promising to return for me in six months. I pretended I was going to Buenos Aires, but I warned Bobby if he left, we were through." She looked down at her tightly clasped hands. "He left anyway. I don't think we'll ever be the same when he comes back—if he comes back."

"What do you mean by *if?*"

Claudia's eyes looked troubled. "I'm worried about his safety. That work is dangerous."

Michaela could see how she would be worried. "Bobby must be tough and courageous to take on that type of work. When will the six months be up?"

"Very soon. Then he's supposed to be off for six months, something like that." Claudia wiped the moisture beneath her tired eyes with shaking hands. "I miss Bobby terribly. I think about him day and night and I wish I could be with him. How do I know he won't enlist again to make more money?"

"I doubt he will. Once you tell him about Mikey, things will work out," Michaela soothed.

"Bobby is adventurous. He's a real daredevil. I don't want him to feel forced to stay because we have a son together."

"He *married* you, so I'm sure he wouldn't feel forced," Michaela said. "This isn't only about your marriage, it's about Mikey now. Bobby deserves to know he has a son."

"That's what Paolo says."

Michaela sighed. "For once I agree with your brother. Did the Woodbridges say if they've been in touch with Bobby?"

"No! They don't know where he is and I won't tell them either," she said defiantly. "Bobby wouldn't want to talk to them anyway." She gave a dismal shrug. "They disowned him because he eloped with me."

Michaela felt affronted on Claudia's behalf, but she knew that unless the Woodbridges came around and made amends with Bobby, Claudia would never be truly content. After all, she came from a close-knit family and Bobby's parents' purposeful dismissal and alienation was foreign to the kind of family life she was used to.

"This is unfair and so convoluted. But one thing's for sure. You have to get in touch with Bobby and tell him he's a dad before his parents do," Michaela said firmly.

Claudia blotted at another surge of tears. "I don't think I can face him without falling apart." She blew her nose and shook her head mournfully.

"Yes, you can. He's your *husband!* You must swallow your pride and do it soon," Michaela urged. "Sounds like you're still in love with him. If you save your marriage, Mikey will benefit. Think of it that way."

Mikey began to fuss and Claudia rushed over to check on him.

Hearing his cries, Michaela yearned to nestle his soft little body close to hers. "Can I hold him?"

"Sure, be my guest. I just fed him, so he's not hungry. He probably just wants to be held."

Michaela smiled. "I can do that." She washed her hands at the kitchen sink and then carefully lifted Mikey from the bassinet. Awed by how much he had changed in just one week, she gazed into his scrunched up little face and then kissed the downy, light brown fluff on his head.

"What's the matter, little guy? Aw, don't cry," Michaela cooed. Mikey found his thumb and sucked it as he looked up at her and blinked, his innocent blue eyes touching her heart. He was no longer crying, just calmly contemplating her. She wanted to tell him how lucky he was to have Claudia as his mother and Paolo as his strong and caring uncle.

"He remembers you," Claudia marveled.

"You think so?" Michaela sat on the sofa and positioned Mikey against her chest with his little head tucked beneath her chin while he noisily sucked his thumb. She inhaled his clean baby scent, the sweetest fragrance she had ever smelled.

"You're so good with Mikey...you should have a baby of your own."

"Maybe in the future. Right now I've got my hands full with too many things."

"You mean the competition, or my brother?"

"Both. You're not expecting Paolo back any time soon are you?"

"Nah. He won't be home till late." Claudia rolled her eyes. "He has a meeting with that Bernice lady tonight for the dinner party she's throwing."

"Oh."

Claudia gave her a pensive look. "I wish you two weren't competing against each other."

"That makes two of us," Michaela agreed ruefully.

"It's hard to see the two of you not getting along. I mean...you're so cool together."

"Cool" was not exactly how Michaela would describe their relationship, it was more like *scorching*. But she knew what Claudia meant. "Did Paolo say we weren't getting along?"

"No, but when I asked him when he was bringing you here to visit us, he made a face and said it wouldn't be any time soon."

Hearing about his reaction made Michaela feel bad. It was one thing for her to avoid Paolo, but it bothered her to hear what he'd said about her coming over. "What else did he say?" she asked, hating herself for asking.

"Well...um..." Claudia stalled nervously. "I'd rather not say. I just wish *both* of you could win."

"Yeah, that would be nice if we could each have our own show," Michaela commiserated. "Anyhow, go ahead and tell me the rest. I won't get mad, I promise." She tried to sound casual even though Claudia's unease was making her apprehensive.

"Okay." Claudia took a deep breath. "When I asked if he was worried you might beat him, he laughed it off and said, 'Are you kidding? My gimmick will wipe her out.'"

"How modest of him." Michaela felt like gnashing her teeth, but it was a wake-up call to stay on track and not let her guard down with Paolo. "I hope you don't feel conflicted because Paolo and I are opponents. You can still count on me for anything."

"*Gracias*. It's hard not to love you, Maki." Claudia rushed over to give her a warm hug and they formed a cozy circle with little Mikey sandwiched in between.

Chapter Fifteen

What is Paolo's blasted gimmick? Michaela wondered impatiently, as she stood at the spa kitchen stove, stirring the risotto with punishing strokes. A whole week had gone by since she had last seen or talked to Paolo, but her plan to keep him out of sight, out of mind wasn't working. They were weeks away from the competition and he had kept a tight lid on his gimmick so far.

"Give the risotto a break, goddess. You're supposed to stir it, not beat it to death," Elliot wisecracked, giving her a haughty, raised eyebrow look. When Michaela didn't respond, he added, "Tell me, lovey, what has your apron in a tangle, your bra in a vise, your thong in a twist—"

"Enough, Elliot. I get your drift," she said dryly.

Elliot cackled and moved away from her to taunt Dan instead. Michaela relaxed her tight grip on the wooden spoon. Lately, whenever she thought of Paolo her hands clenched—it was an automatic response. Somehow, he had gotten a TV appearance yesterday on the South Florida morning show following the *Today Show.* Giddy with excitement, Aunt Magda had called Michaela last night with the news about how "that scrumptious hunk of a man" had looked amazing on TV.

Michaela had to find a way to get some publicity—but how? A press release to the *Miami Herald?* That could hardly compare to Paolo being on TV, and there was no guarantee the newspaper would pick it up. She had to find a way to get on TV or a radio show ASAP! Maybe Tiffany had a connection. She would call her tonight, and if Tiff couldn't help, then she'd consult Aunt Magda as a last resort. The woman was shameless and utterly relentless when she pursued something. But first, Michaela had to come up with a gimmick.

"Goddess, you have a visitor," Elliot called out.

She turned her head toward the entrance and saw Lisa rushing toward her.

"Hey, Lisa," Michaela said, brightening at seeing her friend.

Lisa looked stressed. "Can you take a quick break? I need a huge favor," she said anxiously.

"Of course. Elliot, please take over the risotto." Michaela handed him the wooden spoon. "Make sure it's glossy and creamy."

Elliot slammed the wooden spoon on the counter and covered his ears. "I won't hear such blasphemy! When have I ever failed you?"

Michaela ignored Elliot's theatrics and ran after Lisa who was waiting at the spa entrance. "What's up?" she asked her.

"I was on my way to massage Paolo when I got an urgent call. He's in the massage room waiting for me, but I don't have time to go back and tell him I'm going to be late. I have to deal with an emergency first."

"What's wrong?"

"My roommate called to say that the bathroom is flooding."

"Oh, no!"

Lisa pointed to the empty receptionist's desk. "I have to run over there and get a plumber and Francine isn't anywhere to be found. Would you go in and tell Paolo that I'm running about ten minutes late? He's in room number five."

"Of course," Michaela said without hesitation.

Lisa exhaled a sigh. "Thanks. You're a lifesaver."

Michaela watched Lisa run outside to make the call. Paolo was alone in the room waiting for a massage—she desperately needed a massage herself. Lately, she'd had a bit of a stiff neck from not sleeping well.

Hmmm. She was suddenly tempted to do something crazy and a bit twisted by her standards, but if it worked...she'd be way ahead of the game. A scheme began to formulate in her mind that made her giggle nervously. If there was ever an opportunity to find out the bragging showman's gimmick, this was it! She thought gleefully, rubbing her hands with relish.

Paolo lay face-down on the massage table, naked save for a

small towel draped over his butt. He was looking forward to the massage after the stressful week he'd had. He was tired, but mostly he was horny as hell ever since Michaela had put the brakes on him. Just when things had heated up between them, she had doused his libido with ice water. Now, he couldn't think about anything else but having her and it was driving him nuts. Damn the *caliente* redhead! He was wound up tighter than a steel drum and ready to explode.

Adding to his problems, he'd had to deal with the arrogant Woodbridges and their plot to take Mikey away from Claudia. They had pushed hard for her to divorce Bobby on grounds of abandonment and then tried to bribe her with a large sum of money. Paolo hadn't had a good night's rest since Claudia and Mikey had come to stay with him, yet he was so attached to Mikey that he'd be damned if he couldn't provide a good life for his little nephew. That kid would not want for anything; Paolo would make certain of it.

The soft, tinkling Asian music began to lull him to sleep. He was about to doze off when he heard the door open and quiet footsteps approach his side. Without opening his eyes, he said, "Hey, Lisa."

"Lisa late. I massage," a young female voice said. She sounded eastern European, maybe Russian. Paolo tried to lift his head to look at her, but a soft hand firmly held his neck anchored on the headrest of the table so he could only look down.

"Do not move," she ordered.

Paolo heard her uncap a bottle and squeeze the contents. She began to massage his back and shoulders with feather light strokes. Instead of relaxing him, her silky touch was making his rigid body respond in ways he would rather not... Damn, after that last session with Maki, all he thought about day and night was making love to her and this girl's feathery touch was reminding him of Maki's soft hands.

"That's too soft. Press harder. I'm tied up in knots," he said, his voice garbled.

"Why?" She pummeled his shoulders with tight fists.

"It's been a stressful week. That's it," he grunted. "Give it to me harder. Much harder."

"Gladly." She doubled up the pressure.

"That's more like it. What's your name?"

"Irina."

"I'm Paolo. Where are you from?" He rarely heard an accent like hers on Flamingo Island.

"Ukraine."

There was something familiar about the masseuse. She smelled like roses, just like Maki. There was also something familiar in her intonation, even if she had a heavy, low-timbered accent. Paolo tensed. If he wasn't mistaken, that voice belonged to Maki! Who did she think she was kidding? He knew her soft touch, her delectable scent... He almost shouted with laughter when he realized it was indeed her, but lying buck naked and trapped in the treacherous hands of his rival, he chose not to. Two could play her little game of deception. Paolo decided not to expose her, especially since he was in danger of being exposed himself—literally.

"Never been to the Ukraine. I'm from Argentina." When she didn't respond, he added, "I'm the chef competing against Michaela in the *Miami Spice* competition. Do you know her?"

"Yes. Michaela great chef."

"Eh, maybe, but I'm sure to win," he boasted. He held his breath waiting for her reaction.

"Why?" Her voice sounded snarky already.

"She only serves up rabbit food." Paolo relished the sound of Maki's strangled groan.

"Rabbit food better than lard." She punctuated her words by vigorously thumping his shoulders with her balled up fists.

Paolo's shoulders began to shake with mirth. If Maki thought she was hurting him, she was delusional. Her pounding massage actually felt good, revved up his blood.

"What's funny?" Her voice sounded close to his ear.

"I was laughing because that bossy little spitfire doesn't stand a chance over my gimmick."

She dug her nails into his shoulder blades and worked handfuls of his flesh with a vengeance.

"Watch it, Irina! Your nails are sharp." Their game was fun, but Paolo wasn't willing to become Maki's human pincushion.

He tried to turn around, but she quickly threw a lavender-scented towel over his head. When he reached to pull it off, her hand firmly pressed down on his nape.

"Be still." She switched her attention to his towel-covered buttocks and smacked them with malicious vengeance.

"Hey, what kind of a massage is this?"

"Slavic. Tell me about gimmick," she demanded, the trace of her distinct American accent suddenly surfacing.

What the hell, might as well tell her and gauge her reaction, he thought, biting back a chuckle. There was no way she would want to steal his idea or copy it anyway. Not proper Maki.

"My show will be called *Grill Me, Baby.*"

"*That* is your gimmick?" she asked in a dismissive tone. "Eh!"

"Not all of it. I'm going to pick one lucky lady from an all-female audience and romance her with my magnificent cooking."

She gave a cynical snort. "I do not like this *Grill Me, Baby!*"

"Why? It's genius. The women will *love* it...that I know."

"Sounds lame." The little spy's fake accent was back, thicker than ever. "Is that *all* you have?"

"No, that's not all," he growled. "I am going to whip my opponent's lily white ass!"

Michaela's elbow landed sharply between his shoulder blades and dug in.

"Oof, cut that out."

"Maybe she wins."

"No way. She doesn't stand a chance. Good thing she's hot, because the spoils go to the victor, eh?"

Michaela added her other elbow and intensified the pressure mercilessly.

"Stop that," he roared.

"Ees good for you."

Paolo was sorely tempted to turn over and pull her on top of him when he heard approaching footsteps.

"Sorry I'm late, Paolo. What's going on here?" Lisa asked in a bewildered tone.

Michaela mumbled a hasty good-bye and ran out the room. Paolo's chest began to rumble when Lisa hurriedly said, "Hold on, Paolo. I'll be right back."

Paolo could only nod his head. If he uttered a sound, he would start guffawing and then they would all know he was on to Maki's tricks.

Chapter Sixteen

"I know what Paolo's 'gimmick' is," Michaela crowed triumphantly. Aunt Magda and Tiffany were gathered around the dining room table.

"How did you find out? I thought he was keeping it top secret," Tiffany said.

"He doesn't know that I know." Michaela still couldn't believe that she'd pulled off the outrageous trick on Paolo without him catching on. Thank God, Lisa had been a loyal ally, and hadn't let on that Michaela was masquerading as Irina.

"How is that possible?" Aunt Magda asked.

A giggle escaped Michaela, prompting her to take a sip of ice tea instead of elaborating.

"That was a guilty giggle if I've ever heard one." Aunt Magda's eyes brimmed with curiosity. "I want to hear the story. And please don't leave anything out!"

"It's no big deal, really." Michaela tapped her pen against a yellow notepad and tried to look nonchalant, but the image of Paolo receiving her wrathful massage, big and bare except for the tiny towel over his taut butt, made her squirm in her seat and nearly sent her into a gale of giggles. It served him right for all the rude, chauvinistic comments he had made about her. She almost strangled him when he blithely said, *"I'm going to whip my opponent's lily white ass"*. Unfortunately, he was a little too well acquainted with her ass...

"So what's his gimmick?" Tiffany prodded. "Dish already!"

"The Latin lover plans on having an all-female audience. He will choose one lucky lady—his words, not mine." Michaela rolled her eyes. "And plans to romance her on air with his *magnificent* cooking. His words, not mine again."

"That's the gimmick?" Tiffany asked. "Anything else?"

"His segment will be called *Grill Me, Baby.*"

Aunt Magda nodded. "It's catchy. I'll give him that. Unfortunately, I like it," she admitted, looking a bit guilty.

"Me too," Tiffany said. "You have to admit it, Mic, sex sells."

"That man oozes sex," Aunt Magda cooed shamelessly, her powdered cheeks flushing bright pink. She fanned herself and took a sip of iced tea. "Goodness, gracious me. He is positively swoon-worthy!"

Paolo didn't just ooze sex; he *was* hot sex—uninhibited, forbidden sex and Michaela hadn't been able to get that last night at her apartment out of her head since. "Hey, who are you rooting for anyway?" she demanded, glancing from one to the other.

"You!" Aunt Magda and Tiffany cried in unison.

"Good, let's keep it that way," Michaela said. The doorbell suddenly rang, startling the three of them.

"That must be Willow," Aunt Magda said. "I told her we were brainstorming over how to help you win."

Michaela rushed to the door and opened it with a welcoming smile. She was always delighted to see Aunt Willow.

"I came as soon as I heard you needed my help." Aunt Willow deposited a kiss on Michaela's cheek. "The moment that Magda called, I downed my ginkgo and a few other mind boosters with my herbal tea. I'm full of ideas. They are flowing through my head as we speak."

"Good! I'm certainly in need of them." Michaela gave her a hug. "Come in. Tiff and Aunt Magda are already here."

Aunt Willow glided to the table, radiating serenity. "Hello, my dears." She greeted Tiffany and Aunt Magda with a kiss on the cheek before taking a seat at the table.

"You look amazing." Tiffany gave her Aunt Willow an admiring once-over. It was true. Few women at sixty-three wore their hair, straight, all gray and shoulder-length with such panache, but Willow's hair was just as silky and thick as in her younger days. Her eyes were a clear, radiant blue, just like Tiffany's. Had to be her organic diet. Whenever Willow entered a room, people visibly relaxed. She claimed psychic abilities. Maybe that was what drew people to her, even total strangers. That and her ability to connect on a deeper, emotional level than most.

"All right, ladies, what have we got?" Aunt Willow asked.

While Tiffany filled Aunt Willow in on Paolo's gimmick, Michaela fixed a cup of her aunt's favorite white tea. She placed it on a tray and added a tin of her light version of French *macarons* that she planned to feature on her show. She set the cup in front of Aunt Willow and noticed her eyes were closed and she remained silent.

"Yoo hoo, earth to Willow." Aunt Magda glanced heavenward with a shake of her sleek auburn bob. The contrast between the two women was staggering and what made them unique. Aunt Magda, slim and stylish, wore a periwinkle blue tunic top, black legging capris, and jeweled black patent leather flats. Like Tiffany, Aunt Magda adored fashion, hair and makeup and used it to her advantage. The two of them made an ideal shopping team, always finding the best bargain for their buck, yet looking current and stylish.

Aunt Willow, ever the flower child, wore a flowing tangerine caftan with multi-colored macramé bangles and fringed tan leather sandals. "I was trying to tap into Paolo's macho spirit, Magda. I was almost there, but now you ruined it," she said with a sigh.

"I didn't ruin anything," Aunt Magda replied. "You looked like you were in a trance. Have you been puffing on the wacky weed again?"

"No! I would never drive a car under the influence," Willow protested with wounded dignity. "Magda, really, that was quite unnecessary."

Before Magda could respond, Michaela quickly said, "Here, have one of these." She opened the tin and set it in front of her two aunts—appealing to their sweet tooth to end the bickering.

Aunt Willow selected a lavender-colored *macaron*. Sporting two mood rings on her un-manicured hand, she twirled it from side to side and inspected every angle. "What is this beautiful confection?"

"It's a lavender-infused love bite. The center is Valrhona chocolate." Just like the color of Paolo's eyes, Michaela thought privately. *Stop it*, she told herself sternly. What was she doing thinking dreamy thoughts about Paolo when their job today was to find a better gimmick?

Aunt Magda quirked her perfectly waxed eyebrows and gave Michaela a surprised look. "Did you say love bite?" She picked a coral one and giggled as she studied it. "I like the name, the play on words. It's deliciously naughty. What's this one made of?"

"Passion fruit with Armagnac-fig filling."

Aunt Magda popped it in her mouth and sighed dreamily after she swallowed. "Such sinful delicacies. They're positively decadent. I could devour the whole box. Actually, I could inhale it."

"Thanks, I'm planning on..." The doorbell rang again interrupting Michaela. "Who can that be?" she wondered aloud.

"Paolo?" Tiffany grinned mischievously.

"I sure hope not!" Michaela said, hurrying to the door.

Michaela peeked through the peephole and for a fleeting moment, she wished she could turn her visitors away. Anxiety churned in her stomach at the prospect of letting her parents in, but she couldn't exactly exclude them when the rest of the clan was here. It wouldn't be kind. And in truth, she was curious as to why they had shown up...together. This was a first. She hadn't seen her parents together in a long time. Well, they had been at the taping, but they'd been sitting far apart from each other.

The moment Michaela opened the door, her parents strode into the apartment with the same purposeful vigor they unleashed in courtroom litigation. She was surprised. These days they barely communicated with each other, except through one of their daughters.

Dressed to the nines in a fitted, charcoal-colored silk suit and a Tahitian gray pearl earring and choker set, Mom imperiously confronted Tiffany, Magda and Willow. "Why wasn't I included in this family discussion?" she asked. Accusation and something akin to hurt clouded her keen blue eyes.

"What about me? Aren't I part of this family too?" Dad asked, looking dapper in a dark blue Armani suit. His neatly trimmed goatee was a new addition. "Magda, you did right to call us. After all, we are Michaela's parents," he boomed in his deep, courtroom voice.

"Isn't it ironic that last week both of you were ready to

disown Mic after the show and now you're pledging family loyalty?" Tiffany gave him an accusing look. "What's going on, Pop?"

"Don't be disrespectful. We heard Michaela's been given another chance. But she still needs to beat that shady Latin chef, right?" Mom asked.

"Paolo is not shady." Even if he was her teasing tormentor and formidable competition, Michaela felt compelled to defend him. "He's just full of himself and determined to win. I need to come up with a gimmick that's better than his."

"That shouldn't be too hard," Mom said with her usual abundance of self-confidence.

"We'd better get cracking," Aunt Magda said.

"Do you know what you're up against? What is his gimmick?" Mom's face was a picture of tough ambition as she focused on a worthy new cause—her oldest daughter.

As soon as Michaela finished filling Mom and Dad in on Paolo's gimmick, the room began to buzz with advice, given in rapid-fire succession, as each family member tried to outshine and out shout the other. When the cacophony escalated to an ear-splitting pitch, Michaela covered her ears and was tempted to ask them all to leave. But she kind of liked the fact that her whole family was united for her cause. It was a welcome change to the usual criticism doled out by her parents.

"Hey, everybody. Shut up and listen up. I've got it!" Tiffany cried out, getting their undivided attention at once. Her blue eyes sparkled and her cheeks glowed pink with excitement. "I have the perfect idea. You can't say no until you've heard me out, Mic."

"I'll be the one to decide that, Tiff. What is it?" Michaela cast a wary eye on her wily little sis. Tiffany's ideas were legendary in the Willoughby household. Like when she'd finagled the neighborhood boys who owned cars to give her rides to school so she wouldn't have to take the school bus...and she was only eleven. And when she'd set up a lemonade stand spiked with the vodka she'd "borrowed" from their parents' liquor cabinet.

Tiffany took a dramatic breath and looked around the room as she commanded center stage. She grinned broadly, obviously thrilled with her plan and enjoying all their attention. "Here it is in a nutshell. You invite only male viewers to enter a contest and then..."

"But that's copying Paolo," Michaela cut in.

"Who cares? War is war. Don't get hung up on the tactics, just the outcome."

"No, I'd rather come up with something else. Keep in mind we're running out of time."

"That's why you should hear me out before you start objecting. Okay?"

"Okay," Michaela agreed reluctantly.

"The guys will be invited to email or Twitter you with a personal message about how they got into shape after battling weight gain," Tiffany said. "Then the winner is invited on the show and you pamper him with a special, healthy meal. And you wear that hot red dress I bought you!" She snapped her fingers and made a dismissive gesture. "Giada, move over and let Mic take over."

"I don't know about that," Michaela said, stifling a groan. "That puts me in the same category as Paolo and—"

"No it doesn't," Aunt Magda said. "I like Tiffany's idea."

"Me too," Aunt Willow chimed in. "It sounds like 'The Biggest Loser' combined with those Kathi Lee *Today Show* segments, 'Everyone's Got a Story'. People love an inspirational story."

"Well, I have to agree with my sisters on this." Mom nodded. "The premise works, Michaela. You can create a low-calorie meal to satisfy the contestant."

"And end it with decadent love bites," Tiffany added, her blue eyes alight with mischief.

"Decadent love bites?" Dad repeated, looking appalled. Hearing her burst of giggles, his blustery reaction seemed to amuse Tiffany to no end. Nothing made her happier than to shock her family, especially their stuffy dad. "Really, Tiffany. That's pushing it!" He gave her an admonishing look. "You are out of control, young lady."

Everyone but her parents laughed along with Tiffany. "Don't worry, Pop, Mic's love bites are tempting, but harmless." Tiffany offered him the open tin of pastel-colored *macarons*.

"Here, have one."

"You call those love bites?" Mom arched an eyebrow at Tiffany. "Did you come up with the salacious name?"

"It was my idea. I came up with it, Mom," Michaela said.

"Taste one," Tiffany urged. "They're Mic's take on a French *macaron* and they are amazing."

"Oh my God, a light bulb just went off in my head!" Aunt Willow turned to Dad. "Lawrence, do you know how we can get an 800 number? We can make it 1-800-luv-bite and make it l-u-v instead of the usual way," she said, spelling out the letters. "The contestants can either call in with their story or visit a website called luvbite.com and leave a message!"

"We can do a Facebook page too!" Aunt Magda added eagerly.

"Whose show will be filmed first?" Tiffany asked.

"Paolo's will be filmed in the morning. Mine will follow right after."

"Lawrence, our daughter is in dire need of our help," Mom announced.

"That sounds a bit dramatic," Michaela said.

Mom ignored Michaela's objection as she pressed Dad. "Why don't you call in a few favors and get Michaela some press in the *Miami Herald* and on the radio?"

"I was already planning to offer help, Sylvia," Dad replied, giving her a look of reproach.

"Good, then I'll take care of getting the 1-800 number set up," Mom said.

"Now the question is, what should she call her segment?" Aunt Magda asked.

"Uhhh, we need to brainstorm that one." Tiffany tapped her temple.

Aunt Magda's face lit up. "I know. How about *The Pleasure Palate*?"

"Mmmm, hmmmm." Tiffany giggled. "Love it and so will the men."

Dad cast a stern eye toward Tiffany. "I'm not happy about the name or the concept. It sounds sleazy."

"I agree with Dad. I don't want to put myself out there like that," Michaela said.

Tiffany waved a dismissive hand at her. "Oh, please, don't be miss-ish. You want to win, don't you?"

"Yes, but..." Michaela said.

"No butts, unless it's yours sheathed in that little red dress." Tiffany's blue eyes twinkled as she let out a hoot of laughter.

Michaela rolled her eyes, but she had to admit it was nice to see her family rallying behind her as a unified force. She was most surprised by her parents, who usually couldn't stand being in each other's company, let alone holding a civil conversation. Today, they seemed to have bonded over helping her. There was nothing like two proud, competitive lawyers hell-bent on winning.

"Alrighty then. I'll set up the website and record the message. All you have to do is give me a good headshot of you. Better yet, make it a full body shot." Tiffany chortled. "In a string bikini."

"Now I know you're kidding," Michaela said. "Forget it."

"I was kidding about the bikini, but serious about the rest. Aunt Magda, you're the social media diva. Can you somehow post a message on the Internet dating sites about Mic's show?"

Aunt Magda beamed. "Absolutely! I'll see what I can do."

"What can I do to help?" Aunt Willow asked.

"You can help Michaela choose the winner," Tiffany said.

Aunt Willow looked inordinately pleased. "I would love to."

"Hello? People, I haven't agreed to any of this," Michaela protested. "I'm not sold on the idea. It feels like I'm pimping myself."

"You need to look at the end goal," Mom urged.

"The Willoughby name is at stake and we've got your back. You are going to win!" Dad declared, pumping his fist in the air.

"If we blitz the Internet with your contest, it'll give you an edge over Paolo," Aunt Magda said. "Thousands of viewers can be reached through Facebook and Twitter."

"And just think of the lucky guy who gets chosen," Aunt Willow said kindly. "You'll make his day."

"You always say the nicest things, Aunt Willow. And you're

a wonderful help, Aunt Magda." Michaela looked at her relatives, touched by their passionate enthusiasm. "Thank you, everyone, for being here and supporting me."

"Yeah, yeah, that's all nice, Mic, but you better remember one crucial thing," Tiffany said.

"What?" Michaela asked.

Everyone's attention zeroed in on Tiffany as she grinned at them with an impish expression.

"Sex sells and I'm your new pimp," she proclaimed, gleefully ignoring the collective gasp.

Dad's face darkened with disapproval. "I am not impressed, Tiffany. That is very crass of you to say to your sister. Why do you get a perverse joy from saying outrageous things?"

Shrugging off his tirade, Tiffany giggled and popped another love bite in her mouth. "Mmm, these *are* good! You've outdone yourself, Mic."

Chapter Seventeen

Claudia stood in the living room clutching her new cell phone with a white-knuckled hand as she waited for Bobby to pick up. They were two hours behind in Alberta, making it seven o'clock in the morning there and nine in Miami. She had just hung up after another alarming phone call from Max Weintraub, the Woodbridges' lawyer. The thought of them taking Mikey away made Claudia's blood run cold. Bobby needed to know what his parents were up to so he could stop them! He also had to be told about Mikey. That part worried her because he would be furious that she had kept the news from him.

When Bobby didn't answer, Claudia was about to leave a message, but Mikey started to cry and she didn't want Bobby to hear him in the background—not yet. She hung up and ran to the baby carrier on shaky legs.

"¿Qué pasa, nene?" she cooed softly, peering into her son's red, scrunched-up face. She picked him up and carried him to the sofa. When his mouth nudged her breast, she felt her milk let down instantly. It was barely two hours since he had last nursed, but knowing Mikey's voracious appetite, he was probably hungry again. She remembered the Leche League lady's caution that sometimes she might feel like she was nursing nonstop while the baby was building up her milk. Breastfeeding really was all about supply and demand.

Claudia kissed the top of Mikey's head as she lifted her blouse and lowered the flap of her nursing bra. At least she could feed him well, she thought, as Mikey latched on and slurped like a thirsty sailor.

For what seemed like the millionth time, Claudia gazed at Mikey's little hands in awe. They were shaped just like Bobby's, with square palms and long, tapered fingers. Hands not meant for hard labor in the remote Canadian oil sands. She had no idea what her husband did out there, but she knew it had to be risky, otherwise how could he be making so much money?

The cell phone rang, startling her. *Oh God, was it Bobby returning her missed call?* As she picked up the cell, Claudia felt a confusing mixture of relief and disappointment when she saw it wasn't Bobby calling back, but Señora Fuentes from down the hall.

"*Hola, niña,* do you want a break? I can come over around noon and watch Miguelito for you," Señora Fuentes offered.

"That would be wonderful. Just come in. I'll leave the door unlocked."

"*Perfecto.* I'm making *arroz con pollo*, so I'll bring you some."

"*¡Qué rico! Gracias,*" Claudia said, grateful for a visit from the kind widow. What would she have done without Señora Fuentes? Claudia longed to share Mikey with the rest of her family, especially her mother, but Mamá still couldn't get her visa squared away. At the rate her mother was going, Mikey would be walking before she got here!

As soon as Señora Fuentes arrived, Claudia hugged her and then sat down to devour the tasty chicken and rice lunch the widow had brought. When Claudia finished, she fed Mikey again before Señora Fuentes took over and shooed Claudia away to take a relaxing bath.

Grateful for the reprieve, Claudia squeezed lavender-scented bath gel into the tub and filled it with hot water, swishing it to form bubbles. She stepped in and closed her weary eyes as the frothy water covered her from neck to toes. Her thoughts inadvertently turned to Bobby again. How would it be when he finally returned?

In a dreamy trance, she ran a soft, soapy washcloth down her throat and across her tender breasts, remembering Bobby's fevered touch when he made love to her. She longed for him so much her whole body ached, but they had unfinished business and there were no guarantees that Bobby wouldn't take off again on another adventure, new son or not. If he did it once, he might do it again.

Would he see Mikey as an end to his dream of starting his business of yacht chartering? Now that she had Mikey, Claudia wouldn't be able, nor would she want to join Bobby to work beside him on the yachts. Sailing the open seas was no place for an infant. Would Bobby feel shackled by being a dad? They had always talked about waiting at least five years before having kids because Claudia was so young and filled with wanderlust, just like Bobby.

She exhaled a morose little sigh. As soon as they talked, Bobby would want an explanation for everything, starting with why she never went to stay with her family in Argentina and ending with why she had neglected to tell him she was pregnant with his baby. There was no getting around it though; she had to tell him now.

All too soon, the bath water cooled, along with her nerve, and Claudia reluctantly got out and dried off with a fluffy towel. Rather than call him again, she decided she would send him a text with her new cell phone number. As she wrapped her damp hair turban-style in a towel, she heard a cell phone ringing. She donned her mauve silk kimono robe—a Valentine gift from Bobby last year—and then joined Señora Fuentes on the living room sofa.

"Was that my cell phone I heard ringing?" Claudia asked, wondering if Bobby had tried reaching her.

"*Sí*, I answered it," Señora Fuentes said, not taking her eyes from the TV screen. She was engrossed in watching a Spanish *telenovela*.

"Who called?"

Señora Fuentes pursed her rouged lips. Even in a housedress, the Cuban widow always made an effort to look put-together with nicely styled gray hair, pearl earrings and makeup. "I don't know. It might have been the wrong number. I couldn't understand anything, the reception was terrible."

"Oh. I finally got the courage to call Bobby earlier."

Señora Fuentes nodded approvingly. She had been very vocal about Bobby needing to protect and support his new family. "I'm proud of you. What did he say?"

"He didn't answer. I wonder if it was him trying to call me back," Claudia fretted.

"I sure hope so," Señora Fuentes said emphatically. "Don't worry. If it was Bobby, he'll try again."

"Yes," Claudia agreed, but she hoped it wouldn't be right away. She needed just a little more time to figure out how she would confess everything. "What are you watching?"

"*Pura Sangre*. It's filmed in Colombia." When a commercial came on, Señora Fuentes switched channels with the remote.

Suddenly, Claudia exclaimed, "Stop! Can you go back to the last channel?"

"*¿Sí qué pasa?*" Señora Fuentes drew back and eyed Claudia with curiosity as she asked her what was happening. "I think that was a commercial for Maki's show. I wonder if Paolo knows she has commercials on TV now." If he did, he hadn't mentioned anything to Claudia. Then again, her brother had barely been home. He had been very busy with the restaurant, Bernice's constant demands about Palmentieri's dinner party, and getting his gimmick ready for his show.

"Who is Maki? The girl on the commercial?" Señora Fuentes asked.

"Maki is competing against Paolo to host the *Miami Spice* TV show. But that girl on the commercial wasn't her. Just somebody who looks like her. Maki is a redhead and she doesn't wear sexy clothes like the blonde had on."

"*Qué tremenda,*" Señora Fuentes said, calling the blonde "fresh" in Spanish as her penciled-in brows knitted together. "What did she say about love bites?"

"I think it was something about going to a website for more information about her show. They had www.luvbite.com on the bottom of the screen, so that must be it." Claudia jumped up from the sofa. "I'm going to call my brother. He needs to get a commercial too!"

Señora Fuentes gave her a dubious, raised-eyebrow look and shook her head. "TV commercials are very expensive."

Claudia sank back down on the sofa. "True...so what can he do?"

Señora Fuentes shrugged. "I don't know, but there must be some way Paolo can get more exposure. Many years ago in Cuba, I was an actress on television, but I've lost my contacts."

"Didn't you tell me you still do community theatre?"

"Yes, when they'll have me." Señora Fuentes sighed and raised her arthritic hands in a dramatic gesture.

Claudia smiled and patted the older woman's stooped shoulder. "I'd love to hear all about it sometime. Why don't we go on the website and see what Paolo is up against?" She headed to the kitchen counter and opened the laptop. As soon as she was connected to the Internet, she typed in www.luvbites.com and up popped an interactive website featuring the same blonde on the TV commercial in a video telling about the competition and plugging Michaela's cooking talents. After a few minutes of exploring the website, Claudia found links to Facebook, Twitter and YouTube with a gorgeous picture of Michaela on each.

Señora Fuentes placed a sleeping Mikey in his carrier and joined Claudia at the kitchen counter. She pointed at the laptop screen. "*¡Qué bonita!* Is that Maki?"

"*Sí*, that's Maki." Claudia turned to Señora Fuentes with a worried look. "Paolo had better get busy if he plans on winning. Maki is all over the web with a sexy message."

"Isn't that similar to what he was planning? But he is going to have an all female audience, right?" Señora Fuentes asked, surprising Claudia that she had remembered Paolo talking about his segment called *Grill Me, Baby* a few days ago.

Claudia grabbed her cell phone. "I better tell Paolo. He's not going to be happy that Maki caught up with him in the hottie department."

"I can't believe that little sneak stole my idea!" Paolo stared intently at the computer screen. Claudia was on the other line prompting him to check out Maki's ad campaign. He clicked on YouTube and watched the segment. "Damn, she looks hot too!"

Claudia giggled. "*Sí muy guapa y caliente.* Maki always looks so buttoned-up. Who would have thought she had that hot body?"

Paolo was not amused by his sister's observations. "What's this I'm reading about a competition?"

"She's holding a contest for guys to write in and explain why they should be chosen to be her date on her show."

"What? That sounds like my idea, but now I'm thinking I won't pick just one," he said smugly. "*All* the women in the audience will be romanced."

"Well, you're going to have to step up your game. Maki is calling her segment *The Pleasure Palate*."

"*Grill Me, Baby* is better," Paolo countered.

"Better watch out, *hermano*, Maki is already very popular. She has thousands of people following her on Twitter and..."

"What the hell is Maki doing, putting herself out there with a sexy message on the net?" he groused. "It's foolish and dangerous."

"What are you going to do?"

"I'm going to find out exactly what else that little thief is planning and then beat her at her own game. Thanks for the heads up."

"No problem." Claudia hesitated before adding, "Um, Paolo...there's something else you should know."

"What?" Paolo asked, impatient to get off and get to the bottom of Maki's shenanigans.

"The Woodbridges' lawyer, Max Weintraub, called again today."

"And?"

"They're still determined to take Mikey away from me, so I tried reaching Bobby, but he didn't answer his cell phone."

"Call him again, Claudia," Paolo urged.

"I will." She didn't sound very convincing.

"Do it now."

"I'll try," she said evasively.

"Don't worry about Bobby. If he gets difficult, I'll talk some sense into him," Paolo vowed, unable to take his eyes from Maki's spicy image on her website.

Paolo's jaw dropped as he stared at the screen. In the "All About Me" section, a neck and shoulders headshot depicted Maki leaning slightly forward in an aqua blouse, the low-cut neckline highlighting her round, creamy breasts. Her long hair had been cut and styled in tousled layers with feathery bangs that made her aquamarine eyes appear huge, especially with the smoky eye shadow she wore. Maki's glossy pink lips, slightly pursed and parted, and that look in her eyes was too provocative for a decent website!

A surge of lust made Paolo tighten his hand on the mouse and he had to release it before he broke the damn thing. Proper Maki had transformed herself into a hot babe, a sex kitten, for all the men to ogle. Paolo didn't like it, not one bit! If he was reacting this way, the men tuning into Maki's website would surely be salivating over her. She was doing a stupid thing, putting herself out there as a target for all the weirdos in cyber land.

"Paolo? Are you there?" Claudia asked.

He hadn't been paying attention to what Claudia was saying. All he knew was that he wanted to wring Maki's neck.

"I'm here with Señora Fuentes. I've gotta get off," she said.

"Okay, call you later, Claudia. *Ciao*," he said distractedly.

Paolo was so annoyed by Maki's suggestive message beneath her photo, he barely heard Claudia's good-bye. With mounting ire, he read the words aloud through tightly clamped teeth, imitating Maki in a falsetto tone:

"Hey, guys, write me. Tell me your story. What prompted you to shed unhealthy eating habits and get fit? The lucky winner gets a date with me on my show. At The Pleasure Palate, your dining wish is my command. And we'll end the evening with my specialty...luscious luv bites."

The only one giving love bites would be Paolo and Maki would be on the receiving end, he vowed malevolently, his gaze riveted to the screen.

Chapter Eighteen

Michaela and her favorite aunt sat yoga-style on a silk Balinese rug that partially covered the bamboo floor, sipping white pear tea and munching on crisp ginger wafers. Visiting with Aunt Willow was always a treat and tonight was no different.

"You should see some of the emails that have come in." Aunt Willow's lips twitched with amusement. "Those guys are baying at the moon to get on your show."

"That bad?"

"No...that good! They really like your picture and they seem to think they're going to get a chance for a real date with you."

Michaela groaned. "Oh no."

"What do you think about the website Tiffany created for you?" Aunt Willow asked.

"I've been meaning to check it out, but we had a fire in the kitchen a few days ago and it's been hellish to say the least."

"Maybe you should take a look."

"I will when I get home. I just haven't had any spare time to look. If you don't mind, I'd like you to filter the guys and help me make the final decision."

Aunt Willow looked surprised. "Really?"

Michaela nodded. "Really, it would be a huge weight off my shoulders."

Aunt Willow beamed. "I don't mind at all, dear. I'm honored that you trust my judgment."

"Of course, I do."

After a thoughtful pause, Aunt Willow said, "One entry stood out in particular. Would you like to read it?"

"Can you give me a recap? It's so comfy here, I'd rather not get up."

Aunt Willow patted Michaela's knee. "Me, neither. Let's

see…he sounds like he has a great sense of humor. He said he is a closet glutton, but because of health reasons, which he did not clarify, he has had to reform."

Michaela nodded. "Sounds promising."

"He said he has a great love and respect for butter and cheese, lots of it, his words again." Aunt Willow smiled. "He doubts he will be convinced otherwise, but he loves your approach to healthy eating and wants to believe!"

"Hmmm…sounds like he might be a jokester."

"I don't know about that. He has a self-deprecating humor and his tone seemed sincere. Maybe we should ask for a picture." Aunt Willow's brow furrowed. "Tiffany put a notice on the website not to include one. She said you were adamant about it so the choice would not be biased."

"It's true. I don't want to base the final decision on his looks. That wouldn't be fair."

"I agree. Personality is what counts. This one sounds like he's fun. I like the way he confessed his weaknesses."

"If you think he's the best candidate, then sign him on. I really appreciate you doing this for me, Auntie. Thanks." She leaned over and kissed Aunt Willow's cheek.

"My pleasure, dear. It's been very entertaining going through the entries, I must say. When your contestant is set to go, I'll e-mail you his info." She set her cup down on a bamboo tray resting on a lettuce-green tufted ottoman and turned concerned eyes toward Michaela. "Are you okay? You seem preoccupied."

"I've been dealing with work overload," Michaela admitted. "Every time I try to come up for air, something new needs my attention. Just this afternoon, Mr. Blumenthal's secretary called to tell me that he wants me to cater the desserts for a dinner party he and Bernice are hosting for Palmentieri, the famous tenor."

"That's wonderful!"

"Well, it would have been perfect except that Paolo will be catering the rest of the meal." Michaela made a face to show how she felt about it.

"Why the face?" Aunt Willow studied her niece. "Something tells me this is more complicated than you're letting on."

Michaela sighed. "You know me too well. There is something that's been gnawing at me."

Aunt Willow smiled serenely. "Tell me what's bothering you and we can look for a solution."

"It's Paolo. He's gotten under my skin. No matter how hard I try, I can't shake off the attraction." Michaela knew it was more than just attraction. She was falling for Paolo and couldn't get him out of her mind...or out of her heart.

"Do tell," Aunt Willow said, grinning. "The two of you have combustible chemistry."

"Is it obvious?"

"Absolutely. Such powerful energy! The day of the taping, the air was so charged, I thought the set would go up in flames."

"That is what's killing me. I'm the last person Paolo should be igniting." *But the only one I want to ignite me,* she amended privately.

"I don't know about that. Your kind of connection with him doesn't happen often. You should run with it, not away from it," Aunt Willow stated with certainty.

"I can't," Michaela wailed. "Paolo and I want the same thing and the stakes are high for both of us. How can we fiercely compete and build a loving relationship? I can't see that happening. My feelings for him are deepening, but I have to stay focused on winning."

"I see your problem." Aunt Willow gave a reflective pause. "I'm pulling for you, dear, and I think you are the better chef by far," she said loyally, "but what are you going to do if for some reason Paolo wins?"

Michaela shook her head. "I don't know. I can't think about that now."

"I understand. Just promise me one thing."

Michaela braced herself. "What?"

"Stop thinking so much and start living. Look at Magda. She was always looking for the perfect man, always rejecting one after the other because he wasn't her Mr. Darcy. Maybe if she'd given some of the guys a chance, she wouldn't feel so alone now." Willow clucked her teeth and shook her head. "She sure could use some lovin' and groovin'."

Michaela giggled. "You sound just like a sixties flower child."

"How else am I supposed to sound? I was a sixties flower child and proud of it. Honey, don't laugh. Without the lovin', life ain't worth livin'," she drawled. "It's not a cliché, it's the truth. It's been twenty-four years since Stephen died, and I've dated other men, but nobody has ever come close to making me feel the way he did. We were total opposites, but we clicked and all we wanted was for the other one to be happy."

"I hear you. But Paolo is pretty hot to handle. Our personalities are poles apart. Our family backgrounds are very different too. He comes from a close-knit, loving family and has strong opinions on marriage and children."

"That's wonderful."

"Maybe, except you know what Mom and Dad's marriage was like. I have no idea if I can be the kind of wife Paolo would expect."

"Why do you doubt yourself? Of course, you can. You're loving and generous and..."

Michaela gave a self-deprecating laugh. "Thanks, but I think I got ahead of myself and went a little overboard there. Who even said he wants to marry me?" She sighed deeply. "Anyway, even if we weren't competing, I'm not sure it would work out."

"You won't know unless you surrender to the attraction and separate business from pleasure. Just let it happen," Aunt Willow said fervently. "Peace and love. It's still what life is all about."

"I just wish things hadn't gotten so complicated. I had everything planned out."

Aunt Willow chuckled and gave Michaela a tight hug. "Oh, honey, who ever said life went according to our plans? We have to roll with the punches and be resilient. That's my secret for happiness."

Michaela could not believe her luck. She was about to present her special desserts to the upper crust socialites of Williams Island. Mr. Blumenthal had felt it only fair for

Michaela to be involved with the catering since she and Paolo were competing for *Miami Spice*. He didn't want to give an unfair advantage to Paolo over Michaela.

So here she was in the Blumenthals' mansion, setting up with her assistant Dan's help. The impressive kitchen was grander and bigger than Michaela's living and dining room combined. Sparkling with modern elegance, it was decorated in cool, neutral colors with bisque travertine tiled floors, smoky quartz countertops, and sleek mahogany cabinetry. Taupe glass backsplashes and state-of-the-art appliances completed the glamorous kitchen. Seeing the pristine condition of the stainless steel appliances, it was obvious the Blumenthals rarely frequented their kitchen, let alone cooked or ate at home.

Earlier when she had arrived, Michaela had been surprised to find the Blumenthal mansion was opulent, without being kitschy, which she would have expected given Bernice's gaudy style of dressing. Bernice had probably contracted an interior decorator. The elegantly appointed mansion exuded an impersonal air in spite of the coordinated luxe fabrics and stylish furniture. All the right accents were there to make it look splendid, all except one addition that could not be escaped—portraits of Bernice, in different poses, at different stages of her life—some nude—adorned every room Michaela had passed on her way to the kitchen. There was even a large framed, black-and-white etching of a woman's bare, curvy back, surely Bernice's, on one of the kitchen walls.

Michaela stood beneath the multi-tiered modern chandelier over the island, pinching herself at the incredible opportunity to highlight her deceptively lo-cal desserts. So what if Paolo had catered the rest of the meal? She had made the desserts bite-sized and colorful, tempting samples of her culinary talents. Maybe she would even make a convert out of Bernice. If Bernice had stuck to lo-cal foods, her backside would still resemble the flattering black-and-white etching instead.

"I hope Palmentieri has a sweet tooth, because these are amazing," Dan said, interrupting her thoughts. The big, Texan chef was carefully transferring her dainty key lime tarts to one of the silver platters provided by Jewel, Bernice's long-suffering, elderly Jamaican kitchen maid.

"Sadly, I found out he doesn't care too much for sweets when I called his assistant. She said, and I quote, 'Signore Palmentieri prefers to eat hearty and drink even heartier'," Michaela said in an Italian accent. "Apparently, Paolo is making his favorite meal."

"Don't worry. He's not the only guest."

"True. Williams Island isn't called the Florida Riviera for nothing. The residents here are used to the very best of everything."

Dan lifted a delicate *macaron*. "These are sure to please them."

"Thanks, Dan." Michaela had brought dependable Dan to help her out instead of Elliot. With so much at stake, she could ill afford to deal with Elliot's penchant for drama, especially after his revelation that he had the hots for Palmentieri, whom Elliot insisted was gay. Knowing her sous chef too well, Michaela was sure he would have finagled an introduction to the tenor tonight. Elliot on a mission was more combustible than gasoline and matches.

She had purposely arrived a half an hour early so she could get a head start before Paolo began invading her space...and peace of mind.

Forty minutes later, Paolo charged in, running late as usual. He gave a curt nod of acknowledgment to Michaela and Dan and then got down to business. His accompanying staff of three joined him in transforming the kitchen into a bustling bistro. Michaela wondered why Paolo looked tense and unhappy, with her mostly. It couldn't be that he was behind schedule. He was so self-assured about his cooking skills those things didn't faze him.

Decked in a gypsy-like, garnet corset dress with a red rose tucked into her overflowing cleavage, Bernice peeked in often while the staff labored nonstop. Michaela sighed. The woman was a classic. No doubt, she had dressed for Palmentieri's benefit, since he was reprising the role of Don Jose in *Carmen*, Bizet's lush opera later that week. *Carmen* was about sex, love, jealousy and murder—things sure to intrigue Bernice. Palmentieri would have been more excited had Bernice opted to dress like Escamillo, but not everyone knew that, according to

Elliot.

Michaela stood with her hands on her hips, surveying her glistening desserts. "Looks good enough to eat," she said with satisfaction. Mouthwatering key lime tarts, airy meringue nests filled with raspberries, dark chocolate passion fruit truffles, and the *piece de resistance*: a lavish variety of liqueur flavored "love bite" *macarons* in dreamy pastels.

Paolo was too preoccupied with his meal to give her a second glance. She came up beside him and peered over his shoulder while he stirred the chanterelle and porcini risotto. *Peace and love.* Michaela remembered Aunt Willow's words. Paolo had been studiously ignoring her since he arrived. Granted, he was working against the time, but still...it hurt to be disregarded.

"That smells divine," Michaela said sincerely.

When Paolo didn't respond, she asked, "Are you purposely ignoring me? You seem annoyed with me."

When he finally gave her his full attention, she shrank away from the stark displeasure in his eyes. "I'm disappointed in you. You are not the person I thought you were, Michaela."

Michaela, not Maki, and spoken in a cold tone. Michaela swallowed hard. "What do you mean? Why are you looking at me that way?"

"Don't act innocent. It is beneath you," he said bluntly. He turned his attention back to the risotto.

Michaela heaved a shaky breath as a tremor ran through her. She was baffled by Paolo's harsh words and was about to ask him to elaborate when Bernice stole up behind Paolo and made a shushing motion with her finger over her pursed lips, urging Michaela not to let on she was there. Michaela's eyes bulged incredulously when Bernice's hand slid upward from the back of his firm thigh and meandered over to rest on his taut buttock as he bent over the six-burner stove. From the glazed look in Bernice's eyes and her wet grin, it was obvious she had already imbibed one too many martinis.

"Not now, Michaela. You are not going to sabotage this," Paolo grated, shocking her with the unfair accusation. "This time I'm prepared. I won't put up with your tricks tonight."

Michaela's face burned with the injustice of his charge, and he had made it in front of the producer's wife no less. God only knew what she would relay to Mr. Blumenthal. "I am not trying to sabotage you! That was..."

"I do not like your new image on your website, or the way you've changed just to win this competition," he snarled in a low voice, cutting her off. "You cheated. Now take your hand off my ass."

So *that* was it. Paolo disapproved of her website and was pissed off at her. The revelation stung Michaela; she had never felt his wrath directed at her.

Bernice let out a raucous giggle. "Actually, that's my hand, darling. Just checking to see how things are progressing," she said giving Paolo an inappropriate, proprietary pat on the rump, as if to say "this is mine and you work for me".

Michaela could see the cords tighten in Paolo's neck when he realized that tipsy Bernice was the culprit. His square hand clutched the wooden spoon, his muscles flexing beneath his brown skin. Any doubts Michaela might have had about his relationship with Bernice dissolved as she looked at Paolo's face, taut and dark with annoyance.

"Everything is going fine, Bernice. But I work better without interruptions," he bit out.

One more impertinent pat of her jeweled hand and Bernice was gone—for now.

Once Bernice was out of earshot, Michaela asked, "Paolo...about my website. What's wrong with it?"

"It is all about sex and not about cooking," he said bluntly.

This coming from the master of sexy charisma? How ironic.

Paolo walked away and turned his attention to his sous chef, Gil, who was putting the final touches on the veal *osso bucco*, cooked earlier at the restaurant and waiting to be plated. Michaela remained rooted to the spot, smarting from Paolo's allegations.

Okay, so she had cheated a teensy bit by kind of copying his idea. But what was this about the website? When Tiffany had promised to set it up, Michaela had thought it would be fine. She should have monitored the website, or at least checked to see what Tiffany had done with it like Aunt Willow had suggested, but things at work had been like a roller coaster lately and she hadn't had a second for herself.

Maybe she had been too trusting, given Tiffany's penchant for mischief. A wave of unease made her feel queasy when she remembered how Tiffany had announced playfully, "Sex sells and I'm your new pimp." Dad was probably right. Tiffany needed to be reined in and controlled or she went off the rails sometimes. Michaela should have put a stop to it then, but she'd been swept away with the thrill of having her whole family united behind her.

Michaela's iPhone rang in her chef's tunic pocket. Surprised to see Mercy Hospital in the caller ID, she answered it on the first ring.

"Hello?"

"This is the emergency room of Mercy Hospital. May I speak to Michaela Willoughby?" a male voice asked briskly.

"Yes, this is Michaela Willoughby."

"Please come to the hospital. Magda Talbot and Willow Reese have you listed as an emergency contact."

Michaela's heart almost stopped. "Oh, my God, what happened?" she cried.

Chapter Nineteen

Waiting in the ice-cold hospital emergency room was nerve-wracking enough—but waiting alone was even worse. Michaela had left Dan in charge of everything before tearing off for the hospital in a panic. Just before she left the kitchen, she caught Paolo watching her with a concerned look as he asked Dan what was wrong.

She had thought of calling Mom and Dad, who were out of town at a lawyers' convention, but decided to postpone calling them until she had more information. She didn't want to alarm them yet, but her sister was another story. Michaela had called, texted and emailed Tiffany to no avail. She had left a detailed message about her aunts' car accident and where they were being treated for injuries. Her little sister had an annoying habit of disappearing, often forgetting to charge her phone.

Who knew what Tiffany was up to? Michaela had not had a moment to speak to her recently, but she knew that Aunt Willow had been in almost daily contact about the contest and details of their campaign for her show. Michaela's cell phone didn't work in the ER, but she wasn't going to budge from there until she got more information on her aunts' conditions or at least talked to a doctor. Tiffany knew where to find her. If only she would get there soon!

A long, distressing hour passed in the crowded waiting room with no word on her aunts, save that they had sustained injuries in a terrible car accident and were undergoing myriad tests. Beside herself with worry, Michaela had alternated between praying and badgering the ER attendants for updates on her aunts.

She was about to ask the ER nurse for another update when the glass entrance doors slid open and Paolo rushed inside. Michaela's heart ached with relief at the sight of him as his keen black eyes scanned the room for her. Never had she been so happy to see anyone in her entire life! Their eyes met across the room and Michaela could not stop the soft sob that escaped her mouth. Her heart fluttered wildly in her chest as she ran to him.

Paolo's strong arms closed around her in a tight embrace, dismantling her control and unleashing her pent-up anguish. Hot tears ran down her cheeks and her words came out in a jumbled mess. He patted her back and murmured comforting words, encouraging her to talk about the accident. She kept babbling that it was a miracle her two aunts had survived the head-on collision, but they were in bad shape.

"What if they don't make it?" she blurted out before she could stop herself.

"Calm down, *querida.* Don't think like that," he said firmly, rubbing her back. "Your aunts are in good hands at this hospital."

"I can't get past the fact that they could have died," Michaela mumbled, her voice muffled against his chest. She pulled back and stared at the wet splotches on his shirt. "I'm sorry," she said, feeling her face crumble pitifully. "I ruined your shirt with my mascara. I never cry like this."

"It's okay, Maki. I don't give a damn about the shirt." Paolo gently cradled her face in his big, beautiful hands as he slid his thumbs beneath her eyes, wiping away her tears and the remnants of her mascara. He handed her a napkin from the paper bag he held. "Here. Blow," he instructed patiently.

Michaela blotted her eyes and then blew her nose. She took hiccupping breaths to get a grip on her emotions.

"Everything's going to be okay, *nena,*" Paolo soothed, sliding his arm around her waist as he led her toward the exit doors. "I brought you some coffee and a sandwich. Let's go sit on the bench outside. We can talk there while you eat."

Michaela suddenly noticed that everyone in the waiting room was staring at them. "No, I don't want to leave until I speak with a doctor," she whispered, her voice raw.

She had never expected Paolo to show up; his generosity stunned her. Anyone else with a chance to hobnob with the Williams Island elite before his show would not have ditched everything to go to the hospital and be with his competitor—a sneaky competitor who hadn't been playing fair, she thought with a pang of guilt. Gazing into Paolo's eyes, she could not imagine anyone else she would rather be with during a crisis.

"It's just outside the door. I'll let them know you're there." Paolo led her out to a long wooden bench. He unwrapped a prosciutto and mozzarella panini sandwich and handed it to her along with a thermos of hot coffee. "Eat. I'll be right back."

"Thanks." Chefs never ate during a catering event, often going home to eat a bowl of cereal before crashing in bed. Paolo had known that and brought her sustenance. His thoughtfulness made her tear up again as she swallowed a bite of the sandwich.

Michaela gave Paolo an expectant look when he returned shortly. "What did they say? Can I go in to see them?"

"Not yet. Your aunts have already had a CT scan and an MRI. Now they're getting X-rays taken."

"It's so frustrating. I've only been able to get bits and pieces of information since I got here!"

"How did the accident happen?"

"All I know is that the other driver was a teenager. He ran a red light and crashed against the driver's side. Aunt Willow's side. Her vintage Volkswagen beetle was totaled." Terror welled up inside Michaela. "I can't bear to imagine what shape she's in."

"Then don't. No sense in imagining the worst scenario until we have the prognosis."

"You're right." Michaela felt comforted by Paolo's strong, unruffled manner. Earlier he had looked ready to throttle Bernice when she had dared to fondle him. He had not been too happy with Michaela either, as she recalled. But now he was being incredibly supportive when she needed it most, making sure she knew he had her back. It impressed the heck out of her that he could let go of his earlier irritation so easily.

"Where is your family?" Paolo asked quietly.

"My parents are out of town and I can't reach Tiffany. I left her several messages, but she hasn't returned my calls or text messages."

"I'm sure she'll be in touch as soon as she hears your message. It's Friday night. She might be out."

"Yeah, could be. I'll kill her when I see her though! She has a bad habit of forgetting to charge her cell." Michaela took a breath to calm down. No sense in taking her frustration out on Tiffany. She handed Paolo the uneaten half of the sandwich. "Do you want it? It was delicious," she said gratefully, "but I can't eat anymore. I'll bet you haven't had anything to eat all evening."

"Don't worry about me. I'm not hungry."

"How did the meal go tonight?" she asked, changing the subject to distract her from the anguish eating at her.

"I'm sure it went great. I left Gil in charge and then went home to check on Claudia and Mikey before heading over here."

"How are they? I miss them," she admitted in a soft voice.

Paolo grinned proudly. "Mikey is getting big and strong. He smiled for the first time yesterday. Claudia was thrilled. So was I."

"Aw, he must look so adorable smiling. I want to see it." Michaela took Paolo's big hands in hers and squeezed them, drawing strength from him. "Thank you...for everything...the sandwich, coffee, for being here with me," she said, her voice clogging with gratitude. "I hate hospitals."

"Me too," Paolo admitted ruefully. "I don't like the sterile smell and all those machines. It brings back bad memories."

"Oh, I'm sorry." Michaela rested her hand against his jaw.

Paolo smiled at her. "It's okay, *corazón*. I can handle it."

He had never called her his heart and Michaela liked hearing it—almost too much. "We should go inside now," she said, finding her voice after a few moments.

Another hour passed. Paolo and Michaela sat quietly, his arm slung around her shoulders and her head resting against his chest. She was grateful for the solace of his presence. The solid weight of his arm around her shoulders made her feel safe. She had already tried to send him home, claiming she would be fine, but Paolo had adamantly refused to leave, giving her a stubborn look that held no room for negotiations. She was more than thankful for that. She had lied when she said that she would be fine. The only thing keeping her scattered nerves together was having him at her side.

Pressed close to him on the vinyl couch, Michaela marveled

over how Paolo seamlessly separated his business from his personal life. She was deeply touched by everything he had done for her tonight—leaving the party beforehand, bringing her food, staying with her. He had even thought of bringing her his warm-up jacket, which she proudly wore, engulfed in its warmth. She couldn't stop thinking about how he had come through for her in her time of need.

"Is Michaela Willoughby here?"

Michaela's head shot up when she heard her name called out by a harried young doctor entering the waiting area.

"Yes, that's me." Michaela rushed to him. Paolo got up and followed her.

"I'm Dr. Jackson." He shook her hand and then Paolo's. The tall doctor's arresting green eyes had purple shadows underneath. He looked as if he had been on a long rotation without a break.

"How are my aunts?" Michaela asked, her anxiety so acute her heart hurt.

"They're resting now, but they've been through quite an ordeal. Magda sustained a fractured rib and got some glass in her eyes from the windshield, but we flushed it out and her eyes appear to be okay."

"Thank God!"

"Her vital signs are normal now," Dr. Jackson continued. "With adequate rest, she should be fine."

Michaela sucked in a shaky breath. "What about Aunt Willow? Is she going to be okay too?" Serene Aunt Willow was a different story than Aunt Magda. Willow's health was more delicate, even if she exuded peacefulness most of the time. She lived with the deep-rooted sorrow of having lost her beloved Stephen at an early age and she compensated by helping others and seeking happiness in the beauty of nature.

"Willow's condition is a bit more complicated. The sonogram showed that her kidneys are bruised and there was evidence of some internal bleeding. She has a catheter in now until the urine runs clear. Other than that, she has two fractured bones on the left side of her back and two cracked ribs."

"Oh no." Michaela's hopes plummeted. Not dear Willow!

She was sure to be upset over being poked and prodded by machines. She was such a naturalist, she probably felt like a caged animal in the hospital. Paolo's arm slid around her waist, reassuring her with his solid presence. "Are you an orthopedic doctor? How serious is it? I mean, will she have to be in a body cast?"

"I'm an orthopedic trauma surgeon. Willow's broken bones will heal on their own. No need for a cast," he said. "She'll probably have to wear a brace for a while. With proper care, she should make a full recovery. The next twenty-four hours will be crucial to see how her kidneys are doing."

"Can I go in and see them?" Michaela asked Dr. Jackson.

"Yes, but keep it brief. They were given a sedative and might be asleep already. Given your aunts' ages and the shock of the accident, I have recommended that they remain overnight. Tomorrow morning, we'll assess when they can go home."

Just then, Tiffany flew in and landed before them like a leggy flamingo in a hot pink sequin mini dress and silver stiletto sandals. Her long blonde hair was a tangle of curls on bare, tanned shoulders. "What happened, Mic?" Her frightened blue gaze lurched from Michaela to Paolo to Dr. Jackson. "Are my aunts going to be okay?" she asked Dr. Jackson, her voice choked.

Dr. Jackson repeated what he told Michaela.

"Can we see them now, doc?" Tiffany cried, bouncing with nervous tension.

Dr. Jackson straightened his broad shouldered physique as his eyes flicked over Tiffany. On the outside, Tiffany looked like a wild South Beach club hopper, but what he didn't see was the big-hearted person beneath her party girl get-up.

"I'm working as fast as I can," Dr. Jackson said, his voice laced with irony.

"Please take us to see them," Tiffany said, not hiding her impatience.

"Chill, Tiff. Dr. Jackson already said he would," Michaela said wearily. The last thing they needed was for Tiff to get overexcited and annoy the overworked doctor.

"I'll wait here and follow you home when you're ready."

Paolo's tone was so calm and reassuring, Michaela could have kissed him.

"You don't have to wait for me," she said.

Paolo smiled at her. "I'm not going anywhere."

"Thank you." Michaela heaved a sigh of relief. The sincerity in his dark eyes was a balm to her nerves. She did not want him going *anywhere* without her. Even though Tiffany had arrived, Michaela still needed him with her.

Turned out, Dr. Jackson was right. Both aunts were asleep when Michaela and Tiffany checked in on them. It was distressing to see them laid up like that. Aunt Magda, usually so vocal and dynamic, looked defeated on the narrow hospital gurney. Michaela went in to see her first so she could spend more time with Willow, who was in worse shape. Seeing she was sound asleep, Michaela gently kissed her aunt's cool forehead before she left, whispering, "Feel better, Aunt Magda. Tiff and I are pulling for you and we love you."

Tiffany gave her a peck on the other cheek. "Ditto everything Mic said. I love you too."

Aunt Willow, the older of the two, appeared even more crushed than Aunt Magda as Michaela and Tiffany approached her side. Willow's usually rosy complexion looked oyster white and her fine features were drawn. Michaela carefully laid her hand on her aunt's wrinkled one. Sunspots stood out in harsh relief on Aunt Willow's translucent skin, reminding Michaela of all the weekends she had enjoyed with her at the beach.

Michaela bent forward and whispered softly, "Aunt Willow, as soon as you get better we're going to the beach to celebrate. You, me and Tiff, just like old times. We'll stay and play until the sun goes down. Feel better, dear auntie. I love you," she said, choking up.

"Stop that, Mic. She's going to be just fine," Tiffany stated with certainty. Michaela appreciated her sister's attempt to be optimistic, but she had never seen Aunt Willow look so pitiful. The accident had absolutely trounced her. "I'll stay here until they're both settled in a room." Tiffany's eyes suddenly glinted with a look Michaela was all too familiar with. "Maybe that cute Dr. Jackson can arrange for the two of them to share a room."

"If anyone can pull it off, it's you, Tiff," Michaela said wryly.

"But just don't try to railroad him. He looked a bit tired and might be out of sorts."

"This calls for a big dose of honey," Tiffany said, smiling confidently. Her blue eyes clouded with a look of contrition as she touched Michaela's shoulder. "Mic, I'm really sorry my cell was off and you couldn't reach me. Truth is I was on a heavy date tonight."

"So you turned it off not to be disturbed," Michaela surmised.

"Yeah." Looking troubled, Tiffany gave a profound sigh and shrugged in a helpless gesture. "Unfortunately, after everything was said and done, I had to break things off with Javier."

"Who is Javier?"

"He's the tennis pro at Mom's country club." Tiffany grimaced. "It's a long story. I'd rather not get into it now."

"I understand." Michaela vaguely remembered her mom's phone call a while back about Tiffany dating a guy whom Mom had rudely referred to as a wetback wanting a green card. "We need to catch up at some point, Tiff. We're due for a long chat."

"Yep, when things calm down a bit." She looked at Michaela with concern. "Please go home."

"I can't go yet."

"You must. You've had a long day. There's no sense in both of us staying here."

"I don't feel good about leaving."

"Nonsense, you've been here for hours. It isn't fair to Paolo. He is not going to leave unless you do."

"That's true," Michaela said, wavering.

"Don't keep him waiting any longer. They'll be asleep for the rest of the night. I'll call you if anything comes up. I promise."

"Okay." Michaela didn't have the strength to argue anymore. She was exhausted, emotionally and physically spent. "I'll come back in the morning to check on them. At least their conditions seem stable." She draped Paolo's warm-up jacket over Tiffany's shoulders. "You can wear Paolo's jacket while you wait. It's warm and comforting."

"Just like him," Tiffany said with a smile.

Michaela nodded. She handed Tiffany the brown paper bag.

"Here's a thermos of coffee and half of the sandwich that Paolo brought me."

Tiffany's eyes widened. "Mic, I hope you realize that Paolo is a treasure," she said passionately. "Seriously."

"Oh, I do, Tiff. Believe me, I *know* he's a treasure."

Chapter Twenty

True to his word, Paolo was waiting for Michaela when she returned. Concern was etched in his dark eyes as he rose immediately and headed toward her. The full impact of her feelings for Paolo hit her like a tsunami wave. Oh, God, she thought, *I love this man. I've been a fool not to hold on to him.*

Her eyes lovingly studied every detail of his face as he bent toward her with concern. She adored Paolo's strength and generosity, his warm-hearted loyalty to his family, his sense of humor and the way he handled challenges with ease. He was grace under fire in all things, from providing shelter for Claudia and her baby to the pure grit of enduring Bernice's passes earlier without telling her off.

"Are you okay?" His brow creased as he studied her face.

Michaela didn't trust her voice just yet, so she nodded.

He put a strong, supportive arm around her shoulders and gave her a reassuring squeeze before releasing her. "How are your aunts?"

"They are both sleeping. Sorry I took so long."

Paolo rubbed the back of his neck and rolled his shoulders, working out the kinks. "No worries. I told you I wasn't going anywhere."

"I know, and I appreciate it." Michaela gave him a grateful smile. "I wanted to make sure they were settled in their rooms, but Tiffany pushed me out of there. She insisted on staying with them so I could go home and rest a bit. And she promised to call me if anything came up."

"Good. I agree with Tiffany. Rest and then come back. Let's go." He took her elbow and led her out the sliding glass doors toward the parking lot into the warm night air.

"Wait a minute. I'm parked on the other side," Michaela said, trying to slow his progress, but Paolo didn't break stride.

He reached the passenger side of his car and opened the door, paying no heed to what she had just said.

"I'm taking you home." He quietly uttered the statement as a fact. "I'll come back early tomorrow and drive you over so you can pick up your car."

"But..."

"Don't argue for once, Maki. You are tired and have had a rough day. You shouldn't be driving. Now, please, get inside." Paolo helped her into the car and leaned over to buckle her in before going around to the other side. She wondered at the way he was treating her as if she were fragile cargo. Gone was his usual deep-dimpled grin and sexy Latin drawl, replaced by a serious, reflective manner.

The drive to her apartment didn't take long, but emotionally it felt like a lifetime as she reveled in the fact that she loved him. Paolo had generously stayed beside her all evening, bolstering her spirits with his upbeat, comforting presence during one of the loneliest, most anguished moments of her life. He had moved her deeply by showing how much he cared for her. For the first time ever, Michaela felt cherished and protected by a man and the feeling was utterly intoxicating, especially since that man was Paolo.

She didn't want him to leave and come back in the morning. She wanted him to stay with her all night. If he did, they would surely be intimate and the heady anticipation made her jittery with excitement, wondering how it would all turn out. Paolo's lovemaking would lodge him deep inside the private place she had kept shuttered, protected from anything or anyone who might hurt her as badly as Jeff had. Once she let Paolo in, there would be no turning back.

She stole a sidelong glance at his shadowed face as he drove quietly, his attention focused on the highway ahead. When they arrived at her apartment building, he parked the car and turned to face her. His eyes glowed like coals in his taut face. "I did a lot of thinking while I waited for you to come out tonight."

"What did you think about?" she whispered, her throat clogging with emotion.

"You...and me." He dragged a hand roughly through his

thick hair. "Maki, I'm through playing games. As far as I'm concerned, you're mine."

Michaela gazed into Paolo's stunning eyes, touched by the ardent way he had said she was his. She already knew this; there was no denying it now. She reflected on how fleeting life could be, evidenced by her aunts' untimely accident. Dear Aunt Willow was right. *Without the lovin', life ain't worth livin'.*

Taking a deep breath and a leap of faith, she asked, "Will you stay with me tonight—all night?"

"I'd like nothing more," he said gruffly.

"Good, because I don't want you to leave." Sitting beside this gorgeous man, breathing in air laden with honeyed sexual tension, she knew she had made the right decision.

"If I stay with you, *querida*, there will be no getting rid of me," he warned her softly, a slow, sexy smile spreading over his face.

Paolo's passion was so palpable, it saturated the air and robbed her of oxygen. Michaela's heart fluttered riotously and she gulped deep breaths, sucking weighted air into her suddenly constricted lungs as she imagined the deliciousness of complete surrender to him.

"As far as I'm concerned, you're mine," she repeated his words to her with a tender smile.

When they reached her apartment door, Michaela fumbled with the lock, letting out a near-hysterical yelp when it wouldn't budge. Paolo covered her hand with his and with a soft click, the door gave way. She gasped when his warm, engulfing touch sent wild vibrations skittering inside her. She wanted him so badly, she almost flung herself at him right there at the threshold.

Paolo's head dipped and when his lips touched hers, Michaela couldn't help moaning into his mouth, "Make love to me. I want you."

He held her face in his hands as he kissed her. Hot, sweet and spicy, his mouth on hers stoked a fire deep in her belly. She yanked at his shirt with closed fists, pulling him closer as they backed into her apartment until they reached the living room and the back of her thighs hit the sofa's edge. The loud thud of her heartbeat turned into thunderous pounding as

Paolo eased her onto the sofa.

He knelt before her and pulled down the straps of her dress and bra until her breasts lay before him, bare and tilting upward, beckoning his attention. Her body thrummed and pulsated as he kissed the tips, his tongue swirling and circling her nipples until she almost climaxed from the wet assault.

"*Qué bella*," he groaned. His lips never left hers as he lifted her skirt and pulled her panties off. His hands slid up and down the length of her bare legs, petting her with long sweeping caresses. His fingertips lightly circled her slick feminine core until she was writhing helplessly. Michaela panted, her chest heaving and close to bursting, as she wound her fingers in Paolo's satiny hair.

"Take me," she implored, her torso arching upward as she clawed at his shoulders.

"Not here."

Paolo carried her into her bedroom. He flung the comforter aside and tumbled into bed with her, kissing her, caressing her body until she was out of her mind with wanting him. She whimpered when he tore himself away briefly to get a condom from his wallet. He made short work of shedding his clothes and pulling on the condom. His body was big and strong, corded with hard muscle and sinew.

He returned to the bed and Michaela wrapped her arms around his broad back, molding herself beneath his solid weight. Paolo's hungry palms slid under her bottom and hoisted her upward as he knelt between her thighs and slowly eased inside. The cords in his neck strained as he waited until she adjusted to him before he continued. Michaela's pelvis arched upward and she cried out as his deep thrusts touched her sweet spot repeatedly until she was bucking wildly beneath him. Her fingers dug into his buttocks as he rode her with steady thrusts and she was certain she couldn't take any more pleasure without dying. He looked deep in her eyes, his face ravaged with lust and need, and suddenly she shattered with a keening sob.

"Maki," Paolo murmured, his face flushed dark with passion, his eyes profoundly tender. Braced on his elbows, his biceps bulged as he pushed the damp strands from her face. He

203

groaned, "*Te amo*," and then burrowed even deeper inside until he let go with a hoarse roar.

"I love you too." She gazed at him through a blur of tears, happily replete with the feel of him still inside her.

Paolo turned their bodies sideways and spooned her, his strong knees tucked behind hers. One brown hand languidly rested on the pale curve of her hip. Michaela smiled to herself. It was deliciously erotic and she loved it—the possessive way Paolo held her anchored against him.

Michaela was the first to wake up. At six in the morning, she was ravenously hungry, not for food, but for Paolo. Never in her thirty years had she let go so completely. The second time they had made love had not been as rushed and vigorous as the first. In the darkness of her room, they had learned each other's bodies, taking their time. Paolo was tender and passionate, everything she'd ever wanted in a man. Not wanting to awaken him, she tried to carefully extricate herself from his embrace, but his eyes opened and he tightened his hold on her.

"Hey, where are you going, *linda*?" he inquired in a satiated, lazy drawl. Paolo's jet-black hair was mussed up and his jaw line was shadowed with morning bristle. He looked appetizing and wicked hot. He regarded her from beneath a heavy-lidded gaze, silently luring her back to bed.

Michaela's heart swelled with joy as she gazed into his dark, slumberous eyes. "Oh, no you don't. I have to get to the hospital to check on my aunts."

"You're right." He made a rueful face.

"Besides, I'm already sore in places I haven't felt in a long while," she added.

"Oh?" His black eyes glinted with devilish intent. "Perhaps you need a massage."

"Perhaps," she said coyly, running her hands over the light pelt of hair covering his broad chest.

"You're in luck. I have had a lot of experience with massages lately. I'm just the one to deliver it." He rolled her over onto her stomach and gave her two lusty smacks on her unprotected backside.

"Hey! What was that?" she demanded, indignantly rearing up. Rude slaps on her bottom were the last kind of massage she had expected!

"Slavic massage, Irina," he growled in a Russian accent.

A guilty giggle escaped Michaela as Paolo rolled her over and pinned her beneath him, nuzzling her neck with his unshaven jaw. She slapped at his arm. "So you knew all along that it was me massaging you?" she asked incredulously.

Paolo nodded smugly.

"Why didn't you tell me?" she demanded, embarrassed and not pleased at having the tables turned on her.

A delighted grin lit his face. "I was waiting for the right time."

"Ooh, you are impossible!" She pushed at his chest when he burst into hearty chuckles. "And a handful."

"So are you. A delectable one." With a wicked grin, he cupped his hand, reminding her that he had just had a handful of her bottom moments earlier. "I never gave up on you, Maki. After the competition, I fully intended to make you mine."

"We'll probably spend all our time fighting," she stated, trying not to be enticed by those rakish dimples. "I'm a perfectionist and, and..."

"You are bossy, pig-headed, and a little *rabiosa*, but we both know I won't be bossed around," he interjected.

"Yes, well..."

"But we'll work it out. I can't think of anyone else I want to be with."

"I feel the same way," she admitted. "Even though you turn my orderly life upside down, Paolo."

"And you center me, *amor*." He flashed a cocky grin. "Sounds like a great combination to me."

"What about *Miami Spice*?" she said weakly. Michaela had already decided that she would do her utmost to win and then put it up to fate. No more putting work before her private life. There had to be a happy medium. She was through with being alone. She wanted love and marriage...and babies someday. But mostly she wanted Paolo. He had once told her that he hadn't married because he hadn't found a girl who'd put her husband and family first in her life. She wanted to loudly proclaim, "I am that girl!"

"The hell with *Miami Spice*. I want *you*." His eyes flashed black fire as he held her enthralled, waiting for her answer.

"I'm yours, darling." She flung her arms around his neck and kissed his smiling mouth with gusto. "But we have to get going," she said, remembering her aunts' plight.

Michaela swung her legs over the side of the bed and pulled her discarded dress over her head to shield her naked body from Paolo's hungry gaze. Her muscles, some in quite intimate places, felt deliciously sore as she walked out of the bedroom with as much dignity as she could muster. She blushed when she saw her panties flung on the floor beside the sofa, recalling her total abandon. She had been so far gone with desire she had urged Paolo to take her right here on her pristine sofa.

This time Michaela couldn't blame it on champagne. She had been stone cold sober. Well, not really sober. She had been deliriously drunk with wanting him!

Chapter Twenty-One

Mikey was acting extra fussy this morning and had kept Claudia up most of the night. She was anxious for him to fall asleep so she could finally take a nap. She had just finished changing Mikey's diaper and was trying to lull him asleep when she heard the insistent knock on the door. She hoisted her son's squirming little body on her shoulder and headed toward it.

"I'm coming, I'm coming! Did you forget your keys, Paolo?" Claudia demanded, flinging the door open.

Bobby. Claudia blinked. Her mouth fell open and her blood roared in her ears when she saw her husband standing before her. Shivers ran up and down her arms as if she had been caught naked in a blizzard. She couldn't move, couldn't breathe. Her husband had found her and caught her holding their baby. He was going to *kill* her for not telling him about Mikey.

"Bambi," he said quietly.

Claudia's heart skipped a beat at hearing his nickname for her. He stretched out strong arms—arms that had once held her pressed against his heart while he crooned endearments.

"Come here, baby." Bobby's deep voice hit her at her knees, crippling her with the potent urge to run into his arms and never let him go. His startling blue eyes held her immobile—crystal, sapphire ones that made her breath catch in her suddenly constricted throat.

"Bobby, what are you doing here?" she managed to whisper.

Her husband stood before her, long, muscular legs spread, head tilted to one side as he studied her intently. Bobby robbed her of her senses, just like he always had. But he looked different—more mature, tougher. In six months, Bobby had gone from cute guy to imposing man. When she didn't move forward, he dropped his arms and nodded toward Mikey where he rested on Claudia's shoulder, noisily sucking his thumb. He bridged the gap between them in one stride.

"Is that our boy?" he asked.

Bobby's question almost knocked her to the floor. He already *knew* about Mikey? How? When? A million questions raced through her mind, making her fidget and twitch nervously as she stared at him as if he were an apparition. Even though he was acting calm, she could feel the uncoiled tension in his hard body. The unspoken truth about their baby was a massive weight bearing down on her chest, fraying her last nerve.

"Yes," she finally managed. She looked down at the floor and then closed her eyes, willing strength into her heart. She felt unhinged and vulnerable wearing the mauve silk robe that Bobby had given her last Valentine's Day. With a pang, she remembered that he had always loved seeing her in that robe.

Bobby leaned forward and took her chin in his hand, forcing her face upward as he studied her with those damn blue eyes. "Aren't you going to let me in?"

"*Eh...em...bueno.* I guess so," she babbled, edging away. She realized she sounded like an idiot. All she knew was that her legs were wobbling and she was worried she might start hyperventilating.

Bobby followed her into the living room with a loose-limbed gait. His navy polo shirt strained over his shoulders. Well-worn jeans cupped his muscular butt and hard thighs commanding her undivided attention. She took a steadying breath and averted her gaze.

"Let me hold him," he said, settling on her couch.

"Maybe later. He's a little fussy right now," Claudia hedged, sitting across from him.

"I can handle a tiny baby," he said with confidence. Bobby regarded her with a mixture of love and exasperation.

Why was he acting so composed, so in control of his emotions? Claudia had expected him to be furious that she had not told him she was pregnant. But he was acting unruffled, like nothing was wrong. Who had told him? Paolo?

Her brother, the snitch, had run out last night after throwing a sandwich and a thermos in a bag, making a ruckus about Maki needing him. He had told Claudia he would be gone most of the night. Good, because she was so furious with him for spilling the news about Mikey without giving her the chance to tell her husband first, she didn't know what she would do to Paolo if he suddenly walked through the door.

Claudia reluctantly handed Mikey to Bobby and was amazed when Mikey didn't fuss. Bobby rested him on his knees, holding Mikey's little body in his large hands as he closely looked at his son.

"Hey, son, looks like your *mamá* has been feeding you well." Bobby smiled at Claudia and her heart flipped. "He looks just like me. Same nose. Same eyes."

"He has *my* eyes," Claudia countered, her gumption surfacing to bolster her.

"No, he doesn't, Bambi. You have brown eyes and our son's eyes are blue."

"All babies have blue eyes. They might turn dark later—"

"His won't. They'll be as blue as mine," he stated with smug certainty.

"Well, Mikey has my chin," she retorted.

"That he does." Bobby tapped the tiny cleft in Claudia's chin. "And it's as stubborn as ever."

After a loaded pause, Claudia uttered the burning question lodged in her throat. "How did you know about him? Who told you?"

"Your neighbor. Señora Fuentes."

Claudia was stunned, but he could not possibly be making it up. How else would he know her neighbor's name? "Señora Fuentes? When did she tell you?" she demanded.

"The day you finally returned my calls, but didn't leave a message. When I called you back, Señora Fuentes answered and said you were taking a bath. That's when she lit into me." He shook his head wryly.

"Serves you right!"

"Man, she gave me hell about you having to raise your baby alone and at such a young age. When I told her I had no idea you were even pregnant and that I would never have allowed you to go through it alone, she finally believed me and gave me your address."

"Oh, God," Claudia groaned. "She should have never done that!" Paolo had warned her that Señora Fuentes was a busybody, but Claudia loved her all the same. The kind widow had been like a surrogate mother to her and she was fun company.

"I'm glad she did." Bobby gave her a reproachful look. "At least somebody did the mature thing."

"You think *you* did the mature thing?" Claudia's chin rose defiantly. "I did try calling you, remember? When you didn't pick up, I texted you the next day."

"I was already on a flight over. I figured I'd come see you before you tried to put more barriers between us."

"I had a good reason to put up those barriers." Past resentment mushroomed inside her. "You thought you had the perfect solution to go on your newest adventure—just send the little wifey back to Buenos Aires. As you can see, I never left," she said triumphantly.

"Damn it, you led me to believe you were going back." Bobby's face registered shock, then disapproval.

"No, I didn't," she retorted. "I never agreed to anything."

"I would have never given up trying to reach you if I hadn't thought you were safe with your family." Bobby's jaw worked as he visibly strove to keep cool. "No wonder you wouldn't return my calls. You didn't want me to know where you were."

"That's right."

"Claudia," he began in a strained tone. "We both know it wasn't an *adventure*. I worked damn hard in those oil sands. And I did it only to make good money for us."

"I told you it was over if you left me! But you left anyway," she stubbornly persisted.

Bobby's clear blue eyes turned turbulent. "We're married. I took that vow to mean forever," he stated evenly. "Why didn't you let me know when you found out you were pregnant?"

"I didn't want you to come back to me because of Mikey," she said, her voice rising. "Which is exactly what you did."

"I told you I was coming back," he replied angrily. "I was always going to come back to you when the six months were up.

Señora Fuentes saved me from buying a ticket to Argentina. Remind me to thank her one day." Taking a deep breath, he looked at the ceiling and then back at Claudia as if trying to summon divine patience. He glanced down at his son. "You named him Mikey?"

"His full name is Michael Robert Woodbridge." She fought the hot tears that burned the back of her eyelids.

Bobby nodded. "I like it."

Claudia's heart ached as she watched father and son, alike in many ways, bonding naturally. "Bobby." She paused and swallowed hard against the clogging, emotional knot in her throat. "Did Señora Fuentes tell you about the horrible problems your parents are causing?"

"No." Bobby's body stiffened and his eyes narrowed into sharp blue lasers. "What problems are they causing?"

By the time Claudia finished telling Bobby about his parents and their cutthroat lawyer, Max Weintraub, Bobby's self-control dissolved. His jaw clenched and unclenched as a play of fierce emotions crossed his face—shock, fury, indignation.

"I wish you had told me about it sooner. You wouldn't have had to deal with all their crap," he said, his tight voice laced with disgust. "Don't worry, Bambi. To hell with their lawyer and to hell with them. Now that I'm back, I'll take care of this. They won't mess with us again."

The doorbell rang, startling Claudia and waking up Mikey who had just nodded off in Bobby's arms.

"Who's that?" Bobby asked, glancing at the door impatiently. "Paolo?"

"I don't think so unless he forgot his keys." Claudia hesitated, not moving a muscle to answer the door. She wanted this time alone with Bobby. The last thing they needed was an interruption.

"Want me to get it?"

"No, I will."

Claudia opened the door and almost shut it again when she saw the cute and friendly neighbor she had met a week ago while sunbathing by the pool. Juan Ramirez was a senior at the University of Miami, studying business. They had struck up a pleasant conversation in Spanish when he had gone down for a study break. With a pang of regret, Claudia realized she should have never told him she was staying with Paolo. Juan had misread her friendliness and he'd gotten the wrong idea. Claudia was so starved for friends, she had been thrilled to find someone young and Spanish-speaking in Paolo's building.

Juan held out a white paper bag. "*Hola*, have you eaten yet? I brought you a toasted bagel with cream cheese. Sesame, your favorite. And the crazy Brazilian comedy I was telling you about. We can discuss it tonight over Chinese if you like," he said, blushing.

"Thanks, Juan. That was kind of you. But tonight's going to be impossible." Claudia glanced over her shoulder with trepidation. She worried about the impression they were giving Bobby, chatting as if they were dating. She had only met Juan a week ago and she had certainly done nothing to encourage him. Now the love struck kid was bringing her breakfast and a movie to watch over Chinese food!

Juan followed her uneasy gaze. "Oh, sorry. I didn't know you have company."

Bobby rose from the sofa and ambled to the door, every muscle in his six foot two build possessively flexed as he gave Juan a measured look. "I'm not company. I'm Claudia's husband." He lifted Mikey. "And this is our son."

Poor Juan turned beet red. "Oh. Nice to meet you. I'm Juan Ramirez. Uh, Paolo's neighbor." He swayed on unsteady feet before Bobby's ferocious, territorial stare, clutching the take-out bag to his chest as if it were a life vest. "I guess I'd better get going."

"You guessed right," Bobby said.

"*Adiós*, Juan. I'll tell Paolo you stopped by. Again, that was very nice of you," she said, trying to smooth things over for Juan's sake—and hers. Bobby looked incensed.

"You shouldn't have been rude to him," Claudia said when Juan left. "Juan is a friend, nothing else."

"He's a lovesick kid," Bobby said bluntly, "and you shouldn't be encouraging him."

You are a jealous man, Claudia thought with a glimmer of satisfaction. "I don't encourage him. Juan is a really nice guy and we're friends, that's all. He is friendly with Paolo, too, as are all of our neighbors."

"Where is your suitcase?" Bobby asked, changing the subject. Claudia followed his gaze as he glanced around Paolo's apartment that was cluttered with baby items.

"It's in the closet. Why?"

The fevered glint in Bobby's blue eyes held her captive. "We need some time alone to reconnect. I've booked us a suite at the Mandarin where these 'friendly' neighbors can leave us the hell alone."

Claudia stared at him in surprise. The Mandarin Oriental was one of the coolest hotels in Miami where the rich and famous hung out.

"Why don't you ask Señora Fuentes to watch Mikey for a couple of hours?" he suggested.

Nothing would have pleased her more than time alone with her estranged husband. "I wish I could," Claudia lamented. "But I can't just leave Mikey like that. I'm nursing him and in a few hours he's going to wake up ravenous for his next feeding."

Bobby's gaze dipped to his wife's milk-engorged breasts. "No wonder," he murmured, the corners of his mouth turning upward. "Looks like there's plenty of milk."

"There is. Mikey is thriving," she said proudly. She hid a smile. Bobby was a breast man and the look in his eyes said he loved how her full breasts were nearly doubled in size.

With a wry shake of his head, Bobby tore his gaze away from Claudia's bosom. "Where do you and Mikey sleep?"

"In Paolo's room," Claudia said with a guilty pang. "I feel bad about it, but Paolo still insists on sleeping on the couch. I'm afraid Mikey and I have turned his bachelor pad into a nursery."

"I'm going to find us a big, comfortable apartment." Bobby eyed her and then said cautiously, "There's something else you should know. And before you start getting upset, I want you to listen to reason."

Every fine hair on her body stood on end. "What are you talking about?" she asked in a shaky voice.

Bobby exhaled deeply. "My shift is over. I will be here for six months." He paused. "Then I have to leave again."

"What? You are leaving *again*?" Claudia's stomach took a nosedive when Bobby nodded affirmatively. "No!" she almost shrieked, but she stopped before she frightened Mikey.

Holding her gaze steadily, Bobby said, "I signed on again before I knew about Mikey. I was planning on making as much money as I could for a year and then I would never go away again."

"Bobby, how could you?" Shock and despair tore at Claudia's insides and she couldn't stand to look at her husband. She suddenly hated him. They had a baby now and he was planning to leave again!

Bobby reached out to touch her, but Claudia recoiled instantly. "Stop it, Bambi. You gotta understand. I'm doing it for us...for our son." His earnest blue eyes searched her face, seeking to convince her. "I need to make sure I can provide for Mikey. One more six-month term and then no more." He held his right hand up. "I promise."

A feeling of deceit crept into Claudia's heart as she stared at her prodigal husband. Her worst fear had come true—Bobby still had wanderlust. He was so addicted to travel and adventures that nothing would make him change, not even their baby, and certainly not her!

She snatched Mikey from his arms and held on to her baby for dear life. "Either get another job and stay with us or get out of our lives!" she cried, fury roiling inside her until she thought her skin would break out in angry red hives. Mikey woke up and started to wail. "Look, now Mikey is upset! I mean it, Bobby. Next time you won't find us so easily."

Chapter Twenty-Two

Michaela found Tiffany at the first floor lobby of the hospital leaning against a vending machine, munching on a granola bar and sipping coffee. Her mass of golden curls had gone awry, but she still looked sexy in her hot pink mini and silver stiletto sandals. The addition of Paolo's oversized, gray warm-up jacket slung over her bare shoulders made her little sister look like she was on the walk of shame.

"Well, well, well. Look who's all bright-eyed and bushy-tailed," Tiffany drawled, giving Michaela a sassy once-over. "Did you have a good night's *rest*, Mic?" Her question oozed innuendo. She glanced at her watch. "Hmm...ten o'clock. How was breakfast in bed?"

"Hush up." Michaela grinned. "How are Willow and Magda doing?"

"No trace of blood in Aunt Willow's urine, so they took the catheter out. They both seem to be on the mend."

Michaela breathed a sigh of relief. "Oh, good."

"Everything is under control, as I told you when I called this morning. Remember?" Tiffany raised an eyebrow and gave Michaela an expectant look. "Don't change the subject on me. I heard your Latin lover's sultry voice in the background."

"Let's just say everything worked out fine between us," Michaela said, downplaying the wonderful night she and Paolo had shared. It was so new and so special she wanted to treasure it just for herself.

"I'll say. You're glowing like a candle." Tiffany flashed a knowing grin. "Even if you probably didn't get much sleep last night—"

"Back to our aunts," Michaela said, deftly changing the subject before Tiffany started to dig for details. "Were you able to get them into the same room?"

"Yes, they're together."

"Great! I see you haven't lost your touch," Michaela observed dryly. "That was nice of Dr. Jackson to arrange it."

Tiffany gave her a disgruntled look. "Well...Dr. Jackson didn't exactly agree to help. He wasn't very nice to me," she confided, pushing long curls away from her flushed face.

Michaela wondered at Tiffany's reaction. "What do you mean?" She followed Tiffany to the elevator and waited while Tiff punched the button.

"He was too grouchy to even listen to me. For some reason, I annoy him," Tiffany replied with a mystified look.

"You? Impossible." Michaela stifled a smile. Dr. Jackson had to be a real stiff not to be won over by Tiffany. "Maybe he's married," she volunteered when the elevator doors opened and they got in.

"Nope. He's single. Aunt Magda already asked him. She also found out his first name is Troy and that he's thirty-two years old."

"Troy Jackson. Sounds like a football player's name. Maybe he played in college," Michaela speculated.

"He sure has the body for it," Tiffany said grudgingly.

Michaela smiled. "Aunt Magda can't be that bad off if she's already scouting for suitors."

"I know." Tiffany yawned and tapped her mouth with the palm of her hand. "Back to the grouch—"

"You mean Dr. Jackson?" They got out on the third floor and Michaela followed Tiffany down a long corridor.

"Yeah. When I politely asked him if he would arrange for Willow and Magda to share a room, he lectured me. He said, 'This is a hospital, not a hotel, Miss Willoughby'. Can you believe how rude he was?"

Michaela patted her shoulder. "Don't take it personally. I'm sure he was just exhausted from a long shift."

Tiffany shrugged as if she didn't care. "Whatever. Anyway, by the time Dr. Killjoy's shift was over, they still didn't have two rooms for them. So I sidled up to Dr. Mumford, the new doctor who came on duty, and asked if he could help me. What a great guy! He was more than willing to help, and *voila*, Aunt Magda and Aunt Willow are now roomies," she said with a victorious grin.

"Are they getting along?" Michaela asked cautiously.

"I think Magda is beginning to get on Willow's nerves. She's itching to get out of there."

When they reached Room 326, Tiffany stopped in front of it. "They're in this room. Mom and Dad are in there too." She gave Michaela an odd look and lowered her voice to a confidential whisper. "You'll never guess where Mom and Dad were this week. It wasn't a lawyers' conference at all."

"Where were they?" Michaela whispered back, wondering why Tiffany was acting as if she had something scandalous to share.

Tiffany's blue eyes shined with the fun of revealing juicy news. "They spent the weekend at a marriage retreat—together!"

"*Really?* But they're divorced. I thought Dad had a new girlfriend."

"Me too." Tiffany made a comical face. "Go figure."

The atmosphere in the patients' room was pleasant when Michaela and Tiffany entered. Despite the dire circumstances of their hospital visit, her parents looked relaxed and amiable with each other, which really surprised Michaela.

She kissed her aunts hello and inquired how they were doing.

"I'm just dying to get out of here," Aunt Magda said. "Don't worry, Willow, I'll tend your shop till you're released."

"Thanks, Magda, but I told Jamie to put a sign on the window explaining I would reopen next week." Aunt Willow gave her a wan smile. "It's not as if I have tons of customers coming in."

Seeing how pale and forlorn Aunt Willow looked huddled beneath two blankets on the hospital bed, Michaela rushed to her side. "Is there anything I can do to make you more comfortable? Do you want some juice or a cup of tea?"

"No, dear, I'm just happy you're all here with me," Aunt Willow replied. Her face looked drawn and ashen in the stark fluorescent light.

"I know what would make her feel better, but it's not allowed in the hospital," Aunt Magda teased. "While you were sleeping, I found Manny's number and told him that we're here.

His shift ends at five today. Maybe your firefighter will come rescue you through the window."

"Maybe," Aunt Willow replied coolly.

"Magda, stop baiting Willow. Dr. Mumford went out of his way to arrange for the two of you to share this room," Mom reminded her.

"I wasn't baiting her. I wish I had a boyfriend like Willow," Aunt Magda replied.

Michaela wondered if it was such a good idea for Willow to be holed up with Magda, who seemed to have energy to spare this morning, in spite of her fractured ribs.

"Mom, Dad. You two look great," Michaela said, turning the attention away from Willow, so her aunt could relax.

"Thanks. I just wish we'd been here with you last night during the long ordeal," Dad said gruffly.

"Don't worry. Mic was not alone. She was *very* well-accompanied last night." Tiffany wiggled her eyebrows suggestively.

"Oh? By whom?" Aunt Magda asked, perking up. "A man?"

"A hot, manly one," Tiffany confirmed. "Unfortunately for her show, Michaela has stepped over into enemy territory."

"What do you mean?" Dad asked, looking confused.

"What do you think she means?" Mom's face registered shock. "Tell me you didn't, Michaela."

"She sure did! Paolo Santos didn't budge from Mic's side the whole time she was at the hospital waiting to find out how the aunties were doing." Tiffany paused and made a production of sighing happily, as she put her clutched hands over her heart. "And then he took her home," she said in a wistful voice.

"To his place?" Aunt Magda asked eagerly.

Tiffany gave Michaela a sidelong glance. "I don't know. Why don't you tell us, Mic?"

Michaela face flamed as all eyes turned to stare at her with intense curiosity. "It's nobody's business but mine," she said, drawing chuckles from everyone but her parents.

"Aren't you worried he might be trying to soften the enemy?" Mom asked in her usual brash way. "The stakes are too high for you to be naïve about him."

"Paolo sincerely wanted to be there for me during a time of crisis. He's not trying to sabotage my chances," Michaela said, her feelings wounded and insulted that her own mother would insinuate such a mean thing. "You don't know him. Paolo is a wonderful, decent man." She refrained from adding, *"And I love him."*

"Ooh! Look at that dreamy look on Mic's face," Tiffany squealed. "I want somma dat, sistah."

"I quite agree. Paolo Santos is dreamy," Aunt Willow said, beaming.

"You're defending him too, Willow?" Dad stared at all of them and shook his head in exasperation. "*Women.* I'll never understand you," he muttered as if they were an alien race. "We have been trying to outdo that guy for weeks and now all of you are practically drooling over the fellow."

Poor Dad, between his ex-wife, her two sisters, and his two daughters, he was constantly surrounded by women and he still could not figure them out.

"*I'm* not defending him, Lawrence," Sylvia said, giving her ex-husband a supportive look. She turned to her oldest daughter with a cautionary glance. "Michaela, maybe you should step back and assess the error of letting your guard down only a week before the showdown. Or have you given up your goal to win?" she challenged.

Michaela felt heat rise from the back of her neck, up her ears and over her cheeks, surely staining them scarlet. "Of course not! I want to win just as much as Paolo does, but I have come to realize that I want other things too."

"Such as?" Sylvia's keen eyes were upon her daughter like a hawk watching her baby take the first flight.

"Love, laughter, companionship. I want all those things and more!" Michaela said fervently.

"Hear, hear!" Aunt Magda cried. "We also want those things for you. And for Tiffany too!" Her blue eyes glinted merrily. "Although, from the way Tiffany worked the floor in that little sequined mini this morning, I have a feeling she might be dating a doctor soon."

Two vigorous knocks on the door silenced their laughter as all eyes turned to watch Dr. Jackson enter, followed by a matronly, gray-haired nurse. He strode into the room, looking far more refreshed than he had last night. His wavy, dark hair was brushed back from a square-jawed face that held a straight, high-bridged nose above a firm mouth. Penetrating jade eyes surveyed the room and lit on Tiffany briefly. He nodded and then turned his attention to her two aunts.

From the corner of her eye, Michaela caught Tiffany's frosty reaction to Dr. Jackson's arrival. Tiffany had turned away from him, slouched slightly in a blasé pose and was twirling a blonde lock, not paying one bit of attention to the good-looking doctor.

"Good morning. Would everyone please clear the room? I'd like to examine the patients," he said briskly.

Aunt Magda said, "Can you check me first, Dr. Troy? I'm ready to leave."

Dr. Jackson's stern face relaxed into a kind smile. "Of course." He turned to Willow. "I'll be with you shortly, Mrs. Reese, as soon as I examine your sister." The nurse pulled the privacy curtain dividing the two patients.

"Gee, who would have thought he knows how to smile," Tiffany muttered in a voice loud enough for all to hear as she exited the room with her family.

Even though he had barely slept last night, Paolo felt fantastic. As soon as he got home and took a hot shower, he would shoo Claudia to the mall so she could have an outing. He couldn't wait to spend the morning playing with his little nephew. Poor Mikey; the little tyke needed quality time with his Tio Paolo.

But when he turned the key in the lock of his apartment door, he found Claudia still dressed in her robe, complaining to Señora Fuentes, her eyes red from crying.

"Claudia! *¿Qué pasa?*" He looked from his teary sister to the distraught Señora Fuentes and a chill ran up his spine. "Is Mikey all right?"

"*Sí*, your nephew is fine. But his father *es un desgraciado!*" the meddlesome widow said tartly.

Paolo's eyebrows shot up. She had just called Bobby a jerk. "Tell me what happened." He closed the distance between them with hurried strides.

"Bobby just left," Claudia said, between hiccupping sobs.

"Why do you look so upset? Did he hurt you?" Paolo demanded, hot blood rising to his head. "I'll kill him if he did."

Señora Fuentes sniffed. "He didn't hurt her physically, but he hurt her feelings. Very much! *Pobrecita,*" she clucked, calling Claudia a poor little thing.

Paolo clutched his head and groaned as he listened to Señora Fuentes relay what Claudia had told her. He heaved a profound sigh when she finished. "Señora Fuentes, may I have some time alone with Claudia?"

"*Sí*, of course," the widow agreed instantly. "Remember I'm just down the hall if you need me. I convinced Claudia to leave a bottle of her pumped milk in the refrigerator so she can go out for a little while to clear her head." She waved a hand at Paolo. "I just thought I'd warn you so you don't use it to make a cappuccino," she said, cracking up at her corny joke as she closed the door behind her.

Forty minutes later, someone rang the doorbell. As soon as Paolo answered the door, Claudia's husband strode in like a man on a mission.

"What are you doing here?" Bobby demanded sharply, blue eyes blazing with jealousy as he looked Paolo up and down.

Paolo sat back down at the kitchen table where he had been reading the paper while Claudia fed Mikey. "I'm Paolo Santos, Claudia's brother. I live here. Who are you?" Paolo asked, even though he knew it was Bobby from the picture Claudia had shown him of her husband.

"I'm Claudia's husband. Where is she?"

Claudia emerged from the bedroom with Mikey in her arms. "Lower your voice, Bobby. I was just feeding Mikey. Why did you come back?" she asked disdainfully, making no effort to hide her bad mood.

Paolo noticed how Bobby's face softened the minute he saw Claudia holding his son, even though she was less than welcoming.

"I'll burp him," Bobby said, ignoring her rude question. He took Mikey from her arms before she could refuse.

Claudia looked up at the ceiling with a pained expression.

221

"You're doing it all wrong. Sit him on your lap and lean him forward as you pat him between his shoulder blades," she instructed Bobby in a haughty tone.

Paolo almost burst out laughing when he saw the look on Bobby's face. Clearly, Claudia's husband did not appreciate being treated as a fool by his wife in front of her big brother.

When Mikey burped up the bubble that was making him fret, Bobby handed him to Paolo. "Can you watch him for a couple of hours?"

"Of course." Paolo paid no attention to Claudia's vehement shake of her head.

When Bobby turned his attention to Claudia, his blue eyes burned with loving determination. "Come with me. The Mandarin is a beautiful hotel. You'll like it. We need to talk."

"I am not going anywhere with you, no matter how beautiful the hotel is! You said enough this morning," Claudia retorted, narrowing her eyes at Bobby.

"Come on, Bambi. Don't be stubborn," Bobby cajoled, even though he looked close to losing his patience.

"Yeah, Bambi, don't be stubborn," Paolo repeated, chuckling privately at Bobby's name for her. She really did look like Bambi, but that was beside the point. Paolo was getting sick and tired of their lack of communication. Six months had gone by and neither one had spoken to the other during that time—mostly due to Claudia's stubbornness. She had kept Mikey a secret from Bobby. That was not right. Paolo would be damned if he let Bobby leave before they worked things out. Enough was enough! Bobby had come back to work things out with his wife. Claudia was a married woman and a mother now. It was time to start acting like a grown woman instead of a spoiled brat.

"Claudia, go with your husband and work things out," Paolo ordered, giving her a look that left no room for arguments.

"I don't want to leave Mikey."

"Mikey will be fine with me. I can feed him as well as anyone. There is milk in the refrigerator. Señora Fuentes saw to that." He winked. "I promise not to make cappuccinos while you're gone. Relax and take your time. You owe it to your husband to listen to what he has to say," Paolo said firmly.

"Now quit stalling and go!"

Claudia braced her fists on her hips and faced Paolo belligerently. "Just whose side are you on anyway?"

Looking from Bobby's blistering blue eyes to Claudia's blazing black ones, Paolo drew a long-suffering breath. "Mikey's," he said, kissing his little nephew's forehead.

Chapter Twenty-Three

Claudia could not and would not look at Bobby. She was too furious. Her stomach churned as she rode next to him in the silent car. Neither said a word until they arrived at the hotel.

Bobby grabbed her hand and tugged her along through the hotel lobby. His big hand held hers firmly during the elevator ride—as if he never wanted to let her go. When they reached the suite, he slid the hotel card key in the door and turned to stare at Claudia with intense blue eyes. "I love you and I am not going to risk losing you over a damn job." He opened the door and led her inside.

Claudia gasped when they entered and she saw Bobby's parents seated on the sofa in the sitting area separate from the bedroom.

"What the *hell* are you doing here?" Bobby demanded, his face livid. "Why have you been tormenting my wife?"

Claudia's eyes bugged out at his confrontational tone, but he had every reason to be furious. As soon as the Woodbridges had found out their son had eloped with a Latina, they had disowned him without bothering to meet her and then had tried to force Bobby to get an annulment. When he had refused, his parents had cut him out of their lives. After that, Bobby cut off all ties with them, too, even refusing to show Claudia their picture or talk about them. Small miracle, their pit bull lawyer wasn't there, Claudia thought, remembering how much Bobby disliked him.

"Don't be insolent," his father thundered, looking like a volcano about to erupt. Mr. Woodbridge's thick gray hair was cropped short and framed a scowling, deeply tanned face. Piercing blue eyes zeroed in on his son. "Your mother and I are here to talk some sense into you," he said, ignoring Claudia.

Bobby bristled with resentment. "Don't dismiss my wife, the mother of my son. Claudia is the love of my life." He wrapped a protective arm around her slouched shoulders. "When you mess with her, you mess with me."

It was intoxicating to witness her strong husband stand up to his intimidating parents. Beside him, Claudia felt sheltered, treasured—and empowered. Bobby's declaration of love nearly moved her to tears and gave her back her gumption. She was not about to break down in front of his parents. She straightened to her full five feet seven inches and looked his parents square in the eyes—first Mr. Woodbridge and then Mrs. Woodbridge.

"Bobby is the love of my life too," Claudia said in a strong, clear voice.

Mrs. Woodbridge rose to stand beside her husband. Claudia noticed the woman's perfectly manicured hands were trembling. "If you love your wife so much, why did you leave her alone when she was pregnant?" she asked Bobby, disapproval turning her lips downward. "Dad and I thought you had decided to end the marriage when we heard you disappeared."

"I did not disappear! I went away to earn money fast, since you and Dad are blocking my inheritance from Poppa," Bobby retorted, referring to his deceased grandfather's trust that his parents controlled until he turned thirty-five.

"We're doing it to protect you, son," Mr. Woodbridge said in an even tone. "How do you know your wife is not a gold digger? The Woodbridge name spells money."

"Claudia is *not* a gold digger," Bobby countered, the veins in his neck bulging with wrath.

"Then why did she trap you into marriage by getting pregnant?" Mrs. Woodbridge challenged.

"¡*Por Dios!* I got pregnant *after* we were married!" Claudia cried, fury exploding inside her like a stick of dynamite. "I don't come from a humble family, Mrs. Woodbridge. I do not need or want your money. I married Bobby because I love him! In Argentina, the name Woodbridge means *puente de madera*—a bridge made of wood. It means nothing more. I didn't know Bobby was wealthy when I fell in love with him."

"Apologize to Claudia right now or I'll never set foot in your house again. I mean it," Bobby warned, giving them a baleful look.

Mr. Woodbridge backed down. "All right, there's no sense in us killing each other with accusations. We're here to make peace, not to fight with you."

"Then why were you trying to take our baby away?" Claudia asked, blinking back her stinging tears.

"We were worried that our grandson was in jeopardy," Mrs. Woodbridge said.

"What do you mean?" Claudia asked.

"We found out that the Cuban lady who babysits your son is a dangerous political fanatic."

"A dangerous political fanatic—Señora Fuentes?" Claudia repeated incredulously. "That's impossible. She has been like a mother to me since I arrived in Miami."

"Which is more than she can say for you, Mother," Bobby said with biting sarcasm.

"That may be the case, but the Cuban lady is constantly stirring things up with subversive letters to the *Miami Herald!*" Mrs. Woodbridge replied, looking upset.

"Oh, come on! That is ridiculous. Señora Fuentes is a good woman," Bobby said.

"You know her?" Mrs. Woodbridge's Botoxed eyes widened as she stared at him, flabbergasted.

"Of course. Who do you think kicked my ass and got me down here yesterday? It was Señora Fuentes!" Bobby replied angrily. "Did you run a background check on the poor woman?" His eyes blazed with outrage. "And who found me? A private eye? Or was it Max Weintraub and his viperous cronies?"

"Never mind," Mr. Woodbridge blustered with a guilty look. "Your mother and I are here because we want to be a part of our grandson's life."

"You certainly have a weird way of going about it," Claudia observed, sick at heart that she and Mikey had come between Bobby and his parents. As their only son, Bobby had to feel disheartened over the rift between them, but he had never said so, probably to keep Claudia from feeling like the culprit. It was all so unnecessary. Why couldn't the Woodbridges just be normal, loving parents? She wanted Mikey to have grandparents to love and spoil him just as hers had done when she was growing up.

Mrs. Woodbridge looked close to tears as she gave a mournful sigh. She reached out to touch Claudia's hand. "It's obvious our son loves you or he wouldn't be defending you so fiercely. Bobby is our only son and we don't want to lose him."

"Why would you worry about that?" Claudia took Mrs. Woodbridge's icy hand in hers and looked into her tear-blurred eyes. "I would like nothing better than for all of us to get along, Mrs. Woodbridge. My family in Argentina is very close and loving. That is what I am used to. I would have loved to share Mikey with you. You are his grandmother. I miss my mother so much it hurts," Claudia said, tears wetting her face.

"I'm sorry, Claudia." Mrs. Woodbridge instantly closed the space between them and pulled Claudia into her skinny arms. She exhaled a shuddering breath as she released her. "My husband and I did a bad thing by judging you so wrongfully. Please forgive us." Genuinely distraught and defeated, her eyes welled up as she turned to Bobby. "Dad and I miss you, honey! Please, please forgive us," she pleaded. "Can we put all this behind us and start anew?"

"I forgive you," Claudia said, wanting Bobby to make peace with his parents. She gave him a look filled with love and encouragement. In spite of all the mean things they had done, she felt sorry for his parents.

Bobby exhaled his breath with a loud gust of exasperation. "If Claudia is big enough to forgive you after the hell you've put her through, I suppose I can do the same," he said after a long, awkward pause.

"Thank you!" Mrs. Woodbridge pulled Bobby's rigid body close to hers in a tight hug, her jeweled hands running up and down her son's back. Claudia's heart clenched at the sight of Bobby towering over his petite mother, all brawn and muscles, allowing her to pet him as if he were her prodigal son come back to her.

Mr. Woodbridge cleared his throat forcefully. "I guess we'd better get going and leave the young folks alone."

"Yes, please go. We can hash this out later. My wife and I need some private time. We have celebrating to do," Bobby said,

Sophia Knightly

nodding to a bottle of champagne chilling in an ice bucket.

"I understand." Mrs. Woodbridge smiled. She grabbed her Chanel bag and followed her husband out the door. "Call us when you're ready to talk."

Alone at last, Bobby pulled Claudia in his arms and held her tightly against his broad chest. Beneath her ear, his heart pounded like a locomotive. "I am never leaving you again."

She pulled back and searched his striking blue eyes. "You promise?"

"Yes. I am going to get out of the contract." He pulled her in for a ravenous kiss.

When she came up for air, Claudia asked, "What about the yacht chartering business?"

"We can't do that anymore. A yacht is no place for a newborn," he said decisively. "I made enough money for us to find a nice place to live and get settled in with Mikey. Then we can talk about our next business venture." He hugged her tightly. "Whatever we decide, we'll do it as a team. No more separation."

Claudia let out a joyous whoop and threw her arms around his strong neck. She hopped up and wrapped her legs around his lean waist, clutching his neck eagerly. Bobby's hands supported her hips as he headed to the bedroom, lavishing kisses all over her face and neck.

"Hurry! We only have a little time left before your greedy son will be howling for milk."

"Bambi, we have a lifetime of loving ahead of us," Bobby vowed, his voice rough-edged with need as he deposited her on the bed.

Claudia pulled her white tank top over her head and unclasped her bra, releasing her breasts to his ardent gaze. "Come, *mi amor.*" She crooked her finger at him with a sultry smile. "Let's start now..."

Bobby did not need more encouragement. In a flash, he was on her like a starved man.

"It's my turn with Aunt Willow," Tiffany declared, flouncing into Willow's new private room in the early afternoon with two large shopping bags. "No fair, Mic. You've had her all day while I've been with Aunt Magda."

"How is she?" Michaela asked. Dr. Jackson had released Magda in the morning, but he wanted to keep Willow in the hospital until her blood pressure returned to normal because it was still very low.

"She was in good spirits and even went shopping with me," Tiffany said.

"Sounds like Magda is back to normal," Aunt Willow said. "I hope she stays home tonight and rests."

"I think she will. She finally agreed to spend the night at Mom's," Tiffany said.

"Good to hear it." Aunt Willow looked vastly relieved. "Now that you're here, Tiffany, maybe we should discuss Michaela's show."

Tiffany brought them up to date on everything, including the number of guys who were lined up with free tickets for *The Pleasure Palate*. "So, everything's pretty much set," Tiffany said. "The only thing missing is confirmation that our contestant will be there."

"Oh dear, I need to email my final choice," Aunt Willow fretted. "I had planned on doing it last night after getting home, but I ended up here instead."

"Please don't worry about my show, Aunt Willow. You just concentrate on feeling better." The last thing Michaela wanted was for her ailing aunt to have worries while laid up in the hospital.

"I can get in touch with the contestant. What's his name?" Tiffany asked.

"Hugo St. Paul. His email is hurlyburly@gmail.com," Aunt Willow said.

Michaela didn't like the sound of it. "Really? That's kind of odd."

"What does hurly burly mean?" Tiffany asked.

"Hurly burly means a lot of commotion. But Hugo may be playing around with it because he claims he is burly," Aunt Willow replied.

"I guess we'll find out when he shows up." Michaela turned her attention to the shopping bags. "What did you bring, Tiff?"

"Reinforcements for our auntie," Tiffany said gaily. Her ability to bring cheer into any situation pleased Michaela, and Willow too, from the delighted look on her aunt's face.

Michaela sat beside Willow in an armchair by the window watching Tiffany unload everything and run around the room decorating. By the time she finished, Willow's room looked like Martha Stewart had slept there. Dr. Jackson had been right on when he had warned Tiff that the hospital was not a hotel, because she had gotten carried away as usual. Her little sister was generous to a fault and unfortunately, that often landed her in a financial mess, overextended on her credit cards. Michaela had had to bail her a few times. She glanced around the room in dismay. Every corner was brimming with a collection of art books, *National Geographic* magazines, Lindt chocolates, scented luxury candles and even a big stuffed parrot.

Looking a bit overwhelmed, Aunt Willow smiled. "Thank you, luv. Michaela also brought me a beautiful orchid and a stash of white pear tea. Both of you have turned this room into a groovy pad."

"It's our pleasure." Michaela smiled at Aunt Willow's amusing choice of words.

"I'm touched that you're both here and I know you love me, but you deserve to enjoy your Saturday off," Aunt Willow said firmly. "So scoot out to the warm sunshine."

"But we want to be with you," Tiffany objected. "We can't leave you alone with Dr. Killjoy."

Aunt Willow burst out laughing. "I hardly think he's going to put the moves on me. Besides, I need my beauty rest. Manny is coming by tonight," she said with a coy smile.

"Ooh, listen to her. Manny's coming," Tiffany mimicked in a low, seductive voice.

Aunt Willow blushed and Michaela realized it was the first time she had seen any color in her aunt's face since the accident.

"See those lovely flowers?" Aunt Willow asked, pointing toward a vase overflowing with spring flowers. "Manny sent them."

"They're gorgeous. Looks like your firefighter is more

interested in starting fires than putting them out," Michaela observed slyly.

"Yeah. Better not salsa dance with Manny, or Dr. Killjoy will get on your case." Tiffany dissolved into giggles. "At least one good thing came out of dating Javier. I can salsa now." She hummed an upbeat Latin tune and danced around the room doing rapid salsa moves. Her yellow sundress swirled madly as she wiggled her hips, shimmied her shoulders and shouted "*arriba*" a few times. Tiffany gyrated and kicked up her sandals' dainty heels until Aunt Willow and Michaela were in stitches.

Dr. Jackson entered the room with brisk strides, followed by a severe-looking nurse. He paused to glance at Tiffany with a sardonic lift of his brow. "Are you feeling all right, Miss Willoughby?" The look on his face confirmed he had been privy to her manic dance moves.

Tiffany rolled her eyes. "Perfectly fine, Dr. Kill...I mean Jackson," she corrected impishly. "Haven't you ever salsa danced?"

"Is that what that was? I was going to prescribe something for you," he replied in a deadpan voice before turning his attention to Aunt Willow whose mouth was twitching. Ignoring Tiffany's sarcastic groan, Dr. Jackson checked Willow's medical chart with a serious expression. "Mrs. Reese, how do you feel? Are you having any pain?"

"I've been getting sharp spasms once in a while, but it's nothing I can't handle with deep breathing," Aunt Willow replied stoically.

"Where do you get the spasms?" Dr. Jackson asked kindly.

"Mostly on my left side," she said, pointing to her ribcage.

He turned to Michaela and smiled. "Please take Chiquita Banana with you outside so I can examine your aunt." He made a sweeping motion. "And the candles need to go too. They're a fire hazard."

"*You're* a fire hazard," Tiffany muttered under her breath for only Michaela to hear.

"We were just leaving. Come on, Tiff." Michaela pulled Tiffany's arm and blew a kiss to Aunt Willow. "Bye, Auntie. Rest up for tonight's visit. I'll call you later to see how you're doing."

"I'll call too." Tiffany blew her aunt another kiss as

Michaela hauled her out the room. She barely made it into the hallway without erupting into giggles when Tiffany crossed her eyes and made a face behind Dr. Jackson's back.

"Where are you heading?" Tiffany asked.

"I'm going to Paolo's. I can't wait to see Claudia and Mikey. But first I have to talk to Dr. Jackson and find out where Aunt Willow's pain is coming from."

"Oh."

"Wanna come with me? I'm sure Claudia would love to meet you."

"Maybe some other time. I am not in the mood to be insulted again by that grouch. I think I'll go home and practice my salsa moves," Tiffany said with deadpan face.

"You don't need to practice. You move like a true Latina," Michaela assured her. "It's Dr. Killjoy who needs to get his groove on."

"Eh! Who cares about him?" Tiffany replied, blowing a raspberry.

You do, Michaela thought, grinning at her sister's irreverence.

Chapter Twenty-Four

"Maki, your Aunt Willow is really something." Paolo craned his neck as he shaved in front of Michaela's bathroom mirror. Wearing a white towel wrapped around his lean hips, his bronze skin glistened with water droplets from his recent shower. He chuckled, dimples deepening seductively. "I loved the way she waltzed out of the hospital last week, clutching Manny's tattooed arm. He's a good guy."

"You never know what to expect from Aunt Willow. In that way, she's kinda like Tiff. I don't think Manny's going to disappear on her this time around. He missed her too much when they broke up." Michaela came up behind Paolo and wrapped her arms around his lean midsection. Resting her face on his broad back, she licked the water droplets off his moist skin and replaced them with a kiss as she inhaled the heady combination of Paolo and soap.

"You forgot a spot," she teased, tapping the groove beside his mouth where a tiny speck of foam rested. "I'll take care of it." She snatched the towel from Paolo's hips with a flourish and used it to wipe the foam off.

"Hey!" Paolo laughed. "Wouldn't a Kleenex have sufficed? Or are you flirting with me, Señorita Willoughby?"

"Flirting with you? Why, Señor Santos, you know I am a proper and respectable girl," she replied, feigning offense.

Paolo's eyebrows rose. "I thought I cured you of that."

Michaela rolled up the towel and flicked it at his behind. "Need I remind you that the only naked one here is you?"

"That is something we can easily remedy, *querida*." Paolo flung her over his shoulder, slid his hand under her short robe, and languidly stroked her as he carried her to bed. Within moments, Michaela was moaning and panting, her hips rising to meet Paolo's deliberate thrusts. He took his time with the long bout of lovemaking, fusing their bodies together, bringing her closer and closer to sweet agony until she climaxed with shuddering spasms. Waves of pleasure washed over her as Paolo's release followed, explosive and thrilling to behold. He stayed inside her for a long time, petting and gentling Michaela until she quieted and relaxed against him.

Much later, she lazed on top of Paolo, drawing circles on his chest. "My insatiable caveman," she murmured dreamily. She gazed into his midnight eyes, loving the ravenous way he always looked when they made love, and the tender look he gave her afterward. The hunger of his desire seemed imprinted on her body. It was as if he couldn't get enough of her. She certainly could not get enough of him.

They had spent every moment they could together the past week, making love often and taking sublime enjoyment in getting to know each other intimately. Michaela had never felt so close to anyone in her life. Her love for Paolo was so intense, so all encompassing, it sometimes scared her. He was everything she wanted in her life and everything she admired in a man. They were very different personality wise, but she believed they completed each other perfectly. And she felt she could trust him with her life. Just last night, he had told her he would walk through fire for her and she believed him, because she would do the same. For the first time in her life, she totally trusted the man she loved and it was staggering and humbling at the same time.

However, in the back of Michaela's mind lingered the niggling reality that their competing shows would be taped soon and it might test their newfound love. They had agreed not to talk about their shows when they were together to avoid arguing. The first time Michaela had brought it up, Paolo had silenced her with a kissing game *everywhere* that left her speechless and gasping for a rematch.

"I think we should stay in bed all day." Paolo's hands circled her sides with a slow caress. "Once Mamá arrives we won't have much time alone."

"I like the way you think." A drugging rush of desire made Michaela close her eyes and sigh blissfully when Paolo's weight descended on her.

"I'm kind of nervous to meet your mother," Michaela admitted to Paolo as she waited beside him at the Miami International Airport early Sunday morning. It was just the two of them because Bobby had insisted that they keep it a secret from Claudia so she would be surprised. After their reconciliation, the Woodbridges had bent over backward to please Claudia and bond with her. They had used their influence and money to arrange for Señora Santos to travel from Buenos Aires so she could finally meet Mikey.

"Don't be nervous. She can't wait to meet you. And she'll be happy to meet your family too."

"Yeah, well that's what worries me the most," Michaela revealed. "My parents still can't understand why I didn't wait until after the competition to date you. I hope they behave today." The Woodbridges were throwing a barbecue in Rosa Santos's honor and they had invited Michaela's family too. She had been floored when she heard her parents had accepted the invitation. Knowing Mom and Dad, they had probably done it to scout and assess Michaela's competition, especially since Paolo would be preparing the *parrillada*, an authentic Argentinean barbecue.

"Relax. It'll be fun." Paolo squeezed Michaela's waist. "Mamá is very easygoing. She gets along with everybody."

"Like you." Michaela smiled up at him. "Does she speak English?"

"Yes, of course. My grandfather was American. From Philadelphia," he revealed. "He fell in love with my *abuela* on a business trip to Buenos Aires. After a long distance courtship he came back to marry her. They stayed in Argentina and had three children. Mamá was the youngest of the three girls."

"Oh, I had no idea. I'm so glad she speaks English."

"Even if she didn't, she would find a way to communicate with you and everyone else here. She is ecstatic to meet her first grandchild. Especially since it's a boy. Girls run in our family," he explained. Paolo's eyes suddenly lit up. "Look, there she is! Come on." He pulled Michaela along as he dashed toward his mother who was emerging from customs.

Rosa Santos was completely different from what Michaela had imagined. Paolo and Claudia were tall, with athletic builds. Their mother was petite and round, with twinkly black eyes and abundant salt and pepper hair cut in short, tousled layers framing a jovial face. The only thing she had in common with Paolo was a big, white smile, framed by deep dimples.

"Mamá!" he shouted excitedly.

"Raviolini!" Señora Santos chuckled merrily as Paolo picked her up and exuberantly twirled her around. *"Hijo, por favor.* Put me down!" she exclaimed, dangling in mid-air, her pretty face flushed.

When Paolo set his mother down, there were tears in his eyes. He was so unabashedly male in every way, yet he was comfortable expressing his emotions. Michaela loved that about him. She stood slightly behind them as they chatted in rapid-fire Spanish until he abruptly stopped and pulled Michaela forward.

"Mamá, I want you to meet my girl. This is Maki."

It pleased Michaela enormously that Paolo had referred to her as his girl, especially to his mother. Watching them interact, it was clear that Paolo and his mother shared a tight, loving bond. Michaela's parents were not the touchy-feely types; she rarely remembered being hugged or kissed by either one. Nevertheless, Tiffany had somehow turned out as affectionate and physically demonstrative as a puppy, something that never failed to enchant Michaela.

Rosa looked her up and down with delight. "You are Maki? So nice to meet you!" Her face lit up as she hugged Michaela and kissed her on the cheek, warming her with the show of genuine affection. "I've heard a lot about you. Thank you for taking care of my little Claudia when she was having her baby. I'm forever indebted to you," she said, smiling sincerely.

Michaela waved her hand in a gesture of dismissal. "Oh, please don't thank me. It was an honor to be with Claudia for Mikey's birth. Wait until you see him. He is the most beautiful baby I've ever seen!"

Beaming, Señora Santos said, *"Sí.* Claudia has emailed me many pictures and she always holds Mikey up when we Skype. For a while there, she stubbornly insisted that he looked like her, even though Mikey is the image of Bobby, blue eyes and all."

Michaela nodded. "He does look like Bobby. But now that they're reunited, Claudia is willing to concede it, Señora Santos."

Paolo's mother took Michaela's hands in hers and gave her a warm smile. "You must call me Rosa. Everyone does."

"I will, thank you. My name is Michaela, but your son has christened me Maki." She smiled up at Paolo and her heart fluttered when he winked at her.

From that moment on, Michaela and Rosa hit it off. They went directly to Paolo's apartment to drop off Rosa's suitcases and allow her to change from her travel clothes into something cooler for the outdoor event. After a shower, Rosa emerged from the bedroom, looking refreshed in a white, safari-style blouse, tan pants and brown leather sandals decorated with seashells.

Poor Paolo was bound to end up with a sore neck again because, knowing him, he would insist on having his mother sleep comfortably in his bedroom while he slept on the living room sofa. No matter, Michaela thought, stifling a giggle. Irina would be more than willing to give him a rigorous massage any time he needed it.

By the time they arrived at the Woodbridges' palatial home, Rosa had entertained Michaela with funny stories about Paolo's childhood antics and Michaela felt comfortable enough to practice the limited Spanish she knew with her. Paolo pulled his car up to the guardhouse at the entrance of Gables Estates, the hub of old Florida money. Within minutes, they were parked in the driveway of the most magnificent house Michaela had ever seen, including the Blumenthals' Williams Island mansion.

"This house looks more like a hotel than a home," Paolo muttered, shaking his head. "Good thing Claudia and Bobby already found an apartment to move into."

"Yes, those two need to build their own nest for Mikey," Michaela said. When Bobby moved them into his parents' house temporarily, Claudia had confided that she felt overwhelmed by their immense wealth. Even though they were generous, Claudia didn't want to stay with them. She was anxious to move out and make her new home with Bobby and Mikey.

"It's beautiful, but too big for only two people," Rosa mused. "I can only imagine how happy they are to have a grandson to fill it with life."

The Woodbridges' home was an architectural dream built in French Tudor fashion, but it did seem a bit much for just one couple. Samuel, the uniformed head servant, gave them a tour of the magnificent interior. Rich, oak-beamed, cathedral ceilings soared above massive pristine windows, stone walls and glossy hardwood floors. On their way to the covered terrace, they passed Elizabethan antiques and embroidered rugs in muted floral prints. Samuel told them the house was 14,000 square feet and boasted of a dozen bedrooms and an equal number of bathrooms. He pointed out original European paintings and tapestries, giving historical facts as if he were a tour guide. The walk to the terrace was like going through an elegant hotel lobby.

When they reached the brick terrace that preceded the beautifully landscaped grounds, Michaela felt as if they were entering an opulent park. Lush, verdant acreage extended to the water's edge providing a breathtaking view of the Bay. Flowering jasmine and gardenias perfumed the air. Clay tennis courts beyond the pool area added to the grandeur of the grounds.

On the right side of the terrace, a very long table ran the length of the rectangular pool. The table was decorated down the center with whole artichokes, clusters of red and yellow tomatoes on the vine, and tiny eggplants.

"Look, there's Claudia and Bobby." Michaela pointed to the far left where they sat under a banyan tree beside Mrs. Woodbridge who was humming as she rocked Mikey in her arms. Several others lounged on wrought iron sofas and chairs with blue and white striped pillows, chatting and sipping drinks.

"*Hija*," Rosa called out as soon as she saw her daughter.

"Mamá?" With a look of elated shock, Claudia bolted from the chair and raced to her mother, pulling her into a fierce hug. Mother and daughter rocked together, happy tears streaming down their faces as they exclaimed and chatted in their lilting Argentine accent.

Bobby joined them with Mikey in his arms and together they formed a tight circle. Everyone in the patio got up and approached them, including Michaela's parents, Tiffany, Aunt Willow and Aunt Magda, the Woodbridges, Paolo and Michaela. Even Señora Fuentes was there, carrying on about what a wonderful family they were.

Hours later, Michaela turned her face to the sky and said a silent prayer of thanks. She didn't want the day to end—ever. Surrounded by her family and friends and seated next to Paolo, she felt dizzy with happiness. She was glad she had stopped drinking after the third glass of Malbec, even though she could have polished off the whole bottle. After all, today was for revelry, a jubilant celebration of Rosa Santos and her family. Little Mikey reigned supreme, looking adorable in a striped blue Ralph Lauren jumpsuit that matched his impossibly clear blue eyes as he slept in Abuela Rosa's arms.

The Woodbridges had gone out of their way to make everyone feel at home. The afternoon sun was setting over the Bay, but nobody was in any rush to leave after gorging all afternoon on the feast of *empanadas*, tomato, avocado and red onion salad, and perfectly grilled meats. The *empanadas*, savory meat pies, were stuffed with braised sirloin, minced onions, green olives and raisins, and spiced up with cumin and other exotic spices. Paolo had skillfully grilled every type of meat imaginable including Argentinean sausages called *chorizos*.

"Paolo, did you really make the sausages? I couldn't resist. I ate two of them," Aunt Magda confessed, patting her tummy. Grilled until the outside was crunchy and the inside was tender, the sausages were tucked into freshly baked rolls. "What's the Spanish word for sausage again?"

"*Chorizo*. And when we eat it inside a roll, it's a *choripan*. They're good for you too. Eh, Maki?" Paolo teased, grinning.

Michaela grinned back and reserved comment. She had learned to choose her battles with Paolo and didn't feel like rising to the bait.

"What seasonings give the *chorizo* that savory taste? I can't figure it out," Aunt Willow said. "But it sure is delicious."

"It must be the garlic, cloves and nutmeg I put in with the pork and beef mixture before filling the casings," Paolo said. "I'm glad you liked it."

"Paolo's *chorizo* is the best," Michaela declared, drawing hearty laughter and ribbing. "Gosh, people, I didn't mean it *that* way!"

Replete from the lunchtime feast they had washed down with the finest Argentinean Malbec, Michaela, Paolo and company lounged on the patio furniture gazing at the ocean. Michaela's heart swelled as she watched Paolo interacting effortlessly with her family, as if they had known each other for years. Even her parents were getting along with him and God knew they were difficult to please!

Everyone swore they couldn't eat another bite until Claudia brought out her signature dessert, a three-layered moist vanilla sponge cake slathered with creamy *dulce de leche*. Imagining the abundant calories, Michaela groaned silently, but she ate a small slice and her taste buds went into overdrive as she savored the sweet, rich concoction.

When Mikey woke up and started to fuss, Claudia took him inside for a feeding, followed by Bobby, who hadn't left her side all evening. It was as if he were trying to make up for the time he had been away and caused Claudia so much unhappiness.

Seated at the table, between her mother and Rosa, Michaela almost dropped her fork when Rosa asked, "Are you going to be at Paolo's taping tomorrow?"

Sylvia Willoughby went from relaxed to ramrod stiff as she squeezed Michaela's thigh beneath the table where no one could see. Michaela looked at her mother and gave her a private warning look. She had already told Tiffany and her parents that Paolo's mother had no idea his girlfriend was competing against him. Michaela and Paolo weren't keeping it a secret exactly, they just wanted to avoid the subject altogether while they were gathered today. There was no sense in adding drama to a family reunion and risking getting everyone riled up as they took sides.

"No. Unfortunately, I can't," Michaela said, answering Rosa's question.

Rosa made a clucking sound. "*Ay*, what a shame. Food is

Paolo's passion and he is an expert at preparing it," she boasted, gazing at her son with maternal pride.

"Food is my daughter's passion too," Mom replied promptly, the competitor in her surfacing in spite of Michaela's previous warnings. "Michaela is quite an accomplished chef."

Rosa turned to Michaela with a surprised look. "¿*Verdad?* But you are so slim! You should have seen Paolo as a little boy. He was such a little glutton, we used to call him *raviolini*," she said chuckling at the memory.

"You still do," Paolo said with a hearty chuckle. He pulled his mother into a bear hug and ruffled the top of her short, layered hair. "But I forgive you."

"Paolo is going to be the winner. There is no doubt about it." Rosa affectionately pinched Paolo's lean cheek as if he were still a child.

Paolo shot a glance at Michaela and she shook her head, mouthing to him that it was okay. But Sylvia Willoughby wasn't about to let it go. She immediately countered with, "The best thing would be to have two winners because the other chef competing for the show is quite exceptional."

"Really? He can't possibly be as good as Paolo," Rosa said, pursing her mouth thoughtfully.

"It is a she," Sylvia said through tightly pursed lips. Michaela could see her mother's temper climbing.

"A woman is competing against Paolo?" Rosa's brow knitted as she regarded Sylvia with a bewildered look.

"Yes, not all great chefs are men," Sylvia said succinctly.

"True, but why do you mention her? We all want Paolo to win, don't we?" Rosa asked, glancing at everyone for agreement.

Suddenly, Tiffany let out a high-pitched giggle and all attention landed on her. Unfortunately, Tiff was quite tipsy from making toasts all evening. "Of course we do. And we want Mic to win too!" Tiffany crowed. "They're both great chefs, so they should each have a show. Now that they've stopped fighting, they can't keep their hands off each other. Let's toast to them and may the best man win." She raised her wine glass.

Of all the toasts Tiffany had made, that was the most revealing. Michaela broke the stunned silence with an apology to Rosa. Aided by Paolo, she gave a detailed explanation of what they had kept hush-hush from Rosa and why. When she finally understood their motives, Paolo's mother relaxed. Showing solidarity and respect for their children's love, Rosa and Sylvia proclaimed that whoever won would be celebrated equally, with no bias. After all, Rosa reasoned, it wasn't often that young love was powerful enough to withstand a fierce competition. Sylvia had reluctantly agreed and had remained quiet—a miracle for her.

While Paolo and his family gathered around for some quiet time with Mikey, Michaela walked outside with her family as they were leaving.

"Tiffany, were you able to get a final confirmation from our contestant for tomorrow's taping?" Michaela asked. "I'm assuming he said yes, since you never mentioned it again."

Tiffany's eyes widened. "What do you mean? Aunt Willow was supposed to take care of it."

"Me? But I didn't have Internet access in the hospital. You offered to take care of it, Tiffany. Don't you remember?" Aunt Willow asked, looking alarmed.

"I, um...uh..." Tiffany stalled, glancing from one family member to the other with guilt stamped all over her face.

"Oh, God, Tiff. Don't tell me you were too distracted by Dr. Killjoy to remember anything about that conversation," Michaela said, trying not to panic. "The taping is tomorrow afternoon!"

"Who the hell is Dr. Killjoy?" Dad interjected.

"Never mind." Tiffany waved him off and whipped out her Blackberry. "Chill, everybody. I'll email Hugo now. I'm sure Mr. Hurly Burly will jump at the opportunity."

"Mr. Hurly Burly? Tiffany, how much wine did you drink tonight?" Dad asked with a disapproving frown.

Sylvia gave Tiffany a scorching look. "If he can't make it, you are going to have to find a replacement ASAP! You better not let us down, missy."

"When have I ever?" Tiffany asked with wounded dignity. "It's a piece of cake. All of you are panicking for nothing. The guys were coming out of the woodwork to be on Mic's show."

"They were?" Michaela asked dubiously.

"Yes, why do you look so surprised?" Tiffany asked her. "I'll be at the studio tomorrow at ten to do your makeup and hair."

"Isn't the studio providing hair and makeup for you?" Mom asked Michaela.

Before Michaela could answer, Tiffany said, "They might be providing it, Mom, but I want to do Mic's make-over and she already agreed to it. Right, Mic?"

"Yes," Michaela said.

"When I'm finished with you, you're going to sizzle on that screen," Tiffany said. "Don't wake up too early. We want you to look fresh and well-rested for the camera."

Late that night after they got home, Paolo's mother could barely keep her eyes open. After she retired to bed, Paolo sat at his kitchen counter and opened his laptop. He missed his sexy redhead in his apartment and in his bed, but they had to keep up appearances. His mother would be scandalized if they had continued with the current sleeping arrangements. He hadn't gotten around to reading his e-mails in a long while and decided to log onto his *Grill Me, Baby* web page to keep his mind off Michaela. The last time Paolo had checked the progress of his promo campaign led by Gil, there had been a long waiting list of women angling to be in the audience.

A loud knock on his door got his attention and he hurried to answer it before his mother woke up. When he opened it, he found Juan Ramirez standing before him holding some papers.

"*Hola*, Juan. Come in. What brings you here so late?" Paolo asked, clapping him on the shoulder in greeting.

"*Hola*. I need to talk to Claudia." Juan looked around Paolo's apartment. "Is she here?"

"Do you realize it's almost one in the morning?"

"I know. I'm sorry, but this is important." He blushed. "I haven't seen her all week and I was wondering if she's okay."

"Claudia is fine. She's back with her husband."

"Oh." Juan looked disappointed. "I guess that's good, considering she has Mikey and all."

"Yes," Paolo agreed, wondering why Juan looked fidgety and nervous.

"I...uh...I wanted to show her this." Juan held out two papers and handed them to Paolo.

Paolo read the first one:

Congratulations, Hugo! You have been selected to appear on Michaela Willoughby's show. The sexy ginger-haired chef welcomes you as her special guest to The Pleasure Palate where your dining wish is her command. Attached please find a script for your portion of the show. Please read it and confirm your participation. Looking forward to meeting you! The Luv Bite Team.

The second paper was a meticulously scripted plan for Michaela's *Pleasure Palate* show.

"I don't get it. What are you doing with this?" Paolo asked, searching Juan's face.

"I am Hugo St. Paul," Juan confessed with an embarrassed grin.

Paolo wearily rubbed the stubble on his jaw and stared at Juan. "What did you say?"

"I'm Hugo, the guy who wrote that e-mail," he said in a small voice.

"*You* wrote that e-mail?" Paolo asked, giving him an incredulous look.

Juan gave a sheepish nod.

Paolo shook his head to clear it of the cobwebs that seemed to have gathered there. "I don't understand. Why would you do that?"

"Señora Fuentes got Claudia all worried that a cyber weirdo might end up on your girlfriend, Maki's show. So we came up with a plan that I would send an e-mail and try to get on her show instead."

Paolo couldn't believe his ears. "What an absurd idea. Claudia never told me about this."

"She didn't want anyone to know."

That was not what Paolo wanted to hear. What else had Claudia been up to behind the scenes, he wondered uneasily. "Did she ask you to do it?"

"No, I offered." Juan shrugged and grinned. "I kinda went a little crazy sending a bunch of e-mails with different names so Claudia could relax. Believe me, I was surprised when they picked me. My e-mails were funny and creative, but the one from Hugo St. Paul was the best of all."

"Why? What did you say?"

"I described myself as a glutton who worshipped butter and cheese. I said I admired Maki's cooking and was willing to reform for health reasons."

Paolo's jaw dropped as he saw Juan with different eyes. The poor kid was so smitten with Claudia, he'd been willing to concoct a screwball plan just to win her over.

"So what are you going to do on her show tomorrow?" Paolo asked, wondering if he needed to alert Michaela of their prank.

Juan hesitated and looked uneasy.

Paolo zeroed in on his awkward silence and asked bluntly, "What's wrong?"

"I can't go on tomorrow. That's what I came to tell Claudia. I hadn't looked at the Gmail account I set up for that e-mail until tonight."

"Why can't you be there?" Paolo demanded. "If you don't show up, Maki will be very upset." That was an understatement. Her carefully planned show would be ruined!

"I have a statistics final tomorrow." Juan took a step backward. "I was planning on helping out and being on the show if I was picked. I just didn't know it would be at the same time as my final."

Paolo clutched his head. How could Tiffany have picked Juan's glib entry over other worthy ones—especially knowing what a perfectionist Michaela was about everything? Michaela had confessed to Paolo that she had had very little input in her advertising campaign and had given her family free rein. With no discretion, Tiffany had transformed Michaela's proper image to that of a sexy siren, relishing her motto of "sex sells" on the website. She was an incorrigible mischief-maker and had probably thought Hugo St. Paul would enliven things for her more mature sister.

"What are we going to do? There were two other messages from the Luv Bite Team and the last one sounded urgent," Juan said, bringing Paolo back to the pressing dilemma.

"What did it say?" Paolo asked.

"It said the success of Maki's show was riding on Hugo and to please confirm that I would be there!"

Damn. By the sound of it, Paolo knew it was too late for Tiffany to notify anyone else. Maki would feel betrayed and sabotaged by the Santos family if Hugo didn't show up and she found out Juan's sham e-mail had been orchestrated by Claudia!

Paolo motioned for Juan to join him at the counter. "Come here. You're going to respond to that email now."

Juan looked worried as he approached him. "What do you want me to write, Paolo?"

"Log into your account and I'll dictate it," Paolo bit out between his clenched jaws. He knew he shouldn't be mad at Juan, but the college kid's desire to impress the heck out of Claudia had created a real disaster for Maki.

When Juan logged onto his hurlyburly@gmail.com account, Paolo asked, "Hurly burly? What were you thinking, man?"

Juan shrugged and hung his head. "I don't know. The old-fashioned word seemed funny at the time. I thought I'd make Hugo sound like a dork, so Maki would take pity and choose him. Unfortunately, it worked."

"Here's what I want you to write: 'No worries. I will be there. Hugo.'"

Juan turned to him with desperate eyes. "But I already told you I can't be there!"

"I know. *I* will be Hugo St. Paul tomorrow," Paolo said magnanimously, even though his inner voice warned him he might regret it.

"You will?" Juan looked vastly relieved. "Why?"

"Because it's past midnight, too late to ask anyone else to pitch in. I have to be at the studio at six tomorrow morning, so you need to get going, Juan," Paolo said, incensed by Juan's immature prank.

"Okay, sorry about everything." Juan's face glowed red with embarrassment.

"Not nearly as sorry as I am," Paolo said, disgusted. He had no other choice but to appear on her show or Michaela would be a laughingstock tomorrow. There was no way he'd text her about the change in plans. Michaela didn't do well with changes, especially when it involved the *Miami Spice* competition. If she got wind of Claudia and Juan's shenanigans, she'd be a nervous wreck and not sleep a wink before her show. Michaela needed to be rested tomorrow morning. Somehow, Paolo would have to tell her between his taping and hers.

If not, he was toast—*burnt* toast.

Chapter Twenty-Five

"Oh, boy, listen to the audience," Michaela said, fidgeting in the armchair in front of the lighted mirror of the dressing room while Tiffany applied her makeup. Paolo was in the midst of taping his show and from the loud applause, the all-female audience was delighted. The sound of their laughter to his ready wit and showman techniques was not good for Michaela's nerves, not good at all. Since the night of Aunt Willow's car accident, she and Paolo had decided that their love was more important than anything else, including the thrilling prize of being the winner of the *Miami Spice* competition. This should have provided comfort, but right now it was making her fret.

"Don't pay attention to Paolo's show if it stresses you out, Mic. And please try not to blink," Tiffany said, using a metal eyelash curler on Michaela's lashes. Tiffany's shiny silver train case lay opened on the counter, overflowing with a kaleidoscope of eye shadows, lipsticks and blushes. Makeup brushes and sponge wedges were spread before her on the counter as she focused on her craft, interspersing her work with peppy comments to cheer Michaela on.

"I want to know how he's doing." Michaela tried not to blink as Tiff had requested. She didn't know how much longer she could sit still. She felt like leaping from the chair and running out of the studio and into Paolo's arms. *Cut it out*, she told herself, *you're being silly*. She hadn't expected to have a case of stage fright and actually, it wasn't stage fright, it was fear of the unknown. What would happen after today? Would their relationship survive the competition?

"Let's close the door so you won't be distracted," Aunt Willow suggested from the couch she shared with Aunt Magda. The aunts had insisted on being in the dressing room with Michaela to bolster her confidence.

"No, I want to keep it open. I need to hear what's going on

out there," Michaela insisted, trying to keep the edge from her voice. She was a bundle of nerves, heading toward meltdown. She was competing against the man she adored and wanted to marry, if he'd have her. All along, she had thought she was up to the task, but the minute she had arrived at the studio, she started to get nervous. Now she had cold feet about her show.

"I provided the exact script of how I want to tape the show. What if Hugo hasn't read it and he's not prepared? What if he doesn't even show up? Then I'm going to have to wing it. I'm not funny like Paolo...I'm only a chef!" Michaela fretted.

"You can totally wing it if you have to. Don't underestimate yourself," Tiffany said. "You're a pro at cooking and a natural teacher. Just think of the Munchin' Munchkins. You've taught them so much since they started your classes."

"Exactly! Listen to your sister, Michaela, and stop worrying," Aunt Magda urged. "You don't have to be Jim Carrey out there. You are a beautiful woman and a knowledgeable and experienced chef. Perform to the best of your ability and they will love you for it."

"Right on. I have to agree with Magda. Once you're groovin' to the beat of your talents, things will go great for you." Aunt Willow shifted on the sofa, adjusting the orthopedic brace that wrapped around her pumpkin-colored, embroidered cotton tunic. "Right now, you're being your own worst enemy. Turn that negative aura to a positive one before you face your audience. You can start by trying to relax. Breathe in deeply and hold it a few seconds before exhaling slowly."

Michaela tried to take deep breaths, but she couldn't, she was too revved up. "It's not working. I'm afraid I might have gotten in over my head. I like everything planned ahead of time," she said. "I should have never chosen this type of show just to outdo Paolo. I agreed to have a surprise guest that I haven't met beforehand and practiced with." She clutched her head and moaned, "What was I thinking? It's madness! I should have stuck to what I do best and not tried to upstage Paolo for the sake of winning at all costs. Then I would have a fighting chance."

"Just listen to yourself. Shoulda woulda," Magda repeated, shaking her head. "You are not helping things with a shopping list of regrets. You have had several meetings with the silver fox, have you not?"

"Who is the silver fox?" Aunt Willow asked, looking befuddled. "Have I missed something here?"

Tiffany sniggered as she applied a coat of glossy black mascara to Michaela's lashes. "Aunt Magda has the hots for Ted Marton, a.k.a. the silver fox."

"Who's Ted Marton?" Aunt Willow asked, looking from face to face for an answer.

"He's the culinary producer who has been working with me all month getting things set for my show. The same one I worked with for the taping I did with Paolo," Michaela explained. "Aunt Magda met him today."

Always on the lookout for eligible bachelors, Aunt Magda had taken a shine to Ted Marton, the handsome and urbane, silver-haired culinary producer collaborating with Mr. Blumenthal. She had been giddy ever since Ted had winked at her when they were introduced.

"Why didn't you tell me about him, Magda?" Aunt Willow asked, looking hurt.

"Because you have Manny."

"I have no interest in your silver fox, Magda. I would never flirt with any man you're interested in. Let's concentrate on helping Michaela." Aunt Willow turned her attention to Michaela with a heartening smile. "Try again, luv. Breathe deeply and exhale slowly."

Michaela made a valiant effort to take a few deep breaths and exhale them slowly.

"That's it, dear. Keep going, you're doing great," Aunt Willow said softly in a Zen-like tone.

Breathing rhythmically, Michaela remembered Amy, the spa director's words of encouragement: *Stop sabotaging yourself. You have planned your show to a T. Dan and Elliot will be there, along with the team Ted has put together to assist you backstage. They will make sure the food is picture perfect for the cameras. All you have to do is smile and sell yourself.*

The sound of the audience's laughter interrupted Michaela's relaxation breathing.

"Paolo is probably clowning around and entertaining the

ladies." Tiffany gave an offhand flick of her wrist. "Don't let it throw you. You know how he is. He has his style and you have yours."

"Yes, I know," Michaela said proudly. She knew only too well how at ease Paolo made others feel. It was one of the things she loved most about him, his genuine warmth and friendliness.

"Don't worry, Mic. You will charm the pants off those guys. Just look at yourself. You're a smokin' hot chili pepper in that red dress. *¡Muy caliente!*" Grinning, Tiffany fanned herself rapidly. She added a final sweep of blush on the apples of Michaela's cheeks and then stood back to survey her. "Perfect. Now all I have to do is run a flat iron through your hair. Can't wait for you to knock 'em dead," she crowed, doing a little dance move with her arms and shoulders.

"Thanks," Michaela barely managed to say before she felt a surge of nausea. "I just wish I felt better. It must have been all that rich food I ate last night. My system isn't used to it."

"Neither is mine, but I feel just fine," Aunt Magda said. "I don't think you're reacting to the food, dear. It's the stress of competing against that gorgeous man that you love so deeply, especially since there is so much riding on it."

Michaela nodded forlornly. "I wish the circumstances were different—that I could be sitting in the audience, enjoying Paolo's success. Knowing that I have to compete against him is nerve-wracking," she admitted.

"The stakes *are* high, but your love will win out in the end," Aunt Magda said.

"I want to win. But honestly, the way I feel right now I'll take doing well in front of the camera," Michaela said.

"You'll do great. Don't forget you're going to have that tiny earphone and Ted will be whispering in your ear, guiding you along," Tiffany said.

"I wish he'd whisper to *me*," Magda said under her breath. "I can think of a few things I'd like that silver fox to growl in my ear—"

Aunt Willow let out an exasperated sigh. "This isn't about you, Magda."

"What?" Magda asked defensively. "I was just saying..."

"Never mind." Aunt Willow turned her attention back to Michaela. "What was that Tiffany said about the earphone, dear?"

"It works like a backup. I have to listen to what Ted says and pay attention to the studio director who will be pointing to the camera I'll be facing," Michaela said. "I'm also going to be cooking, entertaining the audience *and* dealing with my surprise contestant." She threw her hands in the air. "All of a sudden, it seems like too much!"

"You can do it. But you must master your nerves. Visualize yourself at the end of your show, triumphant and happy. Relax and focus," Aunt Willow soothed with a serene smile.

"What do you think of your mom sitting in the audience with Rosa and Claudia?" Aunt Magda asked. She got up from the couch and reached for a pot of rosy cream blush to brighten her cheeks.

"Magda, why do you have to bring that up now?" Aunt Willow objected, her face flushing pink with exasperation.

"To try and take her thoughts away from that dazzling man who is now cooking up a storm and charming the dickens out of the crowd," Aunt Magda replied.

"Honestly, Magda, you're making me have a hot flash and I haven't had one in a long time. What has gotten into you?" Aunt Willow demanded, fanning herself rapidly.

"Nothing. I'm nervous myself. Poor Michaela! I don't know why Sylvia agreed," Aunt Magda said. "The families should not have to be together during the competition."

"Mom couldn't exactly refuse," Michaela said. "She had to agree. Otherwise it wouldn't have been very gracious, especially since Rosa is so proud of Paolo."

"Kind of puts Sylvia in an awkward position, but it's good for her karma, I guess," Aunt Willow said.

Magda nodded. "Yes, it is good for Sylvia to descend from her high horse every once in a while."

"Magda, really." Aunt Willow gave her sister a look of rebuke. "Not in front of the girls."

"It's okay, Auntie," Tiffany said. "We all know Mom can be overbearing, but we love her anyway."

"True, but we can't afford a repeat of the other day. I was

worried that Sylvia might start fighting with Rosa if you hadn't intervened, Michaela," Aunt Magda said. "Your mother was getting hotter under the collar by the minute. Every time Rosa calmly stated that Paolo was going to win, I could see the tension build inside her. Small miracle Sylvia didn't take off like a rocket and blast her with reasons why you would be the victor."

"Did I just hear you mention me and a rocket, Magda dear?" Mom inquired, strolling into the dressing room. Her keen blue eyes glinted with purpose as she took the situation in.

"Why aren't you in the audience, Sylvia?" Aunt Magda asked, straightening before the mirror. She patted her shiny auburn bob in place as she gave her eldest sister a questioning look.

"I'm finished spying," she announced imperiously. "I know how you are going to be the victor, Michaela." Sylvia Willoughby's razor-sharp gaze zeroed in on Michaela with the same vigor she had used to push her daughter to win the national Constitution gold medal her senior year in high school.

Michaela felt the aggressive energy emanating from her mother. "How?" she asked.

Suddenly transformed into a dynamic courtroom litigator, Sylvia took center stage as everyone's attention riveted to her. "You nail that sucker with precision. Be cool under fire. Impress them with your skill and knowledge all the while luring them with your self-confidence." Her blue eyes burned with fiery zeal. "The men in your audience will want to be charmed just like Paolo is doing for the ladies. However, there is one caveat...you must do it better than Paolo. He is losing points by not being precise about the measurements and cooking instructions. Oh sure, the women are having a ball out there, but at the end of the day, it will be the producers who decide. And if they deem Paolo cannot give adequate and accurate instruction in a cooking show, he might not win." She paused for effect, her gaze sweeping the room as if she were facing the jurors. "You will be the winner!" she cried, pointing at Michaela as she finished her discourse with a triumphant jut of her chin.

"Mom," Michaela said wearily. "I hope you're saying this for my benefit. I don't want Paolo to do badly. I just don't want to look like a fool out there. I want to do great too." She also wanted Paolo to be proud of her. It warmed her heart that he genuinely wanted her to do her best, in spite of everything they were competing for.

"Don't let your feelings for Paolo get in the way of your ultimate goal, Michaela! You *will* win or my name isn't Sylvia Willoughby," Mom said, not listening to a word Michaela had said.

"Wow," Aunt Willow breathed, her eyes widening. "You certainly were born for the courtroom, Sylvia." Willow loved to tell the family that she had always been in awe of the depth of Sylvia's ambition. Not that she ever wanted to be like her, she had added, she just enjoyed seeing her big sis in action. "I love the way you champion Michaela. She certainly deserves it!"

"Well?" Mom asked Michaela without even glancing at Willow. "Are you up for the challenge?" She placed both hands on the makeup counter and leaned forward to peer into her daughter's guarded eyes. "Are you going to make us proud?"

Moaning, Michaela edged away from her mother's fierce interrogation. "I feel queasy and a little faint. What should I do?" she blurted out, hating the way her mother's fervor dwindled to disappointment in mere seconds.

"Put your head down and let the blood flow to your brain. I'll get a ginger ale from Kraft services," Aunt Magda said. "And maybe some saltines. Be right back." She took one last glance in the mirror to smooth her fitted tan skirt over her trim hips before leaving.

"Hmph. More than likely Magda's gone off to snare the silver fox," Aunt Willow drawled with a knowing look.

"Maybe she'll get lucky." Tiffany exchanged an amused look with her aunt.

"I don't know what you two are babbling about," Mom said testily, "and, frankly, I don't care. All I care about is pulling Michaela out of the doldrums and putting some steel into her spine!"

Seconds later, Dad walked into the room. "How is our star doing?"

"Our star is in the throes of stage fright," Mom reported, looking to the ceiling in disbelief and then back to her husband.

She gave him a pointed look. "Michaela is having major self-doubts."

"Our over-achieving daughter?" he asked Mom incredulously.

When Mom nodded grimly, Dad turned to Michaela. "Seriously? You're not raring to get out there and trounce your opponent?" He regarded her as if she were his alien daughter. "This is your road to stardom, hon."

Michaela gave a feeble shrug.

"Mic is freaking out. She's worried that she's lost her mojo," Tiffany said. "She needs a strong shot of something to boost her. Forget about ginger ale. Magda's probably going to take a while anyway. Can we get her a shot of vodka?"

The thought of having any liquor made Michaela's stomach roil. "No, I'd rather sip some ginger ale." *And curl up in a ball,* she added silently.

"Rubbish, Tiffany. Her mojo is intact," Dad said in a no-nonsense voice. "Better buck up, Michaela. There's a long line of guys outside the studio door waiting to meet you."

"Has Hugo arrived yet?" Michaela asked, hoping with all her heart that Dad would say "yes" and she could at least relax about that part of her show.

"I don't think so. If he is here, he hasn't announced it to the culinary producer yet," Dad said. "I've asked several times."

"Oh, God, I think I'm going to be sick," Michaela said, reaching for the trash bin.

Paolo smiled and bowed before the thunderous applause. He waited until the cameras stopped filming before he descended into the audience and greeted the women, allowing them to kiss him on the cheek and give him congratulatory hugs. From the corner of his eye, he caught sight of Michaela, white and still as a glass of milk, standing to the left of the stage watching him. He motioned for her to come over, but she shook her head and gave him a wan smile, her eyes huge in her pale, anxious face.

Paolo quickly wrapped things up and ran up the stairs toward her so he could explain about Hugo before he appeared on her show, but when he got there, she was gone. He tried to enter the dressing room, but Mr. Willoughby barred his entrance, saying Michaela needed time alone to center herself before the show.

Feeling frustrated, Paolo went to his dressing room and changed into jeans and a polo shirt. He dreaded appearing on *The Pleasure Palate* as Hugo. Michaela had not looked well just now. In fact, she had looked awful, her usually radiant face drawn, her sweet body slumped. Nevertheless, the moment they had locked eyes, her love had reached out to him from across the room, warming his heart.

Paolo's spirits plummeted when he thought of what was to come. Very soon, Michaela's love would disintegrate when she saw him arrive as Hugo St. Paul. She would probably think he had written the email to sabotage her show. There was only one way to salvage things, Paolo decided, his heart surging with excitement at the prospect.

He descended the stairs, two steps at a time, until he reached his mother. When he finished telling her his plans, Rosa was overjoyed.

Now he just needed to convince Michaela...

Chapter Twenty-Six

"Feeling better now?" Aunt Willow asked, patting Michaela's hand gently as she lay on the couch with a cool rag on her forehead.

"Yes, amazingly I do. Sorry about the gross-out earlier." Michaela smiled sheepishly at her gathered family. "I guess I had to purge what was making me sick inside."

She didn't mention that she actually felt bolstered by seeing Paolo just a few minutes ago from across the room. She had been headed to the ladies' room to brush her teeth after being sick to her stomach and had paused to watch him interact with his audience. The love in his eyes had told her they were going to make it, regardless of who won the *Miami Spice* competition. When she saw him motion to her and head her way, she had left quickly because she didn't want to be distracted anymore.

Funny, she remembered how she'd initially disliked him the first time she'd set eyes on Paolo in Mr. Blumenthal's office because he was competing for what she wanted most in life. Of course, she still wanted to win, but Paolo had won her heart and she wanted *him* more than anything else. Whatever today's outcome, regardless of the victor, their relationship would survive and thrive for having crossed the hurdle together as a unified couple. Michaela was sure of it. That certainty gave her such a rush of strength that she suddenly sat up and pulled the rag off her forehead.

"I am ready to get out there and give it my best," she announced to everyone's relief.

"Good girl! Hugo is finally here. Thank God the stage manager told you, Aunt Magda," Tiffany said. "Did she mention what he looks like? Is Hugo hot?"

"No, I wish she had given more details," Aunt Magda said.

"All she said was that Hugo St. Paul had just called and was entering the building now."

"I'm no longer nervous," Michaela announced, stiffening her backbone. "I don't know what got into me earlier, but it's out now!"

"That's my girl," Mom said. "Dad and I have never said this to you, but we are proud of the fine chef you are and the strong young woman you've become. Whether you win the show or not, you are a winner in our eyes."

"Thanks, Mom. That means a lot to me," Michaela said, touched deeply. She smiled at her assembled family. "I'm going to try to make all of you proud. Thanks for being there for me. I couldn't have done it without you. Really," she added, tearing up.

"Don't cry or you'll ruin your pretty makeup." Aunt Magda brushed the tears from her eyes.

"Yeah. I didn't slave over you so you could smudge it by getting sappy on us. You're not the only one who has a vested interest here. I'm hoping to get future business out of this. Thousands of fans are going to be texting and e-mailing me after the show," Tiffany teased. "They'll ask are you the genius who did Chef Michaela's website and makeup?"

Michaela smiled. "You're the best, Tiff. Thanks."

"Now you're going to make *me* cry," Tiffany said, giving Michaela a tight hug. "C'mon guys, we need a group hug."

Led by Tiffany, Aunt Magda, Aunt Willow, Mom and Dad held hands, forming a circle around Michaela and hugging her tight. "Break a leg!" everyone took turns calling out before they left the dressing room.

Michaela took a deep breath, said a prayer and went in search of Dan and Elliot.

Paolo watched Michaela's entrance from the sidelines. He had just had a harrowing moment trying to explain to Mr. Blumenthal, Ted Marton and the studio director why he had to appear on Michaela's show as the mystery guest. With no time to lose, the producers had retreated to what they referred to as the video village just off the set, where they would sit and watch the monitors during the taping. Paolo would have to clear things up with them after the show. Once everything was straightened out, they'd see why he had to go on as Hugo St. Paul.

Paolo was in agreement with the audience when they rose to their feet and greeted Michaela's arrival with hearty applause and a few wolf whistles. She looked beautiful in a flame-colored mini dress that set off her luminous skin and highlighted her slender curves. Her hair shined like copper in the studio lights and her wide aquamarine eyes glowed beneath long, dark eyelashes. Two pink flags on her cheeks suffused her creamy complexion, the only indication that she was excited and nervous.

Filled with pride, Paolo watched and listened as Michaela conducted the first few minutes of her show and talked about her love of food and her quest to keep things delicious for the palate, yet light in calories and fat. So far so good, he thought, impressed by her poise as she competently read the teleprompter, keeping the mood light-hearted and informative.

Michaela faced the camera with a big smile. "I want to thank all of you in the audience today for being here and for writing in to participate in my show. As you know, one contestant was chosen for his unique email. He will now read it as he enters. Everyone, please welcome my mystery guest, Hugo St. Paul."

A drum roll sounded and loud applause followed.

Paolo took a deep breath as he tightened his tenuous hold on the email he had printed out earlier. Feeling like a Catholic schoolboy about to say penance, he read in a clear voice, "I am a closet glutton, but for health reasons, I must reform. I have great love and respect for butter and cheese, lots of it, and I doubt I will ever be convinced otherwise. Chef Willoughby, I love your approach to healthy eating and I want to believe!"

When he looked up, Paolo saw the myriad of severe emotions cross Michaela's face—confusion, betrayal, disbelief and then gut-wrenching hurt. If her heart was breaking, his was already severed in half, Paolo thought, wanting to take her in his arms and make things right.

Paolo hesitantly smiled as he approached her, his eyes trying to convey that he understood the awkwardness of the situation, but Michaela was having none of it. She refused to meet his gaze, keeping her blazing eyes focused on his forehead as if she'd like to send a dagger through it.

Michaela froze and her heart nearly stopped when she heard Paolo's voice reading the e-mail. When he appeared onstage, she thought she was hallucinating. What was he doing there? She blinked several times and tried to say something, but her throat felt paralyzed when she realized that the love of her life had played a dirty, rotten trick on her. She wanted to scream, *why, Paolo, why?* Staring at him now, so damn confident and good-looking yet trying to fool her with a rueful look on his face, she felt pathetic for having believed in him. She was living her worst nightmare before the eyes of her family, her audience and the producers—it was devastating! She had trusted him with her love.

Summoning her last shred of dignity, she turned to face the camera with a smile that made her face ache and her heartache even worse. She could hear Ted's voice in her ear prompting her to *say something*. Michaela's face flamed feverishly and her eyes burned with the effort to hold back tears. She helplessly glanced at her family in the front row of the audience. Dad mouthed *focus* and sent her a fortifying wink. Mom gave her a firm thumbs-up signal. Aunt Willow held up her Tibetan mani stone and rubbed it. Aunt Magda and Tiffany were huddled together in shocked disbelief.

Bolstered by their support, Michaela stiffened her spine and persevered. "Welcome to *The Pleasure Palate, Hugo*," she said, her voice strangled as she forced the words through tightly clamped lips.

"Hugo couldn't be here, so I'm taking his place." Paolo reached her side with an apologetic smile.

"Perfect," Michaela said, her hurt turning into anger. He would not leave the set unscathed, she vowed silently. She would make a mockery of his deceit. "And what is your name?"

"You know my name, Maki."

"Yes, but please be courteous enough to introduce yourself. This is *my* segment and there is a nice family in the front row, the Willoughbys, who just sat down and did not see your show being taped." From the corner of her eye, Michaela could see her family looking aghast as the drama unfolded. "Maybe there are others. Is there anyone here who does not know this man?"

Some raised their hands, prompting Paolo to say, "My name is Paolo Santos." And just like that Paolo's usual self-confidence crumbled.

Michaela looked out at the audience. "Ladies and gentlemen, the mystery has been solved," she announced. "Our guest's last name is St. Paul, which translates to Paolo Santos in Spanish. How clever of him."

"You don't understand. I never—" Paolo began.

Who did he think he was fooling? The fake name was too much of a coincidence. "Let's not waste time with explanations. We have work to do."

Paolo shook his head and whispered, "Maki, you need to know that—"

Michaela held up her hand. "Save it. Everyone is here to learn to cook light, am I right?" she asked the audience.

A round of applause answered her question.

Paolo gave her an encouraging smile. "Let's get started then," he said cheerfully.

Michaela strove to keep her cool, but she was dying inside. "Miami is an international hub of many different foods and my recipes are quite diverse." She continued to force an even tone for her audience. Shawn, the director was waving at her to look at the camera, so she faced it head on.

"Don't keep us in the dark any longer," Paolo said with a wink at the audience. "What are you making? I can't wait to try it."

He had the nerve to wink and make light of this? Couldn't he feel her anguish and rage beneath her forced calm? Lies, blatant lies, that's what he'd been telling her all along. Suddenly, Michaela wished she could stick an apple in the deceitful swine's mouth and shut him up. She kept her gaze focused on the camera lens. "Chef Santos likes to cook lard-ridden foods and he probably would prefer for me to roast a pig. However, I'll start by making crisp and tasty mahi croquettes instead."

"Mahi croquettes? Interesting."

"Mahi croquettes go beautifully served with citrus cilantro salsa." Michaela turned away from him to face the camera. "The freshest ingredients make for delicious croquettes."

"They may be delicious, but how are they lo-cal?" Paolo's brow knitted together. "What about the béchamel sauce that goes in the filling?"

"There's no béchamel in my recipe," she replied with feigned patience even though she wanted to scream, "Quit interrupting me!"

"Can't wait to taste them. Are you going to fry the croquettes or do you have something else up your sleeve?" he inquired.

The lying hypocrite! He actually looked interested in her recipe. Did he really think his teasing would draw her into banter? Michaela refused to look at him as she said, "I will pan fry them quickly in a skillet coated with cooking spray and then bake them in the oven." She held up an egg. "First you must separate the yolk and only use the egg white for less calories and fat."

"What's wrong with a little yolk, eh, Maki? My Italian Nonna says that an egg without the yolk is like a day without sunshine. And she's right. Is it really necessary to skimp on the yolks?"

"I believe in moderation—a quality that is alien to your cooking," she said through tight lips. On top of everything else, Paolo was challenging her on her own show. *Unbelievable!*

Paolo gave a slight bow of concession. "Show us what you can create without the yolk, Chef Willoughby. I am at your mercy." He raised his hands in defeat, drawing chuckles from the audience.

You have no idea how much you are at my mercy, she thought balefully. Mr. Show-Off was so damned cocky he was sure he could win her—and the audience—over with his charm. Well, the egomaniac traitor was in for a rude awakening. Once she finished with Paolo, he would think twice before ever playing with her emotions and elbowing in on her show.

She looked at the camera and smiled. "As I was saying, I only use the egg white in this recipe."

Paolo shrugged and gave the audience a bemused grin.

"Good thing my Nonna isn't here or we'd both be mincemeat."

The audience burst into laughter.

Enough was enough. Paolo was taking over her show...just like she feared he would. Michaela's wrath suddenly erupted like lava, fiery and unstoppable.

"Well, then we'll just have to please Nonna, won't we? Since you both love the yolk so much, here's the whole egg!" she cried, cracking it on Paolo's head. Her action was met by surprised gasps from the audience. Michaela relished the sight of raw egg dripping down the side of Paolo's tightly clenched jaw.

"What are you doing?" he asked, shocked.

"You've been egging me on since you barged in on my show. Now you're the one who's walking out of here with egg on your face." She gave him a snarky look. "Forget the mahi. Since you're the biggest ham I know, *you'll* be the filling. I'm making ham croquettes today!"

Paolo leaned down and hissed, "Stop it, Maki, we're on TV! It's not what you think."

Ted's frantic voice thundered in her ear. "What the hell's going on?" he demanded.

Michaela yanked the earpiece out and flung it on the counter, ignoring Shawn as he wildly waved at her. Her chances at winning were already ruined, but she wouldn't stop until she taught Paolo a lesson he'd never forget.

"Next some salt and pepper," she said, throwing a handful of each over Paolo's head.

"Argh," Paolo roared and started to cough. The muscles in his throat bulged as the audience laughed.

"Let's not forget the breadcrumbs. I use Panko. The Japanese breadcrumbs produce a lighter, crispier coating that I adore." She grabbed a box of Panko and dumped the entire contents over Paolo's head, drawing more loud guffaws from the audience.

Purple-faced, Paolo glared at her, but he remained rigid with self-control.

"Last of all, we cook it. Usually, ham croquettes are fried, but in this case, we will bake them. Chef Santos, will you please open the oven door?" she asked with sweet malice, clutching a wooden spatula.

When he leaned forward to open it, Michaela whacked his tight behind with the wooden spatula. Satisfied when it landed with a loud thwacking sound, she gave a malevolent laugh.

Covered in egg, salt and Panko, Paolo straightened with a cunning glint in his eyes. "Don't think that will go unheeded, my dear," he said in a deceptively calm voice. He slowly advanced toward her. "My name might be Santos, but we both know I am no saint, even though you're determined to make me a martyr today."

Michaela ran toward the counter. In two long strides, Paolo joined her and stood directly behind her. He placed his large hands on either side of the cooking space, anchoring her before him. Michaela pushed back forcefully, trying to dislodge him, but to her growing alarm, Paolo wouldn't budge. With dismay, she looked over her shoulder, expecting to find him glowering at her, but instead the corners of his mouth turned upwards in a triumphant smile. The cad! He was delighted he had her trapped with his big, muscular body. Michaela tried elbowing him sharply, but he was prepared already and wrapped his arms around her while his face descended and his mouth hovered close to her ear.

"Maki, I have endured a lot for you today," he said softly, his warm breath fanning her ear. The microphone must have picked it up because the audience clapped in agreement.

"I'm not finished with you yet!" she warned, drawing lively laughter from the audience. In spite of her bravado, it was hard to act ominous when Paolo held her anchored to the counter, his body pressed against her intimately. "Didn't you have enough airtime of your own, *Hugo*?"

"I did not write that email pretending to be Hugo," Paolo said emphatically.

"Oh, really? Then who did, Mr. Hurly Burly?"

"Claudia's friend Juan wrote it, but at the last minute, he couldn't be here. I didn't want you to be without a contestant, so I came in his place. I did it to save your show."

Michaela desperately wanted to believe Paolo, but she didn't trust him anymore—and she refused to set herself up for more heartbreak. "How chivalrous of you," she said sarcastically.

"I am telling you the truth," he growled.

Someone from the audience who sounded like Dad shouted, "Shut up and kiss her, Hugo!" Wild applause followed his suggestion.

Michaela wriggled furiously, trying to dislodge Paolo's hold on her. "Let go of me, you...you attention-hogger!"

"Not until you listen to what I have to say...all of it," he said, holding her body snugly against his. "Today, I allowed you to turn me into a human croquette only because I understood why you did it, *querida*. But I'm surprised and disappointed that you would believe I would ever be capable of hurting you. I love you, Maki," he said gruffly.

Michaela froze, not knowing what to say or do as she stared at him, stunned and speechless. He had just declared his love to her in front of a rowdy audience—after she had publicly humiliated him! More than anything in the world, she wanted to believe him.

Paolo reached into his jean's pocket and held a big diamond ring set in an antique platinum setting in front of her face. "Will you marry me, *amor*?"

"Say yes!" a guy bellowed from the audience, prompting several more to join him until a loud chant formed. "Say yes! Say yes! Say yes!"

Wide-eyed with awe, Michaela stared into Paolo's soulful eyes and saw the sincerity in them. Her heart clenched with regret that she had believed the worst about him, going ballistic on him before he could explain himself. He had once told her, *"My wife and children will always come first and I'll expect the same from the girl I marry."* She wanted nothing more than to be that girl—his girl.

With shaky hands, she took the ring from Paolo and put it on her finger.

"Yes," she whispered breathlessly.

"Louder!" yelled someone who sounded a lot like Aunt Magda. "We can't hear you!"

Boisterous applause erupted when Michaela yelled back, "I said yes!" before returning her undivided attention to Paolo. "Yes, yes, yes!"

Paolo's eyes crinkled at the corners. "Do you remember that I once told you I would walk through fire for you?"

Wiping at the happy tears running down her face, Michaela nodded.

"Grill me, baby," Paolo said with such fierce love that her heart flooded with joy.

Epilogue

Three months later in Tuscany, Italy...

"Of course I said yes," Michaela murmured, running her fingers through Paolo's mussed-up locks as she lay tucked into his side. They had spent the whole day lounging in a nineteenth century bed in the Italian villa Paolo had rented for their honeymoon in Tuscany. Golden sunlight streamed in through the ancient window of the two-hundred-year-old stone house, warming their bodies. "How could I resist you, Hugo, when you tolerated my abuse like a stoic gladiator, letting me pelt you with food and whack you with a wooden spoon in front of all those men?"

"My ego still hasn't forgotten that, Irina," he said wryly, tapping her bottom. "I'm amazed that Mr. Blumenthal wanted us to do a reality show afterward. He kept saying it would be like Lucy and Ricky in the cooking ring." Paolo flashed a sardonic grin.

"I know, but I'm not too sure about putting Hugo and Irina together in front of a camera again." Michaela shook her head at the memory. "Frankly, after all the anxiety I went through in the dressing room before the taping, I'd rather work on getting my cookbook published. And I also need time to develop my love bite business." Ever since Bernice's party for Palmentieri, Michaela had received a deluge of orders for the *macarons.* "I'll be happy to make lots of guest appearances on *Miami Spice* and let you be top chef. You are a natural before the camera." She started to giggle. "I can't believe you asked me to marry you on TV, covered in egg and Panko!"

"*Sí,* and it was no gimmick. I had intended to ask you to marry me while my mother was visiting so we could all celebrate. But I knew I had to convince you."

Michaela smiled, remembering how he'd told her about borrowing his mother's ring. Her heart warmed at the memory of how he'd gone on her show to help her, not sabotage her efforts. "When I looked in your eyes and saw the naked truth in them, my heart melted on the spot." She grinned up at him. "I knew where we would be headed as soon as the show was over."

"Where was that, *querida*?" he prompted, dimples deepening.

"To your bed and into your heart—now and forever," Michaela said, gazing into her husband's midnight eyes.

"Shall we get started doing what chefs do best?" he asked slyly.

"And what is that, my love?" Michaela drawled. Desire welled up inside her as Paolo's skilled hands began a leisurely caress of her body.

"How about we put a little bun in the oven? Eh, Maki?"

"I'm game if you are." Michaela blissfully welcomed the weight of Paolo's strong body as he rolled on top of hers. Winding her arms around his neck, she drank in his passionate kisses and held tight to the man she loved.

About the Author

Bestselling author Sophia Knightly loves to cook up hot romance and delicious humor in her feel-good stories. Whether it's romantic suspense or romantic comedy, her books are fun and sexy contemporary romances. A two-time Maggie Award finalist, she believes in love-at-first-sight and happy endings, and she always enjoys a good laugh. When not writing or reading, she finds pleasure in walking the beach, exploring museums, going to the theatre, enjoying good food, and watching movies. One of her favorite pastimes remains simply watching people, especially those in love!

Write to her at: sophiaknightly@gmail.com.

Follow her on Twitter: @SophiaKnightly

Join her Facebook page by Liking: http://on.fb.me/vGfJ5t

Visit her website at: www.sophiaknightly.com

Check out the *Grill Me, Baby* trailer:
http://youtu.be/6Y07iUPt3rg

It takes a real man to wear a kilt.
And a real woman to charm him out of it.

Love is a Battlefield
© *2012 Tamara Morgan*
Games of Love, Book 1

It might be modern times, but Kate Simmons isn't willing to live a life without at least the illusion of the perfect English romance. A proud member of the Jane Austen Regency Re-Enactment Society, Kate fulfills her passion for courtliness and high-waisted gowns in the company of a few women who share her love of all things heaving.

Then she encounters Julian Wallace, a professional Highland Games athlete who could have stepped right off the covers of her favorite novels. He's everything brooding, masculine, and, well, heaving. The perfect example of a man who knows just how to wear his high sense of honor—and his kilt.

Confronted with a beautiful woman with a tongue as sharp as his *sgian dubh*, Julian and his band of merry men aren't about to simply step aside and let Kate and her gaggle of tea-sippers use his land for their annual convention. Never mind that "his land" is a state park—Julian was here first, and he never backs down from a challenge.

Unless that challenge is a woman unafraid to fight for what she wants...and whose wants are suddenly the only thing he can think about.

Warning: The historical re-enactments in this story contain very little actual history. Battle chess and ninja stars may apply.

Available now in ebook and print from Samhain Publishing.

It's all about the story...

Romance

HORROR

www.samhainpublishing.com

CPSIA information can be obtained at www.ICGtesting.com
Printed in the USA
BVOW081006160513

320904BV00002B/160/P